THE NEW MAGIC

Joseph Malik

Published by Oxblood Books, Gig Harbor, WA

The New Magic is a work of fiction. All incidents and dialogue, along with all characters, are products of the author's imagination. Any resemblance to any person, living or dead, is entirely coincidental.

Edited by Monique Fischer
Cover design by Lynn Stevenson

V 1.01.180901

Library of Congress Control Number: 2018943529

ISBN 978-0-9978875-7-0 hardcover
ISBN 978-0-9978875-8-7 perfectbound
ISBN 978-0-9978875-6-3 e-book

Register at www.josephmalik.com for updates on new releases.
Facebook/Twitter/Instagram: @jmalikauthor

For my father, who, when asked,
"Where did you grow up?"
still answers, "I never did."

Glossary and Cast of Characters

Adielle Riongoran-Thurdin: Eldest child of the royal family and Princess of **Falconsrealm.** Heir to the throne of **Gateskeep.**

Aever of Black Valley: Knight Lieutenant in the **Order of the Stallion.**

Carj of Bitter Lake: Knight in the **Order of the Stallion.**

Carter Sorenson: Greatswordsman from Earth, friend to **Jarrod Torrealday** and Lord of Regoth Ur. Married to **Daorah Uth Alanas. Carter** accompanied **Jarrod** to **Gateskeep** half a year earlier.

Daorah Uth Alanas: Commander (highest ranking field officer) in the **Pegasus Guard** of **Gateskeep.**

Faerie: A long-lived people, northeastern neighbors of **Falconsrealm**. Although they refer to themselves as **"Faerie,"** humans often refer to them as "elves."

Falconsrealm: Gateskeep's largest territory, a mountainous region traditionally ruled by the heir to the throne of **Gateskeep.**

Galè of Lor: A warrior-wizard and professional demon-killer from the southern nation of **Ulorak.**

Gateskeep: Northwestern country that encompasses **Falconsrealm** and Ice Isle in the north, and the **Shieldlands**, Long Valley and Axe Valley in the south. See map.

Gbatu: Collectively, all the races and tribes of subhumans. There are over a hundred subspecies of **gbatu**. The most common species range from three to four feet in height and are lightly-furred, tool-using, and intelligent. They live in tribes that consider themselves to be at war with every other species in the realm, including each other. Armed with weapons by **Ulo Sabbaghian** in a previous war, **gbatu** are a frequent nuisance for travelers.

Greatsword: A large, heavy warsword built for cutting with a wide blade and a spatulate tip. Typically wielded two-handed but balanced for one-hand use. A heavily customized **greatsword** is **Carter Sorenson's** weapon of choice. A smaller historical version, the *gran espée de guerre* (great sword of war), is **Jarrod's.**

Gwerian of Vella: A knight captain in the **Order of the Stallion,** and **Jarrod Torrealday's** highest-ranking local commander.

Jarrod Torrealday: Lord Protector of **Falconsrealm,** Lord of the Wild River Reach, and Knight Chief Lieutenant in the **Order of the Stallion** of **Gateskeep**. A former stuntman and Olympic saber hopeful from Earth, banned from competition for killing another fencer in a drunken duel. Jarrod has been in **Falconsrealm** for half a year, now.

Karra Talivel: A **Faerie** woman, bonded to **Jarrod Torrealday.** She met **Jarrod** before his mission into **Ulorak,** in which **Jarrod** rescued **Princess Adielle** and defeated the army of **Ulorak.**

Levy: A volunteer or conscripted soldier as opposed to a professional man-at-arms.

Longsword: A two-handed warsword often the length of a **greatsword**, but with a lighter blade, a thrusting tip, and a center of balance affording tremendous maneuverability. A **longsword** is effectively a **greatsword** built for fencing.

Order of the Falcon: Order of **Gateskeep** knights drawn from the Pegasus Guard. Knights of the **Order of the Falcon** have ridden a pegasus in combat.

Order of the Stallion: Order of **Gateskeep** knights officially responsible for the training of knights in other orders, though clandestinely tasked with counter-espionage missions.

Renaldo Salazar: Jarrod Torrealday's nemesis from Earth. A champion in the world of illegal underground dueling, **Renaldo's** attack on **Jarrod** several months prior originally resulted in **Jarrod** awakening in **Gateskeep.**

Rider: In **Gateskeep** and **Falconsrealm**, a chivalric title below true knight, merited by skill at arms or exceptional performance in combat. A rider will rise in social standing upon attaining knighthood. Knights often refer to each other as **"Rider"** as a term of respect.

Rogar Hillwhite: Head of the patrician, ore-baron Hillwhite family. Blames **Jarrod Torrealday** for the deaths of his brothers, Albar and Edwin Hillwhite.

Saril of Red Thistle: Knight of the **Stallion.** Second and Lord Chancellor to **Jarrod Torrealday.**

Saxe: A cleaver-like, single-edged shortsword. Used primarily in the **Shieldlands** of **Gateskeep.**

Sergeant: An officer commanding soldiers and levies. Soldiers and **sergeants** are considered an artisan-class profession, one step below nobility in social standing. **Riders** often serve as **sergeants** as part of their training.

Shieldlands: Southern territory of **Gateskeep.** See map.

Ulo Sabbaghian: King of **Ulorak**. Raised on Earth, **Ulo** is a former Las Vegas illusionist conjured as a demon into the **Shieldlands** twelve years prior. **Ulo's** father was once and briefly king of **Ulorak,** and the most powerful and feared sorcerer in living memory.

Ulorak: A trading crossroads with the Eastern Freehold, **Ulorak** was originally a commonwealth of **Gavria.** It became soverign under Sabbaghian the Black, and was claimed by the Eastern Freehold after his death. Now ruled by **Ulo Sabbaghian, Ulorak** briefly became a **Gavrian** territory when **King Ulo** accepted appointment as Lord High Sorcerer of **Gavria,** but quickly seceded. **Ulorak** is once again sovereign. See map.

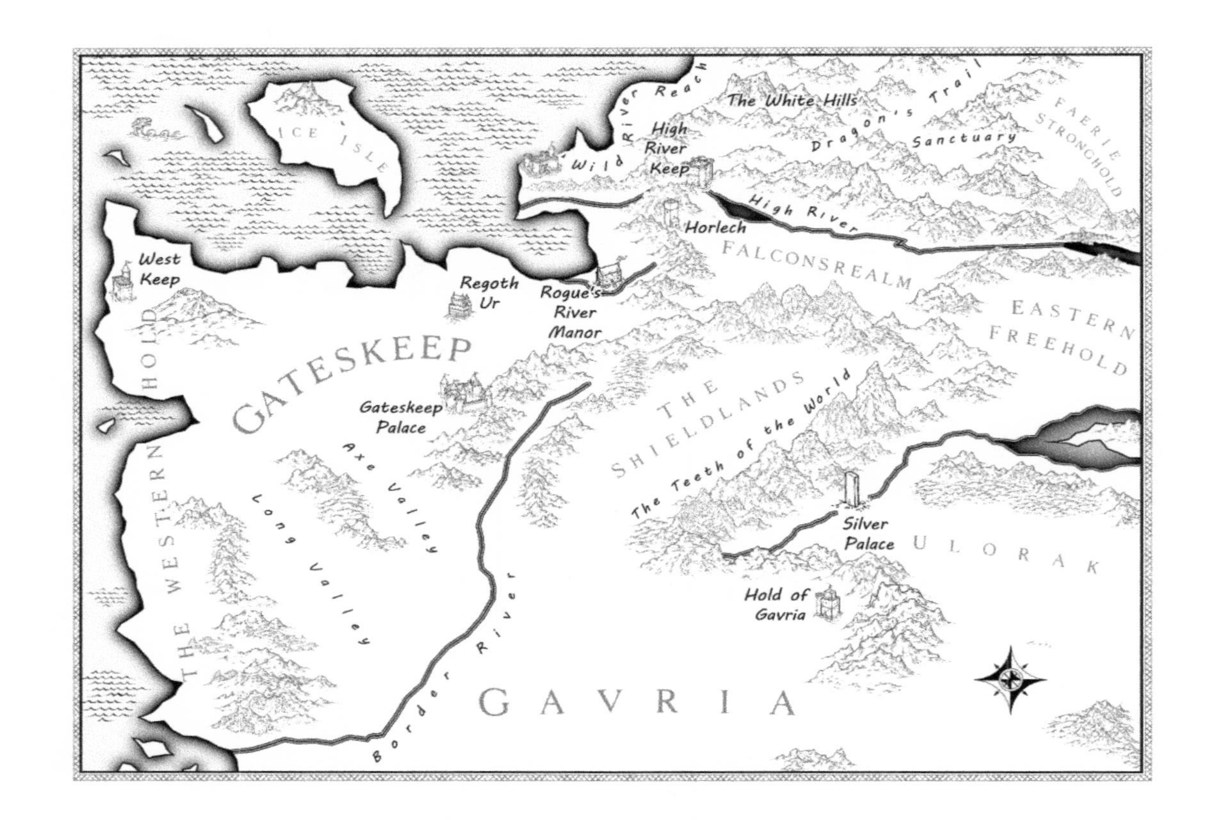
Ice Isle
West Keep
The Western Hold
Wild River Reach
High River Keep
The White Hills
Dragon's Trail
Sanctuary
Faerie Stronghold
High River
Horlech
Falconsrealm
Eastern Freehold
Regoth Ur
Rogue's River Manor
Gateskeep
Gateskeep Palace
Axe Valley
Long Valley
The Shieldlands
The Teeth of the World
Silver Palace
Ulorak
Hold of Gavria
Border River
Gavria

THE NEW MAGIC

HEGGY THE FIRST

"It is better to be a warrior in a garden than a gardener in a war."
- Zen proverb

Heggy was a sloppy, mop-headed boy with a wonderful laugh and no last name.

His given name, Hej, was his mother's father's name and a family name from five generations, but the town knew him as Heggy. "Heggy the First," he called himself.

Galè of Lor was a few shades older, a head taller, a wasteland leaner; a copper-skinned scarecrow clutching a candle in otherwise darkness. The night puffed into the cave, damp with distant winter and the itch of a chill at sandaled ankles.

"And this is safe?" asked Galè.

Heggy added some chalk to the jumble of circles and writing on the floor before a knee-high mirror and stepped back, careful not to disturb the inscriptions.

"The wards are what they are," said Heggy. He still had a child's voice, girlish and funny. "They've worked for a thousand years."

"And where did you learn it?"

"Magister's book. I wrote them down until I could

remember them."

The candle sputtered, nearly died, then found itself again. "I don't trust you," said Galè. He had some magic—he'd been able to make things fly since before he could walk—but he had nothing like this.

"Light it," said Heggy, "and we'll see your father."

Galè touched the candle to each of the red and black candles that dotted the intersections of the inscribed figures.

"Nath of Tanol," Heggy called to the mirror. He did his best to lower the register of his voice. Galè thought it sounded silly. "Nath of Tanol, warrior of Lor," said Heggy. "Rise from death. Rise from rest. Join us in the dark. Your son is here."

The candles flickered in the stillness. The mirror appeared to shimmer. Galè could see the candle in the glass.

"I don't see anything," said Galè.

"Don't blink," said Heggy. "Nath of Tanol," he said again. "Rise from death. Rise from rest. Join us in the dark."

"Heggy, I don't th—"

"Nath of Tanol!" Heggy shouted, the words ringing off the rock walls. "Your son is here!"

"Heggy, I—"

And then he saw it.

A face in the mirror, distant, grayed; obscured as if by smoke and as tenuous as if the wrong thought or even a careless breath could banish it.

"Father?" asked Galè. He blinked, and it was gone.

Staring again, it reassembled, twinkling.

"Father?"

"My son," said the face in the mirror, still a blur and a glint. The voice seeped from all corners of the room.

"I miss you, Father," said Galè.

"Who is with you?" asked the voice.

"Heggy," said Galè.

"Greetings, Heggy. I miss you, my son," said the voice.

"I can't see you," said Galè. "And your voice is not your own."

"You must break the glass," said the face. "Break this glass and open the door. I will return."

Galè shot a sidelong glance to Heggy, who shrugged. "It's his mother's mirror," said Galè. "It's not mine to break, Father."

"A small price to pay," said the face. The voice was now definitely coming from the mirror.

Galè looked again to Heggy, who nodded. Galè, a warrior in his father's footsteps and now under the tutelage of the knights of their tiny crossroads hold of Lor, handed the candle to Heggy and slipped his father's axe out of its thong at his side.

"Go ahead," said Heggy.

Galè stood before the mirror, squared his feet, and drove his axe into the glass.

The mirror collapsed inwards, the shards tumbling multifaceted and breathtaking into a weightless black beyond. The cave erupted in billows of smoke and the roars of wild animals. Unseen hands wrenched the axe from him.

The last thing Galè saw before it all went completely dark was that he had kicked apart the wards.

Galè crawled for freedom in the dark. Images of demons and monsters drove him, his elbows and knees thrashing at the sand, sure of clawed vicious things inches behind him.

He found the opening and rolled down the hill, deafened, throat searing, sulfur on his tongue. Caustic smoke surged from the cave, as if the world itself was on fire and the rocks burning.

"Heggy!" His voice was a hiss, the name held against a

grindstone, uselessly small in the vast waste of stars and sand. The lilac glow of the ringed moon behind the hill cast the smoking cave in shadow.

"Heggy!"

His gut reaction was to run for the magister's house at Lor. He looked down the canyon, judging the amount of time it would take him to reach town, explain, and bring help.

Heggy staggered out.

"Heggy!" Galè started up the hill as Heggy lurched down the slope, stumbling, carrying Galè's axe.

"My father's axe," rasped Galè. He could tell that Heggy was possibly burned, or stunned, or injured. "I owe you a hundredfold."

The face that met his, once Heggy's, was horribly charred, eyeless on the right, hair blasted away, teeth showing through skin burned to tatters.

"Oh, Heggy," said Galè, choking on the words, the back of his throat in shreds. "We'll get you to the magister. You'll be all right. I can carry you."

Heggy raised the axe with a roar of a hundred voices joined in anguish, all the rage and longing of hell itself unleashed at the skies. The stars shuddered at the noise.

Galè threw out a hand and knocked Heggy into the dirt and briars with the force of his heart, the force of the world. He unlocked his knife from his belt and dropped to a knee and drove it, panicked, frantic, into his chest until the last of the voices from the Heggy-thing—no longer Heggy, he was sure—faded and gurgled.

Galè wiped the knife on Heggy's tunic and sheathed it, then took up his father's axe and ran.

Galè slammed his fist on the door to the magister's house, a grip in his gut. He'd killed Heggy. Poor, fat Heggy who loved books and jokes and the magister. His friend. Everyone's friend.

Magister Ramour was the town wizard, a slender, serious man in the manner of many magisters. He opened the door, which scraped on the floor, and the moon reflected on his wisps of white beard and his dark pate.

"Magister," shuddered Galè, "I've done something terrible." He went into a breathless explanation: stealing the mirror, summoning his father, breaking the wards, the mirror collapsing. And, lastly, killing Heggy, although he neglected the part about using his magic. Even Heggy hadn't known he'd had any magic.

Halfway through, Ramour had brought the boy inside and sat him down, made him some tea, and listened with his fingertips pressed together.

It was an odd house, Galè noted. Tidy and sparse and smelling of tea and candles, and yet from the inside it appeared that none of the angles quite came together. Corners met dispassionately and with no readily apparent regularity, and the roof felt like it sagged overhead. All in all, it had a lethargic, unindustrious feel, and Galè was surprised that the town magister couldn't have afforded to have someone build him a better home.

"It's likely that Heggy didn't know what he was doing," said Ramour. "A boy in that much pain may not even have known who he was. If you killed him defending yourself, I don't think anyone will question your actions."

"You don't think there was any chance that . . . that it wasn't Heggy?" asked Galè, sipping his tea, which was remarkable, strong and tinged with honey and whisky. Perhaps the magister had other priorities than straightening his walls, Galè thought. The chairs were comfortable, the larder stocked, and the tea was the best he'd ever had. "The face in the mirror?" he continued. "Was that—" he choked on the words, "—did it become Heggy? Was it the thing *in* Heggy?"

The magister chuckled. "Don't be ridiculous."

Galè felt ridiculous.

"There was no face in the mirror," Ramour explained. "When you stare into a dark mirror, you will see what you want to see. There is always a face in the mirror: yours. Your eyes adjust to the darkness and the face appears to become more visible.

"You kicked over a candle, which set fire to whatever it was that poor Heggy had made his wards from. Sugar, or sulfur, or somesuch. He should have used chalk, if anything at all. I'll have to see what's missing. That's very old magic, physical wards. Marks, as wards," he sighed. "Obsolete. I have to wonder where he learned it."

Galè didn't tell him that Heggy had mentioned learning it from the magister's own books. Had the magister not read his own books? The skin on the back of his neck tried to crawl off his spine.

"This was an unfortunate accident, two boys playing. Nothing more. That you came to me with it, instead of the town marshal, only certifies that you did what you thought was right. Sad about Heggy, though."

"It certainly seemed real," said Galè, finishing his tea. His hand trembled as he set the mug down.

"That's why I'm certain you imagined it," the magister assured him. "It's when it seems *un*real that you need to worry. That's when you've done true magic. Now, we should go wake the marshal, and Heggy's poor mother. Who will replace her mirror?" he wondered, as he pulled on a long cloak and a cap.

"I will work for her until she feels it's replaced," said Galè. "I owe her much more than that, though."

"You're a good boy," said Ramour. "Your father did well with you."

Galè grunted. He wondered how he'd tell Heggy's mother, a town woman named Hun; no last name, no husband, and now no son. His mind spun at the obligation to a woman for taking all she truly had in the world. That's what he was, now, he thought: a thief. He'd stolen Heggy from her, from all of them, in an instant of stupid, childish panic. Not warriorly at all.

He could ask if the small keep here in Lor that had taken him in would take in Hun, as well. He imagined how lonely Hun's house would be without the girlish laughter and infectious smile of fat, funny Heggy.

The boy had been blessed with a laugh.

"I should have carried him home," he said at the door. "I should have calmed him and carried him home."

In a thundering howl that defied the still of the town, Heggy-That-Was smashed the door off its hinges and tore past him into the house.

Galè heard Ramour's screams and the many-voiced wailing of whatever the hell Heggy had become as he ran.

He kept running.

FOUR YEARS LATER

RIDERS

"Tell me who you ride beside, and I'll tell you who you are."
- Falconsrealm proverb

Atop a burly black riding horse, tall and rangy in his green cape and dark woolen tunics, a black woolen watchcap tight to his head, Sir Saril of Red Thistle's face was bright and boyish except for hard slate eyes and a sharp jaw that ground in thought.

Sir Saril looked down upon the settlement of Grach far below, the furthest-flung inhabited corner of the Wild River Reach. The jagged peaks of The Reach, savagely high and sharp, rose against a sky of tarnished silver behind him.

He clicked his teeth together.

Far below the village, pewter breakers smashed at high cliffs, ponderous, blowing spray at a distant tower. The immense pause between rolling impacts betrayed the size of the surf; the waves would have inundated some castles.

The town of Grach was small. Saril counted twenty buildings. It wasn't so much a village as it was a farming and hunting cooperative—maybe a dozen families.

Red Thistle, his home, was such a place. Saril had been born into a town of five families; forty souls. And now, only a few years after leaving home, he was a knight in the King's Order of the Stallion, recently made second and Lord's Chancellor to Sir Jarrod the Merciful, Chief Lieutenant in the Order of the Stallion, Lord Protector of Falconsrealm and Lord of Wild River Reach.

He'd never been home again.

Sir Bevio, as young but rounder and broader and red-bearded, and with a heavy dark cloak pulled tight against the weather, came up behind. His mount, black like Saril's, led a smaller brown horse loaded with weapons, roundshields, and heavy bags shadowed with damp.

Bevio pulled his cloak tighter as the wind snapped its teeth at them.

"No fires," said Saril after a long time watching. "There's no smoke. We're freezing our asses off, and nobody down there has a fire going."

"Maybe their wood's well-seasoned," Bevio offered.

"We'd smell it. The wind's off the sea. That chill comes all the way from Ice Isle."

Bevio unwrapped a hunk of wine-colored cheese, took out a small knife, and offered a slice to Saril. They ate and stared at the village for a while. Nothing moved except the sound of the sea, its measured breathing like a man exhausted and at peace.

The wind screamed at them from time to time, but it brought no sounds of daily life from the valley.

"I hate this," Saril decided. "I hate everything about this, right now."

"So do I," Bevio agreed. "We have to go down there."

Saril watched the sea for a little while longer. It was a violent, unsecure, remote place, the edge of the world. Not a good place.

Not a good place at all.

"Armor up," he decided.

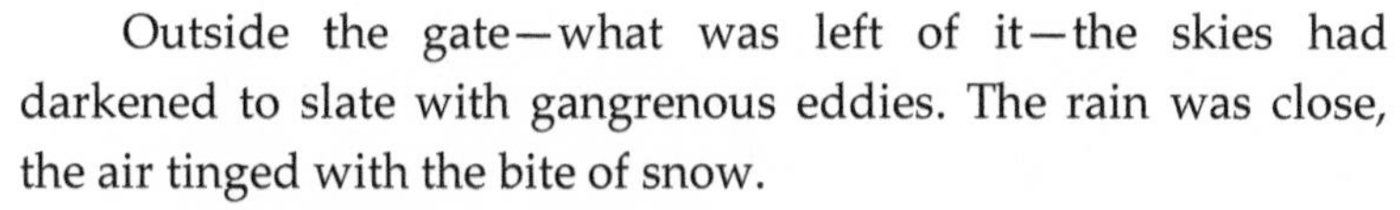

Outside the gate—what was left of it—the skies had darkened to slate with gangrenous eddies. The rain was close, the air tinged with the bite of snow.

Saril waved Bevio to a stop.

He'd never been to Grach, but he knew that the other towns in The Reach didn't have gate towers, or even walls. Grach, however, had been fortified. And, from the looks of it, hastily so.

The walls of the town had been cobbled together with squares of earth cut from a wide and deep trench on each side and augmented with sharp sticks at the top of the wall. It was enough to slow an attacker, but not stop one.

The towers, two men high, were also made of packed earth with simple stone battlements.

And they were empty. Many of the sticks had been trampled. The gate, made of lashed boughs, had been smashed; the ends, and the largest standing poles, chipped and gnawed by axes.

Bevio's voice echoed from behind a curtain of mail that draped from his helmet's spectacles. "What the hell happened here?"

Saril's voice was equally muffled from within a matching helmet. "Why didn't they send for reinforcements? If they had time to build this, they'd have had time to send a rider."

"Be careful," said Bevio. "There's old magic all through these mountains."

"This is not magic."

"No?" asked Bevio. He set his shield, a plain wooden roundshield rubbed dark with years of oil, on his thigh as Saril rode ahead and motioned at him to stay put.

Nothing moved inside the town. Saril could see the outlines

of slain dogs and horses in the rain. A flock of birds flew up from the center yard.

Saril looked at it for a long time, one hand on his swordhilt. He rode back and forth from left to right, looking through the remains of the gate at the town, then reined his horse completely around and trotted it back to Bevio.

"Are we going in?" asked Bevio.

"There's not enough whisky in the world to make that seem like a good idea to me."

Bevio shrugged and patted his horse. "My horse isn't scared."

Saril sighed. "We just spent an entire morning getting his head out of a log."

Bevio shrugged again. "There was an apple in there."

"I'm not trusting your damned horse. Or mine. And I'm not going in there. Let's go check the tower."

The veil of rain whipped over them and they kicked their mounts into a trot.

Maceshadow's Tower had once been the refuge of Vanan the Marauder.

Legend held that Vanan had been a wizard powerful enough to calm the seas off this tower. He had then used the bay as a launching point for a fleet of magical raiding ships whose sailors always found calm waters around them, and as such, stomped the hell out of anyone living along the water for five hundred miles in any direction, until Vanan essentially owned most of the Gateskeep coastline.

The story went on that an enterprising knight named Sir Mathac Maceshadow managed to kill Vanan. This lifted the spells on the ships, which the seas then smashed to slivers against the cliff walls.

It seemed like a lot of work for such a place. Maceshadow's Tower was square, not terrifically tall, and battered to pieces by the world around it, with spiderwebs of dead ivy along the sea-facing wall, which enclosed a courtyard with a three-story manor house and some gabled areas for the daily goings-on that kept a small tower running.

Stubby saltgrass grew in clumps from the wall to the sea. A single-horse trail led back to Grach through a skeletal forest, the trees scattered and leafless.

Saril figured, seeing it now, that Vanan hadn't really been such a great marauder after all. From the stories, he'd expected this place to be magnificent.

The rain hammered sideways off the ocean. The surf was deafening as it shovelhooked the cliffs in long swells a hundred yards from them and not far below, the tide near its highest for the season.

The gate was closed. The windows in the tower, and the windows in the manor that they could see, were completely black. Nothing moved. Nothing glowed.

Saril yelled again at the guardpost; no response.

"They had to see us coming," said Bevio. "There's nobody here!"

Saril kicked his horse and disappeared around the wall. It was a small compound and he came from the far side some time later.

"Nothing!" he said, riding up to Bevio. "We're leaving!"

SWORD DAYS

"Only a fool hopes to live forever by escaping his enemies."
– Viking proverb

Jarrod Torrealday awoke in the pink-gray light of morning in a comfortable bed high in the great tower at High River Keep, several days' ride from his own castle this time of year. The supple and luxuriously tanned body of Karra Talivel wrapped itself around him tighter, filling the bed with hibiscus and heat. He ran his hand through her hair, a snarl of blonde striped with brown.

"Do you enjoy my hair, lover?" she purred. Her accent was distinctly Faerie, sharp and precise on the consonants and slightly lilting. Exotic to him, even here, a million light-years from home.

"I love your hair," he told her, kissing her forehead. "But I thought only predators have stripes."

"I have stripes," she purred, rolling on top of him, "because I hunt the bravest knights." With an expert buck of her hips, they were one.

The room shrieked. The bed objected to the injustice. Gods railed from the beams overhead. Worlds ended and began again outside the window.

The Faerie word for mutual release translated to *the thunder and the rain*.

Grinning, panting, sheathed in candy-scented sweat, Karra rolled off him and dug her head into the pillow, burrowing as she drifted into whatever the Faerie did for sleep. He still wasn't sure. Eyes open, eyes closed, sitting up, lying down. She had said they didn't dream; they used downtime for remembering.

She spent a lot of time remembering.

He slipped out of bed, shook off needles of looming winter with a shuddered profanity, and wished for just one glass window. This was fall chill; winter loomed, silver-black and lethal. The bed beckoned.

An absurd strain of symbiosis had developed between them since their first night together at the start of summer. It was a structure he didn't grasp in its entirety, but it was immediate and effortless, and he shoved aside the occasional digs from his peers about elf magic and illusory charms. Whatever the cause, he was joined at the hip to a feral, magical being, her ferocity kept in check by a fathomless restraint and monastic gentleness, which in turn made her what he needed most: a hardened concrete tunnel under the blazing, collapsing house of himself. A place to forget about the string of bodies he'd left behind him across two worlds, now.

So many bodies.

Her arm snaked out to the spot in the bed where he wasn't.

Jarrod was not particularly tall, but lean and long-limbed despite his size, and hard-shaped with knots of muscle that appeared carved from rock by wind. Between a mat of dark blond dreadlocks and a tight sandy beard resided a pair of powerful eyes, periwinkle in the right light, and a row of perfectly white teeth that many knights here thought smiled too much. A curved scar crossed the muscles of his stomach.

The sky had erupted pink with morning across broken clouds that loomed storm-dappled and dark with cold. He set a log on the coals and blew on it until the fire burst to life.

His armor, a mosaic of bourbon-tanned leather and mail, rested on a mannequin in the corner beneath a banner from the Order of the Stallion, a gold horse's head over a golden key on a green tapestry. A massive warsword leaned against the armor, out of its scabbard and oiled.

Jarrod began his day as he usually did, dressing himself in the uniform of a knight off-duty, a black tunic with a gold officer's brocade at the stiff collar and a black velvet overtunic, known colloquially as "warrior blacks." He slipped his arm through a gold rank braid, tying it to a button atop his left shoulder, and attached the fourragere to his chest with a gold horsehead pin. Above the horsehead, which was roughly the size of a silver dollar, went a smaller pin, also gold: a crossed sword and key, the mark of a Lord Protector, bestowed by the King of Gateskeep for gallantry in defending a member of the royal family.

He buckled on a rapier and its attendant belt, slipping a medical kit in a black leather pouch and a Ka-Bar fighting knife onto it, first.

It was a hell of a sword, a long blade with a breathtaking swept hilt right out of Dumas, the satin-finished cage forged custom by a master smith in northern Maine. One of the last affairs he'd handled before leaving Earth.

Leaving Earth.

The pink-purple moon, down to a sliver as the season ended, peeped through a break in the clouds on the horizon, its lone slender ring canted with oncoming winter. He took a deep breath, as he still did whenever the moon was out.

He'd left Earth.

Not a hundred days ago, he'd rescued Adielle, the princess

of Falconsrealm and heir to the throne of Gateskeep, from captivity in the southern nation of Ulorak. He'd also killed Ulorak's most feared general, along with enough of his small army to stop in its tracks what would have been a costly and ghastly three-front war.

They'd given him an area bigger than Long Island for his troubles, a gorgeous, mountainous region north of here: the Wild River Reach, full of hardscrabble families and the country's largest silver mine. The king had taken it from the family of the late heir presumptive for colluding with the nation of Ulorak to kick off the short war in the first place.

Jarrod had no idea exactly how rich he was; no one on his staff was capable of counting that high. He owned the mine that produced the silver for the country's primary coinage, and coins not in circulation were stored in his castle's lowest basements, a fact that no one here at High River ever let him forget.

The wind slipped through the window, bringing a trace of damp dirt and the hint of rain, as if it stormed on the great ringed moon and he could just smell it here if he held perfectly still.

This was Jarrod's regular trip to the Falconsrealm capital to handle political affairs. He was at High River Keep so often these days that a steward had assigned him this apartment in the princess's tower, though the staff was evasive as to whether he was renting it, couch-surfing, or whether it came with the Lord Protector gig.

This morning's florid shade of hell involved a meeting with several lords from the Shieldlands, who would be airing grievances about Jarrod's proposed moratorium on scutage, the practice of sending paid mercenaries to fulfill the tours of duty expected from knights and lords in the king's service.

Their problem, as Jarrod understood it, was that the lords would send mercenaries to castle duty in their own knights' stead, instead of staffing their castles with mercenaries and sending their knights. As Jarrod had noted, often out loud, most of the mercenaries were cut-rate thugs with inferior gear, surpassed on every level by even the teenaged goons that the border lords knighted. If the lords didn't want the mercenaries, Jarrod argued time and again, why should the king?

This was what the day was going to be about. He had a plan. He had notes tucked in his shirt. He was ready for this.

He closed the door behind him and stepped onto the landing.

A haggard soldier rounded the stairs with one of the chamberlains just as he turned, and several aspects were wrong with it all at once. He wasn't wearing the pin of The Reach knights—a tower with a wave about to batter it—though he had his goatee in fine braids, the style of men of The Reach. The lack of a chivalric pin meant he was a soldier, not a knight or a rider for an order, and he wasn't a soldier Jarrod recognized, although Jarrod's castle garrison was fewer than sixty troops in total and he was pretty sure he knew them all.

It was a long ride from Jarrod's castle at The Reach to High River Keep this time of year, and about to become much longer once the snows came. The soldier's eyes sagged in a wind-burned face. He had his helmet under his arm and he hadn't brushed the mud from his boots, so whatever he had to say, he hadn't stopped for breakfast or even a drink first.

A good man on a horse, sent from an outlying garrison, and sent fast.

"Lord Protector?" the soldier asked, as the chamberlain pointed to Jarrod.

Jarrod grumbled. One constant between worlds, he'd found, was that only trouble knocks before breakfast. "Can I help you?"

"I hope so, my lord," said the soldier. "The Hillwhites have just taken The Reach."

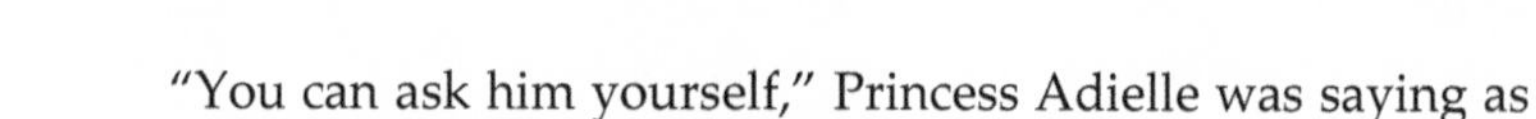

"You can ask him yourself," Princess Adielle was saying as Jarrod entered the audience chamber.

The royal audience chamber was on the eighth floor of the highest tower, and decorated in banners and tapestries, with the two largest on the wall framing either side of a polished wooden throne with a gilded cushion: the green banner of the kingdom of Gateskeep with its gold skeleton key, and next to it, the banner of the principality of Falconsrealm, sky-blue with a diving bird of prey in black.

Flames snapped and echoed from two large fireplaces along the curving outer wall, and the ceiling hung with fat candles in chandeliers lit even in the daylight. Along the walls between the windows hung the smaller banners of the various chivalric orders, including Jarrod's own. The wooden floor was splintery timbers inlaid with stone in the diving-falcon sigil.

Princess Adielle Riongoran-Thurdin stood before her throne. Blonde, slightly taller than Jarrod, and appearing much younger, her eyes were bright blue and slightly watery, and she maintained a poise and grace that made Jarrod have to catch his breath sometimes. She wore a long braid and layered dresses in shades of blue with gold embroidery, along with a gray wolfskin mantle over her shoulders, several beaded necklaces in bright colors, and a sword at her side in a silver-embossed scabbard.

Jarrod knew the sword; he'd given it to her. It had started life on Earth as a leaf spring on a 1971 Cadillac, rescued from a scrapyard and reborn through heat and hammering as a late-medieval arming sword, gleaming, sure, and deadly.

Two Falconsrealm knights in heavy black hauberks flanked

the room, their helmets on the ends of each table in puddles of mail. Jarrod recognized one from fight practice. New to the castle, he was young, aggressive, and stalk-thin, with a tight, clean jaw and narrow eyes. Jarrod remembered that he had good instincts, but he still needed help with his footwork.

The other was Lady Aveth from the Order of the Star, a broad woman, wide-faced beneath a dark bowl haircut. She'd fought beside Jarrod and Carter against Elgast's men a hundred days ago, a sergeant for the Order of the Stallion at the time but knighted to the Order of the Star for it and given the moniker Lady Aveth the Fearless. The Star was a top-tier unit composed of the most elite members of the royal orders, rough and dangerous riders responsible for finding lost travelers in a world made of monsters. It was exhausting, perilous, scary work, and knights of the Star often vanished without a trace. She nodded to Jarrod.

The soldier who'd come up to get Jarrod took a position near the door, pulled on his helmet, and rested both his hands on his sword handle.

Jarrod's eyes flicked around the room. It was quiet and still, which Jarrod knew was not good in a royal audience chamber, ordinarily a place rife with bustle and scribes. That the knights were armored was much, much less good.

He now knew enough about armor to know that knights didn't walk around the garrison in full war gear. Armor is uncomfortable, and it causes ringworm, and it gives you a headache, and nobody talks to you for long because armor stinks.

No one wears armor unless they have to, and even knights specifically tasked with standing watch wore as little armor as they could get away with. Padded jacks were acceptable, as a shirt of mail could be thrown on in a crisis, and some mercenaries working scutage might own little more than a jack and a leather helmet anyway.

Further, Falconsrealm was not at war. High River Keep's vantage point overlooking a crescent of a lake far below meant that any knight would have had plenty of warning to get their armor on, or more armor, if needed.

A lot of people in this room, Jarrod noted, were wearing heavy armor. Also, the two knights in this room were from royal orders, not mercs. Heavy hitters.

A man sat at each table, well-dressed and warm, and Jarrod knew them both. The first was Lord Doravai, the Falconsrealm commonwealth marshal. Tall, thick-shouldered, in gray layered tunics and a black knit cape doubled over his shoulders, he had a heavy brow and a head and face shaved clean even in the chill of the end of fall. He was the levy commander, and essentially a reserve general. If he was in this meeting, the princess was contemplating calling up a yeomanry.

The other was a long-haired bulldog of a man in fine and bright clothing of burgundy and silver, his dark beard in braids. His name was Ravaroth Anganor, informally called Lord Rav. He was a former infantry commander and advised the princess on matters of state security.

A small session meant that this was also a confidential matter.

Jarrod bowed with a flourish to Adielle, fist over heart. "At your hand," he said, a Lord Protector's greeting to royalty.

"Lord Protector," said Adielle.

She had been addressing a man who stood away from the table, a man Jarrod didn't know. He had a tight dark beard, and he wore black baggy silks with knee-high boots and a beautiful black silk cape with gold embroidery on the edges and gold on the reverse, which Jarrod could just see when the man turned to face him.

Black clothes were expensive. Gold embroidery, much

moreso.

Rich as hell, Jarrod thought.

He also had a large knight behind him in mail, dark furs, and a full helmet. It wasn't one of the Falconsrealm half-helms with its skirt of mail covering the face from the cheekbones down, but an expensive full helmet, vaguely Corinthian, the face slitted in a **Y**. Jarrod took him for a mercenary out of some trading crossroads and made a note to ask later.

The rich guy had a huge goddamn sword at his side, too, with a dark red handle jutting nearly to his shoulder, much larger than would normally be allowed in the castle except for nobles, patricians, and knights on duty. Jarrod had to wonder how he'd gotten in, and more to the point, how he'd gotten that close to the princess with a sword that size. It set off every alarm in his body at the same time. All he could come up with was that the guy had to be on a first-name basis with the royal family.

There was a familiar set to his jaw, a unique slant to his nose. Jarrod couldn't quite place him, but he looked like . . .

"Son of a bitch," said Jarrod under his breath, in English. The Hillwhites, the disgraced patricians of Falconsrealm, had sent a representative to meet the princess. With a great big sword and a goon to back him up.

"You just stay right there," Jarrod warned him. "Keep your distance, Hillwhite. And keep your hands still."

The man, who was clearly kin to the late Edwin Hillwhite given his height, broad jaw, and shock of dark hair with flashing eyes, paled. "You," he stammered. "You're –"

"Yeah," said Jarrod. "I am. Which one are you? Nice sword."

"I'm . . . I'm Halchris Hillwhite," the man stuttered. "Cousin to Duke Edwin, the man you murdered."

"I didn't murder anybody," said Jarrod. "Are we back to this, again? We handed him off to the Faerie, who dealt—"

"You killed him!" the man shouted. "You murderous little prick!"

"The Faerie dealt him justice as they saw fit," Jarrod continued. "If you have a problem with that, you can go to war with them. In the meantime, I'm a Lord Protector of Falconsrealm, which gives you the right to meet me in one-on-one combat. Let's step outside."

The large knight—who was significantly larger than anyone in the room, with muscles evident even under his mail— shifted behind Halchris Hillwhite.

Halchris was big, as were most Hillwhites Jarrod had met. He was just over six feet, and Jarrod's boxer's eye put him right at two hundred pounds. The guy behind him, though, would present an interesting set of problems to solve.

"Duke Edwin broke the law," said Adielle. "His lands were forfeit to Gateskeep. My father, King Rorthos, awarded The Reach to Knight Chief Lieutenant Sir Jarrod, personally. Halchris, I give you five days to disband your armies and leave The Reach, or we will remove you."

"I'll be checking the ledgers and talking with the foremen at the mine," Jarrod added. "If your guys take so much as a rock from that hill, you will give it back or I, personally, will come find you and break all your stuff."

The big guy stepped forward. Halchris put a hand on his shoulder.

"We can take The Reach," said Halchris, changing the subject and talking fast, now, because Lord Rav was, literally, growling. "We have it surrounded."

"Maybe," said Jarrod. "And your guys are going to camp through the winter? In the North?"

"No," said Halchris. "We've taken the villages of Grach, Astalia, and Walby, as well as your garrison at Maceshadow, and now Northtown." The town nearest The Reach. "The Reach is ours."

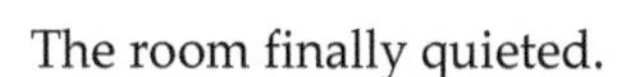

The room finally quieted.

"Halchris Hillwhite," said Adielle, sitting down on her throne. She spoke with a clarity and gravity that Jarrod had never heard from her and had hoped not to. "You have the right to audience with me to settle your grievance. You know the law."

"We're done with your laws," said Halchris Hillwhite. "And we're done with you, highness. We'll take what's ours."

The room went still except for Jarrod's fingers drumming on the grip of his rapier.

Lady Aveth picked up her helmet and seated it on her head, reducing her face to a curtain of mail below her eyes. The other knight followed suit. The message was unequivocal.

"Lord Jarrod," said Halchris, "tell your lord chancellor to surrender the castle. And the mine. And the vault with the coinage. We will take what's ours. And then, you come with us."

Jarrod grunted a short laugh and shook his head, smiling.

"What the hell are you smiling about?" snarled Halchris.

"You've signed your own death warrant," said Adielle to Halchris.

"At your hand," Jarrod assured her.

"Halchris Hillwhite, you've committed treason," said Doravai.

"We're past that," said Halchris. "Kill me if you want—"

"Okay," said Jarrod, stepping forward. The big guy behind Halchris shifted, and Halchris motioned for him to stay.

"—but we'll still take The Reach," Halchris continued, speaking fast, "And Gateskeep can't reinforce you at The Reach and also fight us in the west."

"'The west?'" Adielle asked.

"From Long Valley to the sea. We are The Western Hold," Halchris announced.

"You can't just declare yourselves a kingdom," said Lord Rav. "I mean, you need . . . well, a king, for starters."

"We are the Western Hold," Halchris repeated. "Every lord in Long Valley has sided with us. We have enough troops to fight Gateskeep and win."

"You're jesting," said Adielle.

"All we want is the stores at The Reach, which are rightfully ours. Surrender them without bloodshed. If you do so, we will remain a protectorate of Gateskeep in the west, we will control The Reach, and we will once again be your financiers."

"Or," offered Jarrod to Halchris, "I could just send them your head in bag and we could forget this ever happened."

"We have dozens of families allied to us," said Halchris, turning on Jarrod, exasperated. "Hundreds of knights. Gateskeep doesn't have the troops to fight us. Falconsrealm certainly doesn't. How are you going to fight without Hillwhite iron? Without Hillwhite silver? How are you going to field your knights?"

"How are *you* going to do it?" countered Jarrod. "If your men are *outside* my keep, and not *in* it, then the bridge is gone. We can stay in there for a thousand years. That keep survived the last Cataclysm."

Adielle announced, "He knows this, Lord Protector. His family used to own it."

She stood, then spoke clearly. "I'd say he's here because their initial push failed. I'd say your chancellor held them off, Lord Protector, and now the bridge is gone. They need us to surrender The Reach because if we don't, their forces will starve." The mountains near The Reach gave way to what Jarrod figured was a good three miles of tundra and scrubby grass before ending at the rocks and the massive cliffs under his castle, which spouted stunning waterfalls like faucets for gods. There wasn't much to eat. Or hunt. Or burn for heat.

Halchris's face fell.

"Nice try," Jarrod told him. "Go home."

Halchris licked his lips with a very dry tongue.

"We will take The Reach," said Halchris at last. "And you, Lord Sir Jarrod, if you won't come with me to meet your rightful fate, I'll kill you now."

"I doubt that," said Jarrod.

The big guy in the helmet stepped forward.

"You're right," said Halchris Hillwhite. "He will."

And then Jarrod recognized the muscles, and the ringed guard of the longsword at his side, painstakingly forged and ground with loving detail by the same smith who'd made Jarrod's rapier.

"Hello, Jarrod," said Renaldo Salazar.

"Let me get this straight," said Jarrod, waving his hands to stop the conversation and addressing Halchris. "You go all the way to my homeland to find yourselves a champion, and you come back with *him?* This—" they had no word for *dilettante,* much less for *wannabe.* "—This? What did you do, lose a bet?"

"Lord Blacktree is our champion," said Halchris.

"'Blacktree,'" said Jarrod. "Like 'Hillwhite,' only dumber."

"They made me a pretty sweet deal," said Renaldo, addressing Jarrod in English. "All I have to do is kill you."

"Yeah," said Jarrod. "Good luck with that."

The sword at Renaldo's belt was a four-foot longsword, and

Renaldo, for all his muscleheaded, loinclothed, idiotic preening at Renaissance festivals—where Jarrod had mainly seen him—was gifted with it. He competed in longsword at the international level, and Jarrod knew that Renaldo had made quite a name for himself in the world of illegal underground dueling that had cropped up after "The Incident" in Paris, in which Jarrod had accidentally killed an Olympic saber hopeful in a drunken swordfight.

If they both drew, Jarrod knew he was pretty much screwed. His rapier, even with its heavy blade, would never get through Renaldo's mail, which was certainly welded steel and not the local riveted iron, which Jarrod would still have had trouble with.

Renaldo, facing the unarmored Jarrod, had no such concerns. He might as well have been carrying a chainsaw.

"You understand," said Jarrod, addressing Halchris and switching back to the local language. "If you kill me now, they'll hang you both."

"If we kill you all, we walk out," said Renaldo, in the same. His accent was guttural, monotone, slightly slurred. He hadn't been here long.

Jarrod drew his rapier, and the assembly moved in front of the princess as Renaldo's mammoth blade cleared its scabbard.

Time slows in combat. Men weep as seconds crawl by, as friends fall, as prayers fly and horses scream. A thousand things happen inside a blink of combat time. The world drags.

Jarrod Torrealday relished combat the way others relish dance: consecration of the body, an invitation for a greater power to shepherd worldbound incapable flesh to the realm of the sublime. The cage of his rapier flashed in the light of the chandeliers. His eyes hardened to coals.

He lived in combat time.

Both knights and the soldier plowed into Renaldo as Halchris closed with Jarrod. His sword was very big and very shiny for a Falconsrealm weapon, a massive two-hander even larger than Renaldo's.

A feint, an envelopment, and Jarrod sent the huge sword out of line, steel singing and scratching. He lowered a shoulder into Halchris's belt and lifted him by a handful of pantleg, dropping him heavy and hard. Halchris scrambled up and Jarrod punched him in the face with the cage of his rapier, sending him back to the floor. As he came up again, the tip of Jarrod's rapier, scalpel-sharp, snaked out and caught him under the chin and came out below his ear. The greatsword rang off the floor and blood fanned the room like a thumb over a garden hose as Halchris stumbled back, shrieking and clawing at the side of his throat.

Not ten feet away, Renaldo was fighting off all three troops at the same time, hitting them with armored shins and elbows and throwing them into walls. Jarrod watched the local swords bounce off Renaldo again and again, blow after blow that should have been fight-enders. One—the skinny kid—got to his feet and Renaldo stabbed him through the chest. The point of the longsword came out his back, tenting the mail. The local armor and weapons were just no match.

Beside Jarrod, Halchris's legs kicked as he made creaking noises, blood misting from around his clenched hands and pooling on the floor.

"Sorry," Jarrod said, and charged into the fray to interpose himself between Renaldo and Adielle, who had her sword out as two of the three troops rolled on the floor and the third lay crumpled.

"Oh, really?" asked Renaldo, amused. Jarrod stepped back to make space, and Renaldo shuffled closer and tested him with a couple of feints, nothing elaborate; simple probing fakes sufficient to push Jarrod back.

The issue, Jarrod noted with consternation, was the track of the point of the longsword. No matter where Renaldo moved his hands, the point stayed directly on him. The blade floated, a far cry from the heavy smash-and-cutters he'd been used to fighting here in Falconsrealm.

It had been a long time since he'd actually fenced.

Jarrod circled, turning him around, at which point Adielle threw her mantle over Renaldo's helmet and stabbed him in the back of the leg.

"Mother-FUCKER!" Renaldo roared.

She kicked him in the back, knocking him into the wall. Renaldo spun, fighting with the fur, and she stabbed him, both hands, feet planted—beautiful form, Jarrod noted—dead center in the chest.

For a moment, holy shit, Jarrod thought, she'd killed Renaldo, but all it did was run him back a few steps. Her sword snarled in his hauberk, and she dropped it and leaped back as Renaldo threw the mantle to the floor and came at her, longsword high, screaming, the arming sword dangling wildly and banging off his knees.

Jarrod stepped in, taking the longsword with his rapier, and kicked Renaldo in the chest, freeing Adielle's sword with a yank and a twist. He tossed it to her with a whistle that tore through the room.

Renaldo moved out of Adielle's attacking distance before spinning again to concentrate on Jarrod, heaving, clearly hurting, and out of sorts.

"Highness, run!" Jarrod shouted, at full extension, not taking his eyes off the longsword. "Run!"

"We've got him!" she answered, holding Halchris's warsword. Renaldo backed away from them both, limping. *Goddamn right,* Jarrod thought.

"Run!" Jarrod ordered.

She wouldn't run.

A couple of quick, probing engagements goaded the longsword forward. He caught it near the tip with the rapier, levering it far enough out that it took Renaldo a breath to recover.

Amazing sense of measure and distance, Jarrod thought. Truly gifted. No overextensions, no overcompensations—at least, not while attacking. Surgical.

Scary.

He toyed with the tip of the longsword again, got Renaldo to pull it back into a tighter guard, and followed it in with a glissade, stabbing the inside of Renaldo's elbow. Renaldo shook his head and growled.

It was odd, Jarrod thought then, that Renaldo didn't take pain well. He lacked that measure of physical toughness that made an elite swordsman, and Jarrod could envision him as one of these oddly fragile lumberjack types who winced and swore walking barefoot in the yard. It wasn't much to work with, but he turned it over in his head.

Jarrod eked out another engagement, barely more than a feint, and thought he saw something in Renaldo's reaction that he liked. Another exchange and a scampering retreat out of long attacking distance, and he had it as the bigger man closed the gap and lunged.

Renaldo led with his hands.

It was a minor thing, a bad habit that some swordsmen pick up. Renaldo, like a lot of powerful and self-taught longsword fencers in modern schools, relied on his size and immense strength, and telegraphed his blows by moving his sword at the beginning of the blow instead of using the sword as an extension of his body. Renaldo announced every move a quarter of a second before he did it.

A quarter of a second was enough to keep Jarrod, an Olympic-caliber *sabreur* behind a world-class rapier, alive.

For now.

Renaldo attacked, hands-first again. This time, as Jarrod wrapped up the longsword, Renaldo connected with an elbow shod in mail. The world dissolved into sparks and prickling numbness as Jarrod hit the floor, rolled to his feet, and promptly fell over again.

The room had become a merry-go-round, blurring in the corners, gravity pulling at him in six directions as he watched Doravai and Rav closing with Renaldo and tried to remember what his feet were for.

The last two knights, slow on their feet, joined the fight behind Doravai and Rav. Jarrod rolled to all fours, crutched to a stand using his rapier and stood there a moment until the world slowed its spin, and then grabbed Adielle by the arm and threw her toward the door. "We're leaving!" he shouted. She opened it, and he followed her out at a run. He yelled down the stairs for help as he held the door shut, the wall before him still cartwheeling.

The door barred from the inside, not the outside; he would have to contain Renaldo through sheer force of will. He pulled until his hands ached and his shoulders burned. A tug on the other side would spell the end of the world.

He couldn't see. His eye hurt clear into his brain. He wondered if the socket was smashed and the eye bulging out of his head.

Adielle pulled at him as screams and crashes rang from the room. He shoved her back, then continued pulling on the door.

"If he gets loose in the castle, we all die," he warned. "You can't stop him. Those are weapons and armor from my homeland."

A knight in warrior blacks jumped in and helped Jarrod hold the door shut, while a second ran up the stairs to them with a spear, which they wedged into the handle and against the stone wall. A crowd had gathered, murmuring.

Behind the door, the fighting was dying down.

Jarrod looked Adielle up and down. "Where's the sword?" he asked.

"I gave it to Rav," she said. "What is his armor made of?"

"Steel," said Jarrod. "Good steel, from my homeland." *Case-hardened, welded chrome-moly, I'd bet. Same as mine.*

"Steel mail? How do we stop him?" asked Adielle.

Jarrod bit his lip in thought. "Hold this door until I return," he told the knights, looking up the stairs toward his room. "Keep him contained. You die holding this door if you have to."

"Lover?" asked Karra as Jarrod slammed open the heavy door to their apartment. She wore a gauzy white wrap around her diminutive yet resplendent body. She held his face in her hands and leaned up to examine his eye, which was turning a savage purple, the lid swelling closed. "My lover, heart of my eyes. Did you fight?"

"I fought," said Jarrod, easing her aside and stripping armor off the mannequin, throwing it on the bed. "An old friend, from my world. He's here to kill me."

"Your eye," she said. "Can you see?"

"I'm fine. I need my armor."

"You will fight again?"

"I need to kill him. We have him locked in a room

downstairs." His arming jacket was a motocross jacket of pebbled horsehide with inset carbon-fiber plates. He zipped it on. "If he gets loose, he'll kill us all."

Ten-inch military-grade work boots. Steel toes, speed laces, toggles.

Wrestling into a hauberk, probably the same stuff as Renaldo's but coated in black nitride, felt like it took a year. His mind screamed at him with images of Renaldo loose in the castle, butchering everyone, killing everything—his friends, his horse, the princess's dog—as he smoothed down the links and jumped up and down to seat it.

He locked a belt around the mailshirt, pulled the tie from his hair, and threw a mail coif of titanium over his head, black eighth-inch rings that fell across his dreadlocks like silk. Karra buckled one of his bazubands, a combination forearm and elbow guard, Persian in design, completely alien here and made of tooled leather in whisky and black, as he tucked his hair under the coif, swearing.

She handed him his helm, an enormous Barbute like Renaldo's, but with a locking faceplate and a skirt of heavy steel rings. He jammed it down and one ear bent in half.

He pulled it off, swearing louder, and tried it again. A matted lock of hair hung in his eye.

A third time, Karra helping, and everything seemed to fit.

He slipped the medical kit off his rapier belt and onto the belt of his arming sword, beside a subcompact pistol, and cinched it around the mailshirt, over the other belt. He considered just taking the gun and to hell with the rest of it, but he doubted if a nine-millimeter could drop Renaldo before he got across the room with that goddamn sword.

"This man," said Karra. "He can kill the entire castle?"

"Yes," said Jarrod, slinging his greatsword over one shoulder. He pulled on his gauntlets, which rightfully belonged on a magnificent suit of 15th-Century field armor that was in his bedroom back at The Reach.

"And you want to fight this man?"

"No," said Jarrod, and wiggled his fingers. Scales of steel clacked. "I want to kill him."

She kissed him, leaning up to do so. "Kill him, brave lover," she said. "Go fight him well."

She handed him his shield as casually as if she was his mother sending him off to school with a lunch box. It was a mighty teardrop affair nearly as large as she was, with the Lord Protector's crest on a green field, his sigil as a guardian of the realm. He slipped his arm through it and the world settled into place.

"Stay here," he told her. "I'll be right back."

He slapped his faceplate down and buckled it, then took the steps at a run, six flights down, skipping the trip steps—steps larger or smaller than the others, invisible in a helmet but reflexive to castle inhabitants—which he now knew by heart but had been a real bastard for months. Especially drunk, as he'd often been.

The spear still pinned the door closed when Jarrod arrived. The princess had refused to leave and was surrounded by a group of men and women with knives, swords, and a few axes.

"It's been very quiet," one of the knights at the door said. Jarrod recognized him, a sergeant from the Order of the Star, Lady Aveth's unit.

"Well, that's bad," Jarrod remarked. He fingered the plastic biteguard tethered around a bar inside the faceplate of his helmet, bit it, seated it, and shrugged his greatsword off his shoulder, drawing it with a flourish and dropping the scabbard.

It was a fantastic piece of gear, a reproduction of a 14th-Century *gran espée de guerre*, a great sword of war. Plain, gleaming, enormous. It was nearly four feet of hardened steel with a beefy edge designed to wreck armor and splinter bones beneath. Whether it would be effective against steel mail was anyone's guess, but he figured at the least he could beat Renaldo unconscious in his armor with it, which sounded immensely gratifying.

Someone picked up the scabbard for him.

He wondered about Renaldo's mail. He'd seen the local swords and even that two-hander bounce off it; only Adielle's, that wicked old Cadillac leaf spring, might have dug in, but the rings had bunched up around the tip of her sword and gripped the hell out of it.

The mail hadn't snarled on his rapier, which raised the question: what were the rings made of? Mild steel? Case hardened? Some kind of alloy?

Why didn't it trap the rapier?

He ran the rapier and the arming sword through his head. They were different steels entirely: different carbon contents, different tempers, different hardnesses. Further, there were a hundred differences in the shape of the damned swords alone. It could have been a freak occurrence, some one-in-a-million confluence of edge geometry and distal taper.

Kill him, he thought. *Just kill him and play with his armor later.*

He focused on the moment ahead.

There's going to be blood on the floor. Dark blood, dark floor. Slippery. Keep your balance. Drive from the hips, don't trust the floor. And if you flunge— the airborne, panther-like saber attack that combined a fleche and a lunge, and a short sabreur's lifeline against someone Renaldo's size—*you die.*

He spoke loudly and slowly, his voice muffled around the mouthguard. "After you pull the spear, stay behind me," he told the two knights at the door. "Do you understand me?"

"Yes, my lord."

"If he gets through me, do whatever you have to do to

make sure he doesn't get out of the room."

"How shall we do that, Lord Protector?"

Jarod motioned everyone back. "Hell, I don't know," he mumbled. "Be creative."

They slid the spear aside, and the castle went still. Jarrod's armor creaked in the held breaths of the group as he raised his shield, said a silent prayer behind his visor, and kicked the door open.

Jarrod was no stranger to human wreckage, but this was extraordinary.

He'd seen plenty of wet death in his few months here, and had handed out his own share. What Renaldo had done, however, was another realm altogether.

Blood patterned the walls, the tables, the tapestries. Doravai had been split from shoulder to hip, purple and gray organs glistening in an ocean of ick. Half of Lord Rav's skull above the nose lay upturned on the table, eyes wide, hair dripping.

Both knights and the soldier of the Reach were extremely and spectacularly dead, splayed out in various wide puddles still growing. In a clear space on the floor, a hand held a sword at the end of an armored forearm, the mail and bone sheared clean.

Above it all, the silence. He could hear his breath behind his visor.

No Renaldo.

Halchris was crumpled on the floor where Jarrod had left him, on his side in a quiet pool of black with his arm outstretched toward where Renaldo had been. It was a sad and peculiar way to end up, and Jarrod wondered what had been going through his mind in those last seconds; what he might have thought Renaldo could do for him as he bled out, the world dimming, Renaldo probably blind to him, still beating the shit out of all comers.

Boy, you're just slam-dunking Hillwhites left and right, aren't you?

Jarrod unlocked his faceplate and took a quick look left and right, then flipped it up.

Renaldo was gone.

He spat out his mouthguard and whistled. Half a dozen men and women came running, followed by three men in brown robes. Healers. Castle wizards.

"Where is he?" asked Adielle, adding, "Oh, no," as she saw the mess. "Oh, no."

"I have no idea where he is." Jarrod sighed. "Are there any other doors?"

"No," she said.

"Then stay by me," he advised. Jarrod grabbed one of the wizards by the sleeve. The main healer for the castle, Durvin, was away, studying at Gateskeep Palace. Jarrod didn't recognize the man whose robe he was holding at the cuff. "Did Crius put wards on this place?" he asked.

Crius Lotavaugus, the Lord High Sorcerer of Gateskeep and arguably the most gifted sorcerer in the realm, had placed a series of what amounted to force fields around the great towers of the palaces, preventing anyone from projecting magic through the walls. The lack of these wards had originally been an oversight, leading to King Ulo Sabbaghian, the leader of the bordering nation of Ulorak, stealing Princess Adielle with a brilliant teleport in the early fall and firing the starting gun for a ten-day war, in which Jarrod had rescued the princess and then kicked the Uloraki army in its collective teeth.

Wards kept people from zapping in and out on commando

raids.

Ulo hadn't had wards, either, allowing Jarrod to steal the princess right back.

The wizard was talking.

"What?" asked Jarrod.

"The wards," the wizard repeated. "They stop at the walls. He could—I mean, a man could have jumped, if there was a wizard to—I don't know, my lord. Maybe to catch him, and then teleport him."

Jarrod walked to the window, set his helm on the sill, and looked down. Nearly a hundred feet. Not enough to kill you, but it would make a mess if you landed badly. "How good would you have to be to do that?" he asked. "Catch him," he clarified.

"Better than I," said the wizard. "Far better."

These were castle wizards, part of the staff in simple brown robes and hoods, nothing showy or even notable about them. The other two had started to look over the fallen. One started to struggle with a knight's crushed helmet but the second checked for breath, then told him not to bother.

Jarrod picked up the big red sword from the floor, where it lay next to what had been Lord Rav.

This was not a Gateskeep weapon. The handle was too long, wrapped in crimson leather; the blade was mirror-polished, with no weld lines where steel edging should meet patterned iron spine. Forged and ground from solid steel instead of hammered together from charcoal and iron, the clarity of line and the finish were jeweled compared to even the best Gateskeep swords.

It was a gran espée de guerre much like his own.

A sword from Earth.

Renaldo landed in a splashing heap, shattered by cold. He gasped at the shock, sucked in water, and spasmed. He flailed. He panicked.

He was drowning.

Then he found the bottom and realized that it was just a puddle, crusted with ice and shin-deep. He rolled to a knee and coughed muddy water until he threw up chunks of fish in a searing slop of wine and coffee.

He reached to pull his helmet off, and the world disappeared in flashes and pain, a hammer to his lungs when he moved his arms. Bending over, he shook off the helmet, rinsed it in the puddle, and hurled it away, then threw back his mail hood with a shake of his head, which shot black glass from his heart into his eyes.

He figured his sternum was bruised from the stab the princess had given him, and it crossed his mind that Jarrod might have broken a rib or torn one free with that damned savate kick. He rested an elbow on his knee and squeezed air into his lungs an ounce at a time, swearing. The world was the tang of wet horse manure blowing sideways with rain and snow mixed in.

This fuckin' land. When they give me my castle, I'm going to name it "Mudland," and I'm going to tell these hapless schnooks that in our language it means "shining city on a hill."

He recognized the place immediately; it was the inner courtyard of West Keep, a mighty gray castle overlooking the sea on the northwestern tip of Gateskeep. He knew the smell, the rain, and the twin high towers behind the wall. The weird pink tinge to the clouds. It was a hundred feet from where they'd left when teleporting to High River.

He tried to yell at a figure in blue on the hillside near the inner wall of the castle, but his voice was a pale rasp, little more than a squeak.

A man in a wool mantle heavy with rain pulled at the shoulder of a shorter, stumpier man in a cloak soaked shapeless. They came to him at a run, hands on their swords. "Lord Blacktree!" one yelled.

Well, it is nice to be appreciated.

Renaldo felt around in the water for his sword, found the handle, and threw it out of the puddle as the two soldiers waded in to help him up. The figure in blue strode toward them, moving so fast and gracefully as if appearing to hover.

He put his arms around their shoulders, limping and splashing to the muddy edge and then to the grass, swearing and wincing and holding his leg. His fingers came away covered in blood. That princess of theirs had fucked him up, and good.

His arm was bleeding and stiffening where the tip of the rapier had snuck through the mail. He wiggled his fingers and his thumb sparked with nerves.

One of the soldiers grabbed up his helm and coif and the other handed him his sword.

The two soldiers parted before the figure in blue, taller than either. "Lady Jerandra," one deferred, and added something else that Renaldo didn't grasp. It was a horrid language, simultaneously sung and gargled, like a leprechaun throwing up.

Jerandra was ebony-skinned, white-fanged, and almost as tall as he was, half-Faerie, her mother a desert elf from the Gavrian Wilds. She looked for all the world to Renaldo like a statue of a Nubian warrior princess come to life. A soaked blue dress clung to contours and angles of a magnificent body, and the points of her ears peeked through a chin-length, jagged cut of black hair drenched and dotted with stars of rain and hail. The cold didn't seem to bother her.

She looked down at Renaldo, her eyes flashing turquoise above the dark and knobbed Faerie cheekbones. "They injured you," she said.

"Worse than that," said Renaldo. "They killed Lord Halchris."

"Then you failed," she assumed.

"No," said Renaldo, his tone thoughtful. "He did." Still holding his sword, not wanting to sheathe it wet, he bade them to get him inside.

Jarrod sat on a chair in the audience chamber, his mind coursing, still drunk from the head blow. The pressure of his eye swelling shut was an anvil on his cheek.

"I'm sorry?" Jarrod asked. He couldn't remember the question.

"Lord Blacktree. He knows you. He speaks your language," said Adielle.

"Yes," said Jarrod. "He's a swordsman from my homeland."

"As good as you?" asked Adielle.

"Maybe," said Jarrod. "I've fought him twice, now, and he's gotten the better of me both times. I'm better with a sword, he's just—bigger. And he knows all of my tricks. We studied under the same masters."

It wasn't entirely true. Renaldo had studied Muay Thai; his own sports had been boxing and *savate*. Most importantly, however, Renaldo was a longsword fencer while Jarrod was a sabreur. But the principle held: they'd each had far more training in advanced and alien styles than the typical fighter here.

Jarrod sighed. His competitive edge was completely gone. Renaldo was going to be a world-beater.

Four men were carrying the body of the knight with the

staved-in helmet out of the room. Jarrod watched them, numb, his mind wandering. Lady Aveth the Fearless, a piece of him realized. Judging from the impact to the helmet, Renaldo had likely head-butted her with a case-hardened steel helmet; badass that she was, she'd probably leaned into it, expecting to knock him through the wall. One of the finest knights in the world, dead in what appeared to have been a heartbeat.

Goddammit.

And Christ, he'd lost the mine. To Renaldo Salazar. Literally more money than he could count; he'd likely been the richest man in the kingdom until a couple of hours ago.

An easy job, a fabulous palace, a lover so hot that the horizon shimmered when he looked past her. The princess's ear.

Another incremental set of realizations: the suspicion that, somewhere untended, his higher functions had been conniving a way to fuck the whole thing up.

But the rest of the room was looking to him now, as a healer finally tended to his eye with tender fingertips and an incantation.

"How did they get in?" Jarrod asked.

"Likely, their wizard gated them to the front door," Adielle said. "The same as any Hillwhite, any lord with a sufficient wizard. He requested urgent audience. We let them in."

"With those swords," Jarrod shook his head.

"They were diplomats," she said. "No one would think to—" she cut herself off.

"He's not from around here, Highness. He doesn't think like you."

Adielle took a deep, shuddering breath. "Can you kill him?" she asked. "This Lord Blacktree?"

"I don't know," said Jarrod. "I know he can be killed, if that helps. He'll be able to cut his way through any army we've got, though. He could have murdered the entire palace."

"That's why you locked the door," she said. "Why you doomed those knights to die. And Rav. And Dorovai."

Jarrod nodded.

"You have to stop him," Adielle said. The lacquered calm was back, and he couldn't tell if she was pissed or terrified, and really, he thought, it didn't matter; in his experience, rage was just fear with no place left to go. "You have to find this man," she said, "and kill him. And that sorcerer, too. I entrust you with this. You, alone."

"At your hand," said Jarrod.

"What do you need from me?" she asked.

Jarrod let out a long sigh. "I'm going to need a squad, geared for travel. I need to know where he is, which means we need to talk to the High Inquisitor and find out if we have any spies near him. I need my armor from The Reach, though I don't know how we're going to do that," he admitted. "And then, I guess, the only other thing I need is Carter Sorenson."

HORSEBIRDS

"There is no avoiding war; it can only be postponed to the advantage of others."
– Niccolo Machiavelli

Two young soldiers snapped to attention, spears clacking as Carter Sorenson stepped out into the crisp willow smell of morning. He doubled his cape, cinnamon-colored fur that had once belonged to a bear, and piled it on his shoulders. He could see his breath.

Carter was immensely tall, head and shoulders bigger than the soldiers even in their helmets. His tunics and trousers, lustrous in muted fall colors, draped off slabs of muscle beneath his cape. His hair and goatee were shorn to finger length and speckled with silver, and his teeth were white and even with one gold incisor that flashed in the sun.

He watched from the top of the great stairs as two enormous black pegasi landed in the courtyard, wings hammering at the wind. Amazing creatures.

The local word for pegasus translated to "horsebird."

They were not a people known for their creativity.

Auth-ag, he thought, rolling the Gateskeep word through

his mind and hearing it ring. *Horsebird.*

The knights on the backs of the pegasi, in black mail and furs, unbuckled and swung down. Carter could see the gold commander's fourragères on the shoulder of his wife, Daorah Uth Alanas, the head of the Gateskeep Air Guard, as she addressed the valets. He couldn't hear the words. They led her mount away, its wings tucked in and looking like a hugely fat black horse.

With a grace that belied his size, he skipped lightly down the stairs and jogged out to meet her.

She pulled off her helmet and threw back her mail hood. She was tall and powerful with an honest face, athletic and straightforward with an unset broken nose and a sweaty mop of black hair.

Carter's ex-wife had been a Patriots cheerleader, ten years his junior. Blonde, photogenic, and nail-worryingly useless, she'd left him for an MMA fighter named Blaze two months before Carter had been recruited from Earth to come and train soldiers for Gateskeep.

He wished her well. At least, he did now.

Here, under the great ringed moon, his second wife rode a pegasus.

He strode over to her, the dew steaming off the flagstones in the sunlight.

"Good morning, sweetheart," he said, and threw his arms around her. She kissed him, glowing with sweat and horse and armor stink and the old-penny smell of iron. It was the smell of his life.

"My love," she said. "There's a rider coming from the west. He should be here shortly."

"Well, that will be interesting," said Carter, knowing it was likely the only element of the day that promised to be. He wondered if he would have time to get in some fishing beforehand. A small river fed Regoth Ur, and a mile or so from the castle, in a low valley rimed with willow, it slowed to a series of deep pools with gigantic northern bass that fought like hell. An amazing place to spend a morning.

"Ground pounder?" he asked, inquiring if it was a horsebound rider coming.

"Bird," she answered. It would be a pegasus rider, likely out of Gateskeep Palace, and therefore with big news.

"I was hoping to get some fishing in," he said.

"We'll have lunch ready for the rider," said Daorah. "No need to fish."

"There's never a *need* to fish," he said. "That's the point of fishing."

"Lunch," she repeated.

"Of course. It seems the least we can do." Carter knew that it wasn't a long ride to Gateskeep, but a tough one. It was plains and rolling hills between here and there, and the headwind this time of year bit like knives. Regoth Ur was a half-day's ride from the ocean, and the damp of the sea carried on a northwesterly wind that brought rounds of snow, fluffy hail like beanbag-stuffings, and a particularly shitty kind of slushy hammering rain that, no matter what you wore, always seemed to find its way onto the nape of your neck and sluice frigidly down the crack of your ass.

It was clear this morning, and cold, but the clouds were coming. If the rider wasn't having a bad day already, he would be by the time he got back to Gateskeep.

"I'll open up the wine cellar," Carter offered.

"And talk to The Two," she reminded. "We need to know where those foals are."

Carter let himself into the high tower of Regoth Ur through a set of massive double doors reinforced by iron rivets and bolts, closed it again behind him with a succession of latches and bars, and started up the first of several flights of stairs.

Regoth Ur was a sprawling village in and of itself, with roughly two hundred inhabitants whose jobs combined to facilitate the raising of pegasi and the training of the knights who rode them. The castle was small and understated, with two simple towers and a manor house where a keep would normally stand. Long, low walls encompasssed massive yards for the landing of air assets.

The largest tower in Regoth Ur was central to the breeding operation, and it rose out of the stables and gables that made up one of the largest courtyards and jutted nine stories into the fast-moving sky. The main tower of the keep, within its concentric walled defenses and high on the hilltop, was technically shorter at eight floors, though it stood much taller.

Carter enjoyed visiting the high tower, if for no other reason than it was run by two wizards—The Two, as they were called; again, not a creative people, these folks—and wizards, he'd learned, made their own advantages. Inside the stairwell, for instance, where he'd normally expect to see a candle set on a jutting platform mortared into the rock, a ping pong ball of blue-white light bobbed in the air at his knees as soon as he opened the door and ran ahead of him a few steps at a time like a bumbling puppy. A gentle breeze always blew down from the top of the stairs, the dusty sweet scent of an old library forcing out the ever-present smell of horseshit.

If there was one downside to this job, it was the tremendous amount of shit.

They raised and trained the flying horses for the king's air force. The wizards bred and raised the pegasi, Daorah taught prospective knights to fly them, and Carter taught the knights the finer points of swordsmanship and hand fighting.

There were days, however, when he found himself scraping pegasus shit off his boot and swearing, and then realizing that it was *pegasus* shit, and he'd get dizzy and have to sit down.

Adjustments.

You have not truly experienced a world of magic and wonder, Carter thought, *until your biggest peeve is scraping pegasus shit off your boot.*

Seven floors up, he sat down on the top step and dug his fingers under his kneecap, which hated the stairs. After a lifetime of combat—three years as a defensive end for the Patriots, a moderately successful career fighting in a cage, and ten years as a kickaround medieval buff studying and demonstrating treatises on the greatsword, because you can never have too many hobbies—he had found his place in the universe a good ten years after the end of his left knee's working life.

The light paused at the door, then bounced back down to his foot and danced a quick circle around his toe. Carter stood, rubbing his leg, and knocked on the door. It opened of its own volition a moment later.

Stintlash and Ristan were The Two. They were exceptional wizards, entrusted with the most sensitive of military secrets, and goddamn, Carter thought, you wouldn't know it to look at them. Unkempt, puttering, and short-tempered, Stintlash was a great, fat, bearded man; Ristan was a small, thin, younger man whom Carter would have mistaken at a glance for a farmer or day laborer: stoop-shouldered, dirty, tangles of black hair.

The library was walled with books in cases fifteen feet high, and dotted across its floor with display cases, tables full of parchment, and glass cases brimming with tinctures, powders, and vials of substances Carter figured he was better off not knowing about. The centerpiece of the room was a skeleton of a pegasus, the bones gleaming, spindly wings reaching out directly at eye level. He gave it space.

The floor below was the foaling operation, which no one was allowed to see. As he understood it, the pegasi were birthed through magical means, and all he knew was that several were due a few days ago.

"Greetings, magisters," he said, saluting and, he hoped, showing deference. Stintlash grumbled from his pots and mixing, and Ristan waved over his shoulder from a table where he was absorbed in several parchments and books at the same time. Carter saw that the parchments were shuffling on the desk and the pages of the books flipping without Ristan touching them. "Daorah sent me to ask about the—"

"Tomorrow," interrupted Ristan. "Ask tomorrow."

"I'm here to ask, today," said Carter.

"We'll have them tomorrow, if you leave now and stop asking," Stintlash snapped.

"That looks difficult," agreed Carter, nodding to whatever they were studying. "I'll be back tomorrow."

"Do you want something for that knee?" asked Ristan, still reading.

"What have you got?" asked Carter.

"We're working on a salve for the girth sores," said Ristan. "In the black jar." A white quill pen lifted from the table and shot like a slow-motion dart toward a set of shelves near Carter.

Carter knew now, from months of hearing the knights complain, that conformation of the saddles to the bodies of the pegasi was a bitch. The pegasi were each the mass of a Honda Civic, bristling with muscles and extra moving parts. The rigging on the saddles, which were complex affairs to allow for the motion of the wings, contacted the body at points that were always in motion. The riders had to groom the hell out of the pegasi, and every saddle had to be built custom and fitted meticulously, or the insanely expensive animals came down with tack gall or even abscesses. The knights rode in a kneeling squat, legs above the wings, and the damage was most severe over the withers.

Flying horses, magic flashlights, but they were still working on Aspercreme.

Carter shook his head imperceptibly and lifted up his trouser leg, then rubbed a double fingerful of the ointment into his knee. The result was like shutting off a faucet.

"That is outstanding, gentlemen," he told them after a few long breaths. "How do I get a tub of this?"

"Stop bothering me today, and I'll have some for you when you come back tomorrow," said Ristan.

"Really?" asked Carter.

"Really."

"Done."

He let himself out and jogged down the stairs, the light bouncing happily ahead of him, his knee feeling the best it had felt in years.

He opened the door and the sun shone through a break in the clouds.

He wondered what Jarrod was up to.

Jarrod flung open the door to his apartment. Karra was there to greet him in a mantle of tenderness and patience, feather-light and smelling of fruit-punch candy the way she always did. "Lover, did you fight him?" She handed him a glass of wine.

"He escaped," said Jarrod, emptying the glass in a gulp and setting the red sword against the wall, in its red scabbard that someone had taken off Halchris Hillwhite. "The son of a bitch. He helped the Hillwhites steal my castle. Our castle."

"Your eye," she said. "Can you see?"

"I'm fine. I need to sit down. I killed a man."

She pulled some clothes off of the corner chair near the window, where she knew he liked to sit. She poured him another drink. "You need a healer for your eye. Who did you kill, if he escaped?"

"It's fine," he snarled, then realized he was snarling, and apologized, pulling her to him. She sat on his lap, the heat from her body crawling over his neck and face like a blush. "It's not fine. I hate killing."

"You should," she said, then changed the subject. "You said they stole the castle. How does one steal a castle? They put it under their arms and snuck away?"

"They have it surrounded," said Jarrod, adding, "With a small army."

"Ah," she said. "So, we still own our castle. That makes this easier. Now, how should we get rid of them?" she muttered into his chest.

"We?" Jarrod asked. "You're adorable."

She flashed her fangs playfully and growled at him. "Urrrrrr. I can fight. I will fight for you."

"I have no doubt," said Jarrod. "We can see if Prince Akiel will give you his bear to ride."

"I chose you as the bear I ride," she said, and kissed him. "So, what of your old friend? Must we kill him?"

"I don't know," said Jarrod, looking out the window. "Probably."

"I would find it hard," she said, "to kill a friend."

Jarrod took a long breath. "Some more than others," he said.

THE BEACON

"Peace: In international affairs, a period of cheating between two periods of fighting."
- The Devil's Dictionary, 1911

Ten days' ride to the south from High River Keep, Ulo Sabbaghian, King of Ulorak, paced the bone-colored floors of his map room, the second-largest chamber in the royal apartment.

Ulo was tall, with skin the color of deadened leaves scarified with symbols and flesh-colored tracings. A black tangle of hair framed eyes as blue and brutal as the sky in summer. He wore silver and black clothing and always sandals, never boots.

The Silver Palace was a mammoth black tower built into a monolith of black rock in a world of black dirt and denuded black mountains. The map room and the apartments in which it resided stood in contrast, decorated in white stone with white wooden floors; a refuge from the darkness of the land around him and the tower beneath him.

Out a rough-edged marble window, a sluggish river cut a silver ribbon through the dark valley, pushing its way around the base of the mesa five hundred feet below Ulo's apartment, which spanned an entire floor of the palace. Beside the river wove the fine stone road that led to the Eastern Freehold.

He'd built a world out of roads. And he'd built the roads from the treasures in this room, his maps.

The locals hadn't understood the true value behind maps. Creating detailed maps had been the first thing that he had done when building a war plan to retake this place twelve years ago.

This kingdom—it was once again a kingdom, he reminded himself, though it had for a few tricky weeks last spring and summer been a protectorate of Gavria—had once been called The Black Hold, and troops and tradesmen had simply wandered through, following the river and the mountains, guessing at the locations of passes. They'd died in staggering numbers without good maps.

Maps in this world were rudimentary representations, even at the highest levels of the governments, where representatives had great ornate parchments penned with stunning artistry but little relevant detail. While working with the Gavrian High Council earlier in the year, he'd noted that even the great warrior nation of Gavria didn't have the maps that he had.

He sure as hell hadn't told them about his.

Until the advent of his maps, The Black Hold had been considered an unnavigable void between the Eastern Freehold and Gavria. It was foggy, and dangerous, and the mountains all looked the same. The black soil spawned thorny scrub to eye level, and there was one river, its banks mired with silt. When the fog rolled in—and it did, hot and sulfuric and dark as spun mud—the river disappeared, and when the river disappeared, men disappeared. They'd wander too close to the river and get swallowed up, or they'd drift too far from the river, get lost for days, and pitch over from dehydration and heat.

Ulo looked out over the river.

I am the King of The Black Hold.

Like Jarrod and Carter, Ulo Sabbaghian was from Earth. Jarrod and Ulo had been geographic neighbors at one time; Ulo had been raised in New York, the fatherless son of an immigrant mother, whereas Jarrod was from Connecticut, a banker's boy.

However, unlike Jarrod Torrealday, Ulo Sabbaghian was native to this world.

His mother, Adosa Sabbaghian, had been a neophyte sorcerer and the youngest wife of King Sabbaghian the Black, sent through a time-space rift with a purse full of diamonds to live on Earth carrying an unborn son. Minutes later, a crack team of Eastern Freehold knights had kicked down the door to her chambers, where they proceeded to murder the rest of the family and later bury the pieces in unmarked graves across this valley.

But even those Freeholders had fought their whole war against his family, and won, using shit maps.

In point of fact, Ulo had developed his plan to carve out this valley from the Eastern Freehold and win back his father's kingdom after intercepting a military planning map shortly after his arrival here. The concept of including detailed information about key terrain apparently hadn't occurred to anyone, here. The local maps had the general idea of where cities and villages lay, but militarily, everyone just got to where they were going and then made do, as if constantly fighting wars of exploratory conquest.

He'd sent his teams out over this valley for half a year before he made a move, pacing off every large rock, fighting position, defendable hill, possible ambush point, and quicksand mire in every piece of land that he wanted to take. Battles became a matter of waiting for the Freeholders to show up, and then making sure his men knew where not to step.

After beating back the Freehold, he used the maps to build simple, wide stone roads crisscrossing the valley and the high plain. First had been a road between Gavria and the Freeholds for trade, far from the river banks. It was a safe, patrolled road, with a well roughly at every day's walk and his palace at the center. Another road east, to the Wastes, where Gavria dug its gold and iron but where no nation laid claim. A bridge and a road to Falconsrealm.

Roads brought trade. Trade paid for the wide stripe of silver up his great tower on each face, flashing in the sun on a clear day; a beacon for miles. No one ever got lost wandering Ulorak anymore, although the mountains all looked exactly alike with their tremendous black peaks, and some days the sun hid behind the shitty hot fog that smothered the land like an army of vengeful ghosts.

You followed the road. You followed the beacon.

The roads followed the maps.

A small city cropped up outside the beacon. The city brought taxes, and an army, and eventually a silver kingdom in the black desert. He was King Sabbaghian the Silver.

Now, years later, artisans had carved the maps into wall-sized reliefs of wood and soapstone. Even his roads were laid out, exacting.

His general, Elgast of Skullsmortar, was dead a hundred days, killed by Jarrod Torrealday. The man Ulo had chosen to replace Elgast, an aging warlord and former court adviser to the Gavrian Parliament named Mukul, was doing the best he could in the general's stead.

Mukul was no great speaker. He was no great swordsman. He was no imposing presence. With a dozen battlefields behind him, he had absolutely no business on another one.

He was no Elgast.

But he had his moments. And he was having one, now.

Ulo took a long pull at his pipe, feeling the corners of the world blunting with each heartbeat as he held in the smoke. The tang filled the spaces between thoughts as tendrils of haze drifted through the damp and chill. Amazing stuff.

The valley in Ulorak didn't grow much, but he had to admit, it grew amazing weed.

Ulo and Mukul stood before a map carved into a wooden board the size of a large table hanging on the wall.

Mukul was thin, and not tall, with clipped dark hair graying at the temples and fine clothing that was often purple, and that was mostly purple today. Like most Gavrians, he was dark-skinned. Today, he and Ulo both wore heavy, dark hemp trousers as well as silver cloaks, even inside. Winter was well on its way.

Mukul used a small pushpin to stick a piece of paper with a symbol on it to the wooden map, placing it at the southwestern-most corner of the Teeth of the World. "Here. They'll come through here."

Ulo's voice was low and grating, his words slow. "They won't come up the hill to the high plain?"

"Never. Not after the beating you gave the Eastern Freehold. Nobody is going to attack you uphill. We took that option off the table a long time ago."

"I hate when you use the word 'we,' when speaking about Gavria," said Ulo.

"It's an old habit," said Mukul. "I'm a stranger to treason."

"You get used to it," said Ulo.

"Gavria calls this mountain at the tip of the range 'The Flint.'"

"Why is that?"

"Because if anyone approaches it with steel, they risk starting a fire."

Ulo gave that some thought, and a longer pull on his pipe. "I like it."

"However," he continued, "They'll be looking for a pass. They'll find it here." He pointed to the map. "But they'll have to enter the Shieldlands. And if Gateskeep learns that Gavria has set foot in the Shieldlands, they'll mobilize the border lords, and Gavria will have a much bigger set of problems than they want."

"That's if Gavria and Gateskeep don't reach some sort of truce," said Ulo.

Mukul shook his pipe at Ulo. "How much of this have you had?"

"Just enough. My mind is clear."

"This gives us an opportunity," said Mukul, returning to the map. "Gateskeep hasn't yet deduced that Gavria is not coming for the Shieldlands." He'd been on the Gavrian War Council.

"They're not?"

"Not since you left," said Mukul. "The only strategy for taking the Shieldlands would be to prosecute a war the way you'd directed. Attacking civilians, razing villages, avoiding the military power projection points instead of engaging them. Nobody in Gavria is willing to do that."

"Then the war is ours," said Ulo.

"How do you figure that?" asked Mukul.

"Gavria is scared of me. They don't want to fight on my terms. That's the only advantage I need."

"It might behoove you to consider an alliance with Gateskeep."

"After kidnapping the heir to the throne?" asked Ulo, incredulous. "How much of this have *you* had? On top of that, they have one man who killed nearly half of my best battalion and my top general getting her out of here."

Mukul shrugged. "Which begs the question: why do you want to keep fighting him?"

SECONDS

"The leading cause of death among beavers is falling trees."
- The Farmer's Almanac

Jarrod rolled into the courtyard of the head of his order atop Lilith, his commuter vehicle. She was a big northern racking horse, black and powerful and thick-necked, with wisps at her hooves and a rolling gait that felt like wheels underneath him. His warhorse, Perseus, a Percheron-sized roan half again the mass, was a truck with bad shocks by comparison.

He was dressed for a day in the rain. His jacket was a custom job, a knee-length burgundy coat of soft, oil-impregnated leather that buttoned double-breasted on the sword side—for him, the left—with an integrated *cuir bouilli* spaulder and vambrace. It was functional, flexible, protective, beautifully engraved, and rakish as hell coupled with a cape and his oilskin Stetson, one side of the brim curled upwards.

Fruit trees and statues adorned the muddy courtyard, and a two-story tapestry with the Order of the Stallion's horsehead sigil hung above the gate to the main manor. The knights at the gate saluted, noting Jarrod's gold officer's braid at his shoulder, his Order of the Stallion horsehead pin on the left side of his jacket below his Lord Protector's sigil, and let him pass.

"Other side," he told a valet as he swung down on the horse's right. The valet walked around Lilith's nose and Jarrod handed him the reins. "Left-handed," Jarrod muttered. "My apologies."

A woman in a heavy green winter jacket and black trousers, with a fat two-handed broadsword with a stained leather handle at her side and a black fur wrap around her shoulders, came out to meet him as the valet led the super-expensive horse away.

She was about Jarrod's height, thin and flinty with a tight wet ponytail and blue eyes set in a taut face arranged around a magnificent aquiline nose he'd come to recognize as from western Gateskeep. He noted the Order of the Stallion pin on her cloak, tied to a Chief Lieutenant's gold braid that peeked out from beneath the fur, and then that she was missing the tips of three fingers between both her hands.

"Lord Protector," the chamberlain said. "I'm Knight Chief Lieutenant Lady Dara."

"My lady chief," said Jarrod, saluting and then handing her a rolled parchment from inside his jacket. "That goes to Captain Gwerian. The princess has requested my audience with the commander. I'll wait here, of course."

"Nonsense," said Dara. "You'll come at once."

"Hey, great."

Directly inside the front door, the chamberlain led Jarrod up a curving flight of wooden stairs in a corner of a well-lit three-story anteroom. Everything in the manor was oak and iron, all of it hand-rubbed, dark, and glistening in torchlight. The stairs, though wood, were solid enough to not creak under his boot.

A door off the stairs emptied onto the fourth floor, into a long hallway with doors down either side. The air was cold, thick, and sweet from dozens of candles sputtering in sconces down the length of the hall, a smell he was coming to associate with fall, and soon, apparently, winter.

Dara led him to a heavy domed door at the end of the hall and opened it. "Knight Chief Lieutenant Sir Jarrod of Knightsbridge, Lord Protector of Falconsrealm," she said.

Jarrod saluted and dropped to one knee as Dara crossed the room and handed the scroll to the commander.

Jarrod didn't look up, and it didn't matter, as the room was lit only by fire and the commander's head was down behind an enormous desk as he wrote something for a bit.

Gwerian stood and saluted, and Jarrod stood and approached the desk.

And he knew why the sense of scale in the room was off.

Captain Gwerian, one of five captains of his order and a chief spy in the king's military, answering only to the king, the commander of the order, and the Lord High Inquisitor—the secretive and sphinxlike figure who oversaw all the spies of the realm—was a woman not more than five feet tall and likely not any older than Jarrod. She wore her hair pulled back in a short ponytail like Dara's, and her jaw was severe and angular, her neck cabled and unusually long above her warrior blacks.

Her eyes flashed with intellect, roaming Jarrod and sizing him up: the muscles of his hands, his foreign boots, the cage of his rapier, the lack of armor; every detail slimmed down, streamlined, ready for single combat at a sideways glance.

There were moments, he was finding, when this world gave him a panoramic external view of himself and his place in things, and this was one of them. Brass knuckles in his pocket, rapier at his side, a black eye, good arch supports. The world was a dangerous place.

"You sure kill a lot of Hillwhites," she said.

"One does what one can," Jarrod returned.

"Mm," she agreed. "Sit. Please."

She had a comfortable leather chair before her desk, and the four-foot rapier at his side meant shedding his swordbelt to sit down. As he peeled his gloves and unlocked his belt, she broke the seal and read over the scroll, her mouth twitching to one side a couple of times. Dara stood by the window, attentive, quiet, hard-eyed, that colossal sword by her side and one hand on the pommel.

Jarrod sat, his sword across his lap.

"What were you thinking, locking that fucking door?" Gwerian demanded, looking back at the paper.

Jarrod really wanted to know what the letter said.

"You locked three knights and two lords in a room with a demon," she continued. "Are you an idiot?"

"Arguably," Jarrod admitted. "But I got the princess out. If he'd killed me, he'd have killed her, and there would be no one to stop him now. I had to run upstairs and get my weapons and armor."

"You have weapons and armor that can stop a demon?" asked Gwerian, pushing the letter aside. "Talk to me about that."

"I wish I could," said Jarrod. It occurred to him right then that Gwerian didn't seem to know that, at least by the local definition, he himself was a demon, having been technically conjured into their world. And yet, Renaldo had been classified as one. It was an intriguing double standard, and he wondered if she was merely being polite; if not, he had to wonder who was hiding what from whom.

"I don't know if they'd stop him, but I knew with just this," Jarrod tapped the cage of his rapier, "and no armor, I had nothing. He had a sword that cut through mail like it's chopping wood. I saw him put the tip through a center-chest hit with good mail, through and through, out the back. His helmet is the hardest steel I've seen." He decided not to mention that it was made of steel identical to his own. "He killed Lady Aveth by smashing her helmet with his." He cupped his hands against each other, then pressed them together. "Like that."

"Well, that's concerning," said Gwerian. "Still, it's not your place to sacrifice people who outrank you. *They* should have run. *You* should have died."

"I didn't have that luxury," said Jarrod. "I had one chance to get the princess out, and I took it. I am a Lord Protector."

"Which is the only reason you're not swinging right now. You understand that. You lost the coin vault for the entire kingdom."

"Yes, ma'am." Military custom dictated that Jarrod refer to her as *ma'am* and not *my lady,* as she was his superior officer. A subtle distinction, but an important one.

"And now, she wants you to go and find and kill this . . . Lord Blacktree," Gwerian said, looking at the scroll again. "With more of my knights, after you just killed three of someone else's."

"Well, yes. The princess wants him dead."

"A lot of people want *you* dead," said Gwerian. "Just so you know where you stand."

"To be fair, ma'am, that's just another day for me."

"Don't get sharp with me, Chief Lieutenant. Not today. Not after this."

"Ma'am," said Jarrod, "Since joining this order, I've spent half my career getting yelled at and the other half getting medals, usually for the same thing by different people. So, take whatever side you're going to take on this and be done with it. The princess wants me on a mission to kill this man and his wizard. I'm pretty sure I don't need your permission to do that. I'm here to tell you that I'm going to do it. I'm just open to suggestions as to how."

There was a long silence. "You've got some balls on you," she said, at long last.

Jarrod nodded. "So I'm told," he said.

"Still," she shook her head, "The bottom of my good ideas list right now involves giving you any more knights."

"Fine," Jarrod said. "I can go alone."

Gwerian scowled. "Not by the hallowed and indomitable tits of my ancestors. You will be supervised."

"Yes, ma'am."

"Everybody," she said slowly, "wants you dead right now. With the exception of probably the princess, and me. And even so, she wants you out of her sight. You don't send a Lord Protector out of your reach with enemies coming over the hill. She's really pissed at you."

"Yes, ma'am."

She did the thing with the corner of her mouth again. "Give me a couple of days to figure out who we can afford to lose if you decide to take the knights I give you and attack a castle with just your cocks in your hands. Again."

"It worked last time," Jarrod admitted.

A slow smile crept across her face. "I bet Rav hated you," she said, her voice wide with appreciation. Jarrod knew that Lord Rav, who'd died in the room with Renaldo, had been hard to get along with and difficult in meetings, usually because Rav was right all the time.

"Rav hated a lot of people," said Jarrod. "However, he spoke highly of you," he added, omitting that he'd never once been told the head of his Order in the city was a woman. Not that it mattered, but it would have been nice to know.

"Of course, he did," said Gwerian. "He had a tree in his trousers for me."

"That happens," Jarrod admitted.

Gwerian looked back at Dara, who smiled at them both. "It doesn't have to," Gwerian said.

"Fair point," Jarrod agreed.

"Well, I have to send you to Gateskeep Palace," said Gwerian. "You're right about that. The princess wants it done, but I sure hate to. I can't imagine the shit you're capable of bringing down if you fuck this up, and I see no way that you won't. What I'm going to do is send you along with a couple of knights who are up here visiting from the Shieldlands, Carj and Aever. Maybe you can all keep each other from getting killed."

"We'll try."

"I have no doubt. When you get over there, *do not* go after this—" here, she looked at the paper again, "—Lord Blacktree. We have eyes and ears. Your seconds will know how to reach them. Find out what 'The Western Hold' is up to. Once you've done that, run your ass back here on that pretty horse of yours with a report, directly to me. I don't care what it says. Report anything. Report that there's nothing to report. Just give Princess Dimples some time to cool off. Ride down, ride back. Do you understand?"

"Yes, ma'am."

"In the meantime, I know a few people. I'll smooth this out and send you to get your castle back and see if I can give you a nice big army to do it with. None of this you-and-your-best-friend shit. Hell, I may join you."

"The princess wants me to kill Lord Blacktree."

"And you will," she said. "When we get you your castle back, stand on top of it, look west, and wave. He will come to you."

"Thank you, ma'am."

"Don't thank me," she said, rising. "Be ready to travel in two days. And don't screw this up."

The tomb of Knight Captain Sir Javal of Ravenhurst was simple yet terrific, a one-room home of stone. A slab of gray rock with an inlaid gold key and horse's head stood stalwart under a stone overhang, with a bas-relief carving of Javal's face inscribed with his name, family, and accomplishments. A brief military man's eulogy and a hell of a job of it, too.

Jarrod knelt before it in the rain, his knees sunken in mud even here under the eave, looking up into Javal's face, forever stern, forever proud. Today, it seemed, forever mad at him, as he'd so often been during Jarrod's internship as a rider—more than a soldier, not yet a knight—for the order. In the distance, several men dug a grave in a flatter part of the cemetery, shovels rasping and thucking in the downpour.

"I miss you like you can't believe, my friend," Jarrod began.

"It was a mistake to entrust me with this. With anything," he added. "I may have destroyed the entire country. I may have ended your world. I don't know what to do, now. You might know, but I sure don't."

He tried to imagine what Javal would say, some shred of wisdom or strategy resident in his higher functions that an apparition of his mentor might kick loose, but it wouldn't come. The tomb was still and the graveyard silent except for the crackle of the rain and the grunts of the men working in the distance. It was silent because Javal was dead, and his position in the order was filled, and it's what war was: great men obliterated and the world moving on, its heroes and their moments washed away like chalk outlines in the rain.

Younger soldiers had to step up in their stead and hope.

"Few hear calls to war so loudly as you."

The voice startled him, and he turned to see Karra, a slip of a woman, shoulder-high in a dark hooded cloak sodden with rain. Muddled locks of striped hair fell forward around her face, her chin as fragile as a thought and every inch of her throbbingly, brain-hammeringly beautiful. She slid in beside him, a breath of grace in a whiff of candy, warm as the sun, her arm around his waist. Her voice, crystalline, musical, and exacting—never a wrong word, but all the coughed and tongue-retracted consonants in the Falconsrealm accent focused, precise, and therefore completely fucked up—was the greatest thing in the world right now. "My brave lover," she said. "Today, you become a hero again?"

And, there it is, he thought. *I have officially lost my hero status.*

"I'm nobody's hero."

"Everyone considers you a hero," she said, reaching up to kiss him. "Especially me."

He'd brought her with him to Falconsrealm because the forests at The Reach were stark and thin, and started miles away from his castle. High River Keep was surrounded by trees; she seemed happier here. Still, though, she sang songs of dark, moss-hung forests and stood outside in the rain for hours, and he could tell she'd been doing it just now and had somehow wandered over to him.

Karra could always find him. She couldn't tell direction indoors—time and again, someone would find her standing in a hallway, looking in either direction, confused and sometimes sniffling—but if he was in the building, she could find her way to him like a bloodhound.

So much about the Faerie that he didn't understand. He felt a pinch at the back of his neck just thinking about it.

"I killed a lot of people today," he muttered into the top of her hood.

"You didn't," she said. "They died because of the man who came to kill you. If he'd killed you, he'd have killed us all. Others can't see that."

"No," said Jarrod. "They can't."

"I love you, and bound myself to you, because you can see

it. You saw what the others couldn't, and you chose the hard choice. You always choose the hard choice, which makes you a hero."

"I lost this one," said Jarrod. "I'm no hero."

"Battles make a hero," she said, "not victories. Every hero loses their final battle, anyway. Does it make them less of a hero?"

"No," Jarrod said, looking back up at Javal.

"Warriors fall. Heroes rise." She kissed him again and nodded to Javal. "Make him proud."

Jarrod kissed her forehead, then turned to Javal, saluted slowly, and walked away with Karra on his arm.

ENCAMPMENT

"Who asks whether the enemy was defeated by strategy or by valor?"
- Virgil

Sir Saril of Red Thistle, chancellor of the Wild River Reach and Jarrod's second in command, looked out over the battlements of the Tower of The Reach that afternoon as the sun broke misty and cold.

"That's a lot of fires," he said.

Bevio nodded in agreement.

"A few hundred men," Saril guessed. "A thousand, maybe."

"This far extended, half of them will be support."

"And where'd you learn so much about warfare?"

Bevio slapped him on the back. "I was studying while you were busy beating asses and chasing tail."

"There's no way they're getting in here. This is a bad plan on their part."

"It's never a good idea to assume your opponent is an idiot," Bevio waxed.

"They have to be idiots. There's no way in."

"They have to have a plan. They wouldn't be here unless they had a plan. All we have to do is figure out what they plan to do."

"No small chore," Saril admitted. "We don't even know what they want."

"I'd guess they want this castle," Bevio suggested.

"You are truly a brilliant man," Saril said. "But that I could think like you."

"Keep trying."

They were safe enough up here. The fires were spread across the hill some mile or so distant, flecks of light in the gray. The wind blew the smoke toward the mountains.

Of course, Saril grumbled to himself, the easiest way to determine what was going on would be to send a team out to the encampment and return with the army's demands.

The issue, however, was that he only had thirty-seven knights, and another twenty footsoldiers that he could draw from the city if needed. The people of The Reach, the city which sprawled down the cliffside from the tower and the great keep, were not warriors—no more than anyone else from the North, anyway. If he sent four troops out, and didn't get them back, it would be a considerable loss. Instead, they'd pulled the drawbridge.

"They've got to know they can't starve us out," said Bevio. "We have nets for fish, we have heat, we have water. Do we even know who they are?"

"We haven't been introduced," Saril grumbled.

"No sigils? No flags?"

"Nothing, yet," said Saril, grinding his teeth in thought.

"Their dicks will be frozen inside out in a few weeks. Where are they going to get firewood? What will they eat?" The hillside where the forces had camped was tundra and scrub. "They don't even have wood for siege engines. What do they think they can do?"

Saril shook his head. It was idiotic. A siege against The Reach was an exercise in futility, and with winter a few days away, laying siege this far north—in the rolling tundra of The Reach, far from firewood, far from supply lines, but within the eventual reach of Falconsrealm's heavy cavalry, slowed as they may be by the snowy passes—amounted to an elaborate form of suicide. It baffled him.

A young servant boy named Kyle, who had just started training with the castle swordmaster, brought him tea in a silver mug. Saril blew at it, looking out over the landscape, thinking, as Bevio cut a slice off a large piece of cheese on a platter Kyle had also brought.

"Something Lord Jarrod said," Saril grunted. "About coincidences."

"And?" Bevio knew Jarrod said a lot of things. He was a sharp man, as sharp as some wizards they knew.

"He said that there are no coincidences," said Saril. "That there are only—what did he say? —fragments. 'Glimpsed fragments of relationships far larger.' Connections that we don't realize. Connections we've forgotten."

"And?" Bevio asked around a mouthful of cheese.

"Three of our towns and a garrison tower have been sacked, and all the people are missing. Where the hell did they go?"

Bevio didn't have an answer. It was one of the first times in a long time that he'd wished he'd studied even more.

"Hillwhite sends," said Daorah, reading a note in the waiting hall, as behind them, lunch was served on a table piled high with steaming steaks, breads, and vats of soup. "'Stand with The Armies of the West against Gateskeep or perish.'"

It was a gorgeous room, and comfortable, and one of Carter's favorite places in the castle. Here, the timber floors were covered in thick silk rugs instead of furs. It had a picture window instead of an arrowslit, and faced the snow-capped, cloud-topped Gateskeep mountains to the southeast. The wind rarely came from that direction, so the room stayed comparatively warm. The fireplace was well designed and the view was breathtaking. It was a great spot for easy meetings, with comfortable sofas and chairs and a desk for writing, and a huge table for food.

This was an easy room, but not an easy meeting.

Carter glanced over at his sword, leaning against the wall in its scabbard, chin-high on most men, and then to the rider who'd brought the message. He was a serious, slender young man in warrior blacks who seemed slightly effeminate for a knight, compared to the swaggering, mail-clad bruisers Carter had been used to seeing until he'd arrived at Regoth Ur. However, the knight wore a pin for the Order of the Falcon, showing that he'd ridden a winged horse in combat.

Pegasi cavalry were a different breed of soldier altogether, unshakeable badasses steeped in a secretive craft that blended mayhem with the awesome responsibilities of magic.

"Hillwhites," Carter repeated. "When are we going to stop killing Hillwhites?"

"It says they have The Reach," said Daorah. "'The Army of the White Hills,' whoever they are, 'have taken The Reach,'" she read.

"I find that hard to believe," said Carter. He had been to The Reach a few times. It was a formidable outpost with a good mile of walls corkscrewing up and down a pinnacle that loomed several hundred feet above the ocean. It would be an absolute bitch to assault.

"They haven't taken it," he assessed. "They may have surrounded it, but there's no way anyone took that castle if Jarrod Torrealday is still alive."

As Lord of The Reach, Jarrod was one of the richest men in the kingdom, and the depths of The Reach were the storehouse for the coin of the realm. There was a reason it was built the way it was built. One way in, one way out, a very long way down. *Thou shalt not burgle.*

Jarrod had a thousand people living around the castle inside the spiraling walls. Hundreds of peaked and perpetually spray-damp roofs poured steam, heated by the geothermal activity that warmed the very rocks beneath them. The keep didn't even technically need firewood to make it through the winter.

The Reach remained highly dependent on trade, though, being in the ass end of the continent. And yet, the mighty bridge was only big enough to get two horses and a cart through in each direction, creating, as far as Carter knew, the only traffic jam on the planet.

Jarrod could take them at the bridge. Probably single-handed.

He looked at his sword again. It was made of an industrial steel used for saw blades, hand-forged to an astonishing hardness and durability. He'd taken limbs with it, armor and all.

"Ah," she said, reading further. "The White Hills is, apparently, the area west of Dragon's Trail and north of High River. Mining country. Silver country. The Hillwhites used to administer it. White Hills, Hillwhites. Clever."

"Not really. If those guys ever have an original idea, it's going to die of loneliness," Carter grumbled.

"Well, the Hillwhites have turned from mining to treason," Daorah said.

"Is there any money in that?"

"Apparently not, or they wouldn't be stealing ours," she answered. "This says that we are to relinquish this keep to 'The Armies of the West,' whatever the hell that is, and in return, they will spare us when they get here."

"Well, that's awfully nice of them," said Carter.

"Indeed," she agreed. "Thoughtful, polite. So very Hillwhite."

Carter scratched his head. "So, now we have 'The Western Hold' on one side, and 'The White Hills' on the other?"

"Apparently."

"No one tells me anything anymore," he griped. "Two new countries, just popping up out of nowhere."

"Temporarily, I'd guess," Daorah predicted.

Carter paced for a while. "The West. So, the coast? Over those mountains, way out there?"

"I'd imagine," she said. "It's kind of vague."

"There's a palace between here and the coast, if I remember correctly. A big one. I'm pretty sure it's the capital of the country, and it has a lot of soldiers in it."

"Most of our assets are in the bottoms of Axe Valley and Long Valley, looking south. If there is, in fact, an army coming east across these plains, we could be in trouble."

"You're telling me we're alone up here?" asked Carter.

"Largely," said Daorah. "Gateskeep's troops might meet them here, but we don't know if this other army is moving yet. We're not set up for a long siege, love. The walls will hold them out for a day, maybe, but after that, we'll be fighting them in the halls. If they decide to take this castle, we will lose the town."

"I need a map," Carter mused. "How many soldiers do they have?"

"There's no way to know," said Daorah.

"That doesn't say?" he asked, motioning to the letter.

"It doesn't."

"Someone knows," said Carter. "All we have to do is find that person."

"And then what?"

"Well, beat it out of them, I hope."

"Hillwhite will demand an answer," reminded the rider.

"No Hillwhite is in a position to demand anything of me," said Carter, then turned to his chancellor, a broad-shouldered man with wispy gray hair named Alel, who was standing in the doorway awaiting orders. He'd been a knight in the early days of the Order of the Falcon and had been the chancellor of Regoth Ur for ten years, staying even after Daorah and Carter had taken it over. "Alel, bring us maps, please. We'll be dining in here."

Alel vanished as Carter began clearing a table.

War is weather, Jarrod thought.

Rain hammered the stable as Jarrod set his war saddle in the cart, settling it in among the armor for his destrier, Perseus. A team of squires and valets arranged bags of feed and a barrel of water in the front of the cart, nearest the seat. Perseus, an enormous blue-gray charger—a roan—so massive he needed his own, larger stall, watched the commotion from over the door.

Jarrod's black plastic footlocker with his armor and weapons was the last item to load. It took two men to lift it, as inside were two shirts of mail, his coat of plates and grand steel pauldrons, two helmets, and a handful of weapons. Jarrod shoved a leather case containing the red greatsword beside it.

He was stroking Perseus's neck and the valets were hooking up his ponies to the cart when Jarrod met his two new sidekicks. They were tall, young, serious knights in riding clothes: dark mail, black padded jackets, dark heavy cloaks with the hoods up, warswords at their sides. "Rider," one acknowledged, an informal greeting among knights.

"You're the Lord Protector?" the other asked.

Jarrod turned from Perseus, showing his pin and officer's cord. "I am."

"I am Sir Carj of Bitter Lake," said the first. "This is Knight Lieutenant Lady Aever, daughter-lady of Black Valley."

Aever's father, Jarrod knew then, was Lord Hulm of Black Valley, a knight and lord who controlled a trade shortcut to The Reach through the mountains northwest of here that would otherwise be impassibly dangerous. He was high on the list of people not to be screwed with, renowned for skinning captured *sheth*—the ogres that lived in the tangled wilderness—and leaving their hides for their tribes to find. "We're your seconds," said Carj.

"Riders," Jarrod acknowledged, shaking hands.

"What's all this?" asked Carj, looking at the cart.

"My gear," said Jarrod. "Where's yours?"

"We're not going to war," said Aever. Her voice was the same pitch as Carj's, and she was slightly taller, with wider shoulders. She, Jarrod thought, was also not to be screwed with. Literally nor figuratively. "You ride in there with all this," she said, "and you'll bring down a shitblizzard."

"They have my castle surrounded."

"And you're going to take it back yourself?" she asked.

"Well, I was hoping you'd help," Jarrod admitted.

"No promises until we get there," said Aever. "We'll get a better grasp on the situation once we get to Gateskeep. However, it seems like you're doing a lot of work before you know what you're up against."

"Story of my life," said Jarrod. "But it's worked out so far."

"You understand that if we do this right, we won't have to fight," said Carj.

"You understand that if we do this wrong, we all die," said Jarrod.

"Have you ever been on one of these missions before, sir?" asked Aever.

"Not exactly."

"Then trust us," said Aever.

He found her voice entrancing, with its deep ring and practiced military clarity.

"Riding gear," she continued, "no coats of arms, no armor. No pin. We'll be staying at inns and farms until we get to the palace. We'll want to look like local knights until it's time to show our pins."

"We are local knights."

"Local knights who aren't you." She looked at Perseus. "You're serious about bringing this horse?"

"You bet your ass," Jarrod said.

Half an hour later, Jarrod had dug through his gear and, with their help, picked out what he thought he needed and what they thought he could get away with. He wore his arming sword over the jacket, on a double-loop belt sporting a leather medical kit beside his Springfield subcompact pistol under his left hand. His massive, four-foot greatsword with its black handle hung from Lilith's saddle. And under it all, a shirt of lightweight titanium mail, effectively a T-shirt of tiny rings like his coif, split in the front for riding and hanging short across his thighs.

He had an apologetic head-butt and long and heartfelt neck-scratching session with Perseus, yanking his head back as the big idiot tried to nibble at his hat. He swung up onto Lilith as the stablehands tied Perseus to the back of the cart and two of them, Marc and Hat, jumped in the cart behind the reins.

"Both of you, huh?" asked Jarrod. They grinned.

"You still look like you're going to war," said Carj, on a gray mare much smaller than Lilith. Aever rode a tall black gelding. Behind them on a painted mare, an older, rough-looking man in mail under a wet fur cape, gray-bearded and stoic in the rain, led two warhorses and a fat mule laden with packs and bags. Jarrod noted the scarred grip of the warsword on his saddle and the mail rings sewn into the backs of his gloves. A sergeant, he guessed.

"I am," said Jarrod. "Let's ride."

FISH

"If you ever find yourself in a fair fight, you deserve to lose."
- Jarrod Torrealday

Lord Rogar Hillwhite addressed a table of stern nobles over a breakfast of fresh fish, dried fish, wine, and cakes, in the westernmost and highest tower of West Keep. Sitting on a fjord five hundred feet above the sea, the towers of West Keep gleamed as the sun threw brilliant red beams across the clouds to the west, the small hall still in shadow.

Rogar was unmistakably a Hillwhite, tall and dark haired, with a commanding jaw and rigid posture. He wore the same type of clothes that Halchris had, if gaudier; more flash to the gold, more sheen to the silk. Renaldo had had trouble keeping them straight, and at one point had taken to referring to them as The Boopsie Twins.

"We're awaiting a declaration of war," Rogar stated. "It's just a matter of how long it takes King Rorthos to grow the stones. In the meantime, we need to keep an eye on Gateskeep possibly rallying auxiliaries at Axe Valley. If they move on us before you're ready, they will crush us."

"And how soon until you have access to the stores at The

Reach?" asked a warlord named Gorhius. Broad, bearded, and well-dressed this morning in loose folds of green and black, Gorhius called the shots for most of the lords of Axe Valley.

"It's coming," said Rogar. "Our troops have it surrounded."

"I've been to The Reach," said Gorhius. "Surrounding it is not sufficient. What's your plan to get inside?"

"I have a plan," said Rogar. "It will take some time."

Jerandra caught Rogar's eye from the end of the table, and Gorhius caught her looking.

"You don't have time," said Gorhius. "You're going to be running out of brothers and cousins in short order. In the meantime, Sir Jarrod the Merciful is in High River, not at The Reach. If they give him an army, your days are numbered."

Renaldo leaned against the doorframe, dressed casually in a gray cotehardie and dark leather trousers. He was a ridiculously muscled, olive-skinned man; his chest and shoulders ballooned up from a tiny waist and the cables of his thighs were visible even through the leather. He wore his long dark hair held back with a black band, and though his teeth were white and his eyes serious and dark, there was a marked deformity to his face, one side notably flatter than the other; one eye higher than the other. It was an odd scar even here, in a world of scars.

"I can take Jarrod," he said.

"My understanding is, he beat your ass," said Gorhius.

"Not even close," said Renaldo. "He ran, even though I was outnumbered."

Gorhius laughed, and asked Rogar, "Have you noticed that everyone you send against Sir Jarrod comes back dead?"

"I'm still alive," said Renaldo.

"Say that tomorrow," grumbled Gorhius. "You're talking about Sir Jarrod the Merciful."

"'The Merciful?'" laughed Renaldo. "Oh, no. He's going to be merciful!"

"The last person who tried to take him was Commander Gar," said Gorhius.

Gorhius's second, a tall, dark-goateed man named Cadir, had heard the story. He set his wine down. "You're going after the guy who took down Gar?" he asked Renaldo.

"Yes," said Renaldo. "And?"

"He killed seventeen men—" started Cadir.

"—Vomit," said Renaldo, the local equivalent to *bullshit.* "Let me stop you right there. He did not."

"No vomit," said Cadir. "Commander Gar of House Fletcher went after him with twenty men last summer, at High River. It was the evening that Sir Jarrod was knighted. All twenty of them were House Fletcher boys, most of them from Axe Valley, but some of them knights, trained in the Shieldlands. I knew two of them. Sir Shul and Sir Fal, brothers out of my hometown."

"He beat twenty men?" asked Renaldo.

"Twenty-one, including Gar. How do you not know this?"

"My homeland is far from here," Renaldo admitted.

"They cornered Sir Jarrod in the storeroom under the barracks at High River," said Gorhius. "When it was over, three of them lived, but they're still in prison, and the way I hear it, they're all cripples. Think about that: one man with a sword, against twenty-one good men, in a small room. He walks out. They don't."

Cadir took up the story. "When it was over, he took Commander Gar prisoner. Sir Jarrod was drunk as shit the entire time. It was during a feast, and they let him get good and drunk. He did that *drunk.*"

"I can kill him sober," said Renaldo.

"You're that good?" asked Cadir. "Truly? Because a mate of mine was on castle duty, says it took three days to mop up all the blood. There were brains on the wall. They still find teeth in the corners of the room. If you had twenty more men, couldn't take him."

"I can take him," Renaldo assured him.

"Then, a week later," Cadir continued, "he and Karr, Son-Lord Soren, beat back a battalion of a hundred men sent from Ulorak at the Silver River Pass. Set up at the top of a hillside and ambushed them, the way I hear it. They took a dozen knights with them and went up against a battalion of one hundred soldiers. The entire army surrendered. Sir Jarrod the Merciful killed their general, Lord Elgast of Skullsmortar."

"General Elgast is dead?" asked Gorhius. "First I've heard."

"By that little shit's own hand, in one-on-one combat," said Cadir. "So, you," he emphasized, gesturing at Renaldo with his goblet, "you're telling me that you're going to kill Sir Jarrod the Merciful. I'm telling you that unless you can shit yourself a dragon, you're going to die. And if you get killed fighting him, and they give him an army, we're done."

"I can take him," said Renaldo.

"No, you can't," said Cadir.

"We'll see," said Renaldo.

Rogar addressed Gorhius. "Falconsrealm has to contend with the mountains, in winter. They can't move fast enough to get to The Reach before we wear it down, but we need to move from here, to reinforce them. It will take all but a shadow of our troops, because there will be losses across the northern plains. Those are Rorthos's lords, and they'll put up a fight. That doesn't leave us much to defend The Western Hold with.

"When Gateskeep hears of the siege on The Reach, they will mobilize through Axe Valley to reinforce. It's faster this time of year for them to move up the plains and reinforce across the north than it is for even Falconsrealm to move through the mountains. You must stop them, or at least slow them. They must not catch us from behind. And if they attack the Western

Hold, you need to keep them back. We will also need a contingent of your best, here."

"Why not send my best to reinforce at The Reach?" asked Gorhius. "It's faster. They're ready."

"Because my best are better than your best. We will need my best at The Reach. Not yours."

"You want me to send my best away, and then leave the rest here to take a beating from Gateskeep?" said Gorhius.

"You're here, aren't you?" asked Renaldo.

"Meaning what?" asked Gorhius, incensed.

Renaldo nodded at Rogar. "Meaning, you've got his trousers down. You might as well get on your knees and get busy. No one said it would be pretty."

Cadir rose and straightened his swordbelt as he kicked his chair back. "You watch your tone, foreigner, or we'll find out just how good you are."

Leather creaked in the ensuing silence as Renaldo adjusted his crotch and shifted the sword on his belt.

Cadir took a long breath through his nose and approached to long attacking distance, one hand on his sword handle. "Give me one reason why I shouldn't just kill you right now."

Renaldo stood taller. "Well, it's a very nice room," he suggested.

Cadir drew his sword, a long saxe with nearly two feet of blade. "Someone will clean it."

Renaldo moved to draw, and Cadir moved before the great longsword was clear, lunging to run Renaldo through.

Jerandra stood, Renaldo sidestepped, and Cadir crumpled, writhing, the saxe sticking point-down in the wood where he'd dropped it. Squeaks and mewling noises escaped his mouth.

"What the hell?" demanded Gorhius, looking from Gorhius, to Rogar, to Jerandra.

"She has a gift," said Renaldo. "War magic. She makes his

mind feel pain."

"His mind believes someone has flayed him over his body," said Jerandra. "I can flay his mind to the bone." With a nod of her head, Cadir screamed until the walls rang. "Or, into the bone," she demonstrated.

"Enough," said Renaldo, and Cadir went limp on the floor, his eyes white in his head.

Renaldo grabbed Cadir by the shirt with one hand and dragged him over to the stairwell, then turned him face-down by the shoulders and took a careful moment to arrange him so that his mouth rested on the edge of the first step.

He turned back to look at Gorhius and held the warlord's eyes as he stomped on the back of Cadir's skull with the sound of a bottle breaking in a leather bag. Blood ran in rivulets down the stair.

"We have an arrangement," Rogar told Gorhius, as Renaldo kicked Cadir interestedly and got no response. "Lord Blacktree is here to kill Sir Jarrod The Merciful. She," he pointed to Jerandra, "is here to ensure he does so, and that includes keeping him safe from idiots like your man bleeding on my stairs."

"You could have said as much," Gorhius grouched.

"I enjoy this," said Jerandra to Gorhius. "You would deny me that?"

Gorhius glared at her as Rogar continued. "When Sir Jarrod the Merciful is dead, we give these two lordships in Western Gateskeep."

"I want a castle on the water," Renaldo added. "A big one. I want to be rich."

Gorhius nodded. "Fine."

"Are we clear?" asked Rogar. "Do you have any other questions on this at all?"

Rogar clapped his hands and nodded to Cadir's body when

three servants in warm, if unremarkable, dress arrived. One asked for a healer in low tones, and Rogar told her not to bother.

Renaldo took Cadir's place at the table, picked up his goblet, and nodded at the servants taking away the corpse. "When we get a shot at Jarrod Torrealday, he'll envy that man."

DREAM CATCHER

"Courage is knowing what not to fear."
- Plato

A knock on the door resounded through Ulo's map room; the crisp rap of a spear on a slab of wood as dense as thorns.

Lower doors in the Silver Palace were made of rock, hung on pins finished like jewels so they pushed open with a finger, but up here, in his chambers, the doors were single-plank monstrosities, cut from massive trunks hauled out of the mountains near the Falconsrealm bridge at immense expense.

Ulo and Mukul stood near the largest carved map, each with a pipe in one hand and pushpins in the other. The latch tripped and the door swung open ahead of a powerfully built young man, copper-skinned and serious in a bright silver skullcap and gray robes. He approached Ulo and Mukul with his hands folded.

"Galè of Lor," Ulo greeted him. "My friend. Slayer of demons. Shining star of the Silver School. How do you fare?"

Galè had grown in the years since Heggy. Youthful yet massive, gone was the scarecrow gauntness and gone was any fear. Ulo had seen few men, ever, with less fear.

"I am well, Your Grace." Galè didn't meet Ulo's eyes but kept staring at his hands. His thumbs twitched, tangled, and untangled.

"Go ahead," said Ulo.

"There is a new demon in Gateskeep," said Galè.

Mukul watched from the window, puffing on his pipe.

"A demon," said Ulo, relighting his own with the touch of a finger.

Ulo remembered the destruction of homes in Lor four years ago, the death of the magister, the theft of conjuring components. Hunting down Galè and recruiting him as a student of magic, although the boy had no real gift for it; he was, however, one of a dozen men in history to kill a demon with his own hands, even if only temporarily.

He also remembered permanently killing that damned demon. What a bastard that had been.

Ulo listened as Galè told him of Lord Blacktree and the Hillwhite uprising; what he knew of it, anyway.

Clouds danced outside the window as his pipe glowed, and Ulo finally spoke.

"You're telling me," Ulo said carefully, "That this demon is from my world."

"Yes, Your Grace."

Ulo pinched off the bridge of his nose between his thumb and forefinger. "Twelve years," he said. "Twelve years I've been here, and I've been alone. In the past year there have been three more to follow me from my world."

"I'm sensing a trend," said Mukul.

"Do we know," Ulo asked, with calculated patience and calm, though his pulse charged ahead like a hammer on his rib, "who conjured this demon?"

"Yes, Your Grace. Jerandra of the Wastes."

There are words that stun the heart, and these were Ulo's. In an untended corner of his mind where old things lay unspooled, jumbles of filament reared their tangles and organized them into a tendrilous hand flipping him off.

"I've been wondering how she was doing," he muttered.

It had been two years since Jerandra had graduated from the Silver School, a gifted conjuror and an extraordinary wielder of war magic. And also, he remembered with closed eyes, a spectacular lay. Elves put forth a low-wattage psychic emanation during sex, effectively a drug to humans. He'd known she'd go far.

"Our understanding is that this demon is working with Jerandra, who is under the employ of the Hillwhites, to kill Sir Jarrod the Merciful."

Ulo puffed on his pipe and flicked the bowl with a finger. "Well, if they do, that would be one problem less," he decided.

"Respectfully, Master, would it?"

"Gather your men." Here, Ulo referred to Galè's crack team of wizards and resident axe-slingers, the clandestine unit that responded to demon conjurings throughout the southlands. "Go to Axe Valley. When you find this demon, contact me before you do anything."

Galè saluted and departed on silent feet.

Ulo returned to the task of adding marking pins to the map, each a unit of Gavrian troops gathering for a push into the Shieldlands and eventually across the Teeth of the World. Come spring, the massing collection of pins would spell the end of everything he'd ever done.

A SOFT PLACE TO FALL

"Whoever wishes to keep a secret must hide the fact that he possesses one."

—Johann Wolfgang von Goethe

"By our beloved departed," said Carj as Jarrod's chivalric menagerie came into a small farming settlement and dismounted. "That is a great horse, sir."

Jarrod figured they were thirty miles south of High River Keep, a half-day's ride at a trot, and the mighty peaks of the Falconsrealm mountains loomed far ahead, with Horlech somewhere behind them on the right atop a cliff. The foothills, carpeted with green and draped in mist, yielded to great black shadows beyond, an expanse of forest lowing as needles of snow pricked at it.

Jarrod loved Lilith's single-foot gait. It helped, too, that she was a gentle, easygoing, likable horse, because he was no great horseman and he had the feeling she knew it.

Riding a racking horse was as close to training wheels as he could get. She had an animated, rolling gait that moved as quickly as the knights' horses at full trot, except Jarrod didn't have to post in the saddle since Lilith didn't jar him in the slightest. It felt like riding a magic carpet.

The knights' horses were well-exercised and muscular and could hold an easy trot all day, much longer than a man could hold himself at post and longer than anyone wanted to get their lower spine pummeled in a sitting trot. Every hour or so they'd slow to a walk and the knights would get their legs back under them. Jarrod's legs, however, were still fresh even after a morning of riding.

He swung down and tied her reins to a tree whose broad orange leaves, half-fallen, kept her somewhat out of the spatters and spits of rain. The valets climbed out of the cart and started tending to the horses.

"How do you intend that we find this pass?" Jarrod asked. He couldn't even see the mountains through the fog and rain behind the houses and the hill.

"Well, we keep these mountains on our right, and then when we see bigger mountains in front of us, we turn right," said Aever. "It's over one of these hills. If the weather clears, we'll know."

"It's winter," said Jarrod, snugging down his gloves, which were soaked through and chilled despite the Gore-Tex beneath the oiled leather. "The weather may never clear. Somebody couldn't just, you know, build a damned road right to it? We need to spend a few days dicking around in the rain?" He stopped just short of asking what the hell was wrong with everybody around here, because he knew too well.

They toughed it out; that's what was wrong with them. They all did. It was how they did everything.

"Why build a road?" asked Aever. "We know where the pass is."

"That's not even close to true," Jarrod corrected. "If we knew where it is, we would be there already." He couldn't believe they didn't have a map.

"Is something bothering you, my lord?" asked Carj.

"Time is wasting," said Jarrod. "My castle is under siege. My lover is back at the palace. I'm cold, I'm hungry, my ass hurts, and it's only the first day." The ride would be at least five days—and perhaps much longer—in the snow and rain. It felt punitive. It *was* punitive, he told himself. "I want to go beat the crap out of these guys and then spend the rest of the winter without pants. Let's just get on with it."

Two men in dark and wet clothes came around the side of the nearest house, hands open in greeting. Carj waved back. "I feel you, sir," he said. "This is the first step."

"We'll take that one," said the sergeant, pointing to the next house over, the first words he'd said all day. His name was Thron, and he had a voice like gravel thrown through a tunnel. Jarrod noted a broad scar across Thron's neck where the beard didn't grow and figured that was why he didn't talk much. "You officers can have the close one, here. It's bigger, probably has better beds. Go on, my lords. Get out of the rain."

"We should just put up a sign," the farm owner laughed. He was a gray-bearded, tall man named Vern. And, apparently, a lot of people came through his farm looking for the way through the mountains. "'The Pass. One day west.'" He handed Jarrod a wooden cup of beer, and his wife, a round and smiling woman named Lar, brought out a root vegetable gratin bubbling with cheese and bacon and set it between two huge loaves of bread on a side table. Aever tore off a piece of bread, helping herself.

"Coming back," said Vern, "you'll see two passes. Make

sure you take the pass to the south. The north has a road that looks easy, but it gets steep and it ends at a wall, an old mine called the Strall, and you'll have a quite a fight on your hands getting back down in the snow."

"I remember this," said Aever. "Thanks for the reminder. It's been a while."

With her hair down, out of her armor and riding gear, Aever was striking. Her chin was large, her nose an odd blade, her front teeth had a gap, and her hair stuck out in angles as it dried, but she was a vibrant, tough, joyful woman. And, Jarrod had learned throughout the afternoon, she could whistle with sufficient skill to make a man weep. Birdcalls, melodies. An absolute pleasure to ride with.

A few inches taller than Jarrod, she had the build through the shoulders and neck that he'd seen on female rugby players in college. He wondered how much she could deadlift.

Her sword was expensive, the spine braided from twisted iron bands in a butterfly pattern and the steel edges welded in a laserlike line, with a couple of dings that had been filed out and a scabbard tooled with images of deer and mountains dyed black against red-brown leather to match the sword handle. She wore it at her side, even here, inside someone else's home, and made no apology.

He watched her eat and realized he hadn't seen much bread in his time here, except at formal feasts. He guessed it was expensive, and he wasn't quite sure why, although he assessed—rightly, as it happens—that Falconsrealm spent most of its limited farmland growing hay and subsistence farming. Up in The Reach, where he now lived, they had to import damned near everything. The role of bread in The Reach was filled by a sliced loaf of nuts, seeds, and dried fruit held together with baked eggs. It wasn't bad, just pedestrian. It was essentially fruitcake without the *joie de vivre.*

Mushrooms were the staple of The Reach: mushroom gravies, an odd mushroom ketchup made with vinegar and garlic, and meals of giant mushrooms packed with meaty, dark flavor that put Portobellos to shame. And fish, as well. Mushroom-stuffed fish. Fish-stuffed mushrooms. Fish and mushrooms stuffed into other fish and topped with mushroom paste.

There was, however, a large snail that crawled along the castle walls by the thousands, which grilled up like a tiger prawn, pink and sweet and the size of a man's thumb. They were the one menu item that kept him from losing his mind.

Generally, though, his was a gray world. Gray food. Gray skies. A castle of gray rock. A vast gray sea.

No grocery stores. No supermarkets. Regional cuisines.

He missed bread.

"You Northers need to import our grain," said Vern, as if reading his mind. "And our daughters, to teach you how to make bread."

"I can make bread," said Jarrod. "Though I'm sure, not as well as this."

"You should let our daughters teach you," said Vern. "There are many things they can do well." The innuendo wasn't lost; it was a language rich in vulgarities and double-entendre.

"I appreciate that," said Jarrod, and graciously, he thought. "But I have a lover, at home."

"And that matters why?" asked Vern.

Jarrod started to answer, and Aever stepped in for him. "He's a foreigner," she said. "They have different values than we do. He is extremely loyal to his lover."

"We, however, are not foreigners," Carj assured Vern, speaking quickly and raising a finger to interrupt. "And anything your daughters want to teach us, we'd be happy to learn." Jarrod glanced over to see Aever grinning at Carj around a mouthful of food.

"I'm sure the feeling is mutual," said Vern.

Jarrod knew enough about Falconsrealm women at this point to not ask any questions.

Knights referred to a house that took you in on the road, where the companionship was particularly companionable, as "a soft place to fall," and the women here were as lascivious as the men. Perhaps moreso. Reproductive rates were low, the weather was mind-rattlingly shitty, and the nights were cold, so—as Jarrod assessed it, anyway—giving each other orgasms had developed into a national pastime. Sex involved no obligations of exclusivity and necessitated little, if any, emotional attachment. The nearest thing Jarrod could compare it to was that finding someone to fuck in Falconsrealm or Gateskeep was analogous to finding someone to go running with on Earth.

It wasn't a bad arrangement, and his first spring here he'd cut a respectable swath through the good ladies of Falconsrealm. But holy shit, he missed Karra.

Heart of my eyes.

"With all due respect, sir," he said to Vern. "I would like the bedroom farthest away from wherever all this will be happening."

A lovely young woman appeared in the doorway in rough woolen clothes, tomboyish and bright-eyed with dark hair and a grin to match Aever's. "If you intend to sleep, sire," she said. "Might I suggest you bed down in the stable?"

Jarrod lay awake in the stable, in a pile of furs on his hammock of parachute silk, which he'd slung between two hooks on the walls.

He thought of Renaldo and that idiotic hands-forward quirk.

Speed is a function of perception. Stripping away excess motion makes a swordsman fast. A skilled swordsman moves all at once, shimmering from attack to attack. Renaldo, however, chose muscle over speed, telegraphing his movements, and he was an exceptional swordsman despite it. It was the piece Jarrod couldn't figure out: Renaldo was relying on some other advantage, some unseen edge that compensated for the flaw in his technique but damned if it was readily apparent. His gifts for measure and distance were a middle game; a minor contributor.

Whatever his advantages, leading with his hands was still a weakness.

Jarrod replayed the fight a hundred times, watching the hands, then the tip, then the feet. It was venial, but coupled with Renaldo's tendency to yowl and whine and bitch at the tiniest poke, it hinted at a larger pattern, a tapestry with a thread he could pull.

The first thing that he came up with was that Renaldo had probably never been stabbed, at least not badly.

I'm gonna fix that, you can bet your ass.

A jarring notion: was he scared of swords?

The more thought he gave it, the less ridiculous it sounded, and the more it began to click. It was likely that this was what had driven Renaldo toward the blade: a mastery of the terrifying. Perhaps he was one of those vain sons of bitches who gravitated toward the arcana of something frightening not to conquer it, but to wield it.

He wants to be scary.

The muscles. The helmet. Starting forward several times with Hillwhite holding him back. Threats. Posturing.

Grandstanding.

He knew the type; he'd seen them a hundred times, heard a

thousand of their stories. Men and women who flirted with greatness but never truly embraced the entirety of a craft, who never took the big risks. The dilettantes, the also-rans, those who'd done just enough to convince themselves that they could have been truly great before waddling back to mediocrity and a life of regaling others with stories of That One Time When I Could Have. Renaldo had bullshitted his way into a shot at the title, and he was probably pissing his pants inside his armor.

Jarrod dozed off to what he was certain were the sounds of Aever having an orgasm on the other side of the wall.

As sleep overtook him, her voice melded into birdcalls.

Wind and snow slapped the drapes from the window as Renaldo exploded, lungs aching, muscles twitching, his hands locked with Jerandra, her nails digging into his knuckles until he wrenched them away.

He was ridiculously chiseled, an anatomical model come to life in the morning light, with muscles so well-defined that a running joke in the castle baths held that he'd once been skinned alive. Veins and spidery sinews pushed hard into tan flesh stretched tight over slabs of muscle.

"I'm done," he rasped. "I'm done. You?"

Jerandra was distance-athlete thin, nearly fragile were she not so damned tall, her skin obsidian and sheathed in perspiration despite the chill. She threw her hair back from her face as best she could, but a good bit stuck to the sweat. "Thunder and rain," she agreed, and together they rolled off the woman in the bed beneath them.

"How about you?" Renaldo asked. Her name was Valyn, dressmaker to Rogar's wife, and she was northern, unique out here, fair-haired with soft eyes and astonishing tits. She smiled up at him.

"Three in a bed is a good winter," Valyn giggled. The world outside railed at the walls in answer.

"Holy shit," Renaldo groaned, slipping in between them both. Sex with Jerandra smelled like cherry Nyquil, and it made him want to ram his head through the wall in a fit of testosterone. And he loved it when she "lit him up," as he called it—using her pain-generating magic for the equivalent of dragging her nails up his thighs or biting his lip at opportune moments. "Maybe the winters here aren't so bad."

Jerandra was unlike any woman he'd ever known. She was every bit as athletic as he was, and toothily competitive about it. When it was just the two of them—rarer and rarer these days, as she liked human women as much as he did—it was often difficult to determine exactly who was fucking whom.

In this room, he was a king, a conqueror, a hero.

Greatness awaited.

Jerandra shoved him out of the bed, ridiculously strong, lifting him and tossing him on his feet into the blast of the wind, which was like a knife through his crotch. His sweat pricked at him in the cold. "Feed the fire," she said.

He rubbed himself with his hands. "You could make me warm, you know."

"I will, when you get back in here with us."

He picked up a log and tossed it on the fire, then another. "You're no fun. Come on, just a little magic."

She hissed at him, showing her fangs, and a streak of warmth licked up his spine and spread to his hands and feet.

"Thanks," he said. "That feels—"

The heat from his spine blasted him with a jolt of pain, and he yelped. "Hey!"

She was still showing her fangs; the smile of a cat with a

broken bird. "All right, that's really—*shit!*" he yelled again, as pain savaged him; he froze as his muscles cramped up in spasm, white-hot. He swore he could feel his bones bending. "What the f—" he squeaked, contorting.

"Don't you ever forget who you belong to," she told him. "You will do what I ask, when I ask, and I will ensure that you get everything you ever desire. But never . . ." and here, her voice dropped an octave and became a thing black and necrotic, the words crawling through the room on giant spiders' legs, ". . . *never,* human, forget your place, nor mine. I brought you. I made you. I promise you greatness beyond the dreams of any living man, but we will share the rewards. Our peoples have kept this pact since time immemorial. Ignore it at your peril."

He straightened as the pain relented. "God, that's kinda hot," he admitted. After a deep breath, he asked, "Anything I want, huh?"

"Of course. But first, get back here," she commanded, and he was already moving. "I intend to make you earn it."

He heard the door open, and Rogar Hillwhite let himself into the room holding a candelabra and stood at the end of the bed.

Renaldo still wasn't sure about the rules regarding sex here, but he had the sense that this was unorthodox, and either way, veins throbbed in his shoulders and neck. He stammered through all the profanities he knew in the local language, but none of them seemed to fit.

"Get out of here!" he finally said. "Get your own."

Jerandra's eyes could have burned through Rogar.

"Interesting," said Rogar. "How many more do you have in there?"

"More than you," said Renaldo.

"There is news," said Rogar. "Jarrod Torrealday rides for Gateskeep Palace. He's with a team of spies from his order, looking into our numbers outside The Reach, and likely, our plans, here. Some kind of fact-finding mission."

"Well, that complicates this," said Renaldo. "What do you want to do?"

"I want you to kill him, you idiot."

Jerandra threw back the covers for Renaldo, and Valyn squealed at the cold.

"He has more to do first," the elf said with a grin.

"Yes, he does," said Rogar. "Lord Blacktree, get dressed, immediately. We will have new arrivals in the courtyard shortly."

Renaldo looked out the window and had to wonder who in the hell would be traveling in weather like this, and decided that they were not the sort of people he'd prefer to meet right now, but probably exactly the kind of people they'd need.

Rogar and Renaldo stood just out of the rain, Renaldo tucking into an alcove before one of the castle's smaller tower doors as a blast of sleet hammered them. He pulled a thick knitted cape around him tighter.

"So, who are the new guys?" asked Renaldo.

"If we're going to attack across the northlands, we'll have to contend with Regoth Ur," said Rogar.

"I don't know what a Regoth Ur is," Renaldo admitted. He didn't like it. It sounded dangerous.

"Regoth Ur is a 'where,' not a 'what,'" said Rogar. "Although it was once a 'who.' It's the great keep of the knight lord Regoth Ur, who developed a strain of flying horses for Gateskeep to use in war. It's now the center for the training and breeding operation for Gateskeep's Air Guard. Elite knights with a long reach. They're the eyes of Gateskeep in the northern plains."

"Flying horses?" asked Renaldo. "With wings?"

"With wings," said Rogar. "Horsebirds. Very dangerous. Huge warhorses and very smart knights, keeping an eye on every movement, every border, every battle. On the field, they charge out of the sky—have you ever seen a man run down by a warhorse?"

"Not yet," said Renaldo.

"You will," promised Rogar. "Horsebirds knock over troops and shatter formations. Think of a flying landslide. The riders do this in special saddles that allow them to not be dislodged by a collision."

"What kind of saddle?"

"Very few have seen them," said Rogar. "The design is a secret."

"So, how do we defeat them?" asked Renaldo. "More to the point, when they go to war, how do their enemies contend with . . ." he hunted for the words and came back with ". . . horsebirds?"

Renaldo saw Rogar peering intently up at the low cloud cover, and it hit him in slow motion. "You—" he started. He thought of throwing in the English word *pegasus* and decided on *horsebird.* Because fuck these guys. "You have your own horsebirds?"

"Better," said Rogar, clapping him on the shoulder. "Much better."

Renaldo expected a dragon. He'd been bracing himself for dragons since the minute he arrived here.

He had seen quite a bit in the past few weeks: he'd killed a handful of knights, teleported several hundred miles in the blink of an eye, seen a moon with a ring around it as real as the scars on his hands, stood on a thousand-foot fjord and screamed his name at the stars, and he'd just been shaken out of a three-way with an elven sorceress.

He wasn't remotely ready for the creature that screamed out of the clouds.

It was a gryphon, but more crow than eagle; more alligator than lion. The result was a small dragon, gray and mottled, with a crow's head and wings, feathered talons, and a whip of a tail. It was massive, as well. On its neck rode a knight in what to Renaldo appeared to be vaguely Eastern-looking metal lorica, with overlapping scales and a fully-faced helmet skirted in mail across the back; otherworldly, even here.

The rider sat well forward of the wings, aggressive, lethal, leaning into the crow's head like a jockey and holding a spear large enough to qualify as a lance. It flashed overhead with the shriek of rending metal in its cry and was joined by two others.

They disappeared into the clouds again, and three more charged down in their tracks, winged past, and followed exactly, disappearing up into the cloud bank.

"Gavrian gryphons," said Rogar.

Renaldo watched them go. "Don't the Gavrians need them?"

"They wanted my money more," Rogar said.

"But your money is in The Reach," said Renaldo.

"Not for long."

"How many?" asked Renaldo, still staring at the sky.

"Enough," Rogar answered.

"And this is your big idea," said Jarrod, swinging off Lilith beside a small stream. It was snowing in tiny flecks that dusted the trees but didn't yet stick on the ground. "We hit these hills, and then somewhere in the next hills is a pass."

"That pass will take us south of Rogue's River in another day," said Aever. "Then we hold tight to the mountains until we reach Gateskeep Palace."

"Vern said one day, not two," said Jarrod.

"Vern probably doesn't ride these roads this time of year," she said. "We'll be lucky to make it in two."

"We need to get to the palace before The Dark," said Carj, slinging his reins around a small tree.

"It's going to be close," she said.

Every hundred and four days, signaling the change of seasons, the big moon disappeared for six days and nights. No one had any idea where it went, of course, though Jarrod figured the big moon eclipsed the sun. Those nights were black as a tomb, and everyone stayed inside.

On the Dark Nights the seas rose, the wolves howled, and the monsters came out.

He had been unconscious for his first The Dark, having just had his ass kicked by a jealous palace lord. He'd spent his second The Dark in The Reach, holed up in front of a roaring fire, banging Karra and wandering through a candlelit castle, wondering at the awesomeness of it all.

He'd heard stories about the dead rising for the long night, of monsters, slavering and fanged, lurching forth. Not that anyone had ever seen them, and this past The Dark had held true to form and passed without incident. But nobody wanted to be out here when the moon went away.

Nobody.

This was a world that rarely saw true darkness; the big pink-and-purple ringed moon cast a heliotrope hue to the world and slate shadows on all but the cloudiest nights.

Four seasons—four The Darks—to a year. Four hundred forty days.

The idea that someone could know nothing of a matter as

grave as celestial mechanics made Jarrod grind his teeth. It stressed him out and made him upset just thinking about it.

And that, my friends, is why we're different, he surmised. *That's why we have A-10 Warthogs and the Mars Rover, and they're still beating swords out of rocks by hand.*

"We can push on to Gateskeep once we get through this pass," said Aever. "Or we can ride north to Rogue's River and stay there for the Dark."

"Let's see where the day takes us," said Jarrod as one of the valets tossed him an apple from the cart. He still couldn't tell the valets apart.

"I'm not going to be out here during The Dark," Thron growled, swinging down from his saddle.

"Scared of monsters?" Aever needled.

"Yes," said Thron. Jarrod noted that he adjusted his swordbelt, cricked his back, and scanned in all directions before he took a step away from his horse.

"So, who's your king?" asked Carj. The rain had come again with the night, and the world was ending over their heads as Thron took Jarrod's cup and opened the cork on the beer barrel. Their job tonight was to drink as much of it as possible. Aever had pointed out that a full cask of beer, transported on a cart, would eventually explode.

They'd rigged a waxed canvas tarp over a lattice of branches and poles and parked the cart under it. The horses were tucked under some heavier trees not far away. "Back home," Carj added. "Your king back home."

"We have no king," said Jarrod, leaning against a fallen log beside Aever and taking the beer Thron offered. "Thank you," he said. Thron nodded wordlessly and poured himself another.

"Double-check the tethers on that big bastard," said Thron, addressing the valets and pointing to Perseus. "Make sure he's on something solid. I don't want him breaking free tonight."

"The tree's fairly stout, sergeant," said one of the valets.

"Yeah, you'd think that. I've heard the stories."

"What's that, now?" Aever asked.

"As I heard it, Lord Protector here, is out and about in Lake City," Thron said, sitting down on a fat log. "He takes his big horse out for some exercise, walks him down the lake."

"Took him to the Sticky Pig," said Jarrod.

"Bought him a drink," Carj wagered.

"As well you should," said Aever.

"He's a good horse," said Jarrod.

"Horse walks right into the tavern looking for Lord Protector, pulling a tree behind him. Just dragging it down the street. Pulled it right up, roots and all."

Jarrod shrugged. "He did find me, you've got to give him credit."

"Brilliant horse," said Aever.

When the laughter had subsided, Carj asked, "You have no king?"

"We don't," said Jarrod.

"You should go be king," pronounced Aever, as if that would solve everything.

"We don't have kings anymore," said Jarrod. "We kind of . . . outgrew them, you could say."

"Dangerous words," warned Aever.

Carj threw more wood on the flames. Blankets hung on tripods around the fire, steaming into the makeshift roof. Thron snugged down a line as the wind bit at them.

"Our needs are different than yours," said Jarrod. "Basically, we have a group who want to lead our country. They spend their lives studying policy and economics and warfare. And then, we vote for them every four years. Whoever gets the most votes becomes our supreme leader."

"How do you know who to vote for?" asked Carj. "Are these people you know? I wouldn't want someone I didn't know to lead me."

"Well, they tell us what they plan to do. And then we vote for whoever has the best plan."

"Well, that's easy," Carj assessed. "All they have to do is lie about their plan, and then get all the votes."

"Oh, that happens all the time," said Jarrod. "In fact, that's pretty much what always happens."

"So, you need a king," agreed Carj.

"We had kings," said Jarrod. "Our needs have changed. Kings can no longer provide what we require. Every once in a while, we get a leader, or someone who wants to be leader, who thinks he's going to run the country like a king, but the leader can't really do anything unless other elected people, our representatives, allow him to. And we have a set of inviolable rules, written on a parchment, that everybody we elect has to adhere to. Leader, representatives, everyone."

"But men break rules," said Carj. "That's one of the precepts of men."

"Yes," said Jarrod. "But our soldiers are sworn to defend the rules, not to defend the leaders."

Aever looked to Carj. "That's the craziest thing I've ever heard. You don't swear fealty to a leader?"

"Absolutely not," said Jarrod. "Our soldiers swear fealty to a document."

"But they obey the ruler."

"Well, yes, as long as he obeys the document."

Carj swirled his beer around in his mug for a while as the rain went on around them. "Actually," he said after a time, "that's a fairly good idea. That's a better idea than having soldiers sworn to a person. Swear them to the laws."

"What if the laws are unjust?" asked Thron from his corner, then lapsed back into silence.

"Well, there are judges who decide that," said Jarrod.

"What if the leader decides that?" asked Aever.

"Well, then, he's out of luck," said Jarrod. "He can order the judges to review a law that he questions, but he can't order them to change it. And the judges are appointed by the people, as well, just like the leader." He knew he was oversimplifying by a longshot, but he didn't really know the intricacies. And it sounded good when he said it out loud, or at least it did in their terms. He wondered why Ulo hadn't tried it; he'd come here from Earth, but had made himself king, not president.

He decided that being a tyrant was probably pretty awesome until the last hour or two.

"The leader doesn't appoint the judges?" asked Aever, incredulous.

"No," said Jarrod. "The people appoint the leader, and the parliament, and the judges. The leader can't do anything without a majority of the parliamentarians' approval, and the judges enforce the laws. If the people don't like the laws, then the parliament changes them. If they don't change the laws that the people don't like, the people change the parliament. All the power resides in the people."

"But," Aever said, and belched, "People are idiots."

"There is that," said Jarrod. "Most people have no idea what they actually want. And those who cry out loudest and demand the most radical change usually don't understand that they already have exactly what they want. They're only told they don't have it."

"How the hell could they not know what they have?"

Jarrod thought about this. "Well, it's complicated. We have

an entire profession—an artisan class—devoted to making everything appear to not be what it seems. To make people think they have it worse or better than they do."

"Why would you do that?" asked Carj.

"Mainly, to get people to buy things they don't really need."

"Wait—what?" said Thron, standing up and stepping closer. "Say that again. Slower."

"We have everything we need," said Jarrod, "most of us. Homes, jobs, families, food. Because of this, most of our industry is involved in making frivolous things. Games, toys, time-wasters of one type or another. There's an entire industry responsible for making it seem like everyone else owns more of these things than you do, and that they're all happier because of it. In fact, in our country, there are more people employed doing that than there are making the things that nobody really needs in the first place."

"Sounds confusing," agreed Aever.

"It will make you crazy," said Jarrod, draining his beer. "You can spend your life running in circles, collecting things you don't need, until you die. It's ridiculous."

"No greater sin than a life half-lived," quipped Carj.

"Agreed," said Jarrod. "And yes. It's why I jumped at the chance to come here. Everything is much simpler. Good wine and good war."

"Good wine and good war," said Carj, raising his mug.

"Good wine and good war," the others agreed.

With the onset of rain at night, it was nearly as dark as it gets. Jarrod lay awake, as he often did. By his best guess—and he wished he'd brought a wristwatch—the days here were thirty hours long. After half a year—one The Dark between each season—he still hadn't gotten used to it and figured he never would. He spent a good bit of any given night lying awake and had turned napping into a hobby. Candles lit at dawn and again at nightfall kept time but damned if he knew how long they burned. All he really knew was that he woke up at about half a candle and fell asleep again at about a quarter, and usually had breakfast early and then got on with his day.

There were no candles here. He was adrift in the night, watching the fire.

Thron snored. The rain hissed. Aever was talking to herself in her sleep. Perseus and Lilith slept head to tail, standing out of the rain, best friends, watching for intruders.

He doodled in his blank book by the firelight, sketching a series of mountain passes and noting soft places to fall as he'd been told by the others. He copied the locations onto a folded piece of parchment that he'd bought at great expense, roughing out a map of the Gateskeep-Falconsrealm border.

The horses woke up in a fit, and Jarrod stood, closing his book, hand on his arming sword, and nudged Thron with his toe. Thron leaped up, a lick of flame along a knife in his hand.

"Who's there?" Jarrod called. The others woke and came to their feet. Perseus stamped, and horses answered on the far side of the fire.

"Gateskeep knights," yelled a tall man in heavy cloaks and a brimmed hat to keep the rain off, stepping into the firelight. "We saw your fire. We're from the garrison at Horlech, headed for Gateskeep Palace. We mean no harm."

"You're among friends," Jarrod said.

"I'm Sir Myk, of Three Hills Keep," said the tall man. He motioned to two larger, broader men behind him. "This is Sir Eth of Mud River, and Sir Kel of Gran's Tower."

"Jarrod," Jarrod announced, and introduced his team. "Aever, Carj, and Thron. In the back, there, are Marc and Hat. Our horsemasters."

"You're knights?" asked Myk.

"We are," said Jarrod, adding, "out of High River." He left it at that. He figured that if these guys didn't recognize him, then it wasn't necessarily bad. They also left it alone.

"You three are from Long Valley," Aever noted, before anyone else did. "You're a long way from home."

"Don't we know it. We just finished our tour in the Northern Brigade," said Myk. "Going home."

"Your timing's perfect," Jarrod grumbled.

"What's that?"

"Your timing," said Jarrod. "There's a war brewing. The Reach is under siege."

"If true, then it's all the more reason to go home, if you don't mind my saying, sire. If there's a war brewing, I want to be near my family."

The three knights and Thron stared at each other. "Good answer," Thron decided.

"You're welcome to our fire," said Jarrod.

"If you don't mind sharing watch," added Aever, quickly. "Jarrod, you were up?"

"I was. I'm not tired," said Jarrod. "I can hold watch for a bit more."

"We don't want to be an imposition," said one of the new knights behind Myk; Jarrod didn't have them straight, yet. Hell, he still hadn't untangled Marc and Hat. "We have our own food."

"Please," said Jarrod. "It's a terrible night. Get under here if you can. There's cover for your horses around back. Our men will help you."

Kel, who was half a head larger than the others and had the

biggest beard, stood before Jarrod. He wore heavy mail, battered and rust-worn even by firelight, likely hand-me-down, and a fur cape turned hair-side down, the hide tanned dark, with a tight woolen watchcap over long hair, very northern. "I'll take watch with you," he said. "I'm Kel."

"Jarrod."

"There's a tribe of *gbatu* just north of us," said Kel, settling on a log next to Jarrod. "They've been sending out scouts."

"Kill any?" Jarrod asked. Gbatu were small, goblin-esque creatures; scrawny, child-sized ogres with swords and fangs. He had only seen them but had never fought one. He had, however, maimed a couple of sheth, the much larger gbatu that ruled the subhuman races. He didn't care to ever meet a sheth again.

"Not yet," said Kel. "They won't engage. Frankly, we figured we'd be safer with you all. We've got, what, seven of us? They should stay away now."

"Glad to be of help," said Jarrod, and broke out his book, again, tucking the map away.

"What is that?" asked Kel.

"I keep a journal," said Jarrod. "It helps me think."

"I hate to think," said Kel, folding his arms and staring off past the fire.

Sometimes, thought Jarrod, starting to sketch anew on a blank page, *so do I.*

THE PASS

"Treat your friend as if he might become an enemy."
– Pubilius Syrus

It was a formidable job, Jarrod realized the next morning, moving nine people, all their horses, and a cart through rain- and snow-swept passes and trying to do it at any sort of speed. The more people they added, the slower it went. He would have wagered that there was some sort of economy of force that would kick in at some point, but it had taken the better part of the morning just to strike camp. He basically had a small army to take care of. He was exhausted by the time they got packed up.

The skies were clearing, though, and that was something. However, with the sun came the cold, and it was awful, insidious, creeping into clothing through vents and nibbling at anything exposed. Ice still crusted the puddles on the road by the time they got moving, which was late morning.

The new knights wouldn't answer to his sergeant. This was problematic, because it was Thron's job to wrangle everyone beneath him in rank, and that included knights from the borderlands who didn't belong to royal orders. The complication arose from Aever and Carj's demand that the newcomers not know their order and affiliation. Jarrod simply showing his pins and rank braid would have shut them up and solved everything. Conversely—and Aever had a point here—it could just as easily get them robbed, murdered in their sleep, or any combination thereof. A shouting match had broken out over Thron's demands that the three knights wear armor for traveling, with Myk insisting that a superior show of force would keep gbatu away. And anyway, he continued, everyone was already wet and dirty enough already, and being stuck inside armor would make for a long day on the road.

"Long days on the road are exactly what you signed up for," Thron growled.

Now, Myk rode beside Jarrod at the head of the column on a painted mare, unarmored, in a pair of layered woolen cloaks. He kept looking at Jarrod's warsword, slung left-handed off his saddle, and the huge Barbute helmet hanging by its strap from the handle, none of it moving as Lilith rolled along like a set of wheels under Jarrod even at a walk. "I'm guessing you have mail under that jacket?" Myk asked.

"And I'm guessing you don't," said Jarrod.

"You really expect we're going to get in a fight out here," Myk laughed.

"I expect you might."

"Ooh," Myk mocked. "You're a tough guy. Why don't you put the old man back there in line?"

"I don't need to," said Jarrod. "If you have a problem with him, you two can work it out. I'll pull over and watch."

"Hey," said Aever, riding up on Myk's other side. "Fall back. I need to talk to our commander."

"Commander of what?" Myk called, slowing down as they rode ahead. Aever gave him some space.

"You need to straighten him out," she told Jarrod, leaning

close.

"He's harmless," said Jarrod.

"Are you sure about that?"

"No," Jarrod admitted.

"They're border knights."

"I know," said Jarrod. "But they're *our* border knights. We need to be friendly."

Behind them, Myk was berating Thron again, whose face seared under his hat.

"Thron is going to kill that guy," she said. "You need to step up. Right now."

Grumbling, Jarrod reined his horse to a halt and whistled.

The procession stopped, and Jarrod swung down off Lilith. "Myk!" he called, walking back along the caravan. Myk snapped the painted's head around; she clearly didn't like the way Jarrod was coming at them. "Get your ass down off that horse."

"And what?" Myk called.

"And we're going to set a few things straight," said Jarrod.

Myk looked to Kel and Eth, then back to Jarrod. "Meaning?"

"Meaning, you and me. Right now. I'm going to kick your ass until you're convinced that it's in your best interest to do what I tell you."

"You could just tell me who you are," said Myk, dismounting.

"You're about to find out," said Jarrod. "Fists? Knives? Swords? Call it."

"Fists are good," said Myk, looking to Eth and Kel again. "Let's wrestle for it."

Jarrod fell back, and they circled, hands up, and then all hell broke loose in ten directions.

First the horses, then the valets, then Myk's knights; everyone started screaming at the same time and Jarrod was aware of a crawling, swarming knot of . . . something . . . hitting the road from two sides. Lots of them.

Gbatu.

He'd been here before. He ran to Lilith and pulled his warsword. He'd nearly been killed half a year ago by taking on a gang of armored gbatu and sheth with his arming sword. He seated his helmet—no time for his coif, damn it all—and bit down on his mouthguard.

Instead of the expected clubs, furs, and axes, some of these little bastards were in mail. With swords.

"Swords!" he shouted, as if he'd even had to. Even Marc and Hat had pulled out long knives and were defending the cart from each direction.

He ran to the cart, and found his way blocked by three of them—childlike, fanged, slavering, with swords and armor—and stepped back as they piled into him. His massive greatsword caught one in the side of the helmet and peeled it back, skidding the gbatu along the road. The others backed up, and Jarrod fell into a half-sword guard and stepped into them, taking one of the smaller swords with his tip, binding and winding, slashing the arm, then the face, and then kicking it over just about the time that someone shot him.

The impact was tremendous, a horsekick that dropped him back a step and left him wheezing as the arrow hit the titanium mail and stuck in his jacket under his arm. He wanted to curl into a little ball and squeak for a while, but people would see him.

He forced his feet to move, then a gun went off inside his helmet as another arrow smacked off, and he realized that he wasn't moving fast enough.

He moved for the cart and swept the boys flat in the back. "My shield!" he shouted and ducked behind. They threw him his green teardrop, and he slid it on his arm and charged in the direction of the fire, which came from somewhere off the far side of the road. He covered his head and ran in a crouch; the titanium mailshirt only reached down to his groin, and just about the last thing he wanted was to get shot in the balls.

He peeked around the shield, got his bearings, and found his target, though it took some looking: a twisted little creature made of green-brown skin and sinew under a collage of mail and rotting fur, standing on a fallen log fifty meters or so off the road, with a clear line of fire to the cart. The gbatu showed his fangs and drew again, fired, and Jarrod sidestepped with a snort and charged him.

He got about three steps before snagging a foot on a vine, and as his sword tumbled away, an arrow clattered off his helmet and shoulder guard.

He covered himself with his shield, then opened his faceplate. "Let's try that again," he told no one, and, rolling, he picked up his sword and came to his feet.

Much easier to run through broken terrain when you can see three feet in front of you, he noted, peeking around his shield for a flash at a time.

A fighter's adage in Falconsrealm states, "Flee a knife. Charge a bow." An arrow rarely kills instantly; even a rabbit struck with an arrow will bite and scratch for minutes. The gbatu archer likely knew this, as all archers would, and scrambled away into the trees long before Jarrod could get close.

He sprinted back to the fight, dodging roots and rocks and snarls of ankle-breaking bullshit, slapping his visor down again as he got to the road.

Aever and Carj were fighting back to back, surrounded by half a dozen or so. Thron was at the cart with the boys with shield and sword, kicking and smashing and beating the hell out of everything in sight. Two of the border knights, each fighting solo, were also surrounded.

He ran to help Thron and the boys, and as he neared, he realized he'd made a mistake: technically, Carj and Aever were the important ones for the mission.

But fuck it, he thought. He was here. He shield-slammed a gbatu, hamstrung another, and kicked a third in the back and took its hand. It scampered off, shrieking, the hand twitching in the mud. Two more fled after it. Thron shoved one's face off his sword with a foot on its head.

Where they stood, ankle-deep in crimson-black mud, it was over, but there was more fighting happening at each end of the caravan. Jarrod motioned Thron toward Carj and Aever, and then ran to help the two border knights, both injured, both exhausted, and both surrounded.

They'd seemed to have had the worst luck of everyone. A couple of the gbatu facing them were in decent armor, mail with plates interwoven, with what appeared to be good swords.

Their primary problem, he saw as he slowed, was that the two knights weren't working together. They were fighting within arm's reach of each other, but they weren't communicating, and they weren't even watching each other's backs. Both of them were fighting all six gbatu at the same time.

Jarrod headed for them at a run and turned to see Carj and Aever closing on him.

"Come on!" he yelled, then wished he hadn't; the gbatu turned on him. Like idiots, the knights didn't skewer the gbatu who turned away, but kept fighting the few that were fighting them. Jarrod could see that one of the knights, the big one he'd kept watch with, was injured and clearly favoring his right side. He couldn't tell if it was a leg injury or a back injury, but he was definitely hurting.

Jarrod and Aever joined the fight, Carj bringing up the rear, and it was over fairly quickly. The world was squealing and shrieking and spurts of blood and the smashing of metal, and then long minutes of stabbing the wounded and chasing the stragglers around the road until they fled into the woods.

"Anybody hurt?" Jarrod called, panting, hands on knees. He unbuttoned his jacket, reaching inside, and felt the tip of the arrow outside the mail but holy shit, it had made a dent. He began to work the arrow free, and Aever came over to help him. "Check each other," he told the group. "And don't stand still too long. There's still an archer out there."

No one seemed too badly hurt. Thron's eye looked about the way that Jarrod figured his own had, days earlier. The boys were shocky and banged up, but uninjured, and Jarrod bade them to look to the horses and gear and get ready to move.

He thought that was the worst of it until Carj pulled off his boot. His right foot was swelling black and purple.

"You are shitting me," said Jarrod.

"Little bastard hit it with a hammer," he said.

"Oh, boy," said Jarrod. "Can you ride?"

"Do I have a choice?" said Carj.

"I can carry you," Aever joked.

"Shut up," he snarled.

Jarrod dug in his medical kit and shook out four ibuprofen tablets. "It's not much, but it will help. They're . . . well, they're medicine. It will bring down the swelling. Swallow them."

Carj looked from Jarrod's face, to the pills, and back again. "Elf magic. I'd sooner shove a badger up my own ass."

"I'm ordering you," said Jarrod. "Trust me."

Aever nodded to Carj, who took them from Jarrod and washed them down with a long pull of whatever was in his wineskin. For his sake, Jarrod hoped it was whiskey. He went over to the border knights, who were checking each other. They'd had the hell beaten out of them, and were bleeding from a dozen places, applying makeshift bandages.

"You're gonna put your fuckin' armor on, now, I bet,"

Thron grumbled as he walked past.

"On that," Jarrod said, toeing the armored body of a gbatu and lifting it with his foot. The armor on the corpses was crap: slag iron, the mail simply butted together instead of riveted, with the occasional thin piece of iron sheet knitted into the chain in a style typically attributed to the nation of Gavria, some ten days' ride south. It would stand up to a handful of blows under steel-edged weapons, and was far better than what they usually fought in—furs if it was cold or rotting hides otherwise—but against humans in good armor, it presented little more than an annoyance.

Not that the gbatu knew the difference. It gave them a competitive advantage over neighboring tribes, which was the primary reason that they wore it, and it made armed and armored gbatu harder for humans to deal with. As they'd just learned.

"We're seeing more and more of these guys in armor, aren't we?" Jarrod announced.

"We are," said Eth, the larger of the border knights. "Can't figure where they're getting it, though."

Jarrod knew, but it was a state secret: King Ulo, Sabbaghian the Silver, had worked a deal with the Hillwhites some months back to arm the gbatu and sheth as a way to attrit the Falconsrealm troops. And here they were.

"Where's Myk?" Jarrod asked. The guy he was supposed to fight before all this.

Eth nodded behind them, where Myk's body lay sprawled. Jarrod ran to him. "He went down quick," Eth called. "Arrow, I think."

Jarrod knelt by him, turned him over, and flinched at the blood covering Myk's face, his mouth and eyes wide open and frozen. He checked for a pulse. Thready and fast. "He's alive," said Jarrod, and Eth and Kel scrambled over.

He opened up Myk's jacket and realized he'd spoken far too soon.

It was a through-and-through, near the shoulder, and horrific; he could have set a golf ball in it. Blood fanned off the road and into the grass, and there looked to be gallons of it already. He guessed brachial artery, near enough to the lung to nick it, too, with the one bleeding into the other. He began to swear in English because even in the impressively vulgar Falconsrealm dialect he didn't know enough profanities to express himself. He opened up the jacket further.

"Are you a healer?" asked Eth. Aever took one of Myk's hands in both her own.

"Of sorts," said Jarrod. "I've had some training. Come here," Jarrod told Eth. "Get over here. Hold his hand."

"Why?"

"Because he's *dying!*" Jarrod shouted. "What's the matter with you?"

Eth sighed, knelt, and took Myk's other hand.

Jarrod checked Myk's pulse again, and it was gone. The wound wasn't even bubbling; respiration had stopped. Blood wasn't pumping anymore, just leaking. Jarrod swore again. "I can't do anything, here," he said. "I'm sorry." He stood, and Aever with him.

"Just . . . be with him," Jarrod told Eth. "Just do that. Don't let your friend die alone in the mud."

Eth let out a long breath. "Damned gbatu got themselves one after all."

"That was really kind of you," Aever said to Jarrod. They stood away from Myk and Eth.

"I wish I could have done more. That was an *arrow?*" It was how he would have imagined a large-caliber bullet wound. A hollowpoint shotgun slug, for Christ's sake.

"That's an arrow wound," said Thron. "You've never seen

one?"

"Not like this," Jarrod said. As a stuntman, he'd been "shot" in the chest by archers dozens of times—fewer, recently, as CGI had taken over—and fallen off of something high, clutching theatrically at the arrow. He'd had no idea that it would pass completely through, nor bleed a man out so fast. Not five days ago, he'd seen a throat wound take longer.

Aever went to check on Carj. Thron walked up to Jarrod, holding an arrow sheathed in bright blood. The tip, made of stone, was fractured, but what remained held threads and flecks of meat. Bone shards, not much larger than fingernail clippings, lay in the gore along the shaft. "This answer your question, sir?"

"Where'd you get that?" Jarrod asked.

"Over there," he nodded off the road. "Right through, just like a deer. A hit like that busts the shoulder like it was a dinner plate and keeps going. I'd say a piece of the shoulderblade opened the lung and a bleeder did the rest. Shitty way to go."

"Awful," Jarrod agreed.

"Nothing you could do, sir. At least, if they're not gonna listen to you. Chief Lieutenant," he added with a nod, and glared at Eth and Kel again before walking away.

"'Chief Lieutenant?'" asked Eth. "You're a chief lieutenant?"

"And she's a lieutenant, and Carj is a knight," said Jarrod. "Yes. Thron is our sergeant."

"What order?"

"Doesn't matter."

"You're all officers," said Eth. "My luck. You were about to make Myk look really stupid, I bet."

"No hard feelings," said Jarrod.

Eth stretched out his back, hands over his head, and sighed. "He would have laughed. The crazy bastard."

"Are you hurt?" Jarrod asked. "Did they get you in the leg,

or maybe in the back?"

"I have an injury in my back," said Eth. "Took a hit in practice a few weeks ago, and it won't go away. It's acting up again. Nothing bad."

"If you want to bury him here, we'll help you dig," said Jarrod.

"I appreciate that. Build a cairn, maybe? Plenty of rocks around."

"I think we can manage that," said Jarrod. "If there's someone you want me to talk to when we get to where we're going," he started. "I mean, I'm the ranking officer. He was killed under my command."

"I think he'd argue that point," said Eth. "But thank you. I may need you to speak with our lord at some point or pen a scroll for his family."

"We're going to lose Carj," said Aever, with Marc and Hat behind her.

"Lose?" Jarrod was used to the English definition. "What?"

"We'll have to put him in the cart," she said. "He's mission incapable. But that's not the worst of it."

"Oh, hell," groaned Jarrod. "Let's have it."

Marc looked at Hat, and they both began to speak, then stopped. "The little bastards," said Marc, trembling.

Hat cut him off, saying, "We tried to stop them."

"What did they do?" asked Jarrod. "It's okay. You can tell me."

Hat was nearly sobbing. "They went after the wheels."

Rogar and Renaldo, flanked by stewards, walked through an immense armory in the base of West Keep. Spears in stone jars stretched down the hallways in a forest of points vanishing into darkness and chill.

"We need to move these men, and right now," Renaldo swore. "Time is wasting. If we don't get across the northlands—"

"Not until after The Dark," said Rogar. "Besides, we barely have the steel to outfit the men we have. Swords take time. Good swords take more time. You want more men? It's going to take even more time."

"We give them spears," said Renaldo, picking one up. "That's all they need. You have hundreds of spears here."

"To defend the keep, and the city, as a last stand," said Rogar. "That's not the same thing."

"So? Pay as many men as you have spears, and give them each a spear. Build an army, fast."

"That is a ridiculous idea," said Rogar. "On the field, the only thing more useless than the man who won't fight is the man who can't."

"I don't know anyone in this land of yours who can't fight," said Renaldo, and it was true. Children fought with wooden axes and shields the way that kids in most countries on Earth played soccer.

"They're not soldiers," said Rogar. "Wielding a weapon doesn't make you a soldier."

"There can't be that much to it," said Renaldo, and then winced as Rogar turned on him.

"Soldiering is a profession of honor," Rogar snarled, standing within inches of Renaldo. The presence of him was terrifying. "It's a lifetime of dedication. It's a soul dedicated to battle and a life dedicated to death. You don't just make a soldier by putting a weapon in someone's hand."

"It doesn't have to be all that," Renaldo insisted. "In our armies, we sent farmers into battle with scythes if that was all they had. You just need to adapt your tactics. You're antiquated."

Rogar seethed.

"Take these spears," insisted Renaldo. "Our soldiers traveled and fought this way for ages."

"With spears?"

"With spears," said Renaldo. "You brought me here. You wanted to know what our people know. I'm telling you this. The spear is your answer. Get more soldiers. Give them spears. Train them in a day. Put them in the front lines. Move them before Gateskeep moves."

"You're an idiot," said Rogar. "Every soldier requires more workers in support. You can't just add soldiers to a war like wood on a fire."

"We did exactly that, and we did it using spears," Renaldo said.

"We already use spears."

"You're not using them enough," said Renaldo. He set the end of the speartip on the floor. "You take five or six more, you lash them together at the top, you put some skins around them, and you have a tent to get you out of the rain. Use four of them and make a lean-to. Can't you hunt with a spear? We'll need less food because they can hunt with their spears."

"And they can tie their belongings to the end and carry it over their shoulder like a child running away from home," said Rogar. "So, they don't need packs or carts, right?"

"Well, I wouldn't go that far," said Renaldo.

"Somehow," said Rogar, "I think you would. Where the hell do they get skins? We're going to stop the entire army so that everyone can go hunting?"

"Not everyone," argued Renaldo. "Just a few. You don't have dedicated hunters for your armies? Procurers?"

"Do you know how much work hunting is?" Rogar argued. "We don't hunt for our armies. We lead cattle, and slaughter them as we go. How do you not know this?"

"Well, then, there should be skins," said Renaldo.

"Who tans the hides? Or do you have them under rotting skins in the rain and snow?" asked Rogar, exasperated.

"How long can it take to tan a hide?" asked Renaldo.

"A week!" Rogar seethed, by which he meant one eighth of the hundred-and-four-day moon cycle, a thirteen-day span. "At least! Gods, we recruited you because you were some great genius soldier. You don't know anything about soldiering."

"You recruited me because I can kill Jarrod Torrealday. I know how to do that. Everything else is your problem."

"It is my problem. Shut the hole in your face until I send you to do your job."

"You have the bodies," said Renaldo. Vertigo tugged at him as he realized that he was literally the only person in the world who knew what he knew. "You have the weapons. You just need to grow a set of balls and think about the way that you're making war. There are better ways."

"There are thousands of spears here," said Rogar. "If I field thousands of levies, the cost would be . . ." his voice trailed off. "Incalculable," he concluded.

"Which means that you have the money. It's just more than you wanted to spend," Renaldo guessed. "You need to ask yourself how badly you want this."

"The money it will require is inside The Reach."

"And you can't take The Reach without more men," said Renaldo. "There's no profit in this. Not in the short term. You need to do this now, and profit later." He lay the spear on his shoulder and walked toward the torchlit exit, humming. Had Rogar been from Earth, he'd have recognized the refrain from *I Did It My Way*.

A hundred miles east, Thron tapped a cracked wheel spoke with the butt of his dagger.

The wheels, banded in iron, with iron axles and bearings, had been chipped and broken with hammers and axes. Two spokes were cracked through at the bearing on the starboard wheel. Thron shook his head. "That, right there. When that goes, we stop. The whole cart goes down."

"How long?" Jarrod asked.

"We might get a half day of use out of them," he said. "Once they break, though? We're ass in the air. And those little bastards know it, too. As soon as the cart stops, they're coming after us. Hard. Ten times as many. We can leave it and move on, in which case they get whatever's left on the cart—"

"Not an option," said Jarrod, thinking of his steel mail, coat of plates, and Damascus grand pauldrons. "Absolutely not. No."

"—or, if we stay to defend it, they'll come at us in The Dark." He looked to Aever. "We have what, three days? Two?"

"Two," she said, "Counting today."

"Son of a bitch," Jarrod said. "And that's it? No other options?"

"This is what they do," Thron said. "It's why they didn't go after the boys. They were going at the wheels. They knew they could take us later."

"What if we go slow?" Jarrod asked. "We move slowly, we check it often. It will create less—" they had no word for *torque,* which he found interesting since it was a fundamental principle of combat, "—stress on the wheel if we move slowly, right? Marc, you and Hat take turns walking ahead, steer the cart out of the way of holes, move rocks, and so forth. We'll see if we can keep it alive."

"Until they hit us again," said Eth.

"Yeah, well, we armor up," said Jarrod, which met with groans from the entire group. "Everybody," he ordered. "Every piece of armor you own. Armor is most of the weight on the cart, right? We'll carry it."

"The big problem is water and food for that damned horse," said Thron, nodding to Perseus. "He'll make Gateskeep without food, but he'll be combat ineffective. And, of course, the water barrels. If we leave the water, we'll have to break trail and end up near the river, or the horses will never make it. The gbatu will probably know that, too," he wagered. "They could be waiting for us by the river. In The Dark."

Jarrod sucked his lower lip. "That's not good."

"No," said Thron. "No, it's not."

"Where's your horse?" Aever asked Jarrod at that point.

Jarrod looked around. Lilith was gone. "Wait, what?"

He glanced down the line of people and horses, in one direction, and then the other. He looked to Marc and Hat. "I thought you did a tally of the horses."

"The ones back there," Hat said. "We figured you knew where yours was, sir."

"Oh, holy shit," Jarrod fumed. "You are kidding me."

"She run off?" asked Thron.

"She wouldn't run off," Jarrod said. "I know she wouldn't."

"She would if she was shot," said Eth.

"Aw, crap," said Jarrod. "My girl."

"If she ran off, she's not dead," offered Aever. "She might find her way."

"That's crap," said Eth. "You know they're eating her."

"I will wipe this road with you," said Jarrod, squaring off, and Aever stepped between them.

"Okay," said Jarrod. "Everybody, armor up. Empty the cart as best you can. Marc and Hat, ready Perseus. Then, water the horses. We'll take the cart as far as it will go, and then we'll make do. You two will just have to ride the ponies bareback after the cart dies."

"I can ride with this foot," said Carj, "but not well, and not fast. I won't be able to post, and I can't fight. Much."

"Let's hope you don't have to," said Jarrod. "We can keep you on the cart today, but I promise you it will hurt worse tomorrow, and the cart isn't going to last that long."

"We also need to be ready for another attack tonight," said Thron, pulling a shield and a bag of armor off the cart.

If moving the circus first thing in the morning had been a task, then this, Jarrod realized after what he guessed was an hour, was nigh-on impossible. His particular hell was that he had the most armor to wear, and he really didn't want to leave any of it behind for the monsters to get hold of; the last problem he needed was a gbatu Renaldo.

He loaned the titanium mail and one helmet to Hat and his leather swordsman's jacket to Marc, gave them both spare weapons from the trunk, and wore his heavy mail, coat of plates, pauldrons, leggings, and helmet.

He was no longer cold.

After armoring Perseus and fitting him with the war saddle—and realizing that Lilith had run off with the scabbard and baldric for his warsword, which brought its own set of problems until he just gave it to Marc—he slung the red sword from Perseus's saddle and tied the case on the other side.

Eth and Kel, with Myk's horse and their pony, had vanished ahead by the time the team was armored up and loaded.

Aever watched them go. "Well, that's that."

"How far are they going to get?" Jarrod asked.

"They think they're going to outrun the light," said Thron. "Dumb bastards. They're definitely going to die out there, alone."

Blue winter shag ruffled out as Jarrod unbuckled Perseus's belly strap, waited for him to breathe, and cinched it again.

Technically, the big gelding was a roan, with a combination of gray and black hair that made him look blue in the right light, and which emphasized the colossal knots of muscle that comprised most of him. Jarrod liked to joke that Perseus was half moose.

The big blue horse didn't seem to mind the extra weight of the armor, a short coat of plates over padding that buckled to the saddle fore and aft. It weighed a hundred pounds, but Jarrod wondered if he even noticed it.

He grabbed a knotted leather braid that hung down from the saddle horn and heaved himself up to get one foot in a stirrup, prayed like hell as he always did that the saddle and barding wouldn't slide sideways and dump him on his ass, and then swung a leg over, settled, and looked behind him.

They exactly resembled a team going to war.

It was getting colder. The clouds to the south had ripped apart, and the moon added its odd pink hue to the edges of creation once again. It was now so close to the sun that it hurt to look at it.

Jarrod realized that it had been weeks since the last fully clear day.

They'd wasted the day. It would be night soon. And after that, well, he didn't know.

When evening hit, they rested for what Jarrod felt was an hour or two, and then pushed on. The big moon was gone at night, now, but two tiny ones gave them a thread of light to work with. They took full advantage, moving forward a few steps at a time, with Hat and Marc clearing rocks and guiding the cart horses, Jarrod and Aever riding point, and Thron taking the rear-guard position. The cart was holding up beautifully at this pace, as maddening as it was, and they were out of the pass and, as best Jarrod could figure it, headed across the plain for Regoth Ur.

Jarrod swore he felt it before he saw it; a sense that there was a thing in the air above them, a whiff of feathers at the edges of his perception.

He pulled off his helmet in hopes he'd hear it, again.

He pulled Perseus to a stop and tugged his coif away from his ear.

Whiff.

Whump.

It was far away, whatever it was; a breath, a figment. The tone during a hearing test that you miss because you think you're imagining it, and then goddammit you were supposed to have been hitting the button the whole time and *can I do that again, doc? I missed the—*

Whiff.

Whump.

Closer, now.

The cart crept up on him, and the noise masked anything he might have been able to hear after that. An owl, maybe.

A big goddamned owl.

He nudged Perseus forward, and as they started to move again, he saw the shape in the blackness overhead, blotting out the stars. He would have missed it in a helmet. Serpentine and vast in the fragile moonlight, he got a sense of claws and a whipping tail and then the horses went apeshit all at once and he was yelling at the team to get off the road.

Whatever it was tore through the sky right over their heads, racing down the road from Aever's position to the back of the team—he could feel the wind off it, and with it, an odd, swampy breeze in the chill—and Thron gave a yell as Jarrod ducked. The noise that followed was world-ending, a hundred nails on blackboards dopplering into a thudding series of tumbles and crashes in the dark that shook the ground as if the world was imploding on itself. The horses spooked, the cart horses bolted, and the boys yelled, and even the mighty Perseus, afraid of nothing, walked backwards from the noise, distrustful.

Jarrod could make out a colossal shape, winged, vaguely avian, flapping brokenly in the dark at the edge of his perception amid metallic shrieks of otherworldly pain.

"What the hell was that?" he asked Thron, riding up beside him. Aever joined them in a moment, and Thron dusted off his hands.

"Got 'im," said Thron.

"Damn gryphon," said Thron, looking over the wrecked creature in the shadows. Jarrod wished to God he could have seen the thing during the day.

Thron yanked an axe out of its forehead with a grunt and a foot on its massive beak. It had a crow's head the size of a small car, its body the length of a tractor-trailer. Thron had buried the axehead just above one eye. "They've got bird bones in the front," he said. "Hit 'em in the head, they go down pretty easy. You just gotta stay sharp, and not get scared."

"Is that a dragon?" asked Jarrod, looking at the length of the saurian body and the whip tail.

"It's a gryphon," said Aever. "Gavria uses them. I've never seen one up this far. The last one I saw was at Axe Valley, five years ago."

"The first one anyone's ever seen up here, and you just killed it," said Jarrod to Thron.

"Would you rather it killed us?"

"Fair point," said Jarrod.

"We've got problems," said Aever, walking around the head.

"Do you think?" asked Jarrod, and then strode over to where she was standing. Thron met them a moment later, and they all looked at the new development together.

"That's a saddle," she announced. "And there's nobody in it."

It had been tough to discern the belts and harness among the mess of feathers and broken road, but as Jarrod recognized what he was looking at, he had to agree. "Did he fall out back there?" Jarrod asked, looking behind them.

"We'd have walked up on the body," said Thron. "So, nope."

"Plus, you don't fall out of these saddles," said Aever. "See all the straps?"

Jarrod knelt next to the saddle and pulled straps and buckles from the feathers and felt each one to the end. "None of them are broken," he announced.

"This just keeps getting better and better," said Aever, looking around them. "There's a damned Gavrian out here, somewhere."

"On foot and probably injured," Jarrod pointed out.

"The Dark will be here tomorrow," said Aever. "We need to move on."

"Now, wait, ma'am," said Thron. "A Gavrian this far north raises some interesting questions. He might be able to answer them. He can't be far."

"And how do we transport a wounded prisoner?" asked

Aever. "An injured man, likely combative, in The Dark, when we're already down a man? If we put him on the cart, what keeps him from killing Carj? What happens when the cart breaks?"

"I'm with him," said Jarrod. "I think we track this guy down."

"Sir," she said, "we're going to be stuck in The Dark if we go after him."

"We're going to be stuck in The Dark anyway, at this point," said Jarrod. "It's just a question now of for how long. I say we at least see if he left a trail we can follow."

Thron was already prone, looking across the brush-strewn flat with his eye inches from the ground.

He pointed, otherwise unmoving. The team started out in the direction of his finger.

Jarrod figured it took less than an hour of walking, with Thron constantly kneeling down, and damned if Jarrod knew what the sergeant was looking at. "He's really hurting," he said at one point, noting where he'd fallen down. A few minutes later: "He's been spitting every few steps . . . and . . . yep, he threw up right here. Internal injuries. Can't be far, now."

Over the next small rise, the lump of an armored body was clearly visible in the moonlight, and Jarrod made a note to have Thron teach him how to track someday.

"That's Gavrian armor," said Aever. Jarrod took the red sword off his shoulder and approached, and the other two fanned out and came in from a **Y**, giving nowhere to run.

"I'm Chief Lieutenant Sir Jarrod Torrealday, Knight Officer in the Order of the Stallion of Gateskeep," he announced loudly.

"I'm arresting you."

There was no answer.

He approached a few more steps, his sword out in a fending guard. The knight was face down, hunched and crumpled in peculiar armor, a type of lorica in overlapping bands with a shirt of lamellar beneath it in small interlaced iron plates, very much like what he'd seen on Uloraki knights, all of it vaguely medieval Eastern Russian by Jarrod's eye.

The knight had one arm out in front of him, as if he'd died either pointing or crawling. Jarrod took another step.

"I don't think that will be necessary, sir," said Thron.

"I put a lot of effort into not getting killed," said Jarrod, not taking his eyes off the enemy knight. "I'd hate to ruin a perfect record."

Jarrod stalked up next to the knight and toed his leg. "Hey. Are you well, sir?"

"He may not speak our language," Aever noted.

"Most of them do," said Thron.

"Hey," Jarrod nudged him again, and getting no response, he put a foot on the knight's hand, then knelt on his arm. He got no response. The knight had dropped his helmet some way back, though they hadn't seen it. Jarrod put a hand on his throat and felt for a pulse, and there was none. He was dark-skinned and thin, and Jarrod's first thought was of Ulo Sabbaghian.

"He's dead," Jarrod announced. "Dammit."

"Figured," said Thron. "The crash wrecked him, good. I don't know where he thought he was going." He bent to strip the weapon belts from the body.

"He was going anywhere but here," said Aever. "We need to get back."

"Do we need those?" Jarrod asked Thron.

"Nobody's going to believe us without them, sir."

"Okay, good point."

They began the long walk back, and Jarrod started to wonder why the rider didn't have a partner. No knight, no rider—nobody—went out into the world alone. You just don't do that here, he told himself. No one did.

Watching the skies, wondering if there was another half-crow hellbeast up there watching them, he tripped over the missing helmet and for two terrifying seconds his entire life became a matter of trying to not fall on his sword.

The ground was really fucking hard.

"Hey, you found it!" said Thron, helping him up.

The helmet was an interesting piece, conical, very tall, alien-looking with a tooled faceplate and an aventail around its entirety that would have hung down to mid-chest. "This is beautiful," said Jarrod.

"They do have nice gear," Aever said wistfully. "They have much better iron than we do. Their smiths are better, and everything's heavier."

"You could join their army, you know," Thron ribbed.

"I don't like their food," said Aever. "Too spicy. I could never ride with something eating a hole in my guts."

Jarrod wasn't listening. He was watching the skies.

THE DARK

"We can easily forgive a child who is afraid of the dark; the real tragedy of life is when men are afraid of the light."
– Plato

It was the shadows that he noticed first. A good chunk of the morning had burned away as they'd ridden out of the pass, painfully slow, crushed with exhaustion, but moving into the great plains of Gateskeep with the mountains on their left like a wall of axe heads.

Jarrod could no longer see the moon, as it was immediately next to the sun, and every glance upwards at it left his eyes swimming with blotches.

He wondered where the hell the other gryphon—and he was still certain there was one—had gone. They were still days away from Gateskeep at a normal pace, and proceeding a few yards at a time. There was no way they would make it before they ran out of light.

They crawled. They stopped the cart to move rocks. They ground their teeth. They swore.

They ran out of time.

In early afternoon, the moon bit the sun, and the world

turned inside out.

Jarrod saw the shadow of himself atop Perseus begin to shimmer, and at first, he had to wonder if he was having a stroke. Lines formed and blurred across the shadows, which twisted, smeared, and faded into gray.

The birds went quiet.

The horses stopped. Perseus turned one massive, stupid eye to look back at him.

"Here it comes," said Aever.

Thron was swearing in tirades behind them.

An eternity passed, the world freezing solid and going dark. The horses balked, and the mule sure as shit wasn't going anywhere. They waited.

And when it hit, it hit like nothing he'd ever witnessed, an instantaneous 360-degree sunset, the whole of the sky exploding in flames with towers of clouds, spire-torn, lighting up in an array of reds beneath.

"Okay, that's pretty cool," Jarrod admitted, watching the world turn deepening shades in every direction. The ground beneath Perseus shimmered and elongated and appeared to almost fall away, and he understood why the horses weren't moving. There was no way to tell what was under your feet.

"Give it a moment," Aever said with a shudder.

The moon, a dinner plate compared to the dime of the sun, slammed the door on the light. Twilight faded, the stars came out, and the world was still.

And very, very dark.

"Well, shit," said Jarrod.

It was a simple thing; two forked sticks in the ground, one

taller than the other. And a big, bright star framed between them like a gunsight.

Not that Jarrod could ever explain a gunsight.

A fire crackled far behind him, and he worked by the slender ring of the moon. Two lazy C's end to end, a child's scrawl across the firmament, had clawed their way out of the dark over the past half hour or so as his eyes adjusted. Soon, however, they would spin on their axis away from the sun, and therefore the moon, and it would be seriously, scary dark.

"I don't understand," said Aever.

"The sun rises in the east, right?" asked Jarrod.

"Of course."

"That means, if you're looking east, it goes up." Seeing only blank stares, he explained further, pointing. "It goes up, and overhead, and then it sets west."

"Yes."

"Everything in the sky is going to start in the east and go up."

"How do you know?"

"Because—" *Yeah, better not explain the world revolving.* "—because it does. You've never watched the stars?"

"No," said Carj.

"Well, they do. They come up in the east, and they go down in the west."

"They appear overhead at night," corrected Aever. "They don't rise."

"Yes," said Jarrod, with what he hoped was immense calm and patience, "but they *move* west. Everything up there does. That means that when you look at the stars—" he paused as he lay a third stick in the forks, sighted up it, and moved the stick a little higher in its cradle, "—they will go *up* if you're looking east. Therefore, they will go *down* if you're looking west. So, we watch that star, that big one, at the end of this stick." He motioned to the stick. "Put your eye right here."

Aever knelt next to it. "Like an arrow at a target."

"Yes. See it?"

"I do," said Aever. "The eye of The Bear."

Jarrod remembered, now. The Bear. He still had no idea how that jumble of stars formed a bear, but he felt the same way about most constellations and believed that most people did.

The others formed a line, and took turns looking down the stick, even the valets. Jarrod noticed that one of them was taller and thinner than the other. Now if he could just figure out who was who; he'd been traveling with them for five days and still didn't know their names. He'd remember once they armored up, because he'd given Hat his helmet. *Hat. Helmet.* He could keep that much straight.

"Perfect," said Jarrod. "Now, we wait. In a while, the eye of The Bear—in fact, the whole constellation—will move away from the end of this stick, and we'll know which way we're looking. If it goes up, we're facing east. Down, we're facing west. Right, we're facing—" he had to stop to think about it, "—south, and if it moves left, we're facing north."

"How do you know this?" asked Carj.

"How do you not?" asked Jarrod, straining to hide his exasperation at a world that refused to figure itself out. "Stars move," he insisted. "This is how you don't get lost at night. We need to head west, and the stars are moving west. All we have to do is head the way the stars are moving. Regoth Ur is due west of the pass we just came out of. It's on a plain, so we can't miss it. We keep following the stars over the hills until we see lights."

"Rogue's River Manor is closer," said Carj.

"We'll never find the bridge in the dark," said Thron. "It's Regoth Ur, or we die out here. Now, what if them stars don't move, Chief Lieutenant?"

"Any star that doesn't move is in the north," said Jarrod,

then turned to them. "Do you . . . wow, do you have any stars that don't move?"

"I don't know."

"Mm. So, we wait. Get some sleep. We have time for a short nap. This is going to take a while."

"Where did you learn this?" asked Thron.

The words *Boy Scouts* made no sense when translated into the local language, as "scouts" were either spies, soldiers who worked ahead of a main force body, or knights of the Order of the Star. "My homeland has a school for children that teaches us wilderness survival," Jarrod said. And simply, he hoped.

No such luck. "Children know this in your land?" asked Aever, her tone impressed.

"The smart ones," Jarrod admitted.

"Speaking of children, do we have any idea where those two idiots went?" asked Thron, looking around. It was seriously, frighteningly dark.

"If they don't know this," Carj said, nodding to the sighting contraption, "then I bet even they don't have any idea where they went."

Jarrod lay awake beside the fire, waiting to be wrong.

The world they stood on orbited a gas giant, as best he could figure it. He was ninety-nine percent certain that they were in fact on a moon. However, he had no idea what their own orbital speed around it was. His math was pretty good, and his understanding was that The Dark was a six-day transit; a complete eclipse. His question was the gas giant's orbital period of what appeared to be 440 days around the sun versus their own, as its moon, which he took to be 110 days, with four, 110-

day seasons to a year and what he understood to be a thirty-hour day.

He dismissed the unlikelihood that four of their orbits around the gas giant appeared to line up exactly with a single journey of the gas giant around the sun. He wrote it off as one of those flukes of astromechanics, akin to the moon on Earth appearing precisely the same size as the sun and vice versa. The odds against the math were preposterous, but he had no one to ask and nothing better to go on, so—like everyone else around here—he ignored it. Every world, he figured, has its quirks.

There was one extra epicycle in there compared to Earth, though, so he had to account for the orbit of the moon on which they stood. He could only guess that celestial navigation would still work.

However (and he tried not dwell on this next part), if the gas giant was moving through space faster than their little moon was spinning, he was screwed and they'd die out here.

He doodled in his book. He took two rocks and moved them around the fire in a model.

He lay down, again.

He didn't think that the stars would move nearly as much as a result of their orbit. If there was a merciful god somewhere in that sky, the orbital delta would be comparatively negligible, and they'd see the rotation reflected in the constellations first.

Holy shit, it was dark.

He leaned back and closed his eyes, and awoke what seemed like an instant later with Thron nudging him.

"Hey, Chief Lieutenant. Your sticks worked."

"What?" said Jarrod, rubbing his eyes. He looked over to see the valets taking turns looking up the sighting rig.

"The Eye of the Bear," said Thron. "Damnedest thing. It went to the right."

Jarrod rolled to his feet. "It went right?" He walked to the sighting rig, fighting the urge to run. With his eyes adjusted to the fire, it was black enough to break an ankle. "Did you touch it?" he asked. He put his eye on it, and the big star had, absolutely, gone a hand's breadth to the right. "Well, son of a bitch," he swore. "This stick is facing south. That means," he stuck his right arm straight out to his side. "Regoth Ur is that way. See that big tree on the top of that hill?"

"No," said Thron, and Jarrod remembered that these were a people who rarely saw true darkness. His own eyes apparently adjusted to the night much better than theirs did, and he wondered how much better. The light from two small moons was plenty to see by after a few minutes.

"Well, I can," he said. "We'll aim for that tree. When we get there, we'll build another one of these, and find another target to the west, and do it again."

"This is going to take forever," said Aever.

"Do you have anyplace else to be?" asked Jarrod, and though he knew they couldn't see him grinning, he hoped it was apparent in his voice.

Arriving at the tree, which took more work than he wanted to think about—mounting up in the darkness seemed to take hours, and clearing the rocks for the cart was its own level of aggravation—Jarrod took a long look back and realized that he could still see their fire in the distance if he glanced away for a bit and let it appear in his peripheral vision. It was a simple matter to aim for a star near the horizon with the tree beside him and the fire behind him, and they moved on toward it until it sank, at which point he had identified the next one above, and so forth. They weren't making good time, but they were moving, and he had to convince himself that it was something.

At one point, they found themselves on the crest of a hill, with the road stretching down behind them, and Jarrod numbly realized how tired he was. He hadn't even realized that they'd climbed a hill. He tried to stay coherent and sought another star. He didn't know how long the break in the weather would last, but they were crawling for the coast, and even a moderate marine layer would fuck them all, and good.

There had been a shift in the demeanor of the team, and as they inched through the darkness, Jarrod had to wonder if the glitch with the long night was more psychological than physical. The curtain of black brought with it more than the complication of not being able to see; there was a palpable belief in imminent doom that permeated the group.

In the Gateskeep language, the word for *dark* also meant *dead.* They used the same term for putting out a candle as taking a life. You didn't kill a man here; you extinguished him.

Gonna snuff your ass, that's for sure, he told Renaldo in the coaly evernight.

As the star he was following got ready to sink, a big one, flickering orange and white, appeared under it.

"What the hell is that?" he asked.

Thron rubbed his eyes. "Star?"

"It wasn't there before," said Jarrod. They had no word for *supernova.*

Carj, back on the cart, piped up. "Wayfire," he said. "Someone's looking for us."

~

The wayfire was just that: a waypoint in the form of a massive bonfire on the top of a hill.

The problem, Jarrod noted when they arrived, was that there was nobody around it. No houses, no keep, no village.

"Well, that's great," he said as they stood at the bottom of the slope, looking up at the fire. It was built on a pinnacle, hundreds of feet above them, and it was huge. The rocks glowed beneath it. "I'm open to suggestions," he said.

Thron reined his horse around, looking behind them. "Somebody put it there, Chief Lieutenant. We just have to figure out who."

Aever scanned the darkness to no avail, as the light ruined what little night vision she had. "They can't be far, whoever they were."

"You're telling me that someone lit that fire, then came down that hill, and then took off into the darkness?" asked Jarrod. "That makes no sense."

"It's a wayfire," said Carj. "The whole point is to mark a route for anyone lost out here. Someone must know we're missing. And a damned good thing, too."

"They might not be looking for us," said Thron.

"I'll take what I can get," said Jarrod.

"It was probably lit by the pegasus riders out of Regoth Ur," said Carj. "But to get here, they'd have to light another fire at sight distance, and another one before that, and so on, all the way back to the castle."

"Well, it was due west of us," said Jarrod. "So, it follows that it's a wayfire to Regoth Ur. I have friends there. If the palace knows we're missing, I would hope they'd send word, and Regoth Ur is the closest keep. So, whoever lit that fire probably got here, from there."

"Undoubtedly," said Carj. "We just have to find the next one."

Jarrod looked behind them, then forward, and they rolled on for what felt like a year but was probably half an hour until he saw another flickering star, the same orange-red as this one. "There's another," he said. "How fast does a pegasus fly?"

"About a thousand times faster than us," grumbled Thron.

Jarrod thought about this, and then a terrifying thought struck him. The fires would burn out long before the six days of The Dark were over. And if the weather turned and it rained enough to put the fires out, they would be screwed much sooner.

"Change of plans," Jarrod said. "Unhook the cart. The fires aren't going to last forever. Everybody eat, feed your horses, stuff your pockets, and sling as many bags of food as you can. After this, Marc, Hat, and Carj, you need to mount up. We're running for it."

THINGS BEST LEFT UNFOUND

"Take care that no one hates you justly."

– Publilius Syrus

Jarrod was beyond exhausted when they passed the last wayfire. It had likely been days; he didn't know anymore, but a million miles ahead of them on a plain shimmered a stack of fires.

Regoth Ur.

The sight was enough to wake the others out of their stupor, and the horses and even the mule picked up the pace. In the last ten miles or so, Jarrod got the sense of undulating hills and scrub beneath his feet as the walled village and the towers loomed larger and larger, and disappeared at one point only to reappear below them, and then he must have dozed off, because they were at a castle gate and people he'd never met were asking who the hell they were. Carj was saying something about fires and his foot and refusing to get off his horse, and the knights at the gate were getting cranky about the whole situation.

Jarrod swung down off Perseus and introduced himself.

"Go get Carter Sorenson," he told the guard. "Right now."

"He's on his way, my lord," the knight assured him, and

Jarrod thanked him as Carter, Daorah, and several others, wrapped in furs and holding steins of something frothy, came out to greet them. Everything sorted itself out in short order after Carter hugged Jarrod and offered him a mug of beer. "You could use this, I bet."

"You are a sight for sore eyes, buddy," said Jarrod in English. He saluted Daorah, slammed the beer, and then hugged Carter again.

"You had me worried," said Carter.

"God, it's good to see you," Jarrod said. "Carter, this is my team. We have an injury. We need—"

"Anything," said Carter. "Anything you need. Get inside. We'll take care of your horses and bring in your gear. It's freezing out here. Do you know how much trouble you're in?" he asked Jarrod as they headed for the manor house.

Jarrod clapped him on the back. "Heh. I hope so."

Carter turned the Gavrian helmet over in his hands. "Wow."

Daorah pulled the Gavrian's sword from its scabbard; a short, heavy two-handed sword. "And you're sure it was a gryphon?" she asked.

Carj lay on one of the sofas in the audience room, his foot elevated. The others picked at plates of snacks on the table. Jarrod sat back in a comfortable chair with a beer.

"We got a good look," said Thron from the table. "Feathers in the front, lizard in the back, about fuck-all long," he motioned from one end of the room to the other, "a little bigger, maybe."

"Just one?" Daorah asked.

"That was my question," said Jarrod. "We only saw the

one."

"Well, they can't travel far at night, and without wayfires, we can't fly in The Dark," she said. "So, it might have put down for a while. They'd have to stay within sight of a keep. We can do presence patrols, but that's about it."

"Well, there's a very good chance he's out there," said Jarrod. "Just, you know. So you know."

"So, what happened?" Carter asked. "I mean, you were at High River, right? We got this message about the 'Armies of the West.' You know anything about this? They say they have your castle."

"They don't have my castle," Jarrod assured them. "They're camped outside it. There's no way in. They're just going to stay out there and freeze, I guess."

"That seems stupid," Carter assessed.

"It really does," said Jarrod. "But, it appears that smarts aren't their strong suit. Their champion and resident military genius is one Renaldo Salazar."

Carter perked. "Renaldo?"

"I had the same reaction," Jarrod admitted. "Goddamn Hillwhites drafted him. This is him. This whole thing. I could tell by the way he was talking. This is his idea."

"Gotta wonder how that conversation went," Carter growled. "How did they find him? And why him?"

"I don't know," said Jarrod. "I told them I figured they lost a bet."

"I wouldn't write him off," said Carter. "He's going to be problematic."

"I've noticed."

"Don't discount him," Carter warned. "I mean, yeah, he's an asshole, but he's got the skills and the mindset to go far, here."

"He's an idiot," said Jarrod.

"By our standards," Carter reminded. "But if he so much as went to a community college, he's Galileo to these people. And he's a good swordsman. He beat me, once. If he's hired on as a living blade for a usurper? Brother, that's how worlds turn. The Hillwhites call the shots, and Renaldo keeps the wolves at bay and makes helpful suggestions. It could work. It's a smart play."

"You think?"

"He's doing almost exactly what we did, and look where we are. One thing these guys have going for them: they know talent when they see it, and they're really good at using it to get what they want. And you, my friend, are the biggest thing standing between the Hillwhites and what they want, and they know it. So, they brought in a ringer. I'm surprised it took them this long."

"I'm still trying to figure out how they got over there. I can't wrap my brain around it."

"Well, we have a problem," said Carter. "To teleport to Renaldo—or, I'd imagine, to bring him over—they had to have *seen* Renaldo. Therefore, someone had to either read your mind, or the mind of the Lord High Sorcerer, Crius Lotavaugus, The Bringer of Earth Dudes."

"You know Renaldo. Someone could have read your mind."

"I haven't thought about Renaldo in forever. Not since you woke up here last spring, after the last time he kicked your ass."

"Hey, he sucker-punched me. In the throat."

"Tomato, tomahto," Carter ribbed. "But didn't you say that Crius messed him up?" he remembered. "Renaldo, I mean?"

"Yeah. Crius hit him with a fire extinguisher. I didn't see his face this time, but he ain't pretty no more, I bet."

"Then, Crius saw Renaldo make you his bitch."

"Okay, you need to stop saying that."

"Eventually," Carter said, and winked. "So, they have a wizard who knows Crius, and they have Renaldo. I'm guessing that he brought gear from home?"

"Of course. He has a longsword from Oullette—"

"Ah, longsword," Carter sighed. "The Nickelback of European martial arts."

"There is that," agreed Jarrod. "But he brought a gran espée de guerre that looks like it might be one of Mike Marshall's."

"Oh, shit."

"Nah, it's cool. I have it."

"*You* have it?"

"He gave it to somebody, and I . . . well, yeah," Jarrod dwindled off. "I, uh . . ." He cleared his throat.

"What," said Carter. "You what?"

"I killed a guy," Jarrod sighed. "Another Hillwhite."

"Jesus!" exclaimed Carter. "How many Hillwhites is that for you, now?"

"One," Jarrod emphasized. "The elves killed Edwin, and Ulo killed Skippy."

"Still, though. No wonder they've declared war."

"Ha ha," Jarrod grumbled. "Funny guy."

"Did Renaldo bring armor?"

"Yeah, but I don't know how much. He has a helmet, probably by Daniels, one of those big Corinthian bastards with the rivets. No visor, it's all one piece. And mail and pauldrons, definitely steel. He's probably smart enough to bring case-hardened steel."

"You brought a gun," said Carter. "Why didn't you just shoot him?"

"Didn't have it on me."

"You should've."

"I know. Anyway, I didn't even have any armor on, and he tried to kill all of us. He and Hal-Halchris? Hillwhite—"

"—the guy you snuffed—" added Carter, raising a finger.

"—we covered that—tried to take out Adielle."

"How'd that go?"

"Not as well as they'd hoped," said Jarrod. "She beat Renaldo's ass. Her Grace has got some game."

"Nothing surprises me anymore," Carter admitted.

"Best we can figure it, Renaldo dove out the window, and he had a wizard waiting for him. This guy managed to catch him in mid-air and zap him out of there. This is a problem, too, because they've got themselves a wizard who's somewhere around Ulo's caliber."

"And who was in our wizard cadre," Carter assessed.

"Possibly," breathed Jarrod. "We're on our way to Gateskeep to talk to the Lord High Inquisitor about what's happening at The Reach."

"Well, hell," said Carter. "I can take you to The Reach when the light returns, and you can see for yourself. No problem."

"I appreciate that, but my orders are to go to Gateskeep Palace and check in."

"You're in no shape to go anywhere," said Carter. "I can tell by looking at you, you haven't slept in days. Stay here. Hang out. Relax. When the sun comes back, we'll head up there and take a look and see what's what."

When the sun comes back, Jarrod thought. He wondered how much sleep he could get before then, and hoped the next actual day would be better than the last one.

Jarrod wasn't sure if it was technically morning when he woke. The candle told him it was either mid-morning or early evening, and the clouds were back, so it was absolutely pitch black. He found his way by candelabra-light down to Carter's in-house smith, trading out the candles for a torch at the door, because the wind had picked up.

Carter's smith was an oddly bent little man, humming to himself and smashing something cherry-red with a hammer, just having a great day. Or evening. Anomalous nocturnal event, Jarrod thought. Whatever.

Jarrod pulled a sword blank, a naked blade with a slender metal handle and no crossbar, from a barrel near the door, oil dripping on the floor and his boot. The pungent smack of hot steel stained the air, the blast from the forge tangible even with the winter howling around him in the blackness. The blade was solid, functional, heavy. It was a good Gateskeep sword, with a slenderer point than a Falconsrealm blade but the same wide steel edges. Nice lines, he thought.

"Can I help you, sir?" asked the smith, grabbing the piece of red-hot whatever and putting it back into the forge. "My name is Torvan Daar."

"Hello, Torvan Daar," Jarrod told him, shaking his hand and thanking him silently for not breaking his knuckles. "I need some special work done."

"For you, sir, anything," he said. "Whatever the crown needs."

Jarrod set the black warsword on a table. "First, I need a scabbard for this. How soon?"

"A few days?"

"I'll pay you double if it's done before the sun returns. It doesn't have to be pretty."

"Pay me double, and it will be," Torvan promised.

"Also, this," Jarrod said, and laid the leather case with the red greatsword inside next to the black sword and opened it, revealing the big blade beside its scabbard. The mirrored length of steel appeared to glow with the furnace. Torvan Daar let out a low whistle.

"That is a sweetheart," Torvan said. "I want to have its

children."

"This is why I need a smith of your caliber," said Jarrod. "It needs a rain guard, and a couple of custom modifications."

"Not a problem," said Torvan. "What modifications do you need?"

Jarrod told him.

The Return of the Light was a celebration that Jarrod had been through exactly once, and it had put a few kinks in his patience for the local color.

These were a people catastrophically afraid of the darkness, so when the sun was scheduled to return, they lost their minds to such a degree that Jarrod had to wonder if they didn't, deep-down, fear that the sun would never come back. As the last candle burned down toward the new season, feasts were held in an orgy of self-erasure and reconciliation; a chance to start again. Wine flowed, drum circles erupted, and women danced topless with swords and torches, all of it sweet-souled yet deliriously carnal.

Jarrod and Aever—who was not dancing topless—stood in the east courtyard, drinking and drunk, rested, sated, and generally okay and feeling like they were going to make it as the sun broke on every horizon. The birds exploded in song; the cows lowed; the horses woke the hell up and Jarrod swore he heard Perseus asking where he was from the other side of the castle.

Somewhere far in the distance, coyotes screeched and chattered as the dawn rose and goddamn son of a bitch, it was light again, the skies rising into sheets of iron gray. Jarrod grunted after a time when he realized that this was as light as it was going to get.

Most of the women in the castle didn't put their shirts back on until about noon.

Carter was getting good at flying.

He would never cease being thrilled by riding a pegasus: the speed of a horse at full gallop, but with a fraction of the effort. No jarring, just a slow, rolling lope between wingbeats. Warhorses in temperament, fearless streaks of black murder in the sky.

Behind him, belted in and holding on until his hands hurt, Jarrod thought he would have had a better grip on this. He'd trained in high falls and wire work; he had literally jumped off buildings for money more times than he could count. He was a seasoned BASE jumper and skydiver. Heights didn't even elevate his pulse.

The nature and scope of what they were doing right now buckled his knees and shrunk his heart the same way the first glimpse of the great ringed moon had done, half a year prior.

Feathered wings whiffed through the air; the sky sizzled around them. It was a glorious day, gray and cold with high cloud cover, the mountains a wall on their right and the Gateskeep plains far behind as they screamed north over the vast slate sea. Titanic breakers were visible even from here, meringued with white and roiling in slow fury against the southern tip of The Reach.

Daorah was a speck high and to the left on a smaller and quicker steed named Maila. Carj, Aever, and Thron rode double behind knights of the Falcon on three more pegasi, behind them.

The bite of the wind, the smell of the sea, the sting of rain coming. The occasional glop of horse-foam on his armor.

Jarrod watched the wings. Impossibly majestic, they jutted just behind the shoulders and below the saddle, branching out behind him, unimaginably long. The wizards had done a stunning job with the feathers, he noted, ending the wings in wisps of fur much like the "feathers" at the hooves. Giant Friesians.

Her name was Persephone, and she was Carter's ride.

Jarrod watched the wings.

Carter knelt in the saddle, his legs doubled above the massive knots of muscle where the wings joined the body, in a yoga sit that looked insanely uncomfortable for him. For Jarrod, half his mass and with no knee injuries, it wasn't particularly bad. Jarrod had noted that the other knights of the Falcon were about his size, and many were female. The men were lean, with dancer's builds, not the smash 'em up, thick-chested muscle of the Falconsrealm cavalry.

It was, as best Jarrod could figure it, fifty miles in a straight shot from Regoth Ur to the southern tip of Wild River Reach. The trick was that, on the ground, it wasn't a straight shot: there were mountains to ride through, two rivers to cross, and a great bay to skirt. It was a full day's ride just to Rogue's River Manor, the halfway point.

But a pegasus flew faster than a horse could gallop, and unlike a horse, it could hold the pace all day. They were going to make the tip of The Reach by lunch.

Ahead he saw wide sheets of foam and flume stretching out into a vast rolling world of slate-green, abysmally cold. They would cross over the beaches within moments.

And as they went feet-dry, he saw it.

A mass of fires, flickers in the gray along the edge of the world, spread north along the sea toward the castle. He banged on Carter's shoulder and pointed, and the pegasus tucked its wings and the world turned inside out as they fell out of the sky until Jarrod's armor and helmet slammed against him amidst a hammering of muscles and feathers and wind, and they banked slowly toward the water.

"Never do that again!" Jarrod suggested, and Carter laughed.

"What? You want me to do that again?" he needled.

"Goddammit!" Jarrod punched him in his mailed back. "Asshole!"

"Hey, look!" Carter pointed. "There's your problem!"

Jarrod could see it, too. From here, what he figured was a thousand feet up—about where he'd normally want to consider no longer fucking around and pull his chute—he could see the fires and encampments around The Reach and smell the smoke. The great bridge was definitely withdrawn. Carter spurred Persephone into a gallop, the wind a wall of static through their helmets.

A long, easy ride over the camp— "A thousand!" Carter announced, pointing over the fires, and Jarrod, who had no way to judge such things, took his word for it—and toward the back, hidden from the tower by a hill, what appeared to be a massive corral, packed with people.

Now, what the hell was that?

They circled down. Jarrod squinted. He popped his visor, rubbed his eyes, and looked again, blinking furiously.

And then he recognized it: a ghost from history, an abomination.

Jarrod leaned his helmet next to Carter's.

"Holy shit," they chorused.

Carter and Daorah stood outside The Reach on a covered platform, out of the rain, as a bevy of stablehands took their mounts inside. The wind pulled the tang of salt spray onto the cliffside. Carter wore a tooled leather harness over a shirt of gleaming mail, looking very Gateskeep, his head bare to the cold. The tide was out, and it was hundreds of feet down to the rocks below. He usually loved the view from the landing.

He had never seen Daorah cry before, and it was stunning. Not that he didn't believe her capable; it had just never come up.

She'd teared up at times: being offered the breeding operation; agreeing to marry him; their first morning in the manor, making love in the lavish apartment with the sun coming in the window. But that wasn't crying, as much as it was emotion overflowing.

This was different. Explaining to her what a concentration camp was? Just finding the words in the language had been a battle. They had no word for *genocide*. The concept of making war on civilians—of even aiming war at civilians—was so entirely foreign that it had taken him forever to explain. They didn't even have a word for civilian combatant; their word for *civilian* translated to *innocent*. Fumbling for words in the rain, realizing just how far from home he was and how little he missed it.

Jarrod was speaking with a group of people on the far side of the landing. They saluted, bowed, and ran back into the castle, and he jogged to meet Carter and Daorah as Aever, Thron, and the three knights of the Falcon came over with them. Carj, walking with a cane and a limp, got there last.

"And this is what you've dealt with," Daorah finally sighed. "How did you defeat this? This is . . . this is the most evil thing I've ever heard. Why? How would Hillwhite even think to do this?"

"I don't know," Jarrod snarled. Carter could see him

clenching his fist. "Ulo, I guess. I mean, Ulo worked with the Hillwhites; Ulo is from our world. This is definitely something that we brought with us."

"Holy shit," Carter said. "Oh God. Did we bring this here?"

"Hey, *hey*!" Daorah's voice had a military ring that focused him. "You don't think that," she ordered. "Don't you ever think that!"

She threw herself around him. "This is not you. You are a good man. I love you. You're a warrior, and a hero of our people. This is not you. This is evil. This is what you fight. This is why you're here. This, right here—that—" she motioned toward the camp beyond the tower, "—is why you're all here."

"Okay," Carter said, "but we need to free those people. Right now. We need to get in there and kill everybody that the Hillwhites have put in place. Every one of them. We need to kill those sons of bitches and save those people."

"We're going to need a thousand soldiers, love," she said. "Ten riders can't do that."

"We'll have to find a way that they can," he said.

Bevio appeared at the far edge of the landing and beckoned them inside.

The nine of them, plus Bevio and Saril, stood atop the great tower of The Reach, looking out toward the bridge, where a group of Hillwhite soldiers had gathered.

"I don't know who they are," Saril admitted.

"Hillwhites," said Carter. "Hillwhite loyalists."

"Hillwhite has raised an army?" said Saril.

"So they tell us," said Jarrod.

He counted about two dozen people; counting bodies at a

distance was hard, because they moved around a lot. He called it two dozen. Roughly half of them, he saw, weren't soldiers. Of the civilians, three were women—one elderly—and two were children. Behind them he counted ten soldiers with spears. Two, then three, then four, then one in the back. Ten. He felt proud of himself for counting them; it felt like a knightly, commanderly ability to have. He vowed to get better at it.

"Have they offered any kind of treaty?" Carter asked. "Any demands?"

"Nothing," said Saril. "We didn't even know who they were."

The ten soldiers with the spears marched the dozen or so toward the gap, prodding them along. A few protested, receiving slashes or short jabs for their efforts.

"What the hell?" asked Bevio. "Hey!" he called over the battlement. "HEY!"

As they reached the edge of the bridge, the three-hundred-foot span toward the water below, the screaming started, vanishing in the roar of the surf.

Behind the spearmen, another figure drove them on with orders, his voice lost in the rumble of the waves as the first few tumbled into space. A mother covered the children; a spearman stabbed her and shoved her into space. Children wailed. Men shouted.

Saril yelled epithets, and Bevio with him.

Carter pulled Saril away from the edge of the tower and turned him around, facing away from the scene. Thron did the same with Bevio, and Saril slipped out of Carter's grasp, yelling at him, "We need to stop this! We need to surrender!"

Saril ran to the edge of the tower and began to shout.

Carter put his hand over Saril's mouth and turned him away from the wall, muscling him back. His strength was terrifying. Saril thought of bears, of ogres, of dragons.

"You are not. Surrendering. This fucking. Castle," Carter warned him, keeping a hand over his mouth.

It was over mercifully soon.

Carter looked to Jarrod, who was watching over the parapet, ghost-white and trembling. One of his nails had torn on the stone and was bleeding in the rain. Together, they stared out at the mass of soldiers as they began the long walk down the bridge.

"We need to surrender," Saril muttered, behind them. "They're going to kill everyone if we don't. They're going to push them all off the edge of the—"

"We never surrender," Jarrod said. "No matter what. If we surrender the coin vault, we lose Gateskeep, and Falconsrealm, to the Hillwhites. They will run this country. We can't have the king and Adielle indebted to people who would do things like this. This is where we are," he announced. "This is the war, right here, at the end of that bridge. They're testing our resolve. No matter what they do, *we hold*. Do you understand me?"

"I'm going to kill every one of them," said Saril.

"No, that's my job," Jarrod said, grinding his teeth. "I need you here, Lord Chancellor, and I need you to *not* surrender my castle while I'm out there killing these shitheads. The rest of you, armor up. Let's go hurt somebody."

Jarrod waited for them at the crest of a hill, silhouetted against the silver skies, with Thron and Aever behind him and just out of sight.

Jarrod rested his black greatsword on his shoulder, looking relaxed and casual in his long leather jacket, his visor open so that rain dripped off of it.

The soldiers, ragtag and sloppy, certainly not Gateskeep-caliber knights trained through drill, set spears at about fifty yards out, but didn't do much of a job of it. Their leader called out a hail to Jarrod, who waved.

The leader brought half the force forward to meet Jarrod.

Jarrod slapped his visor closed. "Hi," he said.

The leader, his beard in braids, in a spectacled helmet and a hauberk with a long axe on his shoulder, stayed out of attacking distance.

"Help you, friend?" he said.

"I'm sure you can," said Jarrod, from behind the visor. "What's your name?"

"Tigdin," said the man, looking behind him, obviously uncertain where this conversation was going. "I'm a captain of the Hillwhite Guard. Stand aside."

"Pig Pen?" said Jarrod.

"*Tigdin,*" the soldier emphasized. "I'm a captain of the—"

"Yeah, yeah, yeah," Jarrod waved it off. "Look, we have a problem . . . *friend.*" He used the same northern slang word that Tigdin had used, a word that alternately meant *compatriot, comrade, brother,* and *pal,* but his measured emphasis and hesitation drew it into something ugly. These were not a literate people on the whole, and sarcasm often eluded them, so he'd made a habit of driving it harder than he needed to.

Tigdin straightened his mail with a tug. "Who are you? And what's the problem?"

Jarrod stepped back and brought the warsword into a front guard, exhilarated, as always, with the way it moved. "Who I am *is* the problem. I'm Sir Jarrod the Merciful."

He wasn't sure what kind of response he would get but dropping weapons and surrendering would have been ideal. Weeping and cowering and shitting of pants would have been a nice touch.

Tigdin raised his axe, and he and all five of his knights rushed Jarrod at once.

Swearing in English monosyllables, Jarrod set his feet, changed up his guard, and clenched his teeth as they charged.

One of them threw a spear, which Jarrod knocked aside. Two more followed, and the spearheads hit hard but bounced and lay on the road, and any soldier paying close attention at that point would have thought to fall back and reassess.

Two of them had been paying attention. It was odd enough to see a man in a helmet and no armor; knowing now that he had a shirt of what had to be expensive mail under his very expensive jacket, they were wary of the damage his sword—probably also very expensive—could likely do. Also, most everyone involved at this point knew that the last time Sir Jarrod the Merciful got pissed off, he killed an army.

They broke into a circle, two hanging far back. Three, including Tigdin, made probing attacks, unsure of how to proceed.

Jarrod decided for them. He feinted, threw one aside as he charged, hit another across his helmet and collapsed it sideways, dropping him in his tracks, and engaged Tigdin and his huge axe as Aever and Thron joined the fight. The other five lagging behind ran in to close the gap, yelling and shaking their weapons, encouraging each other, shouting warnings to keep distance and use space. Good soldiers; good friends.

Carter and Persephone crashed out of the sky behind the five stragglers in a freight train of murder, smashing two of them over from behind and launching up into the sky again as if off a trampoline. Tigdin, wrestling with Jarrod, stared at the pegasus and its giant rider in his demonic spiked helmet as they wheeled into the air. Jarrod head-butted him, denting the noseguard, then hit him with the greatsword several times, fracturing and contusing, pulverizing his mail in bites and leaving him crumpled in the mud.

Daorah and the other two knights of the Falcon followed Carter's lead, thundering down and leaving the last three rag-dolled and shattered, limbs askew and yards between them. One tried to crawl. One rolled in the mud. Several moaned.

The pegasi and their riders circled and flashed by overhead. Jarrod watched Aever trip a soldier backwards, deliver a God-almighty stomp to his crotch after he fell, and kick his sword away.

Tigdin, wincing, came to hands and knees before Thron, who snarled, "I have had a very fucking bad couple of days," and raised his blade.

Jarrod poked Tigdin in the ass, under his mail skirt. "Stay down."

Four were alive—Tigdin and three others—all injured to varying degrees. Jarrod and Thron stripped them of their weapons, throwing everything in a pile.

Jarrod used the ensuing pause to explain a few things.

"I am Knight Chief Lieutenant Sir Jarrod The Merciful, Lord of Wild River Reach and Lord Protector of Falconsrealm. These are my lands. That's my castle. You have committed murder against my people. The witnesses are present."

One of them got up to run, apparently the least injured, and Aever shifted sideways and checked him into the road.

"I sentence you to death," said Jarrod, and the words caught him by surprise. Aever and Thron looked to one another, and their demeanor changed, even behind their helmets with their curtains of mail across their faces. Shoulders stiffened, what could be seen of their eyes became impenetrable. A tectonic shift.

Aever lifted the knight who'd run, stood him on his feet, and shoved him back to the others.

Jarrod, Thron, and Aever marched the four of them back down the road toward The Reach, with the pegasi flying a low overwatch.

The rain began, again.

Saril, Bevio, and several knights of The Reach looked on from the top of the tower as Tigdin and the three soldiers stood with their backs to the gap. Freezing death roiled gray and white an eternity below them.

It was interesting to see the turn of fate, though no one said anything.

Jarrod stood before the line, obvious in his burgundy jacket, Aever and that big, quiet sergeant behind him, and Daorah behind them all on her mount, grounded, its wings tucked, barrel-round and black. Jarrod was having some kind of conversation with them that didn't carry to the tower. The other pegasi circled in massive loops that took them over the waves and back, and some knights' eyes tracked them.

"They took out all of those troops," Bevio's voice was impressed.

"I wish I'd been there," said Saril.

"I'm sure we'll get our chance," said Bevio.

The first of the knights, hobbling, his leg or foot apparently injured, saluted Jarrod, then turned, appeared to pray, and jumped off the cliff. Another got up of his own volition and leaped after.

Jarrod approached the last two.

"I thought you were 'The Merciful!'" spat Tigdin.

"I have my moments," snapped Jarrod, but bit down on the rise in his stomach. The thought had reared its head, as the soldiers had leaped off the edge, that he had crossed an abhorrent line. He had no idea what the law exactly was, governing what he was doing. But, he remembered then, he was the lord here; his lands, his laws. He set the greatsword on his shoulder and gripped the handle harder to hide the shaking. "This is not one of them," he admitted.

"I'll make you the same deal," he said, pacing before the remaining knight and Tigdin. The knight, a woman taller than Tigdin with shorn black hair in a soldier's cut, glared at them all. He'd originally mistaken her for a man, an error he was still making no matter how hard he anchored the idea of female knights in his mind.

It was only in the past few months, getting to know soldiers and knights on a first-name basis, that he realized how many of them were women under the mail. In the royal orders, the numbers ran to what he estimated about twenty percent; strong, vibrant women who could kick ass as well as any man, which was likely why it hadn't crossed his mind. It literally hadn't mattered. No one treated them any differently—they received the same bruises and ass-chewings, wore the same armor, and used the same swords—and he even noticed them in the garrison baths from time to time once he started taking his eyes off the cute healers.

"Who told you to do this?" Jarrod asked her.

"A foreigner," she said. She kept looking toward the edge of the cliff every time a wave thundered into the world beneath their feet. "I don't know his name."

"A foreigner," said Jarrod. "Tall? Short? Thin? Fat? Where is he from?"

"He had a strange accent. Tall. An injured face," she said.

"An injured face?" Jarrod thought of Crius Lotavaugus

pummeling Renaldo with a fire extinguisher half a year ago in a hotel room in Maine. He had always figured that it had left a dent. "Like, broken? Hit with something heavy?"

"Yes! His face was broken!"

"Don't you say another word," warned Tigdin.

"And a sword like fire," she continued. "It shone in the sun. It had branches, silver branches, on the guard."

"Shut your mouth!" Tigdin shouted.

"Make me!" she yelled, turning on him. "You knew this was murder, and you went through with it anyway, you faithless shit!"

She turned to Jarrod. "Kill me," she said. "I'm not worthy to bear a sword. Just don't make me jump. Please, my lord."

Tigdin let out an unprintable tirade at the knight, at which point Jarrod sighed, swore soundlessly, and took Tigdin's head completely off. It landed with a kick of wet pebbles and lay blinking.

Jarrod yanked the blade out of mail and meat and the body fell next to it, graceless, empty.

There is a juncture between life and death, a shift from being a person to being a thing. Man to meat; transitory, instant. Steam coalescing to ice.

Jarrod stared down at the thing that had been Tigdin, pumping liters of crimson onto the rock. He bit his cheek. "Goddammit," he muttered.

Aever put a firm hand on his shoulder. "At least he wasn't a Hillwhite."

"He was," the knight corrected. "Tigdin Hillwhite."

Thron erupted in laughter, like a chainsaw ripping through lumber.

"Son of a BITCH!" Jarrod stomped his foot and beat his pommel against the side of his helmet. Thron walked away from the group, wiping his eyes, his armor shaking with laughter.

Every few breaths, he erupted again.

"Pretty good sword, though," said Aever, trying to cheer Jarrod up.

"Yeah," said Jarrod dejectedly, looking at the streaks up the blade, which ran into the fuller like wine. He turned back to the knight. "All right. I'm going to let you live. You're going to have a nice, long life, thinking of what you failed to do today. You can see that as a cost, or as a benefit. You decide. Go back to your army and your leaders and tell them what I did."

She saluted. "Yes, my lord."

"You convince them to release those people," Jarrod continued. "*You* know it's wrong. *You* understand that everyone involved in this is guilty of murder if they don't free my people. And if you don't free them, I swear: *we will kill you all.* Whether we kill you on the field or we hang you one by one, there will be no mercy, and no survivors. Not for this. You're the last one who survives anything. After this, you all die."

"A thousand thanks, my lord," she said.

"What's your name?"

"Regan . . ." she began, and winced, looking away, ". . . Hillwhite."

Jarrod rolled his eyes. "I want you all to notice that I'm not killing her," he told his team. "Does everybody see me *not* killing her? I want to make sure you see me not killing her.

"All right, Regan Hillwhite," Jarrod said. "Tell your leadership what I told you. And then, you leave the northlands. If I ever see you again, you die. Frankly, at the rate I'm going through Hillwhites, I'll probably kill you whether I mean to, or not."

"I understand."

"I hope so," said Jarrod. "This man with the injured face. Tell me more about his sword."

Winter tore at the high tower of The Reach like a mighty dog pulling at its chain. Jarrod and Carter sat across from each other on huge, fur-covered sofas in front of a fireplace, sipping wine as the fire crackled and snapped. The waves thundered through the palace like a snoring giant.

"We're gonna die," said Jarrod.

"Yup," said Carter. "But those are your people and dying for them is your job."

"I'd like to think that fighting for them is my job."

"And what did I say?" asked Carter.

"Fuckin' Renaldo," said Jarrod, pounding his fist against the arm of the sofa.

"Wait, what?" Carter perked. "Renaldo? You think he did this?"

"That last knight. The one we let go. She identified him. Said it was a big guy with a face injury, identified his sword, that big one with the guard by Oullette."

"Dammit."

"That son of a bitch put my people in a concentration camp."

The fire popped and hissed for a while.

"How badly do you think we're going to fuck this place up?" asked Jarrod.

"What do you mean?"

"I mean, our . . ." he searched for a word, and he wasn't sure if it was because he wasn't speaking English enough anymore, or if he was starting to think in the Falconsrealm language, or if he was just used to the feeling of searching for the right word, speaking in a foreign tongue most of the time, ". . . our interference."

Carter looked past Jarrod and visibly formulated an answer, even starting to speak a couple of times before stopping and restarting.

"Are you familiar with Black Tom Island?" he finally asked, his tone professorial.

"No."

"Exactly my point," said Carter.

"I don't follow."

Carter blew out a long breath. "Black Tom Island was an island in New York Harbor. The Germans attacked it in 1916. Blew it off the face of the Earth."

"No, they didn't."

"Yes, they did. There's an exhibit on it at the Smithsonian."

"The Germans never att—"

"Yes, they did," Carter insisted. "They blew up a ship loaded with munitions that was headed for France, and it damned near took out the Statue of Liberty. It's why you can't go up in the torch; it was structurally damaged."

"That's the craziest thing I've ever heard," said Jarrod. "I'm from New York. Well, Connecticut, but I work in New York. I've *been* in the Statue of Liberty."

"Have you been in the torch?" asked Carter.

"Well, no. I mean, someone has, though."

"Have they?"

Carter waited for an answer as Jarrod searched for one.

"I . . . shit, I don't know," said Jarrod. "You'd think, right?"

"Yeah," said Carter. "You would. Black Tom is widely regarded as the first act of international terrorism on U.S. soil. And here's the thing," he added, pouring himself more wine and shaking a finger at Jarrod with his other hand. "I didn't remember learning about it. I have a goddamn Masters in History. Never heard of it. Studied war for six years. And then I was at the Smithsonian, and there it is."

"I don't . . . I don't . . . look, man, I've seen some shit the past few months, but . . ."

"Yeah," said Carter. "I know how you feel. So, I did some digging. There are all these conspiracy theories about Black Tom Island. The most popular one is that it comes and goes."

"What does?"

"The explosion."

"What? *What?*"

"The thinking is, when we develop time travel, it's the first place anyone goes, to stop it. Sometimes they succeed, sometimes they don't."

"That is insane," said Jarrod.

"Yeah," said Carter. "I don't disagree. The working theory is that the first thing the U.S. government does when they invent a time machine, is they go back to 1916 and *interrupt* the American intelligence operation to stop the Germans. They *let* the Germans blow the crap out of New York Harbor, in order to kick off the War on Terror eighty-five years early. The result, they hope, is a massive influx of wealth and the jumpstart of the military-industrial complex, which bomb-proofs the stock market in Twenty-Nine. The Great Depression never happens, we have a fully-tooled military going into the Thirties, we kick Hitler's nuts into the back of his throat a few weeks after he moves on Poland, after which the Japanese don't dare fuck with us, and on and on. By the 21st Century, it's Planet America."

"But I don't see how—"

"I'm getting there," Carter said. "It is possible that you haven't heard of Black Tom Island, because whether or not that explosion happened varies at any given time. Because there is a *separate time loop*—"

"—Oh, Jesus—"

"—in which people go back to stop the U.S. time-travel commandos, or whoever, from stopping American intelligence from stopping the Germans. Black Tom Island is a focal point, a nexus, in the space-time continuum. And here's the thing. Ready?"

"I'm just gonna go ahead and say no."

"In the world we live in—the Earth, the world we came from—Black Tom Island either happened or it didn't, and the result, where we ended up, you and me right before we left, *is the same either way.*"

There was nothing for Jarrod to say.

"The world takes care of itself, is what I'm saying," Carter concluded. "Screw with it all you want. You can change the past, but the present stays the same. It's going to do what it's going to do."

"That is, overall, the craziest thing I've ever heard," said Jarrod.

"Try telling anyone back home where you've been for the past six months," Carter shrugged. "You want to tell me time travel is impossible?"

"We didn't travel in time," Jarrod said. "Holy shit, I have to tell you this?"

"I know that," said Carter patiently, wiping his forehead. "But I'm saying that nothing is impossible, and you're here right now to prove it. And anyway, the principle is the same. There's nothing we can do to this world that it can't—won't—recover from. You and I are here, specifically, because we can make a bigger dent in history—going forward—than anyone else. That's why they brought us, even if they don't put it in those terms. But it's all going to be fine in the end. That's how it works. It has no choice."

"I've gotta wonder what we got ourselves into when we beat up Ulo's guys on that bridge," Jarrod muttered.

"This is about Duke Dipshit. Edwin. That guy," said Carter. "This is not about Ulo. Thank God."

"Either way," said Jarrod. "You realize that this is all—I mean *all*—because of you and me, right?"

"Of course. But we were trying to stop a war."

"Well, we screwed that one up, didn't we?" Jarrod drained his wine. "This is getting worse. And half of me wants to fix it, and the other half is afraid we're just going to set the world on fire if we try."

"I'm telling you: this world has been through enough shit that it can handle anything you or I can throw at it. On that, I'm going home in the morning, because I have a thing to do, and then I'm coming back here and we're going to go out there and wrecking-ball these clowns. You and me." Carter pointed to Jarrod, and then out the window.

"I'm not that good," said Jarrod. "The two of us against five hundred?"

"We've got the bridge," said Carter. "You can get, what, six men abreast on it? You and I can hold that. Hell, I can hold it with Celeste," his five-foot greatsword. "You know your Montante, you can hold territory with a greatsword, right?"

"Sure, but—"

"We can spell each other. We put on our heavy gear, we bring up the birds, we ferry your men out, lure those assholes up the bridge and we pincer them, you and me on one end with ten guys behind us, twenty of your guys on the other. We chew through them and have the birds bat cleanup."

"Do you think they're going to throw all five hundred of their guys at us?" asked Jarrod. "Because I don't. They'll throw fifty guys at us, or twenty. Or none, and just tell us to surrender or they'll kill everybody in those pens. They're killing them ten at a time right now just trying to get Saril to give this place up."

"He won't," said Carter.

"He might."

"Then you need to stay here."

"Yes," said Jarrod. "I do."

Jarrod lay awake late into the night, listening to the storm.

This would be his first winter here, and while he'd been through a few squalls at The Reach—living on the ocean, after all—he'd never experienced anything quite like this. The winds screamed off the water, battering the castle and even powering through the chimneys, pushing the coals from cherry to orange. It was going to be a dreadful season.

They'd bought hundreds of carts full of wood over the summer and fall, tradesmen coming down from the mountains with firewood by the ton, and the larders were full. The tide brought grouperlike granitefish and man-sized sharks into nets thrown down from the town walls, and there were livestock—hogs, mostly—that fed off the remains of the fish. They had cisterns and rain catchments, and most of all, they had the geothermal energy below them that warmed the rocks of the keep and the floors of the town.

The heat radiating from the walls pecked at him whenever he found his mind wandering. Right now, though, he didn't want to consider that his castle was built on top of an active volcano. He had bigger problems.

He couldn't get the pegasi out of his head. The idea of air superiority staggered him, and he had to wonder why Gateskeep didn't throw all their resources into the breeding and training operation. The pegasi could provide overwatch, mapping, insertion of elite troops, and the obvious advantage of flying soldiers through those fucking mountains. It was a three-day ride from here to Regoth Ur—longer, in the wrong weather—and if your horse took a bad step you could find yourself in a three-hundred-foot freefall off a moss-slicked fjord. And yet, Carter could make it in a couple of hours on a pegasus if he really hauled ass.

There were a lot of ideas that they were missing. The concept of using their wizards only as long-distance operators and travel agents, for starters. *I mean, sure,* he thought, *communication sucks, here. Got it. But why not offense?*

Because they're trained not to.

Except, he thought, they used the pegasi for offense, and the pegasi were as magical as it gets.

And then, he thought, there was Ulo. He could clearly kill people with magic; he'd killed Javal, and Albar Hillwhite, and a bunch of other people who'd been in a room with them. Which was probably why Gavria hadn't gone to kick his ass, yet. The idea of someone shooting fireballs from atop the Silver Palace was probably a game-changer. As was whatever Renaldo's buddy had pulled off at High River Keep.

Which made him wonder about Renaldo's wizard. The Hillwhite wizard.

If there was a spy, or a traitor, within the cadre of wizards, then Gateskeep had serious, world-wrecking problems.

The Order of the Stallion was an intelligence-gathering network; their job was to keep an ear to the ground and report possible transgressions against the crown. But a wizard as an enemy spy? He didn't even know where to begin.

He didn't know anything about wizards, he realized. He knew they were essentially high-order psychics—what he'd seen Crius do was essentially telekinesis and telepathy—as well as low-key enchanters. He'd never seen a fireball or a lightning bolt shoot from a wizard's hand, but he knew that one of the local wizards had just been asked to put an enchantment on the mortar of a knight's new home to help it stand up longer. Would it work? Who knew?

Legend had it that King Rorthos's sword was enchanted and could never break. The irony was that the sword had been through so many fights, it was now dinged up and re-filed long past its usefulness. In Gateskeep tradition, when a blade outlives itself, the point would be ground or sheared off and made into a pendant, showing that the bearer had survived enough battles to wear out a sword. But the unbreakable charm on the king's sword couldn't be lifted, so Rorthos was stuck carrying around a blade that was dinged and filed all to hell. Jarrod was sure the king had other swords, but there was an issue of street cred.

Was it possible, he wondered, if it wasn't a wizard at all who'd read his—or Crius's—mind, but someone with a nascent telepathic talent? The telepath who'd taught him to speak the local language had once had the gift of reading minds at a distance, she'd said, and had only later conditioned herself to only read minds when in contact with the target.

Target. What a word.

Ulo could probably do it.

But Ulo had said he wasn't a fighter. Which was interesting, because he had sure killed the hell out of Javal, Albar, and a bunch of others. He could certainly inflict harm with his magic. So, he wasn't beholden to the rules laid down by Crius's masters.

Wait a minute.

What training had Ulo gone through? From birthday clown on Earth to Darth Vader here; he had to have learned . . .

What training do sorcerers in Ulorak go through?

He dozed off thinking of the great black tower of the Silver Palace, and the view from the top.

Jarrod was doing pushups in front of the fireplace, shirtless in the wind and damp of morning, when Carter knocked on his door and let himself in. "Lookin' good," he said.

"Nine hundred ninety-nine," Jarrod grunted, lowering himself, "And *that's* an even one thousand." He jumped to his feet with a wicked grin and Carter threw him the tunic from his warrior blacks.

Carter wore a black and gray ragg sweater and heavy, mud-colored trousers, work boots from Earth, and a black cape with soft fur beneath. The cape was clasped with a silver single-wing pin, showing him as a rider for the Pegasus Guard; a knight in training who had not yet seen combat in the air.

He walked over to Jarrod's field armor, a 15th-Century suit of steel harness, vaguely Italian, though the smith had taken considerable artistic license at points. It was simple footman's armor, bent slender to fit Jarrod, sans scallops or lance rest but gorgeously engraved. Carter noted that Jarrod had added an integrated green tabard with the Gateskeep gold key in two sides, like a priest's stole beneath the gorget and mantle, as a final flourish.

The mail was heavy and dark-burnished beneath the plates, with full-length sleeves; a heavy welded aventail from the edge of the helmet was tacked with rivets to what looked like black goatskin.

He toyed with a plate and guessed at twelve- or maybe ten-gauge steel, two millimeters thick and maybe thicker in some spots, exceptionally tough. It had taken a few scuffs and dings on their last outing against Ulo's army, but nothing had even come close to penetrating it or denting it. Spears and axes had bounced right off; hell, they'd bounced off Jarrod's titanium mail yesterday, and it was no heavier than a set of butcher's gloves. The plate harness design was four hundred years ahead of the local warfighting technology and the metallurgy had a lead of nearly a millennium. On a battlefield here, it was the equivalent of showing up to a bar fight wearing a fusion-powered exoskeleton.

Carter had one, too.

And so, he was sure, would Renaldo.

Which brought up an interesting point, he thought: Renaldo was a longswordsman, used to one-hit fighting, either in tournaments with points scored, or illegal duels to the first blood. One touch, and the fight stops.

Carter had fought professionally in mixed martial arts and done fairly well. He knew the difference between falls for points in a dojo and having someone jump right back up and come after you. And it was stunning the first few times. It took some getting used to, to say nothing of not having a referee.

He wondered how much time on the field Renaldo had seen, and how hard he was training right now.

He pulled Jarrod's great sword of war partially from its scabbard. The edge was dinged in a few spots and needed grinding, but it was a beast, an absolute day-ruiner. Broad, solid, built to hurt and hurt and hurt some more.

They'd be all right.

"We're about to head out," Carter said. "I'll be back tonight, and we'll do this thing in the morning."

"I was thinking about it," said Jarrod, tying his hair back. "And you're right. If we can convince them to come out and play, with you and me at the head of it, we might have a pretty good shot."

With his words came the ringing of the watchman's bell.

"Son of a bitch," said Jarrod, pulling on a shirt. "I really thought I might make it through just one day without killing somebody." He slung his warsword over his shoulder and was pinning on his cape as Daorah came to the door. She was wearing almost exactly what Carter was wearing, and Jarrod guessed that Regoth Ur didn't have many tailors, or if it did, there was one who did the best work and she had a particular flair. He noted that Daorah's cape was fastened with the diving bird-of-prey pin of the Order of the Falcon, the mark of an airborne knight blooded in battle. He'd expected as much, but he'd never seen one up close. It was also, he noted, strongly derivative of the Falconsrealm sigil, which he thought was interesting, because to his knowledge, Falconsrealm didn't have a contingent of pegasi. This wasn't the time to ask.

"Right now," was all she said.

Jarrod grabbed his hat and they ran.

Jarrod's chambers were high in the tower; there were two more sets of stairs that curved upwards and then an inset ladder that led up to the roof with its wide parapets. Jarrod heaved himself onto the roof to find a bunch of people waiting for him.

"I'm too old for this shit," said Carter, as two knights gave him a hand up. "You need to put a goddamn handrail right here— Oh, God . . ." he went quiet as he looked out over the wall, but Jarrod was aware of his presence behind him.

In the night, someone had set a row of heads—men, women, and a few, judging from the size, children—on the low wall along the side of the bridge, facing the castle. Mouths hung open. Hair whipped in the wind.

Foremost among them, set first in the line nearest the keep, was the short-haired head of Regan Hillwhite.

Daorah's face broke out in fast-rising splotches of red until she roared and pounded her hand against the wall. Jarrod had rarely seen a woman's blood pressure rise so fast, and it crossed his mind that this was a woman who commanded battlefields, and who'd gotten there by hacking apart dangerous men with an axe. He stepped back a little.

"Sir, we need to discuss terms of surrender," said Saril.

Jarrod spun on him and grabbed him by the shirt front.

"Never!" Jarrod shouted. "What the hell is wrong with you?"

"It's just money!" shouted Saril.

"It's not my fucking money!" Jarrod screamed.

"Dammit," Aever yelled, pulling Jarrod away. "You don't think they're watching you, right now?"

"There's nobody around," Carter assured her. "They're long gone. Chickenshits did this in the middle of the night."

"No," Aever sighed. "Here. Right in your ass, right here. You don't think they have spies inside this building, right now?"

"Anybody who is, is gonna die," said Saril, shaking his cloak against the weather and giving Jarrod a few yards of berth.

"And do you think they don't know that?" said Aever. "Someone, out there, knows *exactly* how to get to you, Lord Protector. They know *exactly* how to manipulate you. They wouldn't do this unless they had a way to know *exactly* how it would affect you."

"Someone on this rooftop," said Jarrod.

"Probably," she said, looking across the faces of the assembled.

Jarrod looked across Saril, Bevio, Carter, Daorah, Thron, and Aever. "These are my friends. These are the most trusted people I have." A few knights he knew fairly well stood over at the wall with their sergeants, a couple of guards hanging far back. One scout watched the sea, for reasons he never quite understood, but there was a parapet and lookout's platform on that side, and it was always manned.

"They know these are your trusted people," Aever continued. "When we recruit spies, we look for three factors. We look for placement, access, and motivation. Everyone on this rooftop, right now, has ideal placement; they're high in your organization. They have access; they have your ear, and they know the innermost workings of your organization. And now, what we need to do, is determine who, among us on this rooftop, has motivation."

"Motivation?"

"Motivation," said Aever. "Whose interests would it serve to see this castle given over to the Hillwhites?" She turned to Saril. "Why is your immediate reaction to give this castle up?"

"Are you accusing me?" Saril challenged. He was smaller than Carter but far bigger than Aever, and his skill in combat was legendary. He'd been a rider for his order, plucked from a small farm and given a low-grade chivalric rank after sweeping a tournament in both swordsmanship and wrestling. It was well-known that he'd fucked up a lot of people fighting the Uloraki army beside Carter and Jarrod.

"I'm accusing everybody," said Aever.

"You should be asking the same question of me," added Thron. "Do I have a motivation to see this castle given to the Hillwhites? What do you know of me? Maybe my sister is married to a Hillwhite. Maybe the best fuck of my life was a Hillwhite and she married a knight of The Reach. You," and here, he pointed to Jarrod, "need to start digging."

"I don't have time for this shit," said Jarrod. "Look, if someone on this roof was a Hillwhite operative, I'd be dead by now."

"With you dead, their spies would be useless," Thron suggested.

"So, now it's 'spies?'" said Jarrod. "More than one?"

"I can't believe you don't know this stuff!" Aever said to Jarrod, exasperated. "Lord Protector, you're Order of the Stallion! You're an officer! You should know all of this!"

"I was on an accelerated program," Jarrod shot back. "I was busy stopping a war, busting up a treason plot at the highest levels of government, and brokering international deals." Although, he reasoned, he had walked backwards into the

Hillwhites' spy ring out of sheer stupid luck. He didn't know a damned thing about espionage or treason except that he recognized it when he saw it. "I was a little busy," he admitted.

"Enough," said Daorah, the ranking officer on the rooftop. "Both of you. Everyone. None of this, fixes *that.*" She pointed out to the heads.

"That head in the front," said Jarrod, looking over the wall. "I'm pretty sure that's Regan Hillwhite."

Daorah swore. "Didn't you let her go?"

"I told her to take a message back," said Jarrod.

"Well, their reply is unmistakable," said Carter. "So, you have two options. You either have to give this castle up, or we have to go out there and kill them all."

"I'm not giving this castle up," said Jarrod.

"That makes it easy," Carter said.

"We need to report this," said Daorah. "We need to disperse our riders and send word. We will come back with a plan."

"I'm staying," said Carter.

"You wanted to see the foals," she reminded.

"It can wait. I'm needed here."

"I figured as much," Daorah said. "We'll hurry. Don't do anything rash."

Carter grinned. "Who, me?"

"Darling," she started, and then shook her head, smiling and sighing at the same time. "Kill good. I'll see you soon."

It was raining that night at Gateskeep palace.

Evden Isri, a willowy woman in layered woolen dresses the colors of rust and sky, heavy and snug against the cold, set an agate stein of beer in front of Daorah and another before herself.

Daorah could have easily envisioned Evden astride a pegasus; she was tall, and strongly built, with an intense power in her eyes and the set of her jaw.

Daorah worked to envision what a woman of such strength would find purposeful or rewarding in a life of palace service—Evden was a high steward for the War Council, a keeper of the numbers that drive war—that wouldn't be better found in the saddle. Daorah noted Evden's gaze shifting to her rider's longsword leaning against the table in its silver-embossed scabbard and assessed that the feeling was mutual.

It was past supper, and the small feasting hall in the barracks was otherwise empty. Rain pounded at the roof and dripped into the windows. It was, however, warm and protected from the storm. The benches were worn shiny closest to the fires.

"So, how is it at Regoth Ur?" Evden began the conversation, slurping at the head of her beer.

Daorah nodded. "We're managing. However, The Reach is in a bit of a bind."

Evden folded her hands on the table. "We've heard. What do you need?"

"You waste little time."

"It's in short supply. How can we help?"

Daorah took a long pull at her beer. "Hand weapons," she said. "Five hundred. Maybe a thousand. Daggers, knives, axes."

"For what? Are you building an army?"

"Actually, yes," said Daorah. "The Hillwhites are holding the—"

"The inhabitants of The Reach," interrupted Evden. "Yes, we know."

"This is how we plan to rescue them," said Daorah. "We're going to fly these weapons in there tomorrow night, if we can. Fifteen birds, thirty crates. We kill the guards, open the gates, and turn a thousand armed, pissed off northerners loose in their camp to do the rest."

"Absolutely not!" said Evden, ashen. "Absolutely not," she repeated after a moment's thought.

"And why not?"

"You're arming innocents. Putting them in harm's way."

Daorah shook her head in incomprehension. "They're already in harm's way."

"There is no way in hell that the crown will give you what you're asking for. I won't approve it, that's for damned sure."

"This is not a decision for you to make," Daorah said. "I'm the highest-ranking officer in the military who's not on the War Council."

"I understand that."

Daorah cleared her throat. "Apparently, you don't. Do you grasp what's happening, here?"

"No," said Evden, "but I do know what's happening, *here.* We need every weapon we can get our hands on. We are not, under any circumstances, giving a trunk full of weapons to innocents in the middle of a war."

"I was hoping for several trunks," said Daorah.

"Much less that," said Evden, sipping her beer. "Absolutely not," she repeated. "Why would you arm innocents? What are you thinking?"

"They're killing those people," said Daorah. "Ten at a time, in full view of the tower, trying to make us give up the castle and the coin vault."

"So, now it's 'us?'" said Evden, and snorted, at which point Daorah pushed her beer down.

"You listen to me," Daorah said, and Evden pulled her hand back.

"This is something new," Daorah continued. "This is something nameless. This is an evil spawned from a demon that the Hillwhites have conjured. In the world where he comes from, they make war on innocents, and he has brought that evil here. There are *children's . . . heads . . . on . . . sticks,"* she snarled, pounding her fist on the table with each word, "outside The Reach. Right now."

Evden set her beer down, lining it up with a pre-existing ring on the table. "That's troubling."

Daorah spat a laugh. "Troubling? I'd say it's a damn sight more than 'troubling.' I'd say it's downright 'bothersome.' These are *dead children*."

"What do you expect the crown to do? Just give you weapons, so that untrained innocents—among them, children! —can turn into an armed rabble? To give The Reach, allotted a force of fifty, a ready force of a thousand? Do you consider this reasonable?"

"No, I consider it severe," said Daorah. "But it's what I'm asking. This is what I was brought here to do. This is our plan."

"Well, you had better think of a different plan."

"There are no other options. Without your help, either those people die, or we give up the castle and bankrupt the country. So, show some guts, open the armory in the morning, and get me a thousand hand weapons—"

"—A thousand—" Evden shook her head.

"—and we fly in there and give those people a chance to die on their feet. Maybe some of them get away."

"Precisely our point. They'll be slaughtered."

"Isn't that better?" Daorah asked, pounding her hand on the table. "Evden, if you were being held in that camp, would you want to wait to die, or would you want to fight your way out?"

"They're innocents."

"There's no such thing anymore," said Daorah.

"This is going nowhere," said Evden, getting up. "I'm sorry, but this conversation has ended. You're going to have to think of another plan."

Daorah stood, as well. "And what would that be? I have fifteen riders. The Reach has thirty-eight knights and a handful of infantry. Most of their garrison is in those pens. Hillwhite has five hundred troops, and a full support tranche behind them. We're outnumbered twenty to one."

Evden gave a measured smile. "It sounds like exactly your kind of fight."

"Don't fuck me in the dark and tell me I'm pretty. If we fight an extended fight at The Reach, then we lose our eyes on the north between Regoth Ur and The West. We will need every bird up at The Reach if we want to have a prayer of surviving. This has to be over, and over in one night, or we lose Regoth Ur, and you lose the north."

"You'll think of something," said Evden, and Daorah's jaw ground.

"Commander," Evden insisted, "You can't just take it upon yourselves to redefine warfare—"

Daorah's stein shattered in her hand.

"Is that supposed to frighten me?" Evden said, but stepped back, her eyes flicking from the broken stein to Daorah's sword.

"No," Daorah growled, dropping the pieces on the table and wiping her hand on her thigh. "There will be plenty of frightening yet to come, I'm sure. Because we're not redefining war. That's already happened. We need to fight a new war."

"Like I said, we have the utmost confidence in you." Evden smiled, and again, it stayed too long.

"What are you planning?" Daorah asked.

"Find another way, Commander."

"What are you planning?" Daorah demanded.

Evden adjusted her stole. "Good night, Commander."

"This is not over," Daorah said, as Evden walked out. "My

troops and I are staying the night. I swear on my sword, if I don't have an answer I like by dawn, I will kick the king's door off the hinges and ask him myself."

"I wouldn't do that."

Daorah muttered to herself, "Of course, you wouldn't," but Evden was already gone, and she was alone in the hall.

Morning at Gateskeep Palace came with a hard frost and an emphatic blast of sunlight resounding from roofs and battlements that sparkled chalk-white.

It was several flights of stairs from the cavernous anteroom at Gateskeep palace up to the floor housing the king's audience chambers. The doors, mighty iron-banded wooden slabs, were open to a long hallway, and inside, the sun and moon spilled through glassless windows next to fires glowing in massive alcoves. The cold snuck through the corridor on wisps of smoke and candlesweet.

She'd been cold before.

She'd be cold again, flying out of here.

Daorah wore warrior blacks, sword at her side clacking against her leg, and she wondered when the scabbard had started to come loose. She made a note to call on Torvan Daar, their brilliant smith, to get it fixed. He'd established himself as a man with a knack for simple and enduring remedies to problems that other smiths would dismiss as impossible.

She smiled to herself. She wondered what Torvan Daar might say about the plan she was about to propose to the king. It was, after all, his type of solution: simple, effective, permanent.

She wondered, too, what Torvan might say about her plan to talk to the king, because now she found herself standing in the doorway to the audience chamber, face to face with two knights of the Stallion in warrior blacks asking if she had an appointment.

"I'm sorry, Commander," said the younger of the two. "The king is very busy today." Bustle and murmur spilled through the doorway in splashes, unseen but substantial.

"I have no doubt," she said. "Stand aside."

"King's orders," said the knight. "No one goes in without an appointment."

Daorah didn't move. "Stand," she repeated, "aside."

"Are you going to kill me, Commander?" asked the knight, overly confident, she thought as she looked him up and down. He was young, likely recently knighted, definitely born to a lord or higher, with pale skin and a slender build, clean-shaven in the manner of many knights of the Stallion and his black hair shorn close, but this one was different, with a hollow insufficiency in his eyes: a man who lacked the courage to live completely and who had likely sought this appointment because of it.

"No," she said. "But I'll make you look foolish."

The other knight, older, short-bearded, smirked and nodded.

"You doubt me?" she asked.

The older knight saluted. "Not in the slightest, ma'am. Sir Eldon, let her in. Better that she takes her lumps from the king than we take our lumps from her."

"We can't just—" Eldon started, but the other knight cut him off.

"She will beat you like a dying mule," the older knight promised. "And then I'm going to have to get involved, and then she's going to beat *me* like a dying mule, and I don't want the king to see that."

"Sir, we can't just—"

"A dying mule," the knight repeated. "And you'll make the

same sounds, I guarantee it."

"I appreciate your confidence," said Daorah.

"Respectfully, Commander, we haven't formally met, but I know you," the knight said. "You flew cover for me at the Tanover Line, some years back. I saw you kill a lot of people that day. A lot of people," he emphasized to the younger knight.

"Killing's not always the answer," Daorah quipped.

"Not today, that's for damned sure," said the knight. "Sir Eldon, let her through."

The king's audience chambers were either the busiest calm place in the kingdom, or the calmest busy place in the kingdom. It was a place of cold and severe opulence, with floors of gray and black marble, the furniture carved from dark rock flecked with mica and polished smooth as statuary. The doorways were arches of mighty black timbers carved into arm-thick braids, and the chambers had no actual doors beyond the first. Candles and fires worked tirelessly, and the chambers glowed with a chilly and granitic permanence.

Just inside the doorway, a long table of scribes sat on their cloaks, clad in lightweight tunics as they sat close to the snapping fires, occasionally murmuring to each other, their pens twitching and scratching at papers. This was the archival room for laws, taxes, and royal decisions, and it was also the genesis of letters from the king, which Daorah's knights flew from one end of Gateskeep's vast holdings to another. Past the scribes was a short hallway, and at its entrance stood another knight, this one in mail, who let Daorah through with a salute.

King Rorthos Riongoran-Thurdin was in his chambers with three others she didn't know. They were the type of sober, funereal men she'd come to expect among palace lords and high-level staff: gray-headed wisps of men in gold-decked cloaks and fine furs, whose raily physiques and slender hands showed that they had spent lives eschewing other inclinations beyond power and duty.

The king himself was a former knight of the Order of the Stallion, Jarrod's order, broad-shouldered, white-bearded, and fond of food to the point that Jarrod, upon seeing King Rorthos for the first time, had immediately ordered a clothier to make a stocking cap from red felted wool and white fur fringe. He'd presented it to the king upon their first formal meeting, explaining it as traditional among his people denoting a leader of benevolence.

Jarrod's gift had become one of King Rorthos's favorite hats, and he wore it today along with great green and golden robes, his legendary battered sword at his side, as he puttered around his receiving room holding a parchment and dictating a response to a pair of scribes who copied, pens scratching, as they stood at a table. A pile of pastries and a pitcher of wine sat on a small table next to the throne, which was carved from the same stone as the rest of the furniture.

"Commander," the king greeted Daorah, who knelt. "Splendid to see you," he said. "Rise, my child." He called everyone *my child,* which, to Jarrod, made the hat thing even funnier.

She stood, and he sat on the edge of a table and set the parchment down. "This must be urgent," he said. "Tell me you have news from The Reach. Scribes, leave us." The scribes scattered.

"Terrible news, Majesty," said Daorah. "The Hillwhites are making war on innocents at The Reach. They're holding a thousand innocents, and they're killing them a few at a time trying to convince Sir Jarrod to give up the keep and the coin vault. We fear they'll kill them all if they receive word that High River is sending an army."

"We have heard this. How many troops do they have? We heard a thousand."

"Likely that many, Majesty, but half are support. I'm here to ask for weapons for—"

"Where is the Lord Protector?" asked the king right then.

"At The Reach, Majesty."

The king folded his hands, his tone perplexed. "He was to come here."

"Yes, Majesty. His team was ambushed by gbatu south of Rogue's River. Injuries slowed them, and they got caught in The Dark. He led his team to Regoth Ur—"

"In The Dark?" asked the king. "Of course, he did. Resourceful young man."

"—and on the first day of winter, we took him to The Reach on a recon in force. That's when we saw . . ." her voice faltered, ". . . the innocents, and learned what Hillwhite was doing. Jarrod can't trust his Lord Chancellor to not surrender the keep, so he's staying at The Reach. We have a plan to free those people, Majesty, but we need your help. It's unorthodox."

"If it's Sir Jarrod's plan, I'd expect nothing else," said the king. "Every time that man makes a plan, I have to eat chalk."

"It is his plan, but also mine and my husband's," said Daorah.

"How is your husband?"

"He is well, thank you. He's at The Reach with Sir Jarrod."

"I will need more chalk." The king touched his stomach. "Those two."

"Our plan is expensive, but it will stop this."

"You're talking to me because Evden said no." He rested his hands in his belt, jostling his sword, which appeared to nod.

"Yes."

"It's her job to say no," said the king.

Daorah looked out the window at the mountains veined purple and black beneath the snow that blared in the freezing sun. It was a great spot for a room if you had to spend most of your days in just one. "I assessed as much."

"Do you expect me to say yes?"

"No, Majesty."

"But you're here."

"Yes."

"Evden says you want a thousand weapons," said the king.

"Yes."

"To arm the innocents."

"Northers are fierce. We drop the weapons inside their pen at night—"

"*Pen*?" the king roared, coming off the table.

"—they're kept in a pen, Majesty. Next to the meat animals."

Rorthos shook his head, swearing quietly.

Daorah continued, "We kill the guards, open the pen, and the Northers fight their way out. We use the knights of The Reach as shock troops, and the birds fly cover for the innocents as they return to their homes."

"It's the number of weapons that troubles me. A thousand weapons." He shook his head again.

"We could do it with half that."

"There will be no half-measures," said the king, smoothing out his tunic as the wind cut through the room. "Not for this."

"Then please help us," said Daorah, emphasizing, "Let us save them."

"My trouble with this," said the king, sighing, "is that we will then have a thousand good weapons in the hands of northerners. We will have effectively built a yeomanry, with no way to disarm them."

"Jarrod has thought of this," Daorah insisted. "He means to institutionalize training and create a reserve force so that this doesn't happen again."

"And we'll have an army in the north, who barely consider themselves my subjects to begin with, under no one's control," said the king, shaking his head. "What if they decide to rise up? What will he do, then? Do we arm another thousand innocents to fight against them when Sir Jarrod is trapped in his castle yet again?" Behind him, the advisers nodded to each other, and Daorah knew she wasn't telling them anything they didn't already know.

"Majesty, the Lord Protector believes that it's his responsibility to be the kind of leader that an armed populace won't feel a need to rise up against," said Daorah. "I agree with him. Arming them and freeing them should be a considerable step toward earning their good will."

"That is a mighty risk," said the king.

"It's a kingly risk, Majesty," Daorah ventured. "It's not his to take. This is why I'm here."

Rorthos grunted, and stroked his beard for a time, saying nothing. "Leave us," he said, finally. "We must speak."

~∫° ≈/°

(FAERIE COURAGE)

"Secret operations are essential in war; the army relies upon them to make its every move."
- Sun Tzu

Karra Talivel marveled at the human capacity for spiritual exertion.

Adielle wailed and sobbed on her throne in a sputtering display of fruitlessness; a butterfly hammering at a web. Faerie had so long transcended such matters that to Karra, humans appeared to cry for the same reasons that wolves howled. It looked exhausting.

She sat, cold and pacific, at one of the stone tables in the princess's audience chamber and toyed with the missive that one of the knights of the Falcon had brought, the thing that had caused all the pain. It didn't say much, but it said enough. Damning, if read from a certain point of view.

She let Adielle get it all out, because Karra could do nothing until she stopped. The fire cracked and spat while Karra read the note again.

And again.

"I can't believe that Jarrod is allowing those people to be murdered," Adielle sniffed. Five times, now, Karra noted, she'd said as much, but her gestures now seemed final, and she appeared ready to listen. Or talk. Or, ideally, Karra thought, both.

"You must listen to me, Highness," said Karra. "I will tell you much about Jarrod that you appear not to know. Once you know, then, plan. But you must understand the mind of a hero, first."

"I know heroes," said Adielle. "He's not one."

"Then, you don't know heroes," returned Karra. "Effective measures must correspond to the levels of the world upon which they function," said Karra. "Jarrod has grasped the roots of this problem. You have grasped the branches."

"I have no idea what you're saying," said Adielle.

Karra pulled Adielle's wine away. "I need your mind clear. Follow my thinking."

"I don't understand," Adielle sniffed. "I don't understand him, and I don't understand you."

"No, you don't," said Karra, "and I applaud your choice of beginnings. The root of human failings often lies in presupposing an understanding of all things."

"From talking to you, I'm starting to get the feeling that I don't know anything," said Adielle, reaching for her wine again.

"You know plenty," said Karra. "And first, you should know—I believe you do know—that Jarrod will always choose the hardest path. They torture him by murdering his people in front of him. By standing up to the Hillwhites, and his allowing torture, he overcomes it."

Adielle teared up again. "They're torturing him?"

"By killing your innocents," said Karra. "Yes. They torture

him."

Adielle slumped in her throne. "May my ancestors forgive me," she sniffed, and wiped her eyes with her palms. "I'm angry with a man who's being tortured. Well, that just makes me feel so much better."

"He has Faerie courage," said Karra. "Our word for courage means *friend-love. Ab:* friend. *Ed:* love. Courage: *ab-ed.* Jarrod's life consists only of *ab-ed*."

"I may never stop crying," Adielle sniffed again.

"Don't cry, Highness. Understand. He believes, and correctly, that if he gives the vault and the coin to the West, only slaughter, and the loss of your nation, will follow."

Adielle straightened herself in her seat and nodded. "It will."

"Like all warriors, he chooses the hardest path. We expect nothing less from a hero, and we can't fault him. He prevents the collapse of your kingdom."

Adielle looked from the fire, to Karra. "He won't crumble, will he?"

"No." Karra rose and went to the stack of scrolls. "*Ab-ed.* Faerie courage."

"So, we know what Jarrod's going to do."

"He will do what he always does. And we must never undermine it."

"What do we do, now?"

"You rule Falconsrealm," said Karra, picking through the scrolls. "Decide. But, trust Jarrod. Don't fault him for his beliefs. You cannot change him. Work with him."

"Why don't we believe what he believes? The world would be such an amazing place if he . . . if . . ."

"Yes, Highness?"

"He comes from a world where enemies on the battlefield heal each other after a fight. He tells stories of soldiers from different armies calling a truce and drinking together on holidays. His enemy, this Lord Blacktree. Jarrod calls him 'friend.' What an incredible world."

"I saw it in him when I first met him," said Karra. "He had brought one of our people back to us, and with her, her tormentor. He risked his life, and possibly war between our peoples, because of his beliefs. Not a breath later, he began a plan to rescue you—again, risking his life, and war—because of his beliefs. This war results from that. From him, rescuing you.

"When Lord Blacktree threatened us all—you, me, the castle—Jarrod responded by choosing to fight a man capable of killing everyone he loves. A Faerie knight would flee and fight later, when certain of victory. I can't ignore that. He possesses selflessness that Faerie don't—can't—possess. I chose to bond with him because of it."

"Perhaps I should have," said Adielle, staring at the fire as Karra unrolled a scroll on a table behind her and smoothed it out.

"You still may," said Karra.

"You'd give him up?" Adielle asked, turning back to her.

"I would encourage him to mate with you if you both wished," said Karra.

Karra felt Adielle's gaze pass through her in the silence that followed, watching the exceptionally human instance of grasping at a large concept, missing it, and scrambling after.

Karra explained, "Jarrod can never understand love as Faerie understand it. Only another of our own can give me the love that I require."

"You don't love him?" asked Adielle, squinting slightly.

"More than any human ever could," Karra assured her. "But eventually, I will need another of my own, to bring me a thing beyond love as you know it. Jarrod will die long before that, as will you. I have bound myself to him, and have sworn to give him the greatest life that I can while he lives."

"How do I compete with that?" Adielle grumbled into her chalice and drained it.

"We need not compete," said Karra. "You two as mates would balance much in this world, including the two of you."

"That's nice of you to say."

"If you desire each other, I will bind myself to both of you, if you'd like."

Adielle blinked a few times. "I'm going to need a lot more wine before you explain how that would work."

"Ask again someday," said Karra. "A war awaits." She motioned to the map on the table. "Here."

"We want a map of Western Gateskeep, don't we?" asked Adielle. "This is a map of The Reach."

"No," said Karra. "The West started the war in The Reach. What did they do first? How did it start?"

"They took the castle," said Adielle.

"Did they?" Karra asked.

"No," said Adielle after long thought. "They didn't. They don't have the castle. They took the mine. The silver mine," she said, and pointed to the map. "Here."

"If they wanted the vault," asked Karra, "Why the mine, and why the mine, first? Can they spend raw silver?"

"No," said Adielle. "Only coins. It's illegal to trade for raw silver, unless you're an artisan, with a writ from the crown."

"We Faerie rob the mine because our land produces little silver," said Karra. "You don't guard your silver at the mine because it has no worth until it becomes coin. So, why does Hillwhite steal ore?"

"That is odd," Adielle admitted. "It makes no sense."

"It must make sense to them," said Karra. "Why steal ore? And steal it to where?"

The fire snapped for a few minutes, the wind raging

outside.

"There's no reason," said Adielle. "The mine isn't of any value unless they can . . ." Her voice trailed off.

"I see it," she said. "Wait."

A long moment passed, the wind tugging at the fire through the flue.

Adielle tapped the map again, in a different spot. "They're moving the silver from the mine to the mint. They know they can't get to the vault inside The Reach—Jarrod will never give it up—so they're going to take over the mint and make their own coins."

"I agree."

"The coins will allow them to pay the support staff they'd need to move reinforcements from West Keep. What they're doing is expensive, and this is how they plan to finance it. When the reinforcements arrive at The Reach, the money will already be there."

"We understand, now," said Karra.

"If that's how Jarrod wants to fight, that's how we'll fight," said Adielle. "I need my wizard, my generals, and Captain Gwerian."

"May I ask what you plan to do?" asked Karra, as Adielle refilled her chalice. The princess threw back another long slug and clapped it down on the table with a bang.

"We're going to destroy the mint," she said. "We're going to starve the bastards."

Daorah, scrubbed, warm, and casual in a sweater and felt trousers, came into Jarrod's audience chamber, where he, his team, several knights, and Carter were drinking and talking while the storm beat the holy hell out of the tower in the black of evening. It had been a long afternoon of hauling crates of weapons. The largest ones took two troops—or, as Thron had noted with a grin, four stewards—to carry.

"I love your baths," said Daorah. "The water comes right out of the rock, a hot river."

Carj and Aever pored over a long scroll at a heavy wooden table, Carj sitting sideways with his foot on a pillow on a stool. He was moving around better since Jarrod's healers had worked on him. Right now, though, the bones in his foot were knitting, and the itching made him fidget if he didn't keep it elevated.

Next to them, leaning over the table, Jarrod made notes in his book. "It's nice," agreed Jarrod. "We are never cold here."

"Can I ask what this says?" Daorah inquired, approaching them. "Or is it spy stuff?"

"Definitely spy stuff," grinned Aever. "But it's so good."

"We can't thank you enough for bringing this," Carj told her. "This is fantastic."

"So, talk to me," said Daorah.

"We're almost done," said Carj. "There's a lot here. It will help us."

Carter set a goblet of wine beside Daorah, and she put her arm around his waist. "Do tell," he said.

"We're still putting it together," said Carj, "But we can tell you what we know."

"Who's our source?" said Jarrod, scratching in his notepad and unfolding his makeshift map.

"I can't tell you specifically," said Aever. "You know that. They're horse-breeders, allies of the crown, and they keep an ear towards Axe Valley for us. A lot of their soldiers and knights deploy to Axe Valley, and they do a lot of business down there, so this house has current and credible information on the goings-on."

"They were wise to Commander Gar and his treachery long before you were," said Thron, from a corner of a sofa where he'd been sitting quietly with a tall agate vase of beer. "They're the ones who had the Order of the Stallion post our knights under Edwin, when they learned that Edwin and Gar were working together. Way back. You remember," he told Jarrod.

"Well, damn," said Jarrod. "I probably should have known that."

"Yes," said Thron. "You should have."

"The eldest daughter is a telepath," Aever added. "She can read a mind, even separated by several days' ride, after only meeting someone once. Quite a gift."

Jarrod made notes. "Is that common?" he asked. "I've met a lot of telepaths. None of them could do it."

"Among the wizard cadre, it's common," said Aever. "It's rare to see someone so gifted who stays outside the sorcery schools, but as I understand it, she's something of an oddity. She claims to have the ability to receive thoughts, but not send. Consider it a perturbation in the skill set."

"Anyway," Carj interjected, "she's done so much for us by now that we should offer her an honorary position in the order."

"I know where you'd offer her an honorary position," Aever needled, telling Jarrod, "He's got a sweet spot for her."

"So, what does she say?" asked Jarrod.

"There's movement in Long Valley," said Carj. "Troops heading north. Apparently, there was no word to the Axe Valley legions about it, so they're two, maybe three days behind. The Axe Valley troops are heading for Gateskeep Palace to plus up Gateskeep's forces, and should be there in a day or two. That's the good news."

"And of course, there's bad news," guessed Carter.

Daorah interjected, "Gateskeep will take two dozen days to field an army that's worth a shit. At least. They were caught asleep on this one. They have a garrison force and some recon elements, but no major standing power. The Axe Valley troops will be the first ones ready to stand, and they're not a lot."

"I was afraid of that," said Aever. "The lords of Long Valley—"

"Like those three assholes we met on the road," added Thron.

"—those guys," Aever agreed, "have sided with the Armies of the West. Kingdom of the West. Whatever the hell of the West."

"The Western Hold," Jarrod clarified, scratching in his book.

"Right," she said.

"Should you be keeping those notes?" asked Thron, changing the subject.

"They're in my language," Jarrod said. "They might as well be in code. There are four people in this world who can read this."

"Well, it gets better," said Aever. A steward set a plate piled with shelled snails, pink-veined and glistening with fat, on a table and showed himself out. Thron picked one off the top, popped it in his mouth, and set the plate on the table, chewing and blowing to cool it off.

"What the hell is that?" Aever asked.

"Snails," said Jarrod. "They're outstanding. Try one."

Everybody did, and the pile dwindled quickly. "Told you," Jarrod said.

Carj took another one. "So, our source caught word of an argument between your Lord Blacktree—"

"Fuck, yeah," said Jarrod.

"—and a man she thinks is Rogar Hillwhite."

"Rogar," said Jarrod.

Carter grinned, and clapped Jarrod on the back. "One more

for you. Add him to your list."

"Shut up," Jarrod groused.

"Rogar is the patriarch of the Hillwhite clan," said Carj, "now that Halchris is dead."

"My fault," said Jarrod, raising his hand. "That was me."

"We know," said Aever. "This is the interesting part: apparently, your Lord Blacktree was arguing with Rogar Hillwhite about the role of command staff," said Aever, reading the parchment. "It nearly came to blows, according to this. Lord Blacktree believes that, as a commander—"

"That idiot is a commander?"

"Well, this will be easy," Carter suggested.

"—he should, and I quote, here, 'Be in the back of the field, commanding formations.' Apparently, the Hillwhites are not fond of this notion."

"I can see that," said Jarrod.

"Who would do that?" Daorah asked, interrupting. "I'm sorry, but what kind of leader would push his armies into a battle instead of lead them? Does this man think that leadership happens by following?"

Jarrod and Carter looked at each other. "Apparently," said Carter.

"Doesn't surprise me," said Jarrod. "I don't think he reads much."

"'Armies are led from the rear,'" Carter chuckled, aping Renaldo, stooping so his knuckles dragged.

"Someone should have told that to King David," said Jarrod.

"Queen Zenobia," said Carter.

"Phillip II," Jarrod offered.

"Darius III?" Carter asked, and the battle was joined.

"Xerxes."

"Leonidas."

Jarrod raised his glass with a flourish. "Magister Militum Flavius Stilicho," he announced.

"Ooh, nice," said Carter, balancing a pink snail on a cracker of nuts and seeds. "Edward Longshanks."

"Robert the Bruce."

"Alaric the Bold."

"Erik the Red."

Carter spoke around a mouthful of food. "Attila the Hun."

"Krum the Horrible."

"Che Guevara," Carter mumbled, still chewing.

"Charlemagne."

Carter pointed at Jarrod, swallowed, and said firmly, "Obi-Wan Kenobi."

"Dammit," said Jarrod. "General Obi-Wan Kenobi. Yup. You win."

"Who are these people?" asked Daorah.

Jarrod looked at Carter, then back to her. "Leaders," he said. "Military leaders. Generals who were the first into battle."

"Tell us of Obi-Wan Kenobi," said Aever.

"He was a powerful wizard," said Jarrod, "with a mighty sword, who trained many knights."

"Great guy," agreed Carter, draining his wine.

"I would like to meet this man," Aever repeated.

"All we have of him are stories," Carter said. "But he's well-known among our people. You'd like him."

"Tell us his stories," said Thron, throwing more wood on the fire.

Carter looked to Jarrod, over by the stone decanter of wine and filling two goblets. The storm wasn't going anywhere, and tomorrow night was going to be long. It wouldn't hurt them to stay up. "Why not?" Carter asked Jarrod.

Carter filled two goblets as Jarrod settled in on the couch, and Carter bade him to stand up. "Never tell a story sitting down."

"You're telling it, too," said Jarrod.

"You start."

Jarrod cleared his throat. "A long time ago, in a land far, far away . . ." he said, and paused. "Wait," he said.

"Do you not remember how this goes?" asked Carter.

"Wait," said Jarrod, holding up a finger. "Wait, there's a thing, here."

"Yeah, the text scrolls up the screen—come on, don't tell me you had it memorized," Carter rolled his eyes.

"Shut up!" Jarrod snapped. "I'm a little drunk but wait a minute. Just stop talking. I need to think. Get the message out again," he told Carj, who shook it from its case and unrolled it.

"This telepath," Jarrod said.

"Yes," said Carj.

"You said that she can read minds after meeting someone once."

"Yes," said Carj.

"And she can't read from someone she hasn't met in person, right? She has to meet them?" he asked.

"Yes," said Carj and Aever simultaneously.

"This is why we have to assume that it's this, Sir What's His Nuts. Hillwhite. Am I right on this? We assume, because she hasn't met him."

"Rogar Hillwhite," said Aever. "Yes. It's likely, though," she assured him.

Jarrod gazed across the room, to see if anyone else was thinking what he was thinking. "How . . . *the hell,*" he asked carefully, "does she know who Blacktree is?"

A HILL WORTH DYING ON

"You, you, and you: panic. The rest of you, with me."

– Unknown; attributed to a U.S. Marine Corps Gunnery Sergeant

It was moonless and hailing and as dark as it gets. Carter was inside a tent near the edge of the camp, by the paddock, with Daorah and a dozen of Jarrod's knights huddled behind him. Every time he peeked out of the flap, the wind yanked at the canvas, threatening to announce the team to the world.

Shapes in the corral moaned and shivered, and the tent was close enough to hear them. Children wailed. The elderly coughed. Carter seethed. He couldn't see them through the storm, but damn if he didn't hear them, and his heart cracked at the echoes.

There were only six guards—his small force could easily have taken them—but hundreds of soldiers slept just a shout away and waking them would murder everyone he'd brought.

"He said he had an idea," Carter promised, as Daorah glared at him. "We wait."

"What exactly did he say?" she asked.

"He said he had an idea and had me drop him off next to the livestock pen. I don't know what he—"

"Love?" asked Daorah, pointing out of the tent flap. "What is that?"

Carter followed her hand. It was an army. A no-shit, honest-to-God army, hundreds of torches racing down the hill toward the camp in a thunder of hooves and a cacophony to end the world. The horrors before them in the night vanished in a roaring smear like a hundred basso fire engines.

"Cavalry!" said one of the knights behind them, one of Daorah's riders, Lady Frielle. She broke into a grin. "Ground pounders," she said, her voice round with appreciation. "Getting it done the hard way."

"Where did he get cavalry?" Carter wondered out loud, "And whose side are they on?"

"Ours, I'd guess," said Lady Frielle.

"At least, not theirs," added Daorah.

Every Hillwhite knight and soldier charged out of their tents to join the fight, running for the rampaging chaos on the next hill as distant screaming began. Barked orders, strident cries, paroxysms of horror from hundreds of soldiers caught off-guard, all of it rising in volumes above the cannonade of hell that rumbled through the darkness so near, yet mercifully far.

Carter had never heard so much screaming.

"Go!" said Carter, and they raced to the paddock as the guards ran for the fight. Short work with an axe, and the latch came away, and the knights yelled and whistled for the people to get moving.

"Let's go!" shouted Carter, as the shivering hordes began shuffling out of the corral. Women, children. It made his gut ache. They offered Carter and the knights thanks, and hugs, and touches, and tearful oaths. "Just go," said Carter, shoving them away one after another. "Hurry!"

He needed to get off this goddamn hill before whatever was happening two hundred yards away decided to happen right here.

Knights of the Falcon dropped in, black wings smashing the wind in the darkness, and cut loose heavy trunks which broke open on the ground, spilling knives and axes by the score. Carter's knights rushed in and handed weapons to everyone as they passed.

"That way!" Carter pointed away from the hell breaking loose to the north of camp, directing the stream of people toward the gate and eventually the road. "Fight your way out if you have to! Grab a weapon! Go! *Go!*"

In the middle of it all, a man who could have been Carter's son given his stature and musculature, his knotted arms bare to the cold beneath a threadbare woolen vest, stood before Carter, unflinching and carved out of granite in the hail.

Carter noted two children beside him in what had to be the man's overtunic, shared between them, one arm in each sleeve, with his undertunic sleeves on their heads in the manner of stocking caps. "I'm Gat Kabos," the man said. "I'm a smith from Grach township."

Carter shook his hand. "Carter Sorenson. Lord of Regoth Ur. Pleasure to meet you." He rummaged through axes to find a larger one. "Here. Go kill somebody. On second thought," he said, handing him a second axe, "take two."

Gat Kabos sent his children with an older man behind him and started shouting at able-bodied men and women, all of them roiling with murder, piling them behind him into a mob. "Keep doing that," Carter told him, and moved on, clapping him on the shoulder.

To the north, he could see the cavalry ripping through the tents and camp structures, trampling fires, knocking over weapons racks and cooking pots, running absolutely batshit insane and destroying everything. Every now and again, a tent burst into flames.

There was no order or formation to them; they attacked with an abandon Carter would attribute to carousing Mongols.

He had to wonder if gbatu ever rode horses.

Even from here, though, the mayhem in the wake of the cavalry swallowed the edge of the night, and it screamed at Carter's team in wild and reaching disarray. The darkness convulsed against streaks and shreds of unfathomable rage, glorious.

I don't know who you guys are, but I will buy you all a drink when this is over. Also, keep that shit over there, please.

He wondered what Jarrod had planned, then wondered if this was it, then decided that, at this point, it didn't matter.

Persephone knelt for him, watching the next hill with the nominal degree of horseish distrust. He patted her neck and locked his legs in, cinching buckles and double-checking everything, then checking once more, and then he toed her on both hips and she stood and took to the air in a leap, wings whiffing, Carter's neck wrenching.

They didn't fly high; he was a knight in black armor on a black horse on a moonless night, and no one would even see him up here. Besides, he figured, they were really busy down there. He gave it a hundred feet.

He gave it a hundred more just to be sure. They crossed the camp and flashed above the center of the mayhem, banking hard as Carter looked down to the flare-riddled, scrambling insanity below.

What he'd thought were men on horseback with torches were the Hillwhite army's meat animals—goats, oxen, cows—with their tails on fire, berserk with panic. The protective earthen walls around the camp gave nowhere for human or beast to run. The imperative of survival, cranked up to eleven.

A meat grinder.

He watched a burning ox rampage through a tent, soldiers scattering with screams as it spun in circles several times to shake off the canvas. It sprinted away and a few archers, safe on the raised earthen walls, took potshots.

Carter tried to imagine taking down a rampaging one-ton steer by using a broadsword in his underwear at night, and decided he liked it a lot better up here.

He circled higher and did a loop back over the camp, banking slowly over the now-empty paddocks.

At the top of the hill, standing a few feet before the gate to the cattle corral, several figures stood in a knot. A few punched each other on the shoulder in solidarity and satisfaction.

At the head of them stood a man who was unmistakably Jarrod Torrealday. He was smaller than the others, arms akimbo and watching the mayhem below with immense fulfillment. Carter swore he could see him smiling even from a thousand feet away.

THE LIMITATIONS OF REASON

"I'd rather have ten soldiers who keep their heads in a fight than one hero, whatever that word means. Wars are won by the side that makes the fewest mistakes. Armies run on competence, not heroism."

- Daorah Uth Alanas

"You can't do that!" said Carter. "You just—you just can't!"

"It's done," said Jarrod. "What I can't do, now, is undo it."

Carter's glass shattered on the wall, and the very real possibility set in to Jarrod that he was about to get his ass kicked. "Stay back, man," he warned, putting his hands up, open. The storm was abating in the graying dawn outside the great tower but a new one was about to start inside if he wasn't careful.

"You set *animals.* On *fire,*" Carter growled.

"To free a concentration camp!" Jarrod shouted back. "And it worked! Holy shit, Carter, there are no absolutes, here!"

Carter's nostrils flared as he breathed in and out.

"You think I did that for *fun?*" Jarrod asked. "You think I'm some kind of psychopath?"

"The thought," Carter growled slowly, "has crossed my mind. And I'm not alone."

"Yes, I set them on fire. I harmed them. Desperate circumstances call for desperate measures. I know I'll be working this one off for several lifetimes."

"You were laughing!" Carter challenged, pointing. "You son of a bitch!"

"It was hilarious!" Jarrod countered.

"To you," said Carter. "I'm not saying it wasn't brilliant. But damn, Jarrod. Don't you think you've crossed a line, somewhere?"

Jarrod pounded his drink and poured another. "I'm not even close."

"You're looking for a moral justification for your own selfishness," said Carter. "It's going to be a while."

"You have no idea what I'm capable of," Jarrod heard himself say, and realized as he said it that he, himself, had no idea anymore. He stared into a void every bit as real and wolf-howlingly scary as he'd faced coming across the plains to Carter's place. He flashed back to the weeping knight who'd jumped off the cliff. Tigdin Hillwhite's head and the consonant *thuck* it made in the mud next to his boot. Regan Hillwhite's head on a stick.

And he still had Renaldo to deal with.

Cliffs to jump from, every way he looked.

"You got that right," said Carter. "I don't even know who you are, right now."

"Then you're really not going to like what I'm about to become."

Daorah came in, carrying tea and dried fish on a platter, and they switched to the local language.

"I don't want to see," said Carter, "we're taking your ass back after breakfast and you can go do whatever it is you need to do at Gateskeep. I want no part of it. When you get there, though, I want you to think about how you're going to explain this to the king, and I'd implore you to be very careful about how you say it."

"King Rorthos said to thank you for the hat, by the way," said Daorah, intervening with a change of subject and striving to smooth things over.

"What?" asked Carter, turning to her.

"Him," she said, pointing to Jarrod. "He gave the king a wonderful hat."

He turned back to Jarrod and caught him smiling. "What kind," Carter asked through gritted teeth, "of hat?"

"I gave him a hat," Jarrod said with a shrug, but stepped back a little. "He likes hats."

". . . Jarrod . . ."

"It's not like that, darling," Daorah insisted. "It's a very nice hat. It's a beautiful deep red, trimmed with the whitest white fur, and a . . ." she motioned beside her head, ". . . a little white fur ball at the end. He loves it."

Carter slumped against the window, a severed marionette. "Oh, Jesus, God, fuck," he swore in English.

Jarrod shrugged again. "It was the thing to do at the time."

"God damn you," said Carter, digging his palms into his eyes. "You made the king into Santa Claus."

"Is he not?" asked Jarrod.

"Yes," Carter agreed, sighing. "He pretty much is. But holy shit, Jarrod. This. This, right here. This is what your problem is. This is not Disneyland. Every goddamn move we make here, every word we say, has repercussions. This world is adapting to us faster than we're adapting to it. Do you understand that? The things you do, *matter.*"

"I've noticed," said Jarrod, looking out the window at the streams of smoke that still rose from the wrecked Hillwhite camp.

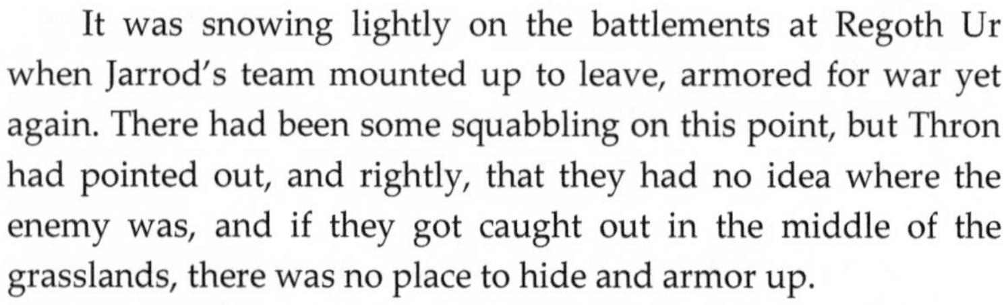

It was snowing lightly on the battlements at Regoth Ur when Jarrod's team mounted up to leave, armored for war yet again. There had been some squabbling on this point, but Thron had pointed out, and rightly, that they had no idea where the enemy was, and if they got caught out in the middle of the grasslands, there was no place to hide and armor up.

A squadron of pegasi—horsebirds, Jarrod reminded himself—roared overhead, wings banging at the wind with a thunder that seemed to draw from the center of the earth.

Jarrod finished tying the red sword into Perseus's saddle next to his black warsword in its new scabbard, hung his Barbute off the black sword's handle, and double-checked all his straps and buckles once more.

"You got this?" Carter asked, dressed for a day in the castle in soft-soled boots and his wolfskin cape. The snow melted on contact with Jarrod's Damascus pauldrons, the tree-ring pattern of the sculpted shoulders and lames a thing of beauty that Carter hadn't really noticed until now. He looked immensely capable. A hint of danger filled the air around him. He was definitely ready, and Carter didn't even know why he'd said it.

Jarrod stuck his hand out, and Carter shook it in both his. "You be careful," Jarrod said. "Don't make me come back here."

"Kill the fucker," said Carter.

"You know I will," Jarrod assured him.

After a short and awkward pause, Carter finally said, "You did good, you know."

"Yeah?"

"Yeah," said Carter, nodding. "I was thinking about it on

the ride down. You saved their lives. And ours. It's not my place to tell you how to be a hero. You have your own thing. It's just not mine."

"We can't all be this awesome," Jarrod said with a shrug.

"I'll ride beside you any day," said Carter. "I mean that."

Jarrod nodded. "I'll hold you to it," he said, and put on his hat and cocked it sideways a bit.

"How do you get up there?" asked Carter, looking up at Perseus. "Seriously. You want a boost?"

"Shut up," Jarrod grumbled, grabbing the knotted lanyard and swinging up.

"We can make it by night if we hurry," said Aever, riding up next to Jarrod with Carj and Thron behind her. Thron led the fat mule, once again laden for the road. Jarrod nudged Perseus into a canter, and they followed him, and Jarrod waved with his hat as they passed through the barbican and out into the Gateskeep plains.

Daorah watched the four of them ride away. "That is a big horse," she said. "How does he get up there?"

Carter put his arm around her and smiled. "The same way he does everything else," he said.

THE MAN FROM GOD KNOWS WHERE

"Nothing is so good for the morale of the troops as the occasional sight of a dead general."
– Infantry maxim

Jarrod, Aever, and Thron lay up on the edge of a birch forest, peeking around trees, their horses tethered far behind.

"That is a lot of knights," said Jarrod.

It was a much larger fight than anything they were used to, and even anything Jarrod had trained for in his days studying to become a knight officer. Instead of dozens of combatants in a border skirmish, this seemed to involve hundreds, with battalions sprawling across the snow-rimmed valley. He looked for the familiar and didn't find it; the formations and the maneuvers he was expecting simply didn't appear, and he had to wonder if a commander someplace was drunk. The fight was unfolding a thousand feet away, and fast.

Everything was wrong. The pace, the movements, the size.

"I have never seen a battle this big," said Aever, and Jarrod wasn't sure if it made him feel better or worse.

"That's got to be the Armies of the West," said Jarrod.

"Who are the Gateskeep guys?"

"Palace knights," said Thron. "Probably scutes under either us, or maybe the Swan."

"You think they'd send knights on scutage into an actual fight?" Jarrod asked. "Are we low on troops?

"That's a recon element," said Thron. "Those horses don't have any barding. They didn't expect to meet enemy forces."

"How many troops do you figure the West has?" asked Jarrod.

"You can't tell?" asked Aever.

"This is new to me," said Jarrod, and it was true.

"Probably two hundred," she answered. "Fifty horse, fifty foot, a hundred more foot behind. Looks like we've got half that."

"This is not good," said Jarrod.

"There," said Thron, pointing right at a front echelon of fast-moving spearmen and a tranche of heavy horse trundling behind, moving up a long slope. At the top, several dozen knights stood under Gateskeep standard, green pennants everywhere. "Those aren't knights, with the spears," said Thron. "I don't know what the hell those are, but we saw that up at The Reach, too. See how the spears are set? Or more to the point, how they aren't? Those aren't knights. Those aren't even heavy foot. Those are levies. Amateurs."

"They raised levies?" Aever asked.

"It sure looks that way."

"Well, what the hell good is that going to do?" she wondered.

"All they have to do is stop those knights," Jarrod said. "A handful of spears and some guys with balls can accomplish a lot. Especially if your horses don't have any armor."

"Our horses have armor," she said.

Jarrod glanced back to Perseus. "Yeah, they do. Let's go."

Thron's voice was a rattle of rocks. "You want to charge up behind, or do you want to flank them?"

"I'm open to ideas," said Jarrod, as they rode along a path near the edge of the forest. He hoped to God that no one saw them. "This is going to suck," he muttered under his breath, looking back at the two knights with him and resting his teardrop shield with the Lord Protector's sigil on his leg. The trail dumped onto the plain ahead of them, and once they walked the last fifty feet, they'd be seen, and it would be on.

"We oughta wait for those spearmen to rush, and then hit them from the side and knock them down," suggested Thron.

"That's not bad," Jarrod admitted. "Let's see what happens." They rode to the edge of the trees. The hill was long, not terribly steep, and grassy, with large granite boulders strewn around that had fallen forever ago from a bald knob at the top. The grass sloped up to an unshrugged shoulder of ridgeline that tilted away from the knob, and the Gateskeep cavalry had the high ground; they rumbled off it with roller-coaster certainty and the distant thunder of worlds ending across town.

Halfway up to the crest, the spearmen met the horses, and sure as hell, the cavalry stopped in their tracks, many of them going over, their momentum devastated, floundering, fucking up the entire reason for staging cavalry on a hilltop. Horses shrieked. Men screamed and scrambled up, launching themselves at the spearmen.

"They're killing the horses," Thron announced. "Bastards."

"We hold here," said Jarrod. "We're not doing that."

Behind the spearmen, slogging up the hill, a wave of footsoldiers formed itself behind a lone hero at the head of a phalanx, moving with a stride and a purpose through the forest of points and knocking any Gateskeep knight dead who came near him. He struck down a horse with one swing of a two-handed warsword, and Aever took a deep breath. "That man," she pointed. "Wow."

Men just fell dead around him, as if he could kill them by touch. "Who have they got, who can fight like that?" she asked, her voice round with respect.

Thron guessed, and started naming people Jarrod had never heard of, but figured he should have. "Lord Tari-dan of Shimros?"

Aever watched, intent. "He's too tall," she said. "And Tari-dan rides. Who can do that on foot? Wow," she said again, as he mowed through a group of knights like a farmer with a sickle.

"Only a few," Thron admitted. "Sir Belgev, maybe. Dorvius of Thossyl is that tall, but he's got to be seventy years old. He could hit like that at your age. I wonder if he has a son."

"Neither of those men would turn," said Aever. "Never. They've been the king's men for generations. That guy's really good," she said, interrupting herself as he fell behind the wall of spearmen as they closed again and shifted his attack, pushing his troops in a sweeping flank across the plain for the next group of unhorsed Gateskeep knights, who had finished slaughtering their way through a group of spear-carriers at the cost of their mounts. The knights formed up and charged, both sides breaking into a run.

Jarrod squinted, and saw the size of the blade and the full helmet, and he knew.

"That's him," he announced. "That's Lord Blacktree."

"Get behind me," he told them. He locked his visor closed, patted Perseus's neck, and kicked him in the ribs with a yell.

Perseus exploded forward under Jarrod in a thundercrack of hooves and muscle, a full metric ton of dumb love and fury moving at the speed of thought. The air tore at Jarrod's visor, muscles shoved at his legs, and he shifted in his stirrups as they neared the knot of footmen and braced for impact.

They'd timed it exactly right. Per Thron's idea, the vector brought them over a small rise and the three of them seemed to appear out of thin air at forty yards out. The footmen had half a second to prepare, and none did. Jarrod felt the shock and the concussions as Perseus slammed men over and charged through, not even breaking stride, and heard the wails of alarm and *kiais* of impact as Aever and Thron came up on his tail, doing the same. He reined Perseus back, wheeled around, and rode them down again from the other side as soon as Aever and Thron joined him in a wedge, men screaming, bodies thudding, dozens crawling and wailing in their wake.

Five footsoldiers in muddy padded jacks now faced them, ready this time with axes and short weapons, and Aever and Thron did the smart thing: they dismounted and shooed their horses, having seen these assholes go after mounts first.

"You got this?" Jarrod asked, and Aever nodded, raising her shield and smacking it with her sword, Thron beside her.

"Go kill Blacktree!" Aever yelled.

Hell of a woman, Jarrod thought, reining Perseus around and heading for Renaldo.

Renaldo was beating the hell out of three knights on foot at the same time with his longsword, in a dark cuirass over the same mail and helmet that he'd worn at High River, black furs on his shoulders.

He was amazing to watch, thought Jarrod, very fluid, tripping and throwing and slipping blows, and every so often the longsword would hit iron mail and punch right through and the knight on the receiving end would fall back.

Jarrod skirted the fight, turned wide, and came up behind the three Gateskeep knights, who broke contact as Renaldo fell back. "Get behind me!" Jarrod roared. The knights flanked him, standing off to hold anyone else away. Similarly, Renaldo's fighters, two spearmen in wet quilted jacks and a third in a rain-blackened leather tabard, backed up as well, and let their champion take the challenger.

Renaldo glanced to each side and saw them backing up, then stepped forward, swearing, and Jarrod realized that Renaldo likely didn't understand how things worked here.

Jarrod glanced around to get his bearings. The true furor and frenzy of the fighting was a hundred yards off, maybe more, and they looked busy. Renaldo had brought these troops this way in an attempt to take the easy route, hit this handful of foot-borne knights, and thin the numbers before flanking the main body and doing some real damage. Smart, Jarrod thought. And, he noted, Renaldo had the endurance to do it all uphill.

Perseus steamed and stamped and eyed the distant mayhem, and the tired Gateskeep knights caught their breath, still wary, as Renaldo settled in behind a hanging guard, flexing his knees and adjusting the blade in increments, yogi-esque and bizarrely balletic for a man of his size.

Jarrod raised his warsword, realizing that Renaldo didn't know who he was.

Right. "Hi, asshole!" he said in English.

There was a glint of recognition, and then Renaldo straightened. "Jarrod?"

"Who else, dumbass?" said Jarrod.

Renaldo's voice echoed from inside his helmet, incensed. "Get down here!" he yelled, pointing at the ground with the tip of the longsword.

"No!" Jarrod answered, kicking Perseus forward. Renaldo jumped back and took a swing at the horse, who ducked aside.

The tip of the longsword banged off the coat of plates under his throat, and Perseus lunged at him. Jarrod got a piece of Renaldo's helmet, and the longsword missed them on a wide swing as the horse leaped out of the way.

Renaldo lunged again, and Jarrod parried, this time Renaldo carried it through and Perseus screamed and lurched as the blade either bit through the iron plate on his flank or found a spot between. Jarrod backed him up, swung over, and jumped clear, landing in the mud in a crouch and a splash, then stood up and shooed him with a smack on his flank.

He beckoned Renaldo from behind his shield.

Wow, the guy was big.

Jarrod carried the warsword high, the shield out, creating room, creating time, waiting for Renaldo's impending hands-first idiocy and thinking through his options with a teardrop shield against German longsword when your opponent was a moron. He liked most of them.

"That's better!" shouted Renaldo, stepping up in an extended guard. "Get that fuckin' horse outta—"

Renaldo vanished with a yell and a blur of impact. The longsword landed, point down and reverberating, almost exactly where he had been standing.

A few horse-lengths away, Perseus was dancing in a circle around Renaldo and kicking the shit out of him. Mud flew in a torrent of screams, curses, and bugling neighs.

Jarrod tried to whistle Perseus back, but he was laughing too hard.

A knight next to Jarrod clapped him on the back, wiping his eyes under his helmet. "You need to call him off, sir," he laughed. "He's going to kill that knight."

Jarrod wrenched the longsword from the mud. "Yeah," he decided, his tone thoughtful. "He might."

Perseus was walking around the twitching body in the

mud, eyeing it distrustfully and stomping toward it from a distance, as if warning Renaldo to stay down. Renaldo's cohort didn't dare approach.

"I guess that's settled," Jarrod decided.

"Respectfully, sir," said the knight he'd been talking to, gesturing to the spearmen, "we should offer them quarter."

"Probably," Jarrod sighed. "All right. Form on me. Stay sharp."

"C'mere!" Jarrod finally yelled. He flipped his visor up and whistled. The big roan trotted over, blowing at him. Renaldo's men gave him a wide berth and didn't seem keen on attacking anyone near the horse. They glanced among themselves and moved a little closer to each other.

Jarrod grabbed his reins and slung his shield on his back. He was thinking up something witty to say just as Renaldo's body vanished, leaving only the hole in the mud. "Hey!" he yelled. "What the hell?" he asked the knight to his right.

"Healer," the knight answered. "They sent him to a healer."

Across the hill, the fighting was dying down. The Hillwhite knights had scattered and were heading out of the valley at a gallop, and the Gateskeep knights had re-mounted where they could and were moving through the piles of horses and corpses and broken spears in cleanup squads, beating the crap out of anyone who didn't surrender.

Jarrod climbed back atop Perseus, and Renaldo's men threw their weapons down and dropped to their knees.

The Gateskeep knights around Jarrod strode forward and took the weapons from the small group. Jarrod looked back at the stream of corpses that Renaldo had left along the hillside, a literal trail of dead in his wake. A dozen, he guessed. He counted; fourteen. Hundreds of bodies littered the hill, all told. It was a disastrous loss.

These were not a people who fought massive wars with

great armies, and that's what struck him as insane about all this as he scanned the field and took a cursory tally. In this world, one did not enlist the general fool for military maneuvers. Unlike Earth, general fools were in short supply.

They didn't have a lot of population to play with—it all went back to the fertility rates, he figured, and the trusty 104-day lunar cycle that affected everything here from the crops to the tides—and it pecked at him that they were using a remarkable amount of manpower for a relatively small amount of territorial gain, and that wasn't something that any commander in their right mind would do, here.

He knew that some of the most decisive battles throughout the history of Gateskeep and Falconsrealm had been champion fights, risking the lives of two knights instead of hundreds. It wasn't unheard of for border skirmishes to be settled with a dozen knights in an afternoon. Ulo had come here twelve years ago and fought a massive war with the Eastern Freehold that had killed thousands and wrecked the Freehold's economy for a generation.

He and Renaldo were here, now; and wow, he thought, look at this mess.

What have we done, brother?

Further, the soldiers he and the knights had just captured were a different breed of troop. The knights and soldiers here generally radiated a hardness to their edges, a conspicuous stoicism that Jarrod could pick out of a crowd nine times out of ten. These guys just didn't have it.

As he scanned the men before him, having given up their helmets, it was that marked Lack of Something More that stood out like so many halos: a hesitance in the gaze; a gut-forward, narrow-footed slouch; every one of them the face of a compulsive flincher who had been promised glory in some form in return for a mere half-measure—or hell, whatever he could muster. It was as if someone had said to them each, *Give us anything, and we'll give you something*, and that wasn't how soldiering worked.

A soldier doesn't give what he can. He gives what no one else can.

The more he looked, the brighter the abberation shone. These weren't soldiers. He had the sense that someone had just jammed spears in their hands and herded them onto the field to bat cleanup for Renaldo and whatever other heroes the Hillwhites had in their stable, which meant they were using these mooks to finish off the wounded, which was also a thing they didn't do here. You gave quarter. You let your enemy drag his injured off the field.

If the Hillwhites were sending hundreds of green troops to kill without quarter, then Gateskeep had a problem that extended far beyond this valley.

"Wait," he said to the knights, as they started moving the group up the hill. "I have questions."

The Hillwhite camp was a ramshackle slum of cookfires, banging smiths, and long canvas alleys booby-trapped with piles of horseshit to slip up the unwary.

Inside his tent at the center of all this, packed in bags of snow but sweating with pain, Renaldo screamed as the healers moved his ribs; the last fractures that needed setting.

Jerandra put her fingertips on his temples, and the pain rushed out in a tide, only to shriek back in again as another bone was shoved into place; she drew it away again.

"Where the fuck were you?" he gasped.

The brightness of her eyes, the sweetness of her long body,

the gentle grin, and those sexy fuckin' fangs. It was impossible to stay mad at her. He grumbled.

Disgraced, beaten—by a goddamned *horse*, of all things—and robbed of the chance to kill Jarrod, his brain rang with pain on levels that she could never dull. Bullshit, all the way around.

He was aware of a thrumming urgency outside the tent. Men and women scrambling; voices torn with concern and getting louder. He hurt too badly to consider what it might be, but it bugged him.

"I would have saved you from him, if I'd thought you might lose," she assured him, kissing his forehead. "This will end soon. You have no more bones to set. Tomorrow, however, you will feel much pain as I speed you through the healing."

"I need a drink," he groused, and someone handed him a wooden cup of whisky.

He had fans.

"We've been routed," said Goun, one of Rogar's generals, and twice the age of any others, coming in the tent. He took no notice that Renaldo was nude, bagged in ice, and black and blue over half his body. "We should discuss surrender."

"Where's General Kur?" asked Renaldo. Kur was the commander for this endeavor, and all deferred to Kur.

"Dead, my lord. We should offer terms of surrender."

"Like hell," Renaldo groaned. "That came out pretty damned even, if you ask me. They're running. They won't fight again. If they do move on us, we'll talk. Until then, wait for reinforcements."

"You're in no position to make those judgments," said Goun. "I make those judgments."

"And you're going to lose this fucking thing," Renaldo grunted as he shifted the bags around him. "We're safe here. They can't find us."

"It's two days until our reinforcements arrive," said Goun.

"Then for two days," said Jerandra, "I will keep you hidden."

"We need to surrender!" Goun nearly shouted.

"She'll kill you if you do," said Renaldo, and Jerandra had spun on General Goun, her fangs showing and eyes flashing. Goun saluted and backed out of the tent flap, and Jerandra returned her fingers to Renaldo's temples. The pain surged away, the void a blessing.

MIRRORS

"The best weapon against an enemy is another enemy."
- Friedrich Nietzsche

Jarrod, Thron, and Aever rode through the outer barbican at Gateskeep Palace along with five knights of the Order of the Swan. Evening loomed in layers of gray above the towers and walls, and a new round of snow squirreled about in friendly gusts of wind. Lanterns and external fireplaces built into walls glowed throughout the grounds, and it had a Christmas feel with an inch or so of squeaky snow on the ground.

They dismounted to a find a team of valets behind them, and they made short work of taking their bags and leading away the horses. "That big one has a wound, left side, on his flank," said Jarrod, and turned to find himself facing three stern nobles in expensive furs and soft castle boots.

One of them, the shortest, was a clearly angry little man, smaller than Jarrod and chihuahua-like, his mouth in a hard line. When he opened it, Jarrod half-expected him to make a yipping noise.

"You," he said, flipping open Jarrod's coat with a tiny hand to reveal the Lord Protector's sigil. "And them—" he motioned to Thron and Aever, "—with me. Now."

"Who are you?" Jarrod asked. Politely, he thought.

"Now," the small man said, and as the others followed him inside, Jarrod fell in behind them.

They stood in a deep, bare, candlelit room off a long hallway on the nondescript third floor of a tower that no one gave a shit about in a corner of the courtyard, and it all combined to resonate with Jarrod as a monstrosity of pretense. Ambiguous evening light strained and clawed its way through an arrowslit along with the tang of snow and the dusty traces of woodsmoke.

"There's a Hillwhite army coming across the northern plains right now," said the small man, who still hadn't introduced himself. He locked his hands behind his back and paced. "I need to know what you know about it."

"I'm sorry," said Jarrod, his tone deferential, "I don't know who the hell you are."

"I'm your worst nightmare," said the small man, his tone shivering with either malice or fear. Jarrod didn't know the difference; it was tough, sometimes, to tell. "Or I will be, if you don't tell me what you know. I have no time to wait for you. Tell me now, or I will certainly make you."

Jarrod took two steps to interpose himself between his team and the small man. It had been exactly six hours, he estimated, since he'd seen someone with such a miscalibrated sense of competence.

"Ask me how my day went," Jarrod challenged, adjusting his rapier. "Go on. I'd love to tell you."

The small man drew himself up until his forehead was at

Jarrod's chin. "You'll tell me everything."

"Everyone, relax," said Aever. "Jarrod, this is Torga Theel. He's the Lord High Inquisitor, the head of our spy network."

"Well, great," said Jarrod. He addressed Torga, who took a step back and crossed his arms. "Don't take this wrong, but I killed a shitload of people today, Mister Spymaster, and I'm still kind of processing that. Do you mind if I sit down?"

Torga Theel smiled. "I like you," he told Jarrod. "I always have. You speak your mind. You're not afraid of anybody, are you?"

"I see no reason to be," said Jarrod, unbuckling his swordbelt and sitting on the floor against the wall. He crossed his legs Indian-style and lay his arming sword across his lap. "We know exactly nothing about the army coming across the north," he said. "All we know is what you told us in that scroll. And thanks for that, by the way."

"We did engage that army," said Aever, "At least, a forward element. They're using what appear to be excellent knights out of West Keep, fielding the best they've got and supporting them with levies."

"Spearmen," added Thron. "Untrained. And lots of them."

"Definitely not soldiers," said Aever. "They're scraping the bottom of the barrel for the spearmen, but they have at least one hero, champion-caliber. Lord Blacktree."

"We've heard of him," said Torga. "He's their champion. Where is he from?"

"We don't know," said Jarrod, and it was more or less true; he didn't know where Renaldo had actually lived. "What I do know is that he's as good of a swordsman as anyone you've got. I also happen to know that he doesn't ride a horse. Hates them."

"Interesting, but useless," said Torga. "It does seem that we've lost the cooperation of the Long Valley legions. A lord named Gorhius took the majority of their knights, and he's fallen in with Rogar Hillwhite."

"Gorhius," said Jarrod. "Okay. What do you need from us?"

"I need you to shit me an army at High River," said Torga. "The Armies of the West have already moved. We haven't even assembled ours, yet. We'll be able to beat them, but not before they take High River."

"They're not going for High River," said Jarrod. "They're going for The Reach. They want the money. They want to go back to financing Gateskeep. They don't want to rule the kingdom. They want to loan money to it."

"You know this how?" asked Torga.

"Halchris Hillwhite told us."

"Before you killed him?"

"Ah, no, just after," Jarrod said, brightly.

"Jokes," Torga mused.

"What else am I going to do?"

"You can stop killing Hillwhites!" Torga roared. His voice rang off the ceiling. "My *stars,* man!"

"Yeah, about that," said Aever, and Torga turned on her, inhaling sharply. "Nothing," she admitted. "It's not important."

"Tell me," Torga hissed.

"We—Okay, I—" Jarrod admitted, "Um, killed another Hillwhite at the Reach. Actually, I guess, probably two. Well, I killed one, and then we let one go, and then they killed her, so . . ."

Torga rested his face in his hands and let out a long groan. "Who?"

"Tigdin," said Jarrod. "And Regan."

Torga winced. "Any others?"

"Not that I'm aware of," Jarrod said. "But, you know. It was kind of a big battle, and—" he shut up. "Well, yeah."

Torga took a deep breath, and started to speak, then took another.

"You were sold out," he told them, after his pulse had visibly slowed. "The Hillwhites sent a team to kill you on your way down here. That was their initial plan. Kill you on the road."

"Those three assholes," drawled Thron.

"Did you meet them?" Torga asked.

"Probably," Aever assessed. "One's dead. They said they were knights from Long Valley."

"They likely were," said Torga. "The palace, and the city beyond, are infested with Long Valley spies, Gavrian spies, and assuredly Hillwhite spies. They have some wizards here, as well, and they're confounding our Finders."

Jarrod didn't know what a Finder was, but he could guess it was a spy-wizard, which sounded like the coolest job in the universe aside from commando-astronaut.

"It is extraordinarily dangerous for you right now," Torga continued. "The Hillwhites are going to send everything they have after you. That army heading across the plains is after *you.* Not The Reach, not the money. The forward element's job, the entire thousand of them, is to kill Sir Jarrod The Merciful. They'll head to High River if they think you're there. They'll come down here if they think you're here. The army following them is to attack The Reach once you're dead."

"They're moving in waves so that he doesn't kill them all at once," Thron joked. "Shrewd."

"So, tell me," said Jarrod, "this Gorhius. Is he a Hillwhite, or—?"

Spit flew in apoplexy as Torga seemed to punch the air in three directions at once. *"Get out of here!"* he screamed. "Get! Go!"

Thron had already opened the door, and Jarrod and Aever ducked under his arm, Torga's curses ended as the slam of the heavy oak and iron bands echoed down the corridor.

"That went well," Jarrod assessed.

"I mean this with all due respect, sir," Thron drawled. "But the man who finally kills you is not going to stop at killing you."

An hour or so later, bathed and beard-trimmed in a set of borrowed warrior blacks a little too big for him, Jarrod learned that it wasn't hard to find a telepath who wanted to be found. She was coming down the stairs from the soldiers' hall in the great keep as he and his team, scrubbed and refreshed, were coming up, and he knew the minute he saw her that she was exactly who they were looking for.

She was a saucer-eyed, redheaded slip of a woman, with the taut physique of a castle-dweller under a gray woolen dress and a fur stole. Definitely a lord's daughter, he thought. A Gateskeeper's heart-shaped face harbored a pointed, girlish chin and approximately ten million freckles. Christ, he was horny. She radiated a dark sensuality that unnerved him, and he reflected on advice a thousand years ago—no, he thought, it was just this past summer—to never date a telepath.

"You're Mirielle Thalborn," Aever said.

She addressed Jarrod. "You're Sir Jarrod."

"You're in danger," she and Jarrod said at the same time, *"You need to come with me."*

The words echoed off the stairwell, and glances collided in the candlelight among the four of them.

"That was weird," Jarrod admitted. "Never do that again."

"You really do need to come with me," she urged.

"No," said Jarrod. "You need to come with us."

"There's someone you need to meet," she said. "This shouldn't wait."

"This is really important," they said again, together.

"Dammit," Jarrod shook his head. "Quit doing that."

"Quit doing what?" she asked.

"Reading my—wait. Really?"

Aever stepped between them. "Okay," she interrupted. "This was fun. You, Mirielle, come with us. There are people looking for you."

"There are people looking for *you*," she insisted.

Footsteps rang on the stairs above, drunken men from the soldiers' hall. "We need to move," Jarrod whispered, and they pushed back down the stairs, slipping out through a door, snow crunching and squeaking under their feet, moments before the knot passed by them. One slapped Thron on the shoulder, and they wandered along the wall toward the next wayfire.

A shadow slipped out of the other shadows, and two more with him. Cloaked, silent, wraithful. Jarrod's hand went to his sword, and Thron's, as well.

"Wait," said Mirielle. "Everyone, wait." The tallest of the ghosts glided forward, with an unusual stride that made him appear to float in the dark. He made no sound, even on the snow.

Jarrod saw the D-ring guard of the sword at his side, which he'd only seen once before, on King Ulo.

A Gavrian weapon.

Jarrod tapped his fingers on his sword handle. Gavrian gryphons. Gavrian knights dying in frozen fields. Now, Gavrian badasses skulking around the king's palace.

Jarrod lifted his hand off his sword. They weren't at war with Gavria. At least, he reminded himself, not yet.

"You're a long way from home," Jarrod told the cloaked man.

"I haven't traveled nearly so far as you," the Gavrian replied, throwing back his hood. He was young, dark-skinned, and massively built, with a shaved bullet head and a fighter's thick neck.

"Sir Jarrod," said Mirielle, "this is Galè of Lor."

"I will bet you my homestead that this is what Torga was on about," said Thron, then addressed Galè. "There is no way, mister, that you got this far without someone saying something. And there are a lot of people in our line of work who would not be keen on you being all the way up here."

"We killed one of your gryphons," said Jarrod, extending his hand. "I apologize for that." Galè took it after a pause, wordless. He had a palm like warm sandpaper.

"I have his helmet and sword," Jarrod continued. "I don't know his name. Can you get it back to his family?"

"You misunderstand me," said Galè. His accent was southern, slurred and musical. "I'm not Gavrian. I'm Uloraki."

"Well, this just keeps getting better," Thron muttered, shifting behind Jarrod.

"You're in no danger from us," Jarrod assured Galè, as the big man sized up Thron. Then, he hazarded a guess. "Did Ulo send you to find Renaldo Salazar?"

Galè's glance ricocheted off the shadowy figures behind him. He glared at Jarrod. "You know the demon's true name," he admitted. "How do you know that?"

"We've met," Jarrod said icily.

"Lord Protector's horse beat the shit out of him," said Thron. "This morning."

"You fight demons?" asked Galè.

"From time to time," Jarrod admitted.

"We fight demons," Galè said, nodding behind him. "King

Ulo sent us to find this one."

"I'll take you to him, if you'd like," Jarrod offered. "He's a half-day's ride from here, probably laying up in a healer's tent."

"The healer," Galè said. "She's dangerous. Her name is Jerandra of the Wastes. She not only heals. She harms."

"Jerandra is the sorcerer who conjured him," Mirielle explained. "She's the sorcerer you seek. She'll be healing him. We need to find the sorcerer, and the demon. Together."

"And I need to kill him," said Galè.

"That's my job," said Jarrod.

"You, demon," Galè told Jarrod, "need to see King Ulo."

"The question," Jarrod posed, as they sat around a table in a corner of the hall above the barracks, the same seats where Daorah had conferred with Evden, as it happened, "is, how the hell did Ulo know where to find me?"

"He probably saw the smoke and heard the screaming all the way down there," said Thron. "You're not hard to find, sir."

The server brought a round of beer and a plate of meat pies, eyeing the dark-skinned, apparently Gavrian, soldiers with wariness.

"They're with me," Jarrod told him, flashing his sigil pin under his cloak, and he nodded and went away.

The others with Galè were whiplike men with deferential, almost penitent body language. They sat in enormous quiet, a blanket of immutable resolve at one end of the table. Religious, maybe? Jarrod pushed beer at them.

Mirielle lapped at the foam on the top of her beer. "I met Galè at a horse auction in Long Valley," she said. "We . . ." her voice faded, and there was no mistaking the flash between the two of them when their eyes met. It crossed Jarrod's mind that Mirielle was probably a beast in the sack. "We connected," she continued. "He was looking for Lord Blacktree, and I've met him, so I understood. I know Galè is Uloraki, I know he's not supposed to be here.

"It's a trait we have," she said, and Jarrod figured she was referring to telepaths. "We know more about you by what you lie about than we do from what you think. I saw what he lied about, and I understood the urgency. I knew that Aever and Carj were headed down, and then they told me that you were coming. I told Galè. I know that he doesn't mean to harm you. Trust me on this."

"We have to kill the demon," said Galè.

"Easier said than done," said Jarrod. "He's a real motherfucker. Tell me you're a sorcerer," Jarrod said to Galè.

Galè set his beer down. "Sorcerers are whores, only they sell what's between their ears instead of between their legs."

"So, that's a no," Thron clarified.

"I trained at the Silver School in Ulorak," said Galè, "but I'm a warrior. I don't sell my magic, and I won't use it to kill."

"Whoa," said Jarrod. "You can use magic to kill? Wait a minute."

"That's why I'm here," said Galè. "We all can."

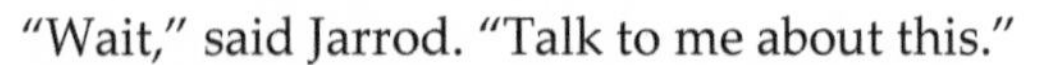

"Wait," said Jarrod. "Talk to me about this."

Thron tore into a meat pie. "Sir, I'd be remiss as your sergeant if I didn't point out that people are looking for these men."

He hadn't finished speaking when several troops came in, shivering and swearing, obviously just off duty, and took up a table at the far side of the room near the other fire.

"Hey," said Thron to Jarrod and Aever. "Don't look now, but it's those two jokers from the road."

"The guys we rode with?" Jarrod asked.

"Pretty sure," said Thron.

"Should we go and say hello?" asked Aever, wiggling an eyebrow.

"Heh. I wouldn't do that," Jarrod admitted.

"Guess they survived after all," said Thron.

Aever interjected, "They said they were going back to Long Valley. That was a lie. They're dressed for watch," she said, and it was true; they carried heavy swords and wore padded jacks under their capes. A few of their group had set their helmets on the table.

"Long Valley is now the Western Hold," said Mirielle. "Why are Long Valley knights here at all?"

"Fuck," Jarrod griped in a whisper. "Those guys are definitely the spies he just told us about."

"Do you think there are three others out there looking to kill you?" asked Aever.

"Hell, at least," Thron told his beer. Jarrod elbowed him.

"The West knew we were coming here," said Thron. "And they have troops here on scutage, I'll bet, probably here to kill us."

"Why didn't those guys kill us on the road?" asked Jarrod.

"They couldn't," said Aever. "We outnumbered them, and they needed us to get them through the pass. Safety in numbers and all that, remember? They weren't lying about the gbatu. Now, though, yes, they're probably going to kill us."

Galè finally spoke. "They mean to kill you, and you are at peace with this?" His tone suggested they were crazy. "You're just here, eating your—whatever this is—" he poked at the meat pie with two fingers, "—and waiting?"

"It's probably fine," Jarrod said. "There are so many people trying to kill me right now, they'd have to stand at the end of a very long line."

"Scutes," Aever swore, and reached for one of the beers in front of Galè's men. "Are you going to drink this? No?" She drank it.

"You know," griped Jarrod into his beer, "When this all started, the first morning of all this bullshit, I was supposed to be arguing for the end of scutage. That was going to be my whole day: arguing in court, then ordering in food, fucking my girlfriend, and taking a succession of naps. And this, right here, is why we need to end scutage. The Hillwhites pulled this shit with Commander Gar. They have one trick, and we keep falling for it."

"We need to get out of here," said Thron. "You all, head on up. I'm bunking down below."

"Like hell," said Jarrod. "We have apartments in the west tower. Get your stuff."

"I'm a sergeant, sir," said Thron. "I'll bunk with the troops."

"You're my sergeant," said Jarrod. "You'll bunk where I tell you. All of you, come with me. We'll find someplace safe for you to stay tonight. Grab another pile of food," he told Galè's people. "And wine."

Jarrod and Aever shared his apartment. Aever's apartment at the end of the hall housed Mirielle, Thron, Galè, and Galè's seconds, whom Jarrod had nicknamed "The Flying Elvises" because of their odd, hovering stride. Jarrod unlaced his boots and kicked them off before the fire. He threw a couple of fat, stumpy logs onto the coals before sitting on the edge of the bed. "I am beat," he said. "That was a strange day."

"Did you take any hits out there?" she asked, motioning to his armor, which was sitting on a mannequin.

"No," he said, his hands on his face. "Not even a dent. You?"

"A couple," she said, stripping off her tunic. She wore a woolen wrap around her breasts. He tried not to stare as she pulled it off and hung it by the window. "I'm not hurt," she promised. "I'm just a little sore."

She turned to face him in a locker-room lack of reserve, four distinct nuggets of abs tucked between a broad curve of hips and a pair of breasts that would have been pendulous on a woman with lesser shoulders.

He stood, shucked his tunic, turned it inside out, and lay it on a padded bench near the door. When in Rome, and all that. He tried to find the fire interesting.

"Good scar," she said, looking at his stomach. "Wow."

He touched it absently. "I missed a parry."

"I'd say."

She rubbed her ribs on one side and moved in front of the fire. And goddammit, now he had nothing else to look at.

"Is that a tattoo?" he asked, nodding to her left arm, where slashes and loops of Falconsrealm script, ribbon-thick, ran down the spurs and valleys of muscle from shoulder to her elbow.

She glanced down at it and smiled. "I got that a long time ago, in Axe Valley. They have wonderful artists down there."

"What does it say?"

She cleared her throat. *"Eat mail and shit nails."*

He wasn't sure what an adequate response would be.

She changed the subject for him. "That man must really hate you. Blacktree, I mean. And if he didn't hate you before, then he really does, now."

"Oh, he did before," Jarrod admitted. "He traveled a long way to kill me."

"What the hell did you do to him?" she asked, sitting and pulling her legs into a butterfly stretch. She let out a series of groans and sighs as she leaned forward and rested her forehead and those majestic goddamn breasts on the floor.

Jarrod considered saying something, then let it go. The longer she was topless, the weirder it would be to say anything about it. Besides, a half-naked Amazon doing yoga in his bedroom was in no way a legitimate complaint.

"It's complicated," said Jarrod. "I've been . . . better . . . than him, at everything he's ever done. And, instead of working harder to get better, he blames the world for conspiring against him. And then, every time, he takes it out on me. Back home, he was trying to draw me into a fight for over a year."

"Why didn't you fight him?" she asked, straightening up and stretching her interlaced hands overhead. Jesus, he thought.

"He never gave me the chance," Jarrod said. "The one time we did fight, he ambushed me. He beat the hell out of me first, and then wanted to fight me afterwards."

"How did that go?"

"Crius Lotavaugus smashed his face in," Jarrod noted.

She put her hands down. "The Lord High Sorcerer?"

Jarrod nodded. "It was a weird day."

"If you don't kill that man," she decided, "he's going to take everything you've got."

Fuck it, Jarrod decided, and took a good, long look at her, and not just the tattoo. She didn't appear to mind.

"It's not enough to kill you," she continued. "He tried to take your castle. He's taking your damn country. Even if he kills you, he'll go on to take everything that was yours, and erase you from the world. He's a conqueror. I saw him out there. I know the type."

"What would you do?"

She leaned forward again, and again with the animal noises. "Oh, the things I'd do," she moaned. "I'd fuck him until he couldn't remember his own name. I'd bear that man's children and raise a brood of warriors to set the world on fire, and then I'd march an army through its ashes."

He blinked at her as she stood up.

"But," she continued, her tone more pragmatic, now, "since he's on the other side of this, I'd kill him." She shoved her breeches down as if in punctuation and stepped out of them, standing nude before the fire. "If I was you, I'd put forth a formal challenge," she said, folding them and setting them before the fire next to Jarrod's boots. "I'd meet him one-to-one and finish it. Give him what he wants but make it the last thing he ever gets."

She walked over next to Jarrod, her breasts directly at eye level. He literally couldn't not look at them.

"Do you mind?" she asked. "I like this side of the bed."

Jarrod awoke by firelight at half a candle, the way he always did, except this time he found Aever draped around him, the intensity of her presence breaking a sweat across his back. He lifted her arm and started to roll out of bed, and she pulled him closer and tucked her face into his neck. Her strength was startling.

"I could go for a fuck," she slurred, reaching down his stomach. "We survived, today. We should celebrate. We should break this bed into pieces small enough to burn."

"I . . ." Jarrod began to rationalize reasons why, but let the thought trail off. "Yeah, no."

"You are really wrapped around that elf lover of yours, aren't you?" she murmured into his neck.

"I like it better when she's wrapped around me," Jarrod admitted.

"Understandable," Aever muttered, and snuggled closer.

As he lay there, now ridiculously awake, Jarrod's eyes traveled to the door, and then over the bench where he'd set his clothes and noticed that something didn't line up: his tunic and trousers were balled up on the floor.

"Get up!" he said, pushing her. "Get up!"

"What?" she asked.

"We've been robbed," he said, and leaped out of bed. "Son of a bitch," he swore.

A few minutes later, in the light of every candle, and with the fire roaring, Jarrod and Aever took inventory, half-dressed.

"I don't see anything missing," said Aever, digging through her belongings. "Are you sure?"

"I'm telling you," Jarrod said. "Someone went through my—"

He saw it. Or, more to the point, didn't see it.

"My book," he said, holding his forehead. "Shit, my book. And Blacktree's sword. The red sword."

"The book you were making notes in?" Aever asked, and gasped. "Jarrod!"

"Yeah," he said, biting his lip. "The book, the map, the sword. The fucking Hillwhites have it all."

"All right," said Aever, not panicking, yet. "You said no one could read it, right? It's in some kind of code?"

"I said four people in this world can read it," said Jarrod. He lay back on the bed, sighing and swearing. "Blacktree is one of them."

Aever stood before him and stared at him until he opened one eye.

"What?" he asked.

"There's no way I'm getting laid tonight, is there?"

MONEY TOWN

"Thus, what is of utmost importance is to attack the enemy's strategy."
—Sun Tzu

Knight Captain Sir Attas of Ghas was a three-battle veteran from the Falconsrealm Order of the Swan. He stood mountainous and undauntable at the head of fifty knights sprawling down the road, armor crashing in the distance as horses shuffled. Mud pulled at hooves and boots. Snow loomed.

He stood before an equally enormous man named Shon Tollrith, the head of the moniers' guild and effectively the mayor of the small town that employed them all. Shon was a likeable man upon first meeting, smiling beneath a gray beard and gnarled in heaps of furs and heavy cloaks against the cold.

Captain Attas handed Shon the scroll he'd been given, unread and unopened, and watched the older man's eyes carefully as he read it, then read it again.

"You're destroying this," said Shon, looking back up the hill to the town and the small mountain beyond that housed the mint. It was a mammoth operation, employing an army of refiners, furnace workers, assayers, and artists. At the head of it all were Shon's men, the coinsmiths known as "strikers," who could turn out a thousand coins a day apiece if so ordered. If the chivalry was the heart of the kingdom, the moniers' guild was the blood that it pumped.

Three of Shon's soldiers stood before Attas, and they clearly didn't like what they were hearing.

"All of it," Shon continued. "We have thousands of dies. You understand what you're asking. This is a lifetime's work. This is our art."

"I don't ask it," said Attas. "The princess asks it. My duty is to ensure that you do it. Today. Now."

"Does the crown ask that we starve?"

"You will be compensated," said Attas. "This is critical to the war effort. Our enemy has taken the silver mines in the White Hills, and they are transporting the ore here. If they can make it into coin, we stand to lose a great deal."

"We can keep them from making it into coin," said Shon.

"No," said Attas. "This is an army that kills innocents. They will murder your children in front of you to keep your strikers working."

"You're jesting."

"I'm not," said Attas. "The mint comes down. When the war is over, you will make a new foundry, design new coins, rebuild it all. There will be enough work to last you for several lifetimes."

"My people won't like this," said Shon.

"I don't expect this to go easily," said Attas. "That's why we're here. I need you to get the captain of your guard to assist us, however, because I'm fairly certain that we're going to need their help convincing your people to destroy their own livelihood."

"I suppose I have no say in this," Shon assessed.

"You don't," said Attas. "I'm sorry to do this, but our mission is to destroy the mint. Your people can do this themselves, or we can go in there and do it. If we go in there and do it, your people will interfere, and some of them will die. Also, some of my men will die. Nobody wants that."

"This is not going to be an easy sell," said Shon. "Give me time to explain it."

"Time is the one thing you don't have," said Attas. "That army is coming up behind us as we speak. We can hold them off, but not for long."

The last dies were melting in the fires when horns blared from Attas's troops at the mouth of the box-canyon.

Attas came at a gallop, with Shon Tollrith and his troops not far behind.

Shon swung down from his horse, no athlete, graceless and winded, to find Attas's men squared off against a ragtag army that, while armed and armored to a fraction of the degree, outnumbered the Falconsrealm knights by what he estimated to be a factor of six. He was better than most with numbers.

Attas was in a shouting match with a man in fine armor but no chivalric affiliation; Shon knew him in a moment as Aron Hillwhite. He was an ore baron—*the* ore baron around here, now that Duke Edwin was dead—and Shon had no idea what he was doing here, least of all in a knight's getup looking like a worm that had stolen a snail's shell, and at the head of hundreds of troops. He looked ludicrous; tall, pasty, and thin, in leather pauldrons much too large for him but padded in extra layers either against the cold or to give his aristocratic build some degree of warriorly heft. As Shon looked down the road, he saw horses, and even men, hauling carts.

The army he'd been warned about, he realized.

They'd finished exactly in time. He was glad they hadn't argued.

Aron Hillwhite, brittle and slight in his preposterous armor, was yelling at Attas, who waited his turn, and yelled back when Aron was done. A few steps separated them, and Shon didn't see any way that Attas couldn't or wouldn't kill Aron outright, except that the disparity of forces was clear.

"You can surrender your troops, now," said Aron, and Shon's immediate reaction was to not trust the bastard. He said as much, and Aron turned on him.

"And here's the zealot," Aron announced. "You soulless shit. I could buy and sell your operation with the silver my troops are carrying."

"You can't," Shon told Aron. "Silver that's not coin is worthless. You're carrying rocks."

"You idiot," spat Aron. "I could have made you rich."

Shon shrugged. "The orders came from the crown. Our dies are destroyed. It will take us days to create even one, and a full season to return to production. There is nothing you can do."

Aron Hillwhite bit down on his lip, furious. "There is no way?" he asked Shon.

"None," Shon told him.

"We should kill you all."

"You could," Shon agreed. "I don't doubt you there. But you'd have to train a new generation of moniers. You'll lose the knowledge of our guild, and you'll be dead of old age before those rocks become money," said Shon, motioning to the army stretching behind them.

"We can't kill them," Aron told Attas, ignoring Shon, now. "But we can kill you. Sure as the mountains. Your troops won't make it out of this valley alive if you don't surrender."

Attas scanned the road and appeared to do some quick math. Shon watched, and guessed that he'd arrived at the same answer.

"You'll guarantee our safety?" Attas asked.

"I'll let you lead them home," Aron promised.

Attas's first observation upon entering Aron Hillwhite's tent that evening was the intense heat, and he immediately made a Gavria joke to the guard on the door, who didn't laugh.

"Aron," he said. Aron was seated in a comfortable chair near the fire, and Attas didn't know how he stood it. It was infernal. He was sweating inside his armor, and Aron was still decked out in all of his.

"I can't help but notice that you've stoked that fire with coal," Attas said, and it was true. "If you've made some kind of deal with the minters—if you think you'll wait out the winter while they rebuild the coinery . . . I mean, the princess will never—"

"That is not my concern, nor my intent," said Aron. "And regardless, your concern should be getting your men back to High River. You have quite a task ahead of you."

"We've given up our weapons," Captain Attas stated.

"I'm well aware," said Aron. "Thank you."

"You can promise that we won't be attacked?" asked Attas, looking to his seconds. "I have your word. We'll be weaponless, on a long stretch of road."

Aron nodded, and put his hand out. "You have my word. You will not be attacked."

Attas unbuckled his sword, and Aron received it, and the lieutenants offered theirs, as well.

Late into the night, Aron Hillwhite forced Attas to watch as his men blinded each of the Falconsrealm troops with molten silver.

They left Captain Attas unharmed, in order to lead his army home.

FALSE GODS

"No enterprise is more likely to succeed than one concealed from the enemy until it is ripe for execution."
—Niccolo Machiavelli

Muted daylight fell on the canvas walls of Renaldo's tent as he thumbed through the book. He was still moving slowly, but Jerandra had assured him that he'd be healed in another day, by the time the reinforcements arrived.

He couldn't get over his incredible luck. The book was written in English, clearly left-handed script, definitely Jarrod's writing. "Jarrod, you incredible idiot," he said quietly, and smiled.

His eyes fell back to the red sword, lying across his table, battered and rain-worn, the pommel tarnished, and with one small bite out of the edge of the blade that had been expertly filed out and re-sharpened, but really none the worse for wear. Jarrod could take care of a sword. He'd even added a rain guard, two wide semicircles of oiled leather at the crossbar to keep water out of a scabbard, the handle almost indistinguishably rewrapped by an outstanding smith. It was a smart addition, and he realized that he should have done it to all his blades before he came here.

It was good to have the sword back. He mourned his prized longsword, but he couldn't have everything.

"He really thought he was being smart," he announced to Rogar, who stood behind him. "He wrote this in our language, so if anyone captured it, they couldn't read it. It's going to take a little time, but I can do this." He opened up one page, fat and loose inside the front cover, folded several times. He unfolded it, and unfolded it, until it sprawled across the table.

"What is it?" asked Argis, a small and scraggly man who reported such things back to Rogar Hillwhite, though Renaldo wasn't entirely sure how.

Renaldo's eyes roved the huge paper. "It's everything," he said.

Argis looked over Renaldo's shoulder. It was clearly a map, huge and intensely detailed.

"We don't have a map of the mountains," Argis assessed. "Gods. Even Gateskeep doesn't have a map of Falconsrealm like this. All the passes. This will save us weeks."

"More than that. This is the whole war," Renaldo admitted, his eyes roving the script. "Each of these," he pointed to numbers on the map, "Refers back to these pages." He pointed to the book. "Every page is notes about a location on the map." He flipped to a page, and another. "Unit strengths, names of commanders, towns, farms, loyalties, stories about them, assessments of their troops—here, he's got a note about a commander who's fucking his lord's wife." In English, he muttered under his breath, "Bless you, Jarrod, you beautiful OCD moron."

He leafed through the pages. "He has the names of Order of the Stallion soldiers and spies in each of these towns, locations of their weapons caches, their supply networks. It's all here."

He clapped Argis on the shoulder. "Congratulations. Go and find General Goun. Then tell Lord Rogar that he owns Falconsrealm."

"You understand that Torga Theel is going to want to talk to you," said Aever, as they sat over breakfast in the lords' hall, one floor above the soldiers' hall. "About your book. About the map."

"He is the last person I want to discuss this with," said Jarrod. "Try the eggs."

"Jarrod, we have to go back to Regoth Ur. It's their next stop. It's where he's going to be. As soon as he's healed up, they're going to take—"

"I don't *have* to do a damned thing you tell me," he snapped, albeit quietly. "Now, you listen to me. I am your commanding officer, and I am telling you what we need to do. This is me, commanding. Understand?"

She nodded.

"We need to get Galè in front of Blacktree," Jarrod said. "That's the only way this is going to work. Before that, we need to talk to the Lord High Sorcerer here, Crius Lotavaugus, and find out how the Hillwhites learned about Blacktree. There's a leak, someplace, and we need to stop it before this gets out of hand."

"I don't understand why that's so important."

"If people in my homeland find out about this realm, we will be facing an army of Blacktrees."

She swore under her breath.

"After that, we need to get me a meeting with the king of Ulorak, and then we all need to get back to High River and put together an army big enough to take them out. Carter can handle anything the Hillwhites can throw at him in the next few days. But we need to do all the rest of these things, no shit, today."

"Then we should get started," said a man standing next to Jarrod.

"Crius!" said Jarrod, standing.

"Lord Protector!" said Crius, embracing him. Crius was a tallish, shambly young man, with a tangled dark beard and tangled dark hair, dressed for a day indoors in plain and comfortable clothes and a jeweled necklace. "It's good to see you! Also—" Crius stood back and threw up the rock sign. "Dude," he said. Jarrod returned it.

"A salute from my homeland," said Jarrod to Aever, who folded her middle fingers under her thumb with her other hand, attempting to make the sign, "and a traditional greeting."

"I pride myself on my cultural knowledge," said Crius. "I did not know you were at the palace. I got your note."

Aever hadn't known that Jarrod had sent a note. When had he sent a note?

"I was hoping to keep a low profile," said Jarrod.

Crius nodded and leaned in conspiratorially. "I'm glad you're here. We have a lot to discuss. I was trying to find you. I'll dine with you." He extended his hand to Aever. "We have not met."

"This is Crius Lotavaugus, Lord High Sorcerer of Gateskeep," said Jarrod to Aever. "My lord, this is Knight Lieutenant Lady Aever, daughter-lady of Black Valley."

"It's a pleasure," said Crius with a wide smile. "And please extend my best to your father. I trust he's still giving them hell up there."

"Every chance he gets," she said.

"Your children will be fine and strong," Crius told her.

"Professional prognostication?" asked Jarrod.

"Best guess," Crius admitted, and sat as a server poured him wine and another placed a handful of shelled, tiny eggs on a dark wooden plate before him. "So, what are we talking about? What brings you to the palace? Tell me everything."

Jarrod told him everything, starting with the recruiting of Renaldo, and working his way through to the gryphons, the spear carriers, and the Uloraki sorcerer hiding four floors above.

The room had emptied out and they were sipping mugs of dandy, the roasted dandelion-root tea that Gateskeepers drink nonstop, and eating honeyed pastries by the time he was done.

"The man they brought back," Jarrod concluded, "Lord Blacktree, is the same man you clobbered in my room last spring. The man who attacked me before we came here."

Crius brightened. "Ah! Yes. That was a good fight."

Jarrod goggled at him. "You hit him with a fire extinguisher."

"Yes," said Crius, excitedly. "It was exhilarating!"

Jarrod looked to Aever, then back to Crius. "Who would know how to get to Earth, but would also know this Hillwhite sorcerer?"

"Ah," said Crius. He closed his eyes in thought, muttering to himself for a bit. Jarrod sipped at cold dandy and picked at his pastry.

"That would be me," Crius said, finally. "We had a sorceress in here, an elf from the Gavrian Wastes. Half-elf, actually. Intelligent, highly skilled, but I couldn't get a truthful answer out of her when I asked her where she'd received her training, and I didn't like that. She didn't last long. She left the palace after a few weeks and went to work for Rogar Hillwhite. She's the one you're looking for. We'd talked of Earth. She was very interested in demons."

"That's odd," Jarrod said. It seemed incongruous. "I understood she was a healer. Or, had been, at one point."

"She had an exceptional gift," Crius remembered. "However, she wasn't a healer, although she worked with our healers."

"What did she do, exactly?" asked Aever.

"She controlled pain."

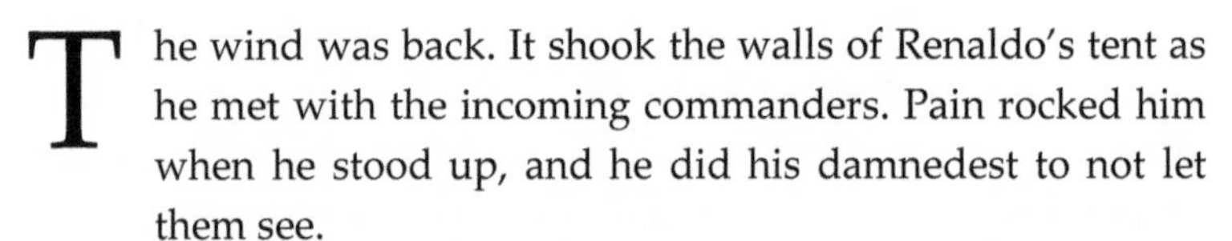

The wind was back. It shook the walls of Renaldo's tent as he met with the incoming commanders. Pain rocked him when he stood up, and he did his damnedest to not let them see.

"Heard you got hit by a horse," said a commander named Torl, who had a fat beard and a hearty laugh. "Happens to the best of us." He clapped Renaldo on the back, and Renaldo thought he was going to die.

"Hell, if that's all that happens to you on the field, you're a lucky man," said another commander, coming through the tent flap in a burst of frigid wind. "I'm Dras. I brought you two hundred troops out of the Four Keeps of Arth."

Renaldo sat down with Jarrod's map and gathered the team around the table.

"Intelligence," Renaldo explained. "The enemy used this to maneuver from Falconsrealm into Rogues' River during The Dark."

The commanders and their officers murmured among themselves. "That's a trick," said Torl. "Where'd you get it?"

"We have our ways," said Renaldo, and loved the way it sounded when he said it. "If you see this map, there's an inset, here—"

"What language is this in?"

"My language," said Renaldo. "One of their officers is from

my homeland. We got it from him. This, right here, shows this pass—" he put his finger down on the end of a line from the inset to a point on the map, "—as the only one usable in winter. The Rogues' River, it says, doesn't freeze, and the road to the bridge is too steep to get a horse up when it's icy, so we can't go north."

"First I've heard of that," said Torl. "Crossing the Rogue's River was the key to this."

"I've never tried it in winter," Dras admitted. "It's better we know this now. However, it also means that Wild River troops can't come south," said Dras. "They have to come in from this pass. It looks like there is one way into Falconsrealm from where we sit."

"Yes, but first, we need to hit Regoth Ur," said Renaldo.

"Seems like a waste of a day," said Dras.

"We've thought about going around, but they have horsebirds, and we need to get rid of them. We need to tear Regoth Ur apart, stone by stone, so they can't launch from there. If we scatter those air assets, then we still have a dozen gryphons, and the air will be ours. They won't be able to see us."

"They have wizards. They can scry."

"Our wizards can keep us safe from scrying," Renaldo insisted; at least, it's what Jerandra had told him. "We haven't been found yet. We can move through this pass, hold the high ground, build a winter camp, and no matter who comes at us first—Falconsrealm or Gateskeep—we have them in a chokepoint, and we have the elevation. We hold them off, we attrit, we eventually reinforce from the White Hills."

"That's a long fight in the snow," said Dras. "The troops won't like it."

"They'll like winning," said Renaldo. "They're going to be cold for a while, but they'll be able to rest up in Falconsrealm when it's over. We've got locations of farms and weapons caches once we get to the other side of the pass."

"Quite a find," said Dras, gesturing at the map and the book.

"Thank you. This gets easy once we destroy Regoth Ur. That's next."

"Regoth Ur is easy," said Torl. "If we leave now, we could take it this afternoon."

"Do we have enough troops?" asked Renaldo, and Torl and Dras laughed.

"I think so," said Torl. "We have enough troops to do any damn thing we want."

HIDDEN WEAPONS

"There are only two forces that unite men: fear, and interest."
– Napoleon Bonaparte

It wasn't raining outside the Silver Palace, and the lack of it startled Jarrod.

The sun hammered him, beating his eyeballs in as he stood, a little disoriented from the teleport and sick to his stomach. It gleamed off a stripe of silver up the middle of the tower jutting from the massif of black rock like an obelisk, five hundred feet above the valley floor. Damned thing could signal the mothership, he thought.

Grand steps, fifty feet wide, led up three stories to a titanic set of stone doors flung wide, and Jarrod had to wonder how anyone would ever close them. A twelve-foot tall obsidian gargoyle stood on each side of the doorway, crouched to spring, and they were detailed enough that he had to wonder if they could.

He wore his leather trousers and his swordsman's jacket, with his rank braid and Lord Protector's sigil, and his rapier, and hoped to God he didn't run into anyone from the fight last summer.

Merchants brushed past him on their way down the steps, yammering in a froth of inconsequential bullshit. He didn't catch much of it, and he didn't care.

Jarrod stood on the top step and turned, looking out at the city, carved and hammered out of flat black rock, sprawling blackly up the black mountain from the northwest side of the black keep. He hadn't even seen it when he'd jumped off the top of the tower in a BASE rig with the princess of Falconsrealm; he had been too damned scared about catching a squirrely gust down the canyon and grinding her into raspberry jam.

In return for which, she'd sent him into a one-man war.

Ingrate.

Jarrod stepped through the doors into the anteroom, fifty feet high and carved out of black stone, the floor polished and inlaid with white marble.

Beautifully dressed men and women strolled in a hundred colors; a group of fighters or knights in heavy lamellar, laughing and joking, brushed past Jarrod and didn't give him a second look; a knot of gray-robed adepts in steel skullcaps vanished up one of several stone stairwells that spiraled into the ceiling forever above.

As massive as it was, every inch was exquisitely carved. He couldn't imagine the amount of work it had taken.

"Can I help you, sir?" asked a slender, dark-skinned, bald man in black and gold silk pajamas. His feet were bare and gnarled.

"Yeah," said Jarrod, looking around. "I'm here from Falconsrealm—" he tapped his Lord Protector's brooch, "—to see King Ulo. His Majesty has asked for my audience."

The chamberlain smiled deferentially, showing brilliant teeth. "I am Wud Qari-Rad," he said. "We are honored to have guests from the great land of Falconsrealm, and if you will allow me, sir, may I formally apologize on behalf of my people for any prior hostilities between our nations."

"I appreciate that," said Jarrod. "And may I say, likewise."

"Please," Wud said, bowing. "I will take you to our king." Jarrod followed him to a set of white marble stairs that spiraled up into nothing, and Wud started up without another word, feet padding on the steps. Jarrod had to run after him.

There was no handrail on the stairs, and Jarrod was still dizzy from the teleport. Looking out into space, he vowed to make all of his mistakes to the right, into the central pillar of the stairwell that corkscrewed up from the black and white floor so terrifyingly far below. Wud wouldn't have to do more than spin around and give him a gentle shove, and that would resolve a great deal of problems for everybody really fast.

It didn't happen.

The stairs wound into the ceiling, and then became a closed stairwell with doors at regular intervals; what Jarrod figured were floors.

He lost count. They were way up in the tower. He remembered jumping off the top and guessing it to be four hundred feet—thirty stories.

"It's this door," said Wud at long last. "Would you like to rest before seeing the king?"

"I'm okay," Jarrod breathed. "The teleport. It gets me sometimes."

Wud laughed a gentle, polite laugh. "We understand. The king awaits."

"Let's not keep him waiting," said Jarrod, and wiped his forehead, threw his hair back, and stepped through the door when Wud opened it.

Ulo sat on a great black throne in a great black room, torchlit and cool, attended by dark-skinned women wearing jewels and nothing else, a line of them coming and going like beauty contestants.

"Jarrod," he intoned. His voice had the same low, grating rasp that Jarrod remembered from the first time they'd spoken, sounding the way Jarrod would imagine a talking Easter Island head.

"Majesty," said Jarrod, approaching the throne and bowing at about the same distance he would King Rorthos.

"I'm touched," said Ulo, in English. "Can I get you something? Wine? A woman? Food? Anything you desire."

"I'm fine, Majesty," said Jarrod. "Thank you, though."

Ulo stood, and the women surrounding him—Jarrod literally couldn't count how many—knelt. He walked up to Jarrod, gray and black robes flowing, and beckoned him up with a finger.

Jarrod's eyes met Ulo's, and flicked to the dozens of scarified symbols and runes on the russet skin of his face.

"You brought a sword," Ulo noted.

"It's one of those 'don't leave home without it' things," said Jarrod. "I wasn't sure if any of your troops would have a sense of humor about what happened the last time I was here."

"That's understandable," said Ulo. "But we have more pressing concerns today. Can we put that whole episode behind us?"

"I'd love to," said Jarrod. "I do have the feeling it's going to come up again at some point."

"Without a doubt," Ulo agreed. "I have a private chamber, through here. We need to speak."

"Secondary crime scene?" Jarrod joked, as Ulo led him through a black stone door into a black stone room lit blue.

"Don't be fatuous," said Ulo. "We don't have the time." He

waved his hand, and the door slammed behind them. Jarrod felt his ears pop.

"I should kill you for killing Javal," Jarrod started.

"But you won't," said Ulo. "Because, if you're here, then you're beginning to understand the workings of this world, and what's required of men like us. Gavria wanted my country. I needed it back. Those people in that room were in the way."

"I could kill you right now," Jarrod said.

"I don't doubt it," said Ulo. And with those four words, his voice lost its measured cadence and its unearthly, grating overtone. While it was still inhumanly low, it had a slight New York accent. Bronx, Jarrod realized. "But you won't."

"Wait . . ." it was too much for Jarrod to process. "Majesty . . ."

"My name's Eric Blackheart," said Ulo, his demeanor suddenly one of an aging metalhead, and Jarrod expected the king of Ulorak to call him *bro* any moment. "Okay? Well, before 'Blackheart,' it was—you know what? It doesn't matter. Right now, this is you, and me. Jerry and Eric. You follow?"

"I—I don't," Jarrod admitted.

"I brought you here, knowing you might kill me, but trusting that you needed to get out of here alive. I need to talk to you. This is important. Are we square?"

"Fair enough," said Jarrod. A moment passed in the blue light. Jarod shifted his swordbelt, then realized he'd just touched his sword in the presence of a king. He pushed it further behind him and stuck his thumbs in his belt and leaned against the wall. "So, talk."

"Time is short for both our kingdoms," Ulo said, which sounded now like the kind of thing he'd have said in his Sorcerer Voice, and it was unpleasantly weird coming out of the person who stood before Jarrod, now. On a stone table that looked remarkably like an altar, Ulo poured two ornate metal goblets of wine from a crystal pitcher that sat next to a goblet made of an upturned skull on a braided stem that gleamed silver in the azure glare. He offered one of the goblets to Jarrod.

Jarrod stared at the cup in the sorcerer king's scarified hand as if he'd just been offered a *Watchtower* magazine. "Yeah, no," he said.

"Oh, fuck," said Ulo, and took a sip from one goblet and held it out again. "Here."

Jarrod accepted it. "All right. Cheers." He clinked it against Ulo's and had a sip. It was outstanding, beautifully aged with overtones of leather and cherries and a soft, vanilla finish. It was everything the berry-wine homebrew of Falconsrealm wasn't, and he missed it.

He missed refinement.

"Wow, that's really nice," he said.

"Thanks," said Ulo. "You wanna smoke a bowl?" he asked levelly. "I grow killer weed."

Jarrod set his wine down. "Who are you, man? I mean, what the fuck? And where does the light come from?" he asked, peering into the ceiling. "Seriously. That's really cool."

"I am a king, soon to be at the end of his reign," said Ulo. "Gavria is coming to get me. They're massing armies. Not an army; *armies.* Plural. They can't come up through the southern pass, so they're going to need to enter the Shieldlands to get here. Probably in the spring, once the passes clear."

"Yeah, that's not going to go over real well."

"Tell me about it. However, you have your own problems. The Western Hold."

"What do you know about the Western Hold?" Jarrod asked.

"I have people up north," said Ulo. "You've met some of them. I know enough to know that Hillwhite is going to walk right over the top of any army you throw at him."

Jarrod finished his wine. "You sound very sure about that,"

he said.

"I am," Ulo said. "I know their wizard."

"And you can help me with this?" Jarrod asked.

"Yes. I can give you my wizards," said Ulo.

"We have wizards," said Jarrod.

"Not like these," Ulo promised.

"We've heard rumors about wizards who can kill," Jarrod said.

"She can," said Ulo. "And here's the thing: mine can, too. I've got a school here. The Silver School."

"I saw the stripe," said Jarrod. "Very nice."

"Thanks. We train these wizards, Jer. They're weapons. Pyromancy, weather control, pain, disease. Wizards who can function as siege engines. Psychic battering rams."

"You have my attention."

"A mutual defense treaty," said Ulo. "You save me, I save you."

"Why do you need us?"

"I don't have enough wizards, yet, to stop Gavria. Do you know how big their armies are? We're talking legions. Thousands. They've never mobilized, before. Not like they're planning."

"What's our end?" Jarrod asked.

"Your king sends a message to Gavria that you stand with me against any aggression. In return for which, I give you a battalion of my wizards. You knock down your rebellion, I keep all this." He gestured around the room. "Well," he motioned to the door and gestured wider. "That."

"Yeah," said Jarrod. "I . . . can't . . . even . . ."

Ulo poured two more goblets. "Are you sure you don't want a woman and a toke before you go? You look like a man who could use a fat bowl and a blowjob if I've ever seen one."

"I'm good," said Jarrod, and waved off the wine, as much

as he wanted it.

"You seem flustered," the king admitted.

"I'm fine," Jarrod insisted. "I'm just working out the odds that some common existential thread could just be conjured up when we both needed it. It seems unlikely."

Ulo drank Jarrod's wine in one long pull. "You actually think I'm evil, don't you?"

Jarrod rubbed his forehead, flustered. "I don't think you're evil, Ulo—"

"Eric."

"Right. I do, however, think you're devoid of any kind of enduring principles."

Ulo set both goblets down. "Well, ouch."

"Look, it makes you an effective leader. I get that. But I don't trust you. No one, in my position, can trust a man in your position. That's not how this works. That's not how men like me keep our heads attached."

"Join me for dinner," Ulo asked. "Old friends. Compatriots. Then, take my offer back to your princess—"

"Yeah, she doesn't like you very much. Or me, really," Jarrod admitted.

"She doesn't have to. Have her take it to Rorthos. Just see what she says."

"Your wizards for our agreement?" said Jarrod.

"I can teleport them in, right now," Ulo said, "I can end this. I can put them in front of the Hillwhites and blow their army off the map. Nobody else has to die. At least, not on your side. Take my hand, and this all ends."

Jarrod blew out a long sigh. "Goddammit," he muttered. "I can't take your hand on this. It's not my call. But send me back, right now, and I'll take it to her."

"You're turning down dinner with a king," said Ulo.

Jarrod smiled at him. "Just this once," he promised. "I have work to do."

Ulo handed Jarrod the skull goblet. It was heavy, the stem cool to the touch. Gold, he realized.

"This belonged to the general you killed," Ulo said. "It was the skull of an adversary he held in high regard. I thought it fitting that it goes to you, now. You earned it."

RAVENSONG

"Shakespeare? I ain't never hoyd of him. He ain't in no ratings. I suppose he's one of them foreign heavyweights. They're all lousy. I'd moyder the bum."

– Tony Galento, American heavyweight boxer, 1910-1979

Carter watched out the window from the tower, and saw the army stretching out across the plain outside the village like so many ants under the tarnished gray carpet of sky. Far, far more soldiers than he'd seen at The Reach. And he had far fewer soldiers within his walls than they'd had.

"That is a lot of troops," he said, and his chamberlain, Alel, nodded.

"I should get my armor," said Alel, tying his wisps of gray hair back in a ponytail.

"It wouldn't hurt," said Carter, and wished Daorah was here. Or that she'd hurry back from the palace.

It wasn't the organized lines and fronts that he'd expected from . . . well, from whatever he'd expected an army this size to look like. It was a rabble, a spear-carrying riot. Most of them were on foot; not even knights.

So many spears.

They'd moved fast, too, emerging at dawn like some hellish machination.

A pair of knights appeared at the edges of the room. "We make it two thousands of soldiers," one told Carter. Their language didn't have a number above a thousand. They hadn't needed it; it had no practical purpose.

The world was changing so fast, now, and Carter felt that he was somehow at the center of it. What was brewing outside was a brand of war he'd never heard mentioned.

And holy crap, he thought, looking again, that was a lot of troops. The plain shimmered with them. Literally more soldiers than they had the words to count.

"They didn't bring that many men to take this castle," Carter announced. "They're going through us. We're an obstacle, not an objective. We need to get everybody the hell out of here." The villagers, a couple hundred of them, were piling into the inner courtyard nearest the towers and the manor. He had no idea where they were going to stay, much less how he would feed them for any length of time.

"And go where?" asked Alel.

"Anywhere," said Carter. "Go get the magisters, get them on the remaining birds and get them as far away from here as you can. Have my pages meet me in my chambers, and send a message to that army to send the best they've got to meet me one on one."

His boots echoed on the steps as he ran up to their apartment, the highest floor in the tower, and the entire floor, at that. Just beyond the entryway stood his armor, a monstrosity of demonic angles and skulls and black dragon scales, high-speed tool steel hardened with molybdenum to the toughness of industrial bearings.

Whoever they sent at him, he would give them a run for their goddamn money.

He pulled pieces of armor off and tossed them on the floor, digging down to the mail and the padded jack beneath. He was wrestling into it when his squires came in and started helping: leggings, mail for the tops of his boots, two of them lifting his enormous hauberk over his head.

They were buckling him into his pauldrons when Alel reappeared, in mail and a helmet with his sword at his side.

"Lookin' good, friend," said Carter.

"And you, my lord. There's an issue, however," Alel stated.

"I can only imagine," Carter said.

"The Two," said Alel, referring to Ristan and Stintlash, the wizards in the tower. The brains of the operation. "They refuse to leave," he said. "They won't abandon the foals."

"Tell them this is not optional," said Carter. "They need to get out of here, so we can make more foals. Without them . . . dear God." He imagined losing the entire body of knowledge resident in those two and shook his head. "Just, go back there and see if you can talk some sense into them." He strapped on a vambrace and buckled it. As he moved his arms, blackened dragon's scales rippled from his elbows to the skull-shaped black pauldrons on his shoulders. "Do we know who they're sending as a champion?" His knees were also skulls.

"We haven't heard," said Alel. "We sent an envoy, but she hasn't returned."

"Well, that's not good," Carter decided. He slipped on massive spiked gauntlets and tucked his helmet under his arm, a black demon skull that grinned with chrome fangs.

He slung Celeste over one shoulder. "I can't believe I get paid for this," he said.

Exactly halfway between Gateskeep and Regoth Ur, Daorah saw the gryphons coming out of the clouds, straight into her path from two sides. It had been years since she'd seen a gryphon, and never this far north.

Knights of the Order of the Falcon don't fight in the air; they fight on the ground, diving into footsoldiers and shattering formations, specifically functioning as a counter to the larger formations of heavy footsoldiers that Gavrians employ. Gavria created gryphons to destroy horsebirds in air combat. Knights of the Falcon fled from gryphons, counting on their greater speed and maneuverability, because air combat is insanely dangerous; a collision can stun a mount or damage a wing, and after that, it's a long fall.

She punched Maila downwards. A gryphon charged by overhead, so close that the wind from its passing overwhelmed the wind tugging at her from the speed of her fall.

And then, the impact. The sky shattered. Maila screamed, and the gryphon, catastrophically big, dragon big, was in the air with them, and they were locked with one talon around her mount just aft of the wing, crushing Daorah's leg, pinning the horse, and the world pinwheeled, graying, blackening, everything melding into screams and blood and horse and bird.

She could see the knight on the gryphon leaning into the black bird-head, into the center of the spiral, and that's what they were doing: spiraling, like two eagles fighting, spinning for the ground in a game of courage. The gryphon was unharmed; it would let go first, she knew, and hurl Maila into the rocks below, and that would be it.

Daorah screamed, raw fury blistering out of her soul, the sound lost in the hugeness of the sky and the fists of the wind as the world went insane and damn it, she was a sky warrior, she was not going to die like this.

Clouds, ground, clouds, ground.

Not like this.

Cloudsgroundcloudsgroundcloudsground.

She drew her warsword, a long and elegant weapon, distinct from the heavier blades of ground troops. Had Daorah seen Renaldo's custom longsword, she would likely have pegged him as air cavalry.

She'd outrun gryphons. She'd evaded them. She'd never fought one in the air. Few knights of the Falcon had, and certainly none had lived. She might die struck against the ground, but she would fight in the air. And damn it, she would fight the fight she was given.

She stabbed at the gryphon and felt the blade sink through feathers and meat, easy and soft. It shrieked, disintegratingly loud, and snapped at her, beak clicking. It struck mail and shrieked again, louder, furious. She stabbed it again and it grabbed the sword, and Daorah hammered its beak with her fist until it let go, gravity and gyration ripping at them. It bit at the blade and missed, and she feinted and it missed the blade again.

The feint was the thing. It couldn't feint. She cut over the end of the beak and slipped the point of the sword through its eye.

The world exploded in feathers and bird-howls and the screams of the knight as they fell away, the sword torn from her hand. Daorah leaned into Maila as the sky righted itself, and beloved departed, the ground was right *there;* Maila hammered at the air and Daorah slammed against her as the big horse recovered and bolted.

The gryphon hit the rocks with a bang and all the screaming ended.

The ground tore past under them, and Daorah pulled for altitude in a slow circle, looking for the other gryphon.

Her leg was hurt. Maila was hurt and slowing down.

The other gryphon was winging for Regoth Ur, a speck in

the distance. She'd never catch it, and even if she did, she'd have no chance against it.

She wheeled Maila around, shouting curses, and made for the palace, the great horse hobbled and struggling, but aloft. And aloft was victory enough.

~

In Renaldo's tent—the command tent, he reminded himself—in the center of the makeshift camp, a fire burned and breathed through a smoke hole in the roof, but he could see his breath regardless as several men worked to get him into his armor. This was a part of it that he loathed, and he felt that they were doing more harm than good, literally slowing him down. But, he thought, such was the life of a champion. People waiting on him hand and foot, beautiful women in his bed, a glass of wine at the ready. The role suited him.

Besides, they'd built him a tent, with a fire and wine, while everyone else was out there freezing their balls off.

"They've decided on a champion," said General Goun. He tucked a note into his jacket. "They're sending Karr, Son-Lord Soren."

Renaldo shifted his helmet a bit and shrugged under his pauldrons with a rattle. "Should I be concerned?" His breastplate, which locked together front and back, was dark leather tooled in gold with a raven centermost and surrounded by knotwork. He put his helmet under his arm as a page/squire/flunky settled his coif for him and another futzed with the buckles on his chest rig.

"No," said Jerandra, standing near the fire. "You should not."

"He is a mighty opponent," Goun warned. "He guards the

tower and the horsebirds. He is not to be trifled with."

"I don't trifle," Renaldo said, and pulled the red sword from its scabbard and thumbed the edge. "Let's do this."

It was a long walk to the edge of camp, and Renaldo didn't ride. He never rode, which he didn't think was that big of a deal. The men, however, thought it was hilarious, not that anyone would say it to his face. The few times he'd gotten up on a horse, it had become painfully clear to him just how far out of his element he was. It looked simple enough—swing up, put your leg on the other side—but a horse was not a Harley and he found it clumsy and alien. The whole "moving with the animal" concept struck him as oddly bestial, and he'd decided some time ago that he wanted no truck with it.

He walked.

The ranks parted, and he seated his helmet, saluted Rogar, and squelched out onto the plain, General Goun behind him.

Goun stayed back after a few steps, and Renaldo found himself standing on the plain, facing the castle, alone in the rain.

This is it, he told himself. *This is where you show them what you're made of.*

He was suddenly and horrifically unsure of what he was made of, though, when a horned demon atop a winged horse touched down in front of the wall. Mighty wings folded into the sides of the beast, and the rider, clad in spiked black armor, dismounted in the rain and took a moment to slip a baldric off his shoulder, draw a massive sword from it, shuffle some things around, and shoo the flying horse away with a slap on its hip.

This guy, Renaldo immediately noted, was huge. A giant, or an ogre in full field harness, striding vengefully through the rain with a cartoonishly big sword on his shoulder. An apparition out of a video game; the Final Boss.

He himself, Renaldo, was used to being the biggest one in the room. No one he'd met since his arrival could match his size, or his strength, and he took a deep breath, thinking this through.

His advantages of mass and speed wouldn't apply, here, and that armor—much heavier and more comprehensive than he was used to seeing; Blessed Christ Jesus, that was really full harness—would wreck the hell out of his sword, and that wouldn't leave him much to kill Jarrod with, when the time came for that.

First things first.

He had one advantage that the approaching giant didn't: the giant was already on the field, having chosen his weapons without having seen Renaldo. He motioned for Goun, who came running.

"In my tent," Renaldo said. "You'll find a long hammer with a pick on one side. I need it."

As the black-armored, dragon-scaled warrior strode across the field, Renaldo got a sense of the sheer size of him. He was seven feet tall. Four hundred pounds, in that armor. And light on his feet, practically buoyant. His visor was a grinning skull mask, chrome fangs gleaming against the black armor and the mud and the gray of the day.

A pang in Renaldo's gut, a tremble in his hand. This was going to hurt. A lot. "Holy shit," he said to no one, and bit down on the rise in his throat.

Greatsword and pick notwithstanding, he would have no margin of error. One mistake, he realized, and he would be buried, here.

The giant stood before him, just out of range now, monstrous and bristling in his lethal black armor. He was human, Renaldo could see that much; there were human eyes, hard and deadly, behind the fanged mask. What he'd thought were spikes turned out to be scales and skulls.

The knight set his sword in the grass tip-down, a full foot of hardwood handle and an egg pommel dripping and glistening above a squared ricasso for close play. The blade was four fingers wide if it was anything, though he had no doubt it danced in the hands of a man so large. It was a horrific weapon, built for a swordsman who knew many ways to use it.

The knight reached up with one hand to unlock and flip up his visor, revealing a salt-and-pepper goatee and a gold incisor.

"Doctor Livingstone, I presume?"

The rain poured off Carter's helmet and dripped from his scales, and Renaldo's brain turned backflips.

Karr, Son-Lord Soren.

Karr, Soren's Son.

Carter Sorenson.

His immediate question was how many other people were here that he knew, and how far this went. Jarrod was here; Carter was here; who else? He shoved the thought aside and tried to figure out just how much trouble he was in, because this was—holy shit, he realized—Carter Sorenson.

The difficulty, he realized, was that he himself wasn't good at getting into trouble. He was a careful, calculating, shrewd man, and had always prided himself on going into a fight knowing exactly how to win, or at least, exactly what his advantages were. He had little experience with surprises that could potentially kill him, and this was definitely one. His brain rang with echoes.

He assessed that he was in severe, life-threatening jeopardy. Carter was as good as they got, and while Renaldo knew he could take him in longsword—and had, years before, in Germany, fighting for touches and points—Carter was one of the best greatswordsmen on Earth, and God knows how good he'd become here.

Longsword and greatsword were completely different styles, and against a man in armor with a greatsword, longsword was a loser, and fencing longsword-style with a greatsword—he had the red greatsword with him—would get him killed in seconds against Carter.

He'd counted on the greater mass of the red sword and his superior knowledge of swordplay and martial arts to get him through whatever this fight would be; whatever champion they'd thrown at him. To that end, he hadn't expected the guy in the skull armor to have a bigger sword than he did, and he damned sure hadn't expected him to know more about it.

Carter was also a former professional MMA fighter with a propensity for making people look stupid while beating them up. Renaldo thought back to a video of Carter winning a cage match by lifting up an opponent and throwing him to the mat time and again like a sandbag he'd really hated. No amount of martial arts training—and he'd had plenty—would give him any advantage. Carter would simply kill him. One way or another.

He could see that Carter could see him thinking.

"I don't want to kill you, Renaldo," Carter said, sounding sincere. Then, he raised a finger and corrected himself. "Okay, that's not true; I really do. I mean, I really, *really*—I *so* want to kill you. But you can give this up right now, go back to them," he said, pointing, "and go around my castle. Because, no shit: if that sword comes off your shoulder, this is happening," here, he wiggled the pommel of the huge sword resting tip-down in the wet grass, "and you die where you stand." He flipped the spiked mask down over his face again and locked it with a twist of an expert hand.

"Your castle?" Renaldo repeated.

"Mine," said Carter. "And the king of Gateskeep, who has given me permission to use any means necessary to defend it."

"Well, we have a problem, then," said Renaldo, stepping back. "Because Lord Rogar Hillwhite has entrusted me to take this castle, and then kill Jarrod Torrealday."

His sword came off his shoulder.

Carter kicked the tip of Celeste and popped it up into a fending guard.

They didn't bother to salute.

Carter had a fleeting prickle of sweat and alarm when Renaldo came in superfast on beautiful footwork, the red greatsword gimbaling from three angles and looking for an opening. Then he choked up on Celeste's handle, adjusted his footing for the wet grass and Renaldo's considerable stride, and caught the smaller blade and bound it. As Renaldo fought to free himself, Carter wrapped it up under one arm and flipped Celeste around in his hand by the ricasso. He powered the end of the crossbar into Renaldo's helmet like a claw hammer hard enough to leave a half-walnut of a dent and stagger him sideways.

Carter kicked him in the thigh, shoving him back and dropping him to his knees, then righted the two-hander and blasted it down, denting the shoulderplate and sending links skittering. Carter stomped him in the face, sending him into the mud. The red sword flew away.

Renaldo rolled back and forth, shaking his head and swearing.

"Game, set, match," Carter said. "Quit now."

"Like hell," said Renaldo, rising. The red sword twitched on the grass a yard away, then lifted up and launched itself for Carter.

He slipped it, batting it aside, and it flashed past.

"Interesting," Carter admitted, watching it go, and turned to keep his eyes on it.

"You don't know the half of it," said Renaldo as the sword leaped from the grass and flew back into his hand.

"Okay," said Carter, squaring off. "That's kinda cool. Let's go."

The next blow from Renaldo was uncharacteristic: straight, heavy—a simple sweep from the side with both hands. Idiotic. Carter put Celeste in the way, five feet of industrial band-saw steel. The impact was stunning, shocking, blowing both swords into him; Carter had no doubt that there had been a magic component to it. Renaldo was probably counting on the blow to break Celeste and bust him up.

He shifted sideways under the impact but kept his feet, and Renaldo fell back, holding the red sword's hilt and nothing more. Carter heard the blade hit the grass far behind him.

"So," said Carter interestedly. "I'm guessing that's the sword that Jarrod stole from you?"

Renaldo threw the handle into the mud.

"Lemme guess," said Carter. "He filed down the tang and then rewrapped it. And then, he waited for you to steal it back."

"Motherfucker," Renaldo spat.

Carter laughed, moving Celeste in loops as Renaldo retreated. "Guy fucked up a magic sword," he assessed. "That must really piss you off."

"You're gonna kill an unarmed man?" asked Renaldo, still backing up.

"Not yet," said Carter. "I'm giving you one more chance to quit and go around."

Someone was running up to Renaldo with a warhammer, a big, two-handed son of a bitch with a long pick on one end.

Carter stepped back, adjusted his guard and extended a bit,

because Christ, Renaldo was quick.

He was waiting for Renaldo to come in with the hammer when his back cramped with a lash of pain through his spine. "Fuck!" he grunted through gritted teeth, then laughed as he stretched it out. "I should've limbered up," he said. "Getting too old for this sh—"

Another cramp, much worse, ripping the air from him, and Renaldo was running at him, the pick over his head. Carter sidestepped, caught the pick on Celeste, and drove an elbow into Renaldo's head with a leg behind. The world erupted, his skin on fire, his eyes going black in a blur of impact as they both ended up on the ground.

He rolled to his knees to see Renaldo climbing to his feet, and all he could think as he saw the hammer going back over Renaldo's shoulder and his body flared with rockets of pain, immobile, was *magic.*

Oh, Christ, it hurt.

But the hammer was coming down, and hurt was a thing he could work through, and he leaped to his feet and dove into Renaldo in an explosion of sparks, broken glass jammed into nerve endings, driving his helmet into Renaldo's face. Celeste's solid foot of crossbar blocked the hammer's haft and Carter drove him back and down, and looped the huge sword into a mighty overhand blow that would end this fucking thing right now.

Except pain choked him—noiseless, senseless, burning him alive—and he faltered. The big sword fell awkwardly and out of tempo where Renaldo had been.

The scalding on his skin crawled through his armor. His skin blistered and cooked, his muscles seized, his vision blurred. He shoved himself forward, his lungs searing, chest tightening. He couldn't take in any air.

It had to be magic. Some kind of hurt magic. Pain magic.

They have a healer in reverse.

He ground his teeth and stepped forward, and his foot exploded in a burst of impact, as if he'd tripped a mine. But there was no mine, and looking down, he saw that his foot was there, although everything told him it wasn't, that his leg was off at the knee. His mind screamed at him. He stumbled.

He looked at his foot again and it was numb, as if he'd been sitting on it for an hour. Why didn't it work? He slammed it into the ground and felt the resonance in his hip.

Good enough.

He limped forward another step, slipped halfway on wet grass, recovered onto another empty leg and *what the hell?* And then Renaldo's pick appeared from his left in a wide arc, and there wasn't a damned thing he could do about it.

Carter lay on the grass. His body klaxoned at him, flares of yellow-orange panic among thudding spasms of damage.

There was a lot of blood. He could feel it, hot, then cold, pumping from under his armor, no hole he could get at.

Men running. Healers. Renaldo shouting at them to get back. Others shouting to let them through. Renaldo threatening them with the pick. *Let him die.*

Kiss my ass.

Death—if this was death—wasn't what he thought it would be. Not much pain, no regret, just a sense of loss that there wouldn't be more to see. Disappointment. With it, though, the feeling of slipping into a warm tub: limbs growing heavy, muscles deflating even while he raged at them to stand up and fight again.

Flaccid defiance.

He found himself hyperaware of the edges and swirls of low clouds overhead, spitting rain, intensely sharp. When had he seen the edges of clouds before? He shoved his visor open, feeling the cool air and watching the skies tearing by. The rain was rapturous.

He thought of clouds, and wings, and castles. The smell of a pegasus. The feel of Daorah. The slam of a fish on the line. Jarrod's laugh.

Cheering crowds, lethal tackles. A field with enemies before him and friends behind him.

A warrior's life, executed beautifully.

A little sadness.

He wished Daorah had been here to see it. He'd fought pretty well. She'd have been proud.

Renaldo stood over him, that fucking pick in his hand, warning anyone who came close.

"Ass . . . hole," Carter stammered, spitting. "H-had to cheat, didn't you?" With a flash of drowning, scrabbling panic, the sky clouded over; The Dark once more. Shadows twisted. Edges blurred. He pulled against it, and the world straightened in a lull of normalcy before smearing along its length again.

And suddenly, like a collapse, nothing hurt.

God, the sky was beautiful.

Persephone charged out of the heavens, hooves flailing, driving Renaldo away in a thunder of noise and threat, a horse and a half.

He stepped up with his pick, menacing. "Shoo! Go on!"

She lunged at him, wings whipping, and he scampered as she trotted back to Carter, leaned in and nosed his helmet, sniffed his face, and then stretched out her wings to cover him.

Carter stroked her cheek with a hand made of lead. "Lovely lady." The sky swirled with rainbows.

"I'm okay," he assured her, and he didn't know why he

said it, because he most definitely wasn't.

"I won!" yelled Renaldo, awash in auroras, twisting, and beginning to fade. "I beat you!"

"For now," said Carter.

He touched Persephone's face once more, and from a hundred miles away he heard a voice saying there was nothing to be done. Whose voice? A healer's voice. He knew the voice.

Don't say there's nothing to be done, he thought, as the clouds went dark. *There's so much more to be done.*

The sky turned a brilliant shade of white, and at the end of a tunnel waited a roaring stadium. The announcer brought the crowd out of their seats as Carter strode onto the field, fists held high, finally home.

ALL THE COLORS OF MORNING

"The penalty for exceeding the time limit is the forfeiture of the game."

- Howard Staunton

Jarrod staggered up the slope of High River's courtyard, moderately drunk and completely turned around by two teleports in an afternoon. He hit the front door to find people waiting for him. No one even asked him how he'd gotten there, they just grabbed him by the arms halfway to the steps and ran him inside. Jarrod didn't get all of it: *manor, war, burned,* and as he asked for the third time, he caught that they were talking about Regoth Ur.

As they crossed the anteroom, the crowd around him quieted, and parted, and in strode Princess Adielle with Karra beside her and a team of advisers behind them, heading right, dead-nuts on for Jarrod.

Adielle was clad in travesty, her mouth a hard line, her eyes puffy. She wore dark clothes, unusual for her, and no jewelry.

The staff around her were forlorn and disconsolate, atypically haggard in rumpled clothes and undone hair. He knew the look of a man who'd slept on a couch in his own office, whether in a woolen tunic or a button-down Oxford, and they all wore it now.

A tide of blackness washed over Jarrod and brought a cramp beneath the scar on his gut, that same haunting feeling that he'd had walking into the princess's audience chamber to find Renaldo. The world hung unresolved, a piano on a string above him.

Karra ran ahead and fairly tackled Jarrod, clinging to him so hard that he couldn't breathe. "Lover," she said, seeming to bury herself in him. "Terrible things," she said.

"It's okay," he put his hand in her hair.

"No," she said. "Not yet."

Jarrod saluted Adielle and knelt.

"Please," said Adielle. "For this, you stand."

"This will hurt," Karra whispered, and put an arm around Jarrod again as they stood. "But it will pass."

Jarrod looked down at her, then back at Adielle.

"The Armies of the West took Regoth Ur," said Adielle.

She gave it a moment, which Jarrod appreciated.

"Survivors?" he asked.

"Few," said Adielle. "The Armies of The West destroyed the castle."

Murmurs rippled through the crowd. Jarrod's voice squeaked out. "Carter?"

"Karr, Son-Lord Soren, met their champion on the field, and failed."

"Failed?" asked Jarrod, looking around for an explanation.

Adielle's mouth seemed to spasm around the word: "Extinguished."

Karra was there, beside Jarrod, holding him tight. It wasn't remotely enough; that word, *extinguished,* echoed and twisted and spun into a void somewhere above as he hit his knees, a child's unflinching faith in the goodness of the world lying shattered. Monsters were real.

"How is that possible?" Jarrod snarled up at her, and then checked himself. *First denial,* he thought, *then anger. Which is good, because you're gonna need that second one here in a minute.*

"We understand that the Hillwhites have a champion who . . . reports are that the—" Adielle's voice faltered, and she deferred to Karra.

"Lord Blacktree refused to allow a healer," Karra said. "Your friend died on the field."

Jarrod screamed and beat his fist on the floor as Karra draped herself over his shoulders.

The crowd went silent and as he stood up, Jarrod realized they were looking at him.

Adielle bit her lip. "I'm sorry," she said. "Not every man gets the death he deserves."

Jarrod's words could have chiseled themselves into the wall. "He does if I can help it."

The walls of the keep wobbled in and out of focus as Jarrod screamed obscenities in his head. Karra tugged at his arm, half-pulling, half-steadying, as he lurched along, fighting to make some sense of it; of anything.

Carter Sorenson was dead.

It had to be a mistake.

His feet tripped on steps and stumbled over nothing in empty hallways, the world fighting him handlessly from every aberrant bearing of this candle-punctured, balls-chilling, pink-gray hellhole. Fuck this place, anyway.

He followed the group forward through frigid, uncaring hallways blurred with tears, the very essence run out of him. His chest ached. He quit breathing for a while just to see what it felt like, and when the world tunneled in on him, it still wasn't enough.

Carter.

The biggest, bravest son of a bitch in the universe, dead a million light-years from home, alone on a field. Against Renaldo, of all people.

The group around him spoke, and he wasn't hearing any of it over the shrieking in his skull.

He straightened his rapier, clinging to some frantic despotism of ego, recognized it as such, and shoved it around on his hip, furious, powerless. Beaten.

No sword would help anything.

He held his breath again, harder. He needed to hurt more.

Carter.

Afternoons of judo and swords, ten thousand years ago, picking Carter's brain when he, Jarrod, was still a sweet-souled idealist: the Bruce Lee of the Broadsword, Rambo of the Round Table, an unkillable genius with a black belt and a swept-hilt sidesword; and Carter, his spare brain on loan. Carter, with the mighty laugh and the ever-present smirk of trouble brewing.

The excitement of this new world. Carter's ability to just slip into the water around him, to put on the mantles of lordship and leadership, here, as if born for it. And maybe he had been.

The anger. The disappointment.

The animals on fire.

Jesus Christ, I'm sorry.

And this is what war was. He'd seen it before: Javal, Elgast. Myk. Myk, a spy, but still his first combat loss, a man he'd barely known, dead from an arrow to the shoulder of all things.

Now, Carter. Every inch as senseless. A skeletal, aching surrealism. The world, robbed. Ghosts howled, rattling chains of absurdity.

And more to the point, he reasoned, if Renaldo with that sorceress backing him was good enough to kill Carter, then he—he himself, Jarrod—was sure as hell going to die. And that creatine-sodden, spray-tanned asshammer was going to inherit this entire goddamned world, because that was how it worked, here: the strong made the rules.

He could not believe the degree to which he had fucked this up.

He was losing a war. To Renaldo. He ground his teeth on the rise of bile it called into being.

It should have been me.

Goddammit.

Carter should be the one in shock right now, with Daorah on his arm, begging him not to go fight Renaldo. Strapping on his armor, punching walls. Yelling for his horse and his seconds.

Eating mail and shitting nails.

He felt Karra's hand tighten on his, and he looked around. Something had changed, now.

They'd stopped.

He recognized the door—Adielle's audience chamber—and as three people opened it, he and Adielle stepped through, just the two of them, alone.

He found himself wiping his eyes, right back where he'd started, as the door slammed behind them. She stared holes through him and he stared right back, his eyes cinders.

"Let's try this again," he growled.

Someone had done a bang-up job of cleaning the audience chamber. Daylight and moonlight hammered down on the planks and the stone tables, washing out the coaly glows of the fires in the walls. Even the tapestries had been cleaned.

Jarrod decided not to mention it. He also tried not to watch her taut nectarine of an ass under her dresses as she strode over to her throne, as this was definitely not the time. Actually, he thought, it might be the perfect time. Shared grief and mutual disaster evoked some frazzled declaration of privilege, even with Karra right outside the door.

He'd never thought to ask Adielle's age, and he wondered about it for the hundredth time. She was suspended in that moment when young women are softly, heart-stoppingly beautiful. She seemed to shimmer in the light, as if manifested out of cosmic dust. And here he was, in his swordsman's jacket, his rapier at his side; masculine, furious, and capable of world-shattering mayhem. The door was locked and the night was theirs inside these walls. The broken, leaking disaster they'd left in their tracks cast a rippling smear of permission that startled him.

He imagined her pushing him onto a table, kissing his neck and unbuttoning his jacket, then slammed a mental hatch shut on it.

"Your job was to kill Lord Blacktree, and that sorcerer," said Adielle, settling herself. "This is what I told you to do."

So, this is an ass-chewing, he decided. *That's exactly what I needed right now.* "I haven't got that far, yet," he told her, adding, "Your Highness."

"Shall we look at what you've accomplished?"

"I'd rather we didn't," Jarrod admitted, and sat down at one of the stone tables. He wiped his nose with his hand.

"You defeated an army. You secured our coin vault. You freed a thousand innocents, at the cost of a hundred of them; maybe more. We're still balancing the ledger on that. However, you did lose a team of knights, and I do mean 'lost'—no one has seen them in days—"

"Border knights," Jarrod pointed out, then wished he hadn't after the look she gave him.

"You colluded with Commander Daorah to go over my head and requisition weapons from the royal armory, building your own army—completely unauthorized and against all tenets of warfare, might I add."

"It wasn't exactly—"

"Yes?"

"—an army," Jarrod admitted.

"The hell it isn't," Adielle said. "It's marching south."

"Wait, what?"

"Your chancellor put out a call for able bodies, two days ago. He and your knights are leading five hundred levies south to meet the Armies of the West. It turns out that nearly every man and woman you freed wants to fight for you. They're camped at the headwaters of Rogue's River. They should be crossing in the morning."

"Well, wow," said Jarrod. "Way to go, Saril."

She stared knives at him.

"But, I can see how that constitutes a concern," Jarrod added quickly, and she shook her head and sighed.

"We're resupplying and reinforcing your army with soldiers out of Horlech," she said. "The cost of this is coming out of your coin vault. There will be a considerable bill."

"That's fair," he admitted.

"We had to destroy the royal mint. All of it."

"Damn, good thinking," he admitted after reflection. "Wow, that's great. They held the mine, so they had the silver. But now they can't—wow. That was really smart."

"The troops we sent to do it never came back," she added. "We just sent several hundred to find them."

"Well, shit," said Jarrod.

"If you were anyone else, I'd have you stripped of your

knighthood and horsewhipped."

"I'm not anyone else," said Jarrod, locking eyes with her. "And you know that."

"Don't test me," Adielle said.

"I test no one," said Jarrod. "I also threw the Hillwhites a trick, a phony map that's going to tie them up for a while. I bought you some time. I saved the lives of my team and negotiated the Rogue's River Flats in The Dark under constant threat by gbatu. We lost one horse.

"We killed a gryphon," he continued. "We fought the Armies of the West on the plains, just below the West Wind Rise, and I got a piece of that motherfucker. He was there.

"Further, we didn't 'lose' those border knights. We let them get away. They were spies, and they were the ones who took the phony map back to the Hillwhites. I destroyed a weapon that could have killed any knight in this world, and I beat a thousand troops with fifty and got you your money back."

She grunted. "You still haven't done what I ordered. Had you done that—"

"Had I done that," said Jarrod, "I'd be dead right now, and you'd be capitulating. That sorceress would have killed me. She probably killed Carter."

"Sorceress?"

"Her name is Jerandra of the Wastes. She's one of the graduates of King Ulo's sorcery school. I thought this is what we were here to talk about."

"What school?"

"I'm glad you asked," said Jarrod. "King Ulo has a school in the Silver Palace, teaching profane magic."

"Profane," the princess repeated.

"Pain magic, war magic, pyromancy. That's where this sorceress, Jerandra, learned it. She hired out to Rogar Hillwhite, and he sent her to my homeland looking for a hero to beat me.

She came back with Blacktree. They killed Carter together. They used magic—war magic, probably pain magic—on Carter so that Blacktree could kill him. Renaldo's not that good. He's good, but he's not that good."

"If she used magic to kill, she'll be pulled apart," said Adielle. It was Falconsrealm's ugliest form of execution, tied to four horses whipped in four directions.

"We need to defeat the Hillwhites and capture her, first," said Jarrod. "And even then, we have a much larger problem. King Ulo is building an army with wizards who can kill. Jerandra, this sorceress, is the first of a wave of them. He has dozens like her. He may have hundreds. I don't know how many are in his ranks, and I don't know how many are loose in the wild."

Adielle swore under her breath in tirades. "You know this, how?"

"Ulo invited me down to talk to him. I just got back."

"You what?"

"He made us an offer," said Jarrod. "I'm loathe to bring it up, but I'd be remiss if I didn't."

She put her head in her hands. "No," she said. "Just, no."

"I need to say this," said Jarrod.

She spoke from behind her palms. "What does he offer?"

"He proposes a mutual defense treaty—"

"—this is not happening—"

"He will give us sorcerers from his army to defeat the Hillwhites if, in return, we send word to Gavria that we stand with Ulorak against Gavrian aggression."

"Is this a jest?" Adielle asked, looking out from between her fingers.

"No," said Jarrod. "This is deadly serious, and it might be the only chance we have to stop the Hillwhites once and for all. I don't like it any more than you do. I think it will succeed, but that doesn't mean it's not still a terrible idea."

"What did you tell him?"

Jarrod shrugged. "I told him I'd tell you. I told him I was in no position to make that kind of decision."

She sighed and threw herself down in her throne, sagging. "Well, that may be the first smart thing you've said in a while."

"Probably the last," he admitted.

"I could have you killed for going down there, you know," she said.

"But you won't," he said. "Because you need me to kill Blacktree. Nobody else has a chance."

"I know," she said.

"I might not even have a chance," he admitted after a moment.

"I know."

She rose, at once immense in the room, as if the fires brightened when she stood. Imperiled, likely doombound, but upright and glowing nonetheless. An astonishing woman.

He stood, eyes on his feet, a smudge of horseshit on the rubber toe of his Merrill hiking boot and a bubble of apprehension forming under his belt as the world unfolded around him, readying himself for whatever might be next.

He realized, then, that this—charging into darkness and making do, not out of duty or loyalty or justice or even suicidal abandon, but out of being divorced from any ability to see beyond the hair-trigger catastrophe of himself—was his normal state of affairs, and that was the problem. They'd needed a hero, and he'd stepped up, instead; a coyote on a rocket with a match.

He realized that she wasn't saying anything.

Had she said something? Was she waiting for a response? What had he missed? The flames crackled in slow motion.

When she did speak, her voice was nearly lost in itself, choked and sandy. "Hold me," she murmured.

"Highness?" he asked as she came to him, wobbling.

In a floundering, spinning moment, the princess's arms were around him and she was melting, her face on his shoulder, weeping soundlessly.

He put his hands on her hips to steady her, and she gasped a shuddering intake of breath at his touch. She folded herself into him, lavender and book dust and candlesmoke, immensely breakable; spun glass in his hands. He put his arms around her and felt her spine tremble.

"Just hold me," she sniffed.

Emotions he'd never examined in enough depth to name erupted misshapen and stumbling and looking for the wrong address. It had all the raw eroticism of helping up a friend who'd sprained an ankle.

He held her until the candles burned down.

Jarrod lay awake in his apartment. The light from the tiny moons screamed at him.

Now what?

At least you didn't bang the princess, he answered himself. *That would really complicate things.*

Yes, because they're not nearly complicated enough.

The line keeps moving.

And yet, you manage to keep crossing it.

Shut up. Work to do. Jarrod punched his pillow and threw his head against it. Karra stirred, mewled, and tucked herself into crooks of him. *Gonna give that asshole the death he deserves.*

Like Elgast?

Shut up.

You're griping about Renaldo using magic, and you're the guy who brought a gun to a swordfight.

To stop a war.

And this is different, how?

Because, he told himself. *Because . . .*

He pictured the bullet blowing through General Elgast's helm last summer, the massive wound channel from the expanding round and all that hydrostatic pressure with no place to go. Literally blowing his brains against the walls of his helmet. Knights looking up, thinking of thunder. Horses jumping. If that wasn't magic, what was it?

Images of blood and gunsmoke swam through the room, his true eternal self splayed out on the ceiling in the candlelight. His own insufficiency, shrouded in an egocentric orgy of dualism and feigned competence, now unmistakable. Monolithic. The world knew. Or, they would.

Cheater.

He couldn't comprehend the idea that Carter was dead. He just couldn't put it into terms that he could understand, much less mourn him. It still seemed like a mistake; like Carter would show up at breakfast tomorrow wondering what everyone was so worried about.

Karra snugged herself closer, a tiny fang digging into his shoulder.

They all think you cheated, too, you know. This is what Ulo was driving at.

Ya think?

And that stumped his imaginary adversary for a time, as he rolled the conversation through his head.

No, came the answer at last. I don't think he knows you brought a shootin' iron. He legitimately thinks you're good enough to take down the best he's got. Little Mr. Springfield brought you to the bargaining table just now.

124 grains of jacketed hollowpoint stopped a war. Was that a bad thing?

And the war was the thing.

He looked at the skull goblet on the table, the purple of the moonlight around collapsing singularities of eye and nose holes.

You're no different from Renaldo, chided his ego. *It's just a matter of who's looking.*

It's different, he told himself. *It's different because I'm not arming a contingent of knights with AK-47's. I have control of this. That's the difference. Ulo's students are out among us, and they're fighting in his army, and he's making more. And I'm lucky he didn't send one of them after me last summer instead of ol' Johnny Skullcastle and his marching band. I'd be discussing this with Javal right now.*

And Carter.

The quickest relief lay in finding someone to blame. He settled on himself, if for no other reason, he thought, than there was nobody else handy.

Jerandra of the Wastes is going to waste you.

I probably deserve it.

Be that as it may, you can't let Renaldo rule this world. Imagine King Renaldo. Just let that seep into your brain.

It was worth dying to stop it.

And that was the math: it was worth dying—really dying; being buried next to Javal with Karra weeping and the princess shattered—just to kill Renaldo and end it.

Even with no way to live through it, he could still save this place by ending everything they'd started.

Kill Renaldo. Die in the process. A hard reboot of the Western World.

Karra stretched, stirring up vapors of warm candy. "Can you sleep, lover?" she asked.

"No," he admitted. "I can't stop thinking."

She rolled atop him and he felt her body shift along his legs as she dragged her fangs lightly down his chest. "Then think of this."

TELL THEM NO LIES

"The life of spies is to know, not to be known."

- George Herbert

In the light of morning, faintly pink and gray and dimmed by snow, Jarrod stood before Captain Gwerian, his local commander and by all rights his boss, who strode back and forth in front of him, her hands locked before her. Aever and Carj waited in the hall.

"First off," said Jarrod, "My troops bear no responsibility. This is on me."

"You're damned right, it is," she began. "My understanding is that you left your room unlocked, and enemy agents were able to steal all of the intelligence that you have been keeping. Copies that you weren't supposed to be making in the first place. Is this correct?"

"More or less, ma'am."

She looked Jarrod in the eye. "What did I tell you? I told you not to screw this up."

"I didn't," said Jarrod.

"They robbed your room!"

Jarrod stared straight ahead. "Respectfully, ma'am, they

didn't."

"What do you mean?"

"Everything they stole was fake," Jarrod said. "I have a second set of books. The real notes were under my mattress."

"What?"

Jarrod ticked off on his fingers. "Fake contacts, fake towns, fake mountain passes—"

"What?"

"—fake caches," he continued, "entire phantom armies, fraudulent troop strengths, detailed blackmail information on lords who don't exist. All my notes were horseshit. The map I gave them is fake, too. They're going to get lost if they use it. In fact, right now, I'd guess you'll find them a half-day's ride from Rogue's River, headed up a trail into a dead end. If we get an army together fast enough, we should be able to box them in."

"Oh." She put her hands to her head.

Jarrod stuck his thumbs in his belt. "Yeah."

"How can you be certain they were Hillwhite agents?" she asked. "That was a huge risk."

"Because they stole my notes, not anyone else's," said Jarrod. "They would have to have someone who speaks my language. That's got to be Blacktree. There are four people in this world who can read my language. Okay, shit—now, three: King Ulo, Blacktree, and me."

Gwerian's mouth twitched. "Go on."

"What gave it away is that those three goons were waiting for us. Somebody sold us out. They knew we were leaving before we did, so it was either you, or someone in your organization between you and the Lord High Inquisitor.

"Now, only you and I know that they have the wrong maps. So, if they head across the correct pass for High River, it's because you told them. If this doesn't screw their army up—if we go up there and don't find them jammed up their own asses—I'm coming back here to kill you. No offense. Ma'am," he added.

Gwerian blew out a short breath. "I'm really glad you're on our side."

"Yeah, me too," said Jarrod. "Now, if memory serves, I believe you owe me an army."

"You already have an army, as I understand it," she said.

"That doesn't mean that you don't still owe me another one."

"Don't get sharp with me. I can get you a hundred riders."

Jarrod glanced at Dara, then back to her. "You promised me a thousand."

"You have a thousand," she said.

"I have five hundred," he countered, "and they're levies. I need a thousand actual soldiers. They have a big army, and a couple of real badasses at the head of it."

"We don't have it."

"Why not?" said Jarrod.

"Because we didn't expect you to live!" Gwerian shouted, slamming her fist on her desk. "There is an entire army out there trying to kill you—you, personally—and *you rode into the middle of it,* and you're still here. I don't even know what to say to that," she shook her head.

He shrugged and adjusted his rapier a little.

"Your horse turned up at Rogue's River," she said, trying to make friends.

"When?"

"Two days ago."

"Is she okay?"

"I don't know. Probably. The sorcerers are preparing a gate to Regoth Ur," she said. "You should go. The princess is going, and she'll need her hero. Take the day while we pass along new orders and get you as many riders as we can. In the morning, we'll send everybody we've got to the—where did you send them?" she asked.

"North of the actual pass," said Jarrod. "The Strall."

REMAINS

"War is a dangerous place."
 – George W. Bush

Desolation. The rain wailed.

Jarrod stood in the courtyard of Regoth Ur, a layer of furs over his swordsman's jacket against the cold, the manor house charred to its bones.

Jarrod had only experienced castles here as places of animation, and enterprise, and life. The hulk around him was staggering in its noiselessness. It was, by any definition that mattered, dead. A corpse. The town within the walls was abandoned and still, and his immediate reaction was to wonder if there was another prison camp nearby although he was in no position to go and look for it.

The shops were burned away, the carts overturned and empty, the fires in the walls long cold. Piles of bodies, more than he wanted to count, stood heaped and frozen outside the steps to the manor when he rounded the tower, and he sank when he realized Marc and Hat were probably in there, along with scores of others who'd had no business on the wrong end of a sword; all of it an utter and murderous fuckup.

A dozen knights of various orders poked around, and a few healers, though there was absolutely nothing for them to do. The princess was here somewhere, as well, though he'd lost sight of her, and losing her wasn't the kind of thing that he figured a Lord Protector should have done but he guessed someone was taking care of her. He kicked an axe handle out of his path.

A good dozen of the man-sized Gateskeep bulldogs, black and brindle with bowling-ball heads and two-inch fangs, lay butchered across the yard. Jarrod hoped that they'd fought hard and hurt the hell out of some people. "Good boy," he muttered, passing one.

The carnage was gratuitous, and it concerned him, because this was a monumental failure of foresight and his experience had always been that failure was contagious. The dogs had fought as hard as they could, and it hadn't mattered.

Carter had fought as hard as he could, and it hadn't mattered.

This was not a disease he cared to catch.

And Renaldo had beaten Carter. He'd cheated, and he'd killed him. And moved on.

Were they coming back? Why hadn't they used this as a base of operations? Where were they going? Why level this place?

He waited to hear the hoofbeats of an army coming to end the world. That would be it, too. Kill them all, take the princess, Gateskeep quits.

But there was no approaching roar of cavalry, and he guessed that Renaldo's goons were headed for the pass he'd outlined in the map they'd stolen. He wished he could see the expressions on their faces when they got there.

He almost smiled.

Almost.

He recognized where he was, now: the smith's shop,

Torvan Daar. Completely burned away, the roof gone, the sword blanks stolen, and on the floor when he pushed through the half-doors, the little smith frozen in a sprawl on the floor with the red sword blade through his face, snapped at the tang. It had done what he'd wanted it to, all right. "Son of a bitch," Jarrod swore, and closed his eyes for a bit and breathed.

"Lord Protector!" called a woman's voice, and he looked to see the princess, in a shirt of fine black mail that moved like liquid and a golden-trimmed black helmet, at the base of a tower on the other side of a small courtyard, nearly an alleyway between the walls. Before her, a set of substantial double doors lay blown open as if by a cannonball, the iron bands bent, the wood shattered.

Psychic battering rams, Jarrod remembered. He jogged over, cautious not to lose his footing on the snow and the blood. All he needed now was a slipped disc.

Someone had sure done a number on the doors.

He stepped up to them, waved the princess back, and drew his rapier and slipped inside.

It was cold, and pitch black beyond the hesitant reach of gray where the steps curved—in the wrong direction, he noted—circling up and to the left in a tight hallway. It was a small tower, and there was no room to fight in the stairwell.

His rapier had considerable reach over a typical Gateskeep soldier's sword and almost a foot more reach than a Long Valley saxe. He'd be all right.

As he turned into the blackness, a light danced against the wall ahead of him, a flashlight beam, tenuous and then gone again.

"Stay back!" he yelled down the stairs.

"You!" he yelled up at the light. "It's all right! I'm a friend."

The light flashed on the wall again, and then again, and then it came around the corner: a blue blip, a golf ball, luminescent and damned if it wasn't alive.

The light bounced on the stair, hovering low, and then flashed to his side and stayed there at knee height, quivering faintly.

"Hey," he said, gently, unsure if it was a living creature—a sprite, a pixie, a will o' wisp—or some spell that had hung in, its caster long gone. There was no heat that came off it that he could tell; it was definitely magic. "It's okay," he told it. "I'm here to help."

It bounded ahead of him a few steps, flew back to his knee, and then back up the stairs.

"Okay," he assured it. "I get it. I'm coming."

"Who are you talking to?" said a voice behind him, and he nearly jumped out of his own skull.

"You scared the hell out of me, Princess," he said, and then added, "There's this . . . thing—" and motioned.

She saw it and cocked her helmeted head, obviously as confused as he was. "There sure is," she said. "What is it?"

"I don't know," he said, "but it appears to want us to follow it."

She drew her sword, that glorious old leaf spring, and it glimmered in the light. "Then let's," she said.

Up the stairs, a few at a time, as it buzzed their legs and flew ahead, puppyish and bumbling, steps after steps until they reached a wrecked door high in the tower where the light paused at the doorway and Jarrod swore it sagged and dimmed a little.

He pushed through the shattered wood, and the ball of light shot ahead of him. There were windows here, though not many, but there was enough light to see the room, and the world was worse for it.

It smelled of horses and snow and housed a number of heavy wooden tables at the front, and a row of small stables further back against the wall. Jarrod set his helmet on one of the tables and picked his way through in the half-light, the floor dotted with broken gadgets and papers scrawled with runes and symbols. His eyes roved the papers and he thought of Ulo's skin—*Eric's,* he reminded himself. *Eric the Evil Sorcerer.*

Incantations.

The stall doors were open. Inside the first, he could make out the shape of a horse on the floor, black, small, feeble, clearly a colt. One wing lay splayed in the straw.

"Oh, God," he said. "They killed the foals."

He kicked the stall door with a yell and a bang that resounded through the tower.

He could hear the princess sobbing in the dark behind him. "Hey," Jarrod said, and went to her. The light was winding around her legs. "Hey, it's going to be okay."

She threw herself around him and her helmet hit him in the face, numbing his cheek. She pulled it off and threw it to the floor, unlocked her swordbelt, and then bent over and shucked her mail with a jingle and a bang.

". . . uh . . ." he said.

She grabbed him by the back of the head and smashed her mouth on his, tongue searching, salty with grief, and he was lost to a frantic, urgent world of wants and needs and this goddamn confining armor.

They fell against the wall, and then the table, scrabbling and tugging at buttons and ties, and suddenly this cadaver of a building was freezing but everything else exploded with warmth, and the table was hard but her breasts were soft, and death glared from every unlit corner but they were breathtakingly alive and out to prove it. She pulled him down onto the table and he entered her like the world was ending.

Hearts thundered and walls screamed until the castle came down around them, or so it felt.

"Oh, shit," he panted into her hair, breathing in lavender and armor, and eased himself free.

"Not yet," she said, her lips on his neck. "Stay with me. Please."

"Princess, I—"

"Please. Just be here with me."

He took her face in his hands.

"At your hand," he promised.

THE PROMETHEUS MANDATE

"As the well-trained soldier is eager for action, so does the untaught soldier fear it."
- Vegetius

"So, you're a war wizard," Crius said, looking Galè up and down a few times.

"I am," said Galè.

They spoke in Crius's office at the palace, which was walled with bookshelves and scroll cabinets stretching to the vaulted timber ceiling twenty feet above them. Crius's desk was perfectly suited to such a room, made of black wood and dotted with strange skulls, knickknacks, and odd weapons and trophies, the whole thing framed by tapestries sewn with mountain scenes.

Galè was not impressed by opulence.

"What can you do?" asked Crius. "What's your magic?"

Galè shrugged. "I can throw things," he said.

"Big things?" asked Crius, interestedly.

"Big things," agreed Galè. "I also move things."

"You can throw things and move things," Crius repeated. "You're a telekinetic, then; not a sorcerer."

Again, Galè shrugged. "Magic is magic."

"Is it?" Crius asked. "I can throw things. I can probably throw this castle, or at least move it a few steps. But I can't throw that skull at you and hurt you with it," he said, motioning to a gbatu skull on the table. "I couldn't throw it at a rat if I saw one."

"You have rats?" asked Galè.

"No," said Crius. "We have neophytes with animal talents who rid this place of pests."

"Your wizards are rat-catchers," said Galè.

"We like to think of ourselves as more than that," Crius admitted, "but there are days."

"You can drive a rat out; why not bring a rat in? Why not a horde of rats attacking your enemy army? Why not a swarm of insects on the battlefield?"

Crius sat down on the edge of his desk. "Because it's against the most ancient of laws," he said. "And you know that."

"Your laws," said Galè.

"Universal laws," said Crius. "These are the laws of the world."

"If they are the laws of the world," said Galè, "then they'd be enforced by the world. These are laws of men. They're enforced by men. You choose to follow them. We do not."

"Have you cast these spells? Forbidden spells?"

"If I tell you yes," said Galè, "then you'll have me killed, yes?"

"You have my word, I won't. I'm just curious as to why you would do it."

"I have cast magic to harm, yes," said Galè. "But I made my own law: I use my magic to harm only demons."

"King Ulo is a demon," said Crius. "Sir Jarrod is a demon. You haven't harmed them."

"They haven't harmed me," Galè countered. "They're

beneficial demons. You don't persecute beneficial sorcerers, do you?"

Crius poured two agate vases of wine. "That's fair. Wine?"

"Please."

"King Ulo sent you to kill Lord Blacktree with your magic, is this correct?"

Galè sipped at his wine. "He did."

"We're sending Sir Jarrod to kill Lord Blacktree. Without magic. With steel."

"That will never happen," said Galè. "The demon Lord Blacktree has a sorcerer of his own, Jerandra, who was trained by King Ulo the same as me."

"I know Jerandra."

"She conjured the demon Lord Blacktree, and she helps him kill, I'm certain of it. She will kill the demon Sir Jarrod. She will do it in such a way that you won't see. It will appear that Sir Jarrod loses the fight against their champion."

"You know this?

"I'm certain of it. Hillwhite is offering Jerandra, and Blacktree, lordships to kill the demon Sir Jarrod. Together."

Crius grunted. "And there's no way Jarrod can win against this Blacktree?"

"Not with her magic," said Galè. "No one can stand against her. She's far stronger than I am. If they have a champion's fight, Jarrod will die, and you will lose Falconsrealm. This is what they want. They want the fight. Don't give it to them."

"I can't stop him from fighting," said Crius. "That's his right, as Lord Protector."

"Then he's an idiot," said Galè.

"I don't disagree," said Crius. "But he's the bravest and most capable idiot we have." He let out a long sigh and paced around the office. Galè was on his second glass of wine when Crius finally spoke.

"My question to myself, is this," Crius said. "How many sins am I committing if I put you at the head of an army against them?"

Galè tipped his wine at him. "You should be asking how many sins you're committing if you don't."

Jarrod stepped dead-bang into the middle of Saril's makeshift army, with Thron and Aever behind him, Crius behind them, and Galè and the Flying Elvises behind the lot.

A momentary detour to The Reach had allowed him to gather his armor—his real armor, his field harness—and grab a few things, although three teleports in a day and he was feeling like his head was scrubbed out from the inside with a scouring pad. He stood bent in half, with his hands on his knees, and Crius clapped him gently on the back. "All done," he promised.

"Hello," Jarrod said, and introduced himself to the alarmed group of people around a cooking fire in which they'd almost appeared. "I need to see Sir Saril, wherever he is," said Jarrod. "Well, we all do," he added. Upon seeing the glazed faces, he assured them, "It's okay. Really."

It wasn't much of a camp, a tangle of dissymmetry that would make an Eagle Scout weep. Disheveled, disorganized, a lot of people with small weapons and piecemeal armor. Although, admittedly, they were breaking it up and getting ready to move, so maybe, he thought, he wasn't giving them a fair shake.

Saril and Bevio came at a run, no armor, in cloaks against the cold.

"Great to see you," said Saril. "I'm glad you're alive, sir."

Jarrod clapped him on the arm. "Well done. This is

outstanding." Actually, he thought, looking around, they were all going to die. The Armies of the West were going to slaughter these amateurs wholesale.

"All I did was put the word out," Saril said. "They started showing up that night, ready to go."

"Falconsrealm is sending a few hundred heavy horse," said Jarrod. "They left yesterday, so they'll be here in two days. We think the enemy is headed up to the Strall. We need to wait for them to head back down, and if we're lucky, we'll hit them when they're tired. If we're really lucky, our reinforcements will get here, first."

"Who's this?" Saril asked, motioning behind Jarrod.

"Crius Lotavaugus, Lord High Sorcerer of Gateskeep," Jarrod introduced, and Crius and Saril and Bevio all bowed to each other and shook hands. "This is Galè of Lor," Jarrod said, and Galè bowed, "and I still have no idea who these guys are," Jarrod motioned behind him to the three soldiers, now in Gavrian armor. "They're here to kill Blacktree if I can't."

Saril scratched his head. "What makes you think you can't?"

Jarrod told him. It took a while.

"You don't want to meet them at the bottom of the Strall," said Bevio, when Jarrod had finished telling the story of Jerandra, and Renaldo, and Carter, all of it as best he could figure it.

Crius asked first. "Where would you have him meet?"

"At the base of that peak," said Bevio, and he pointed into the distance, two hills away. "Dead Man's Reach. There's an old battlesite, there. Ancient ground."

"I didn't even think of that," said Crius to himself. "How do you know that?"

"I read a lot," said Bevio.

"I'd say you do," said Crius. "Sir Jarrod, your man is right.

We fight them there. We want the high ground, and you need to meet their champion in the flat. I will show you where. But we need to get them to come to us. Find a way."

Galè stepped up, his voice insistent. "That wizard is going to kill him if he fights their champion. He will die badly. Immeasurable pain," he promised Jarrod.

"Thanks," said Jarrod.

"No," said Crius. "I don't think he will. I need you four, right now, and we need to borrow some horses, sire," he told Saril.

"All right," said Jarrod to Saril, as Bevio led the wizards and demon-killers off. "What's next?" Two valets grabbed his bags of armor and balked at the weight.

"Be careful with that," Thron warned.

"Get it into the headquarters tent," added Aever.

"Don't drag it!" Thron yelled, running after them.

"We get this army up to the top of that ridge," suggested Jarrod, warming his hands over the fire. A dusting of snow on the ground, scarred with footprints, was getting slogged away by a light but steady and achingly cold rain. "We'll reset this camp up there. On the way up, we'll gather a shitload of wood, we build some big, smoky bonfires tomorrow morning—I mean, big ones—and let those assholes know we're here. We also need big smoky fires to give the Gateskeep forces a signal, because they're expecting us to box the Hillwhites in at the bottom of the Strall, and we're, what, half a day's ride outside of that? They'll need to know where to find us."

"Assuming they get here in time," said Saril. "And, besides, if you're fighting them, we won't have to."

"I'd be ready for them to fight us even if I win," said Jarrod. "And I'd be ready for them to kill you all if I lose and you surrender."

"If you fight their champion, and they fight us, that's

against . . .well . . . pretty much every law of warfare, ever," Saril stammered. "I mean . . ."

"And?" asked Jarrod, rubbing his hands. "Do you expect them to start following the rules now? They've been cheating this whole time, and they've been winning. The only thing we can expect at this point is for them to cheat even more."

"If they're going to fight us either way, then why are you meeting their champion?" Saril asked. "Why not just meet them army to army?"

Jarrod glanced out over the mountains as the wind kicked up and brought a blast of rain with it, mussing his dreadlocks and chilling his ears. "Because these people have no business fighting out there," he said. "They're not warriors."

"They can fight," Saril insisted.

"That's not the point," Aever interjected. "It's our duty to protect these people, not to lead them."

Jarrod nodded. "If I kill Blacktree, or he kills me, there's a chance they won't have to fight. This could end."

"But it might not," Saril suggested.

"No," Jarrod agreed. "It might not."

"I don't understand you," Saril said to Jarrod. "You were willing to sacrifice these people for your money, but now you won't—"

"It's not about the goddamn money!" Jarrod yelled. "And it's not mine!"

Jarrod checked himself and kept his voice in a growl, not wanting to broadcast to the civilians around him that he'd intentionally let them die a dozen at a time. "We did what we did," he continued, his voice a hiss, "because if they took The Reach, we'd lose the country. We'd lose everything we love, everything we're sworn to defend. That's not this. *This* is me, and him—" he pointed, "—out there."

"You're fighting a battle that doesn't need to be fought, to stop a battle that will happen regardless," said Saril. "That doesn't sound like you."

"I'm fighting this one because there's a chance, Saril. Maybe I can beat this guy. Maybe if I do, they don't kill you all."

"Maybe you die."

"Maybe," Jarrod admitted. "But that son of a bitch is coming with me."

DEAD MAN'S REACH

"He never killed a man that did not need killing."

- Tombstone of gunfighter Robert Clay Allison, 1840-1887

Jarrod stood in waves of sleet, alone in the valley, feeling unexpectedly territorial and imposing; actually feeling, for the moment, like he had this.

The Hillwhite army was a cheerless mass in the rain and fog in the south end of the plain, and he could make out flags on spears if he squinted. His army—*his* army, he reminded himself, turning back to look at it and there were a lot of them—sprawled up the hill, rice grains of men silhouetted at the top against a sky of iron gray streaked with columns of smoke far beyond.

It was a good place for a fight. A wide, rolling, spongy plain between two tree-crested ridges, with a blanket of moss beneath his boot from eons of glacial runoff and heavy rain, rubbery and tough and saturated, with a lot of give. The air was just above freezing, warm enough to not crust the ground over; or maybe, he thought, the dark moss absorbed just enough heat to keep the ice away. Whatever it was, it was ideal. Not rocky, not slick with dust or gravel. No vines, no holes hiding under tall grass, no hillocks to run up, no high ground to defend. It was as perfect an arena as any swordsman could ask for.

Champion's ground.

He dug his toe into the matted moss, slid his boots around, pivoted on the ball of one foot, felt the mail shift atop his boot as the stirrup tugged. The matted moss gripped nicely even wet, though it would rob a thrust of some power.

He toed a large white rock, granite or whatever the hell these mountains were made of, insanely heavy and smoothed into a dinosaur egg from God knew how many years of rain. He nudged it back to exactly where it had rested. He took a pull from his waterskin.

Raising his head toward the Hillwhite ranks, he saw a figure in black striding toward him in the downpour, a hundred yards out.

He gripped the handle of his gran espée de guerre—*Baby, don't fail me, now*—and squeezed it until his hand stopped shaking. Water, wrung from the goatskin pad of his gauntlet, dripped off the steel plates at his wrist. Base layers of polypro and merino kept him warm beneath his jacket, mail, and engraved plate-steel harness. He only looked the part of a 15th-Century man at arms. He might as well have been wearing a spacesuit.

Magic was what you make it.

At fifty yards, he recognized the dragon-scale armlets and the silver spikes in the mask, and for an eyelash of hope it was Carter— there was some kind of misunderstanding, and Carter had been healed and had just killed Renaldo, and he was coming over to tell Jarrod that it was over—and then the world sagged once more when he realized that Renaldo had stripped Carter's armor, the motherfucker.

Renaldo still wore a dark leather cuirass over his mail. Jarrod figured, rightly, that Carter's wouldn't have fit him, and then it hit him that if the helmet was intact, then Carter's breastplate probably had a hole in it, and that bummed him out. On his shoulders, Renaldo carried the same set of heavy pauldrons and black fur that he'd worn however many days ago at High River. Weeks, months, millennia.

Jarrod counted, and it stunned him that this entire world-rocking clusterfuck had taken less than twenty days.

An enormous sword on his shoulder, Renaldo strode through the rain, visor down, spikes gleaming, armor murmuring in the tick and putter of the sleet. He stopped well out of attacking distance.

He'd brought one weapon—just the sword. Menacing. Leviathan.

Celeste.

Jarrod eased his visor up. The rain smashed snowflakes off it. "Nice sword," he said in English.

"I thought you'd like to see it one last time," said Renaldo from behind the helmet.

Jarrod leaned on his sword, feigning disinterest. "My horse says hi."

"Fuck you, man."

Jarrod laughed quietly.

"You think that's funny?" Renaldo growled.

"I do," said Jarrod, "The running joke in my army is that he oughta be out here, not me."

"You got that last part right," Renaldo said.

"You're feeling pretty sure of yourself," Jarrod noted.

"Is there a reason I shouldn't?" said Renaldo, but Jarrod saw him shift; a minor tell, but an important one. As he'd assessed, this was a man who put a lot of effort into making himself scary.

"Nothing is certain," Jarrod assured him.

"This is."

"Yeah," said Jarrod, lifting his swordtip from the moss and walking a bit, feeling the ground squelch around the edges of his boot. "Let's talk about that."

"About what?" Renaldo turned to face him as he paced.

"You murdered Carter and stole his sword," said Jarrod.

"We fought," said Renaldo. "I won."

Jarrod stopped, and pointed his sword at him. "No, you didn't. You used magic to kill him, which is murder, and they know," Jarrod nodded behind him. "What you have done is punishable by death. And it's not a good death. Have you ever seen someone pulled apart?"

"They won't touch a champion."

"A champion, no; a murderer, yes. You have violated a very old, very sacred law. There's a reason they placed a prohibition on war magic. It's the only reason we didn't roll in here with a hundred war wizards of our own. It's why my guys aren't packing shotguns. This is how things are done. You, me. This."

"That's why I'm here," Renaldo agreed.

"So you can cheat again?"

"So I can win."

"Boy, you just don't get it, do you?" Jarrod muttered, pacing again.

"There's nothing to get," said Renaldo. "They brought me here to kill you."

"We don't have to do this, you know," said Jarrod. "You can surrender."

Renaldo snorted. "Why would I do that?"

"Because it's the only way you leave this valley alive," Jarrod said. Renaldo shifted uncomfortably again. A gust of wind battered them.

"Surrender," Jarrod repeated, "and come with me. I have negotiated with the Princess of Falconsrealm—"

"—oh, fuck her—"

"I have," Jarrod admitted, and let that sink in. "She has agreed to let our wizards send you home."

Renaldo blew out a spiteful breath that steamed through the spikes. "And you stay here and be a hero," he sneered.

"That's my job," Jarrod admitted. "Go home. You've had your big adventure. It's over."

"It's just beginning!" Renaldo insisted. He dropped Celeste into Fool's Guard, settling back, the tip inches off the ground. Jarrod rested his sword on his shoulder and stood back. His words sizzled.

"You don't want to do that," he promised.

"Yes, I do," said Renaldo, gesturing with the tip. "If you know what happened to Carter, then you know you can't win. And once you're dead, this whole world is mine. I'm going to be king."

"Not for long, I'd wager," Jarrod predicted.

"What the hell do you know about it?"

"More than you. Surrender. End this."

"And you have me killed," sneered Renaldo.

"No. You go home. We execute your leadership, and Jerandra."

"Like hell," said Renaldo. "Wait—how do you know about Jer—"

"I'm a spy, dipshit," Jarrod said. "I'm Order of the Stallion. We're the king's spies. We know who she is, we know how she found you. We know about the school that trained her."

"Not a lot you can do about it, though, huh?" Renaldo offered. "We're going to kill you here in a minute."

"I doubt it," Jarrod countered.

"I don't."

"She dies, today. You can die with her, or you can walk away. Your choice."

"You're not going to kill her," growled Renaldo. "I won't let you."

"It's not up to you," said Jarrod. "Right now, it's only a matter of whether or not you're waiting for her when she gets there. That's your call."

"*You* came out here to die," said Renaldo. "Didn't you? You can't win. You have some kind of bullshit code, some sworn—whatever. You *have* to fight me, because you're a . . . fuckin' . . . whatever . . . and you know you're gonna die doin' it."

Jarrod bit his lip. "I might."

"And that's all this bullshit about me surrendering. You don't want to fight me."

"I never want to fight anybody," said Jarrod. "That's the difference between you and me."

"You idiot!" Renaldo laughed, letting his sword down and waving one hand, exasperated. "You dumb-assed, shell-shocked, PTSD motherfucker. 'Sir Jarrod, The Merciful!' God damned knight in shining armor who doesn't want to fight anybody! This is what we're *here for!*" He flicked the tip of the sword to each side. "Look around you! This is you and me, the best in the world! We're *heroes,* Jarrod!"

There was nothing for Jarrod to say. The rain said it for him.

Calmer, now, sword at his side, Renaldo took a step closer, and then another. Seeing it was safe, he took another, so that his chin was almost at the top of Jarrod's helmet. "You know that even when I kill you, you'll still be a hero. That's why you're here: to go out a hero. What else is there for men like you and me? Huh? What else matters?"

Renaldo stepped back, just out of attacking distance, and squared his feet. "What else matters, Jarrod?" he called.

Jarrod looked back at his army stretching up into the drizzle and mist, and the blurred masses far behind Renaldo. The mountains, the rain, the thick alien sponge under his boot. A kingdom in the balance. A world poised on his next moments; maybe his last moments.

Jarrod turned the words over in his head. *What else matters?*

He closed his visor. "Ask Carter."

"Carter couldn't beat me," said Renaldo, raising Celeste but backing up and not engaging as Jarrod stayed well out of range, his own sword tip twitching at knee height like a cat's tail. "What makes you think you can?"

"Well," Jarrod spat out his mouthguard so that it dangled inside his visor. He let his sword down. "Funny you should ask."

"What do you mean?"

"You're on your own."

The tip of the two-hander dropped a hair. "What?" Renaldo asked.

"You're standing in a ward," Jarrod said. His voice rang heavy and metallic from inside the visor, and it appeared to take Renaldo some horsepower to work it out.

"Wait—what? A *what*?"

Jarrod enunciated and raised his voice to ensure that Renaldo heard everything. "Physical wards," he called. "Protection from magic. You walked right over them. Way back there," he motioned behind Renaldo with his sword.

Renaldo turned quickly to glance behind him and back again. "I don't see anything."

"You wouldn't. It's under the moss. Blocks of chalk, laid out long before this world ever thought about us. Magic won't work, here. Not for, oh, a couple hundred yards in each direction." He toed the white rock at his foot that now seemed obscenely out of place, and he couldn't believe Renaldo hadn't noticed that they'd walked right to it. "Midpoint."

Renaldo raised Celeste a bit higher, but his voice cracked. "You're bluffing."

"Would I be here if I was?" asked Jarrod. "Believe me, we tried it. There's no magic here. If you run, you die," he warned, as Renaldo glanced toward his army in the distance, clearly considering it. "If you run from me, it'll be construed as a forfeit. They take your head for that."

"You thought of everything," said Renaldo.

"You have no idea," Jarrod admitted, flipping his head back and chewing the rubber piece into his mouth again. He dropped into a short guard, half-deep on the front knee, pommel at his hip, statuesque, inviting the attack. A flash flood of white noise approached from behind him, screams and cheers and weapons drumming on shields.

"Last chance," he said. "Surrender or die."

It wasn't until Renaldo came at him that he realized just how long it had been since he'd faced somebody good.

Holy shit, the guy was big. An armor-plated bulldozer with a five-foot chainsaw.

Jarrod side-stepped, parried hard, and barn-doored himself well behind the greatsword as Renaldo charged past. The roar of the armies was mind-wrenching.

That fucking sword, Jarrod grumped. He wasn't sure what it would do against case-hardened steel, but he didn't want to find out. He'd seen it take limbs in iron lamellar.

Renaldo recovered, struck the same guard as before, and closed the gap.

Jarrod adjusted for Renaldo's odd sense of timing and predilection for leading with his hands, parried low, and Celeste cut over and went high, and he parried it down and the huge greatsword slammed into his shoulder and buckled him. He threw himself upwards with an uppercut and stabbed Renaldo in the chest, one hand at the balance of the blade to stiffen it against the mail.

It was steel mail, and welded; he felt the tip pierce the leather but there was no satisfying crunch of mail parting. He heard Renaldo grunt, though, and he slammed the pommel up under Renaldo's chin and disengaged.

Celeste couldn't cut through his armor, and he couldn't cut through Renaldo's. This would be an interesting afternoon.

Renaldo charged, piling into him. Jarrod tripped him, but Renaldo got him by the tabard and they went over, and then Jarrod had a serious problem: Renaldo had a hundred pounds on him. They grappled, they smashed each other with pommels and crossbars, they threw knees and elbows and steel-shod foreheads, and it all seemed idiotic and exhausting to Jarrod until Renaldo, wrenching his hand free from Jarrod's grip, flipped Celeste over and grabbed the last two feet of blade and slammed it tip-first into Jarrod's visor, puncturing the steel under the eyeslit.

Jarrod felt it bite his cheek, and then his mouth flooded with blood and he was on his back and Renaldo was passing the guard, sliding up his chest, all that weight fulcruming down and pinning him. Renaldo leaned on Celeste, forcing the massive blade through the steel a hair at a time, driving Roman candles of pain into Jarrod's skull.

Jarrod reached out to swing his greatsword, found he couldn't get the leverage to do a damned thing, and felt his gauntlet smack against something solid.

The big white rock. The dinosaur egg.

His fingers closed around it.

Renaldo's right arm was up, his elbow raised as he braced himself on the blade. Jarrod twisted in a short, heavy hook with the rock, driving it into the liver with the force of an asteroid ending the world. Renaldo sagged, wheezing.

Jarrod stove in the side of the great spiked helmet with the stone—Jesus, it was heavy—and Celeste left his visor as Renaldo went over.

Jarrod's army went nuts, roaring in approval and rushing forward. He rolled atop Renaldo and hit him with the rock several more times, both hands, smashing in the beautiful visor and pummeling him under the mail, again and again, until Renaldo quieted.

Jarrod stood up, started to toss the rock away, then changed his mind and hurled it at Renaldo. "Fuck you." He toed his sword into his hand. He could see daylight through the hole as he flipped up his visor, and when his mouthpiece came out, it brought a lot of blood with it.

"Get up," he said, and choked, snorking up a mouthful of gore and blowing it out in a mist. Blood chilled the front of his jacket under his mail. He said it again, gargling and growling. "Get up!"

Renaldo lumbered to his feet, crossing them and staggering sideways before righting himself. The armies had formed a ring, giving them plenty of room, but wanting to see the end. The roar had dulled to a murmur.

Renaldo bent to pick up Celeste, albeit slowly.

"You're done," said Jarrod. "Leave it."

Renaldo lifted the huge sword and dropped back into a long-tail guard, the blade behind him and off to the side. "Death," he growled.

"Dude," warned Jarrod. "Seriously?"

"This is everything to me!" Renaldo yelled, and Jarrod realized that he probably hadn't hurt him nearly as badly as he thought he had. "You will not take this, too!"

"What the fuck do you mean, 'too?'" asked Jarrod, circling with his sword up.

"You get everything!" Renaldo screamed. "Girls, Hollywood! Goddamn drivin' a fuckin' Ferrari on TV!"

"You want a Ferrari?" Jarrod asked, and spat another mouthful of blood. "Shit, you could have said so. I'd have given you one just to go h—"

"I'm better than you!" Renaldo shrieked. "At this!" he stomped his foot and gestured around them.

"You're not," Jarrod said.

Renaldo stayed in his guard, and Jarrod could see him getting his bearings. Recovering fast. "You're a fucking *actor!*" Renaldo shouted. "This is *real!* This belongs to *me!*"

"No," said Jarrod, his tone level. "This," he gestured around him, "belongs to the Princess of Falconsrealm."

"Who you're fucking," Renaldo rolled his eyes.

"Now and again," Jarrod said with a shrug, "yeah."

"That's what I'm talking about!" he shrieked, nearly throwing his sword down, and Jarrod knew he'd hit a nerve with it. He grinned and raised an eyebrow, and Renaldo screamed in fury and stomped his foot.

"I found a way to do this," said Renaldo, calmer, now. "I found a way to win. Finally, I'm winning at something real. And *you!* You're the only thing fucking it up."

Jarrod slapped his visor shut again and bit down on his mouthguard. "That's why I'm here."

Renaldo lunged and Jarrod, keying on the hands, saw it long before it landed and went full saber in a modified *passato sotto:* a front split, slipping his head sideways as the greatsword went wide by inches. He hooked a leg and rolled, and Renaldo hit the moss with a jangle. They came to their feet, and Jarrod slammed him across the helmet with the big sword, driving both feet into the planet and knocking him back down.

Renaldo rolled away and lurched upright. "You little fucker!" he wheezed, kicking the tip of the greatsword up and coming in with an overhead out of *Vom Tag*—the weapon cocked ridiculously, ready to split a stump—and Jarrod, seeing the wind-up long before the strike, side-stepped it and caught the big greatsword in a way that Carter would never have allowed. He flipped it sideways with a flick and wrapped it in one arm, grabbing it by the crossbar with the blade trapped in the crook of his elbow, then yanked Renaldo to him and rolled across his legs. The armies roared an ovation.

Renaldo crawled for Celeste, gasping and dragging his left leg. Jarrod leaped up and dropped on him with both knees, feeling ribs shatter and splinter under armored greaves, the unmistakable kindling snaps and thick surrender of bones driving into organs.

He did it again.

Renaldo stopped crawling.

And again.

The crowd went silent, rent to babbles.

Behind him, Jarrod could hear a woman shrieking, and he turned to see who it might be, and there she was, a tall, dark-skinned woman in blue at the edge of the Hillwhite army who was undoubtedly Jerandra of the Wastes. Several men held her back.

Jarrod grabbed Renaldo by the shoulders and rolled him over, then scrabbled at the latch of his—Carter's—damaged visor and flipped it up.

A froth of pulmonary hemorrhage, pink as the moon, spilled in fits down Renaldo's cheek and neck. He was drowning.

Jarrod cradled Renaldo's helmeted head in one hand. He spat out his mouthguard and cleared his throat; he wanted him to hear this. "Hey," he rasped. "Renaldo! Look at me!"

Renaldo's eyes, drifting in separate directions, came together to meet Jarrod's.

"You lead with your hands," Jarrod told him as he died.

Jarrod picked up Celeste from where she lay on the moss, toed his warsword into his other hand, and walked back to a cheering army.

The Armies of the West were scraping Renaldo onto a shield and Aever was handing Jarrod a skin of wine—he still didn't understand how someone could drink right after that much exercise, but damned if the Falconsrealm knights couldn't—when Crius Lotavaugus and Galè of Lor tore through the lines, with the Flying Elvises in their conical helms and strange banded armor behind them and a handful of knights of the Stallion bringing up the rear in a rattling run, demanding the arrest of Jerandra of the Wastes. The Hillwhite army sent its own delegation, and the yelling started.

"There goes the neighborhood," Jarrod said, handing the skin back to her.

"You should probably go help them," Aever said.

"I'm too goddamn tired to do anything about it," Jarrod said. "You know what I could really use? Water. Just water, with maybe some juice in it."

She offered him the wineskin again.

"Yeah, okay," he agreed. "Close enough."

He was corking it when a fight broke out; the Gavrians, it

looked like, against the Hillwhites, as the Falconsrealm knights tried to pull them back. He heard the peals and bangs of steel and a man's scream, and the Hillwhites were moving forward, the whole line of them in the storm, and then the horns, and the roar as a thousand troops rumbled to life.

"Oh, shit," said Jarrod. Shields went up, shouts went out, and Jarrod threw his helmet on and tossed the wineskin away, offering the black sword to Aever as they closed. "You'll need this," he told her.

"I'll need that," she griped, looking after the wineskin. She sheathed her sword, taking the big greatsword from him, and settled in behind her shield as the Hillwhite army became screaming shapes in the rain.

"I'll buy you a beer in hell," he offered.

"Footrace!" she yelled as the thunder increased to subway levels. "Loser pays!"

FALLOUT

"Faeries, come take me out of this dull world,
For I would ride with you upon the wind,
Run on the top of the disheveled tide,
And dance upon the mountains like a flame."
- W.B. Yeats, The Land of Heart's Desire

The adrenaline under Jarrod's skin boiled over and burst through his arm, and Celeste went through a spear's shaft and the spearman's helmet, which broke apart and vomited torrents of pink and gray. The wall of spears ahead of him shattered and collapsed as they scattered from the massive blade, and Aever, on his right, drove ahead with several mooks—Jarrod didn't know what else to call them—on her heels, and this is what it was going to be, he realized, jumping back from an axe and crunching the sword through a mail-clad arm and kicking the man away. Innocents with hand weapons fell in behind him, and innocents with spears fell in behind the Hillwhite knights. This was going to be a shitshow.

The Hillwhite levies had better weapons and more armor, though not comparatively much, as far as he was concerned in his steel carapace. As spears and swords and axes banged off his armor, he struck their wielders down and punched and kicked and elbowed them away, one after the other, indomitable. They couldn't scratch him inside his 15th-Century, chrome-moly field harness, but knew it was just a matter of time before exhaustion, dehydration—or hell, heatstroke, even at two degrees above freezing—took him over. He couldn't stay out here forever. He was already tired and sore and stabbed in the goddamn face, for fuck's sake.

He reverted to Montante, holding a piece of terrain with huge loops and figure eights that nobody wanted to come near. He fought to catch his breath, but he was spitting gobs of blood into his faceplate and it was a lot of sword. He was already feeling his hands tire, and his arms would be going soon after. He was in shreds.

He had to wonder, dully and quickly, if a healer could give him a shot of go juice or maybe do something for his face, and then it occurred to him that he'd lost sight of where they'd started. They might not be outside the wards at all, come to think of it; he might be in an area where no healers could use magic, nor teleport the wounded off the field.

Looking around at the stacks of bodies and the screaming, howling, crawling masses, he guessed this was the case. Absolute, blood-spurting butchery for a hundred yards in any direction. A slaughterhouse of flying knives, bodies pouring in as if on rails and stacking in the middle.

Son of a bitch.

They were all going to die, right here.

And he'd led them to it.

He grabbed Aever, who was fighting on his right, and pulled her back, yelling at her to run for the edges of the wards. "Fall back!" he screamed. "Fall back, and left! *LEFT!!*" He motioned with his sword, and went left, and some of them followed. Some didn't. "Get the footmen out of here!"

He stopped to pick up a roundshield and threw the big sword in one-handed loops at anyone who came near him, propping the shield up and locking off his elbow like a rock climber against his side. Holy shit, he was tired.

The horses broke through on both sides, and the world ended.

It took only moments before a Falconsrealm knight fell from his horse near Jarrod, and Jarrod slung his shield, grabbed the saddle horn, and swung up, hoping the horse would have some sense of humor about all this. He was swinging up from the right side, and the horse shifted left, not wanting any part of it. He jumped down, bucked up and kicked it in the head as it looked back to see what the hell he was doing, and swung up again just in time for another knight to knock the horse right out from under him.

A moment of insane, spinning, zero-g vertigo as he flipped in the air like a tossed coin, and he saw the ground beneath him and righted himself and more or less stuck the landing, flat on his back in the mud with a world-rattling bang that smashed the world into blackness. He lay there for long seconds before rolling to hands and knees. He had no idea where his sword had gone; the horse got up and ran off and goddammit he needed Perseus, but he was fifty miles from here.

Another horse tore by, and Jarrod leaped back, then forward as another one went past.

It wasn't nearly as funny, being on the ground with the horses going every which way.

He found Celeste.

He flipped his visor up for peripheral vision. The horses

were mostly shifting to his right, and he stumbled off to the left and found another horse walking around, confused. He tried it again; grabbed the saddle horn, this time on the left side, and swung up the way a right-handed knight would.

So far, so good.

He grabbed the reins and threw the shield off his shoulder into his hand, then closed his visor and scanned for targets, and kicked the horse forward into the mayhem.

Every now and again, this world gave him a panoramic view of himself, and the universe, and his exact place in it. Under the swirling coal sky, the rain hammering down on a thousand-odd men and women beating the shit out of each other for absolutely no good reason except that they really liked the people who were telling them to, steam and blood pouring from his face, his arms burning, Jarrod had a moment of clarity. He turned the horse left and raced for the edge of the fight, skirting back to the rear ranks.

It's possible that Renaldo hadn't been wrong, after all, and commanding from the rear made a modicum of sense. Somebody had to take charge of this rolling disaster, or they were certainly all going to die. It was squad fighting, writ large, he could see from back here; scores of armed mobs meeting, hacking, killing, and dying, then breaking off and doing it again.

He saw what he was looking for and rode up to a group of knights or riders, he wasn't sure which. "I need you!" he yelled, pointing at them, "over there!" He pointed in the other direction. "Reinforce the center! Grab everyone you can and *reinforce the center!*"

The knight lifted his sword, rallying troops to him, and several dozen cavalry shifted from their small battles and fell in behind him as he and his troops charged down the center line. The footmen parted, the knights smashed a hole through the middle of the Hillwhite levies, and The Reach fighters poured through. It worked beautifully until the Hillwhite knights met the horsemen from a flank and ran about half of them underfoot, and the whole thing pinwheeled for the horrific.

The Hillwhite cavalry in the center surrounded Jarrod's footmen, reduced to a circle and fighting outward, and the Falconsrealm heavy horse were scattered and marginalized and reduced to skirmishes, and his guys were being pushed back and squeezed in as he watched.

The day was lost, on one blown call.

His blown call.

He raised his shield and yelled, gathering knights and soldiers around him. *This is it.*

He wouldn't even live long enough, he realized, to learn from this mistake.

This is where you die. Not by Renaldo, but by the thousand assholes on his left and right. Because you didn't think this through.

Jarrod raised his sword, kicked the horse, and set off for the end with a handful of strangers screaming behind him, realizing as the world smeared under his visor that he was crying. It was over; he'd done it. He'd set it right. They could settle the rest.

Karra's voice in his head. What had she said? *Every hero loses his last battle, anyway.*

Jarrod stood in his stirrups as they closed, and threw his shield out to one side and his sword to the other, crucifying himself in the saddle, tears freezing as the wind ripped through his visor. The horde behind him screamed even louder, electrified.

Hero time.

He heard horns to his left. Horns he knew. Horns he'd trained with.

Jarrod reined back, looked left, then shoved his visor up and rubbed his eyes. Up the slope, a forest of spears and an army of horses appeared in the whirling rain, silhouetted against the clouds; the Falconsrealm cavalry. They spurred into a gallop, spilling off the hill in an avalanche of murder, and holy shit at the front of them was a loping, sprinting, goddamned *grizzly bear* with a rider in Falconsrealm armor, bareback.

The fresh knights chewed up the Hillwhite cavalry, and the bear ripped its way through horses and humans alike, its rider thrashing away with an axe in one hand and a sword in the other. Jarrod's army cheered and went after the wounded and he wished to fuck they'd stop doing that.

He kicked his horse forward into the fight, covered up with his shield, and the levies rallied behind them, and the Hillwhite troops were surrendering, already, and that was that.

"Quarter!" he boomed. "Give mercy!" He repeated it until his voice was a leather-lunged shout.

The fighting died down as if someone had thrown a switch. It was amazing, he thought, what a few hundred heavy cavalry and one giant, pissed-off bear could accomplish.

He trotted the horse forward through the dwindling calamity, the world melting down around him, screams and shrieks and hundreds of people dragging hundreds more out of the wards so that the healers could work on them.

The knight on the bear, he could see through the rain, was in expensive Falconsrealm mail, fine rings coated black, with a black helmet trimmed in gold, and his first thought was of Adielle—it sure looked like her armor—but that was impossible, because what the hell was she doing riding a bear? And then he saw the sword, and sure as shit, it was that gorgeous old leaf spring arming sword, blooded in war and soaking up all the glory a hunk of cast-off Detroit steel could ever ask for, and nothing made any kind of sense at all except that the princess had given some elf her war gear. Maybe, he figured, Karra had sent up a rocket on whatever the Faerie used as an equivalent of emergency radio, and the elves had sent a ringer of their own.

Jarrod popped up his visor and rode forward to where the knight was scratching the bear behind its gore-matted ear.

Jarrod's horse wanted nothing to do with the bear, and that made sense to him; he raised a hand from several lengths' distance. The knight jumped down off the bear, the sword resting on his shoulder, and swaggered over, ten feet of attitude in half the height. But then, he'd been riding a bear.

"Greetings!" Jarrod yelled in Faerie, one of the few things he knew how to say.

The knight stood before Jarrod's horse, set the sword tip-down in the mud, and pulled off his helmet, tucking it under his arm.

"Hello, lover!" said Karra.

WHAT THE STRIKER SAW

"When other generals make mistakes, their armies are beaten; when I get into a hole, my men pull me out of it."
- The Duke of Wellington, after Waterloo

Jarrod awoke in a tent. The wind rattled the canvas like an angry foe at a shirt front.

Everything hurt, six feet of exposed nerve; a dry socket the size of his body. The cold bit at his head, at his teeth. His tongue touched the inside of his cheek and found stitches.

Pain shoved through his veins when he tried to move, and fuck this place, he decided. Fuck swords, and castles, and horses, and waking up feeling like this. This whole thing was a sucker's bet from the starting gun half a year ago, the return far below the wager. He wished the world would just hurry up and kill him for his compiled transgressions already.

So many bodies.

A female healer, quiet and gentle and dressed in furs and long dresses against the cold, put her hands on his, and the pain lessened a bit.

"I'm alive," he said to her. His armor stood on a mannequin to his right, near the back of the tent. It looked like it had been hit by a series of cars. Celeste leaned against the dented and scarred breastplate. Holy crap, he thought. He'd had no idea it had been that bad. He had memories of axes.

"You are very much alive," she said.

"Can I get up?" he asked.

"Not for a while, as I understand it," said a woman's voice from the far side of the tent, and it was Aever, with Karra by her side, both of them bundled up in heavy, drab cloaks. Aever rose slowly and with a groan, but she grinned. "Hey."

"You owe me a beer," Jarrod told her.

"Lover!" Karra exclaimed, and threw herself gently over him, her hands in his hair, candy and sunshine and peace.

"I got hit in the head really hard," Jarrod said, touching her face, "but did I see you riding a bear?"

She smiled and bared her fangs. "They needed someone to lead them through the forest and find you. You know I can always find you."

Jarrod's eyes misted over. "Yes, you can," he said. "I do love you, Karra."

She put her head in the crook of his neck and purred. "And I love you, my brave hero. I will fight for you any day."

"Apparently," Jarrod noted.

Aever put her hand on Jarrod's and squeezed. "I need you to keep an eye on her from now on. She causes trouble."

"That she does," Jarrod admitted. "Are you injured?"

"I'm fine," she said, and winked. "A few dents."

Two more healers appeared in the doorway and held the flaps as Adielle, Crius, and Galè, along with Saril, Bevio, Thron, and several more people he didn't know, entered the cramped space of the tent.

Adielle looked more tired than he'd ever seen anyone look, and he had to wonder if she'd ridden all night to get here, or if they'd gated her in and she'd just been up for a long time. He hoped she hadn't been worried about him, but he kinda really hoped she had.

"At your hand," he said. "Forgive me for not rising."

Adielle's smile was the warmth of the world, her hands composed in front of her. "You're alive," she said.

"More or less," Jarrod admitted. His heart hit bottom and collapsed on itself. Karra at his hand, Adielle before him, and Aever behind them, the adjudicator. The world had figured him out. He prayed for an aneurysm.

Adielle put something in his hands and folded them around it. "I thought you'd want to see this," she said.

He fought to focus. It was a small wooden box, dark and simple. He pulled at it, tried to open it. Nothing happened. He shook it at Karra, and it rattled. "Make it go," he said.

Karra took it gently from him and slid out a dovetailed drawer, revealing a shiny silver coin, a little larger than a half-dollar, on a black velvet bed. She tucked it into his hand.

It was heavier than he'd expected. He lifted it to his face and held it away, rubbing one eye with his other hand as his head screamed at him.

It was a new design, he could see, and clearly a fresh pressing. The Lord Protector's standard, the crossed sword and key, stood proud, superimposed over a teardrop shield—his shield, he noted—with **FALCONSREALM** imprinted around the top edge in their vaguely runic, crooked-stick lettering, and the words **HEROES RISE** around the bottom.

"That's beautiful," he said. "You're back in business," he told Adielle. "Congratulations, Highness."

"You should turn it over," Karra suggested, and when he did, there was no more air in the room.

On the front, in profile, it was clearly him in low relief: dreadlocks, a goatee, the short fighter's nose, and the grin he always felt threaded the needle between mischievous and slightly dopey. He felt his center of gravity shifting, and the world seemed to shimmer around him and reappear six inches to the right and considerably brighter.

"We made it while you slept," said a broad, bearded man behind Adielle who looked like he could have imprinted it with his teeth. "We did the side without the scar. If you don't like it, my lord, we can alter it. You can sit for another when you're healed, or—"

"No, it's beautiful," said Jarrod. "Thank you. I'm very honored."

"Respectfully, Lord Protector," said the man, kneeling, "It was an honor to create it."

Jarrod nodded at Adielle. "And thank you, as well, Highness. I'll cherish this."

The princess smiled at him, her eyes glowing with a depth of consequence he'd never beheld.

"It's our new coin," she said. "It's called a Hero."

BELOVED DEPARTED

"Sing your death song, and die like a hero going home."
- Chief Aupumut, Mohican, 1725

Jarrod and Daorah, in warrior blacks, capes, and accoutrements of station, stood in the snowy courtyard at Gateskeep Palace with several hundred knights and onlookers before a ten-foot tall, carved-stone reproduction of Celeste next to a full-sized statue of a pegasus on its hind legs charging into flight.

A genius artisan had captured the greatsword in smooth gray rock, right down to the wrap on the handle and the dings on the blade. It erupted from a three-foot-square block of granite chiseled with Carter's name and achievements.

Jarrod couldn't read the entire inscription, but he recognized the diving-falcon crest below it, a sky-warrior's pin fixed in the stone forever. It all stood atop a hill in the main courtyard and collected a glaze of new snow.

Daorah held herself up with a heavy black cane, her eyes red, her neck taut. Jarrod watched as a single tear broke loose and rolled down the clenched muscle of her jaw.

He wondered how many people she would murder for this

once her leg healed up.

He wanted to be next to her when she did it.

King Rorthos, in his Santa hat and layered golden robes, strode up to the monument with a gaggle of courtiers, and the assembly knelt except for Daorah, who bowed, and Jarrod figured it was because of the leg. The king saluted the sword wordlessly, and then turned to address the crowd in a voice that, even for a king, stunned Jarrod in its clarity and power.

"For valorous service, loyalty, and unrivaled skill in combat, I present to you: Sir Karr, the Unbreakable! Knight of the Falcon!"

A cheer went up from those assembled, and they all stood, and saluted, and then cheered some more. The king walked back down the hill, his courtiers saluting the statue in suit and trailing him back to the keep.

And that, Jarrod thought, was that. He watched the king go.

"The Unbreakable, huh?" he asked Daorah, his voice nearly lost in the ruckus.

She cleared her throat and wiped her cheek. "I think it's fitting."

Jarrod put his hand on her arm. "Are you okay? I mean, really okay?"

"No," she said, and placed her hand on his and squeezed. "I may never be."

"She's still out there, you know. You'll have your chance."

Her voice cracked with grief but didn't waver. "This is not over," she assured him. "We have much to do. But not today." She gestured to the giant sword. "Today is his."

"And yours, Commander," said Jarrod. He saluted her, and she returned it, then limped away on her cane to be with her comrades.

Jarrod approached the monument as soldiers and knights milled and the crowd of civilians—*innocents,* he reminded himself—came closer.

For the first time that he could remember, he had nothing to say. His pulse thickened. The scar on his cheek throbbed in the cold as he dug at the bottom of a dry well for words.

He fished the new coin out of his pocket, cleared away some of the snow, and laid it on the block.

"I'll ride beside you any day."

A line had formed behind him, and he saluted the statue and started the long walk down the hill to the main building of the palace. He stopped at the top of the stairs just outside the doors, and as the guards snapped to, Jarrod turned to look back, wiping his eyes clear.

The ringed sliver of moon rose behind the wall in the broken clouds. A file of knights and civilians paying respects before Carter's monument had grown until it sprawled down the hill. A few laid something on the block as they left.

Coins.

Jarrod watched the moon, and the line of people, and the clouds drifting in wisps above the towers, rubbing at his eyes as they blurred over time and again. Beyond it all, soldiers milled on walls. A flight of birds wheeled in the sky. The world went on.

He wondered what tomorrow held.

THE END

ACKNOWLEDGMENTS

First and foremost, I want to thank my wife for putting up with everything it takes to be married to an author, and for being smarter about it all than I am. She drew the map, wrangled the contracts, planned the marketing, created the video trailers (and learned to sing in Elvish), spec'd out my Fortress of Solitude behind the garage, had the final sign-off on series artwork, and all in all, she rocked the hell out of this entire endeavor. I have the incredible fortune of having my best friend as my business partner.

Monique Fischer is my editor, and she continues her amazing work of calling me on my bullshit without screwing with my voice. If you're an author and you're reading this, find an editor who gets you. Don't settle. It's worth the hunt.

Sarah Hershman is my agent. Justin Hargett at Kickflip PR is probably the reason you're reading this.

John Terpin, Esq. handles any and all conversations that involve me and the word "frankly."

Lynn Stevenson designed the cover, the badges, and pretty much everything else.

My American Bulldog, Ator L'Invincible ("Tor"), was the basis for Jarrod's courageous and thick-headed warhorse, Perseus. Tor pulls security at the door of the Fortress of Solitude, and has long been a sounding board for scene and dialogue ideas. Such a good boy.

I receive a lot of questions about the types of swords used in these books and their historical accuracy, and many others about where it might be possible to buy a sword like the one used by (insert character here), so a little about that follows.

Renaldo's longsword is based off of a complex compound-hilted longsword design by E.B. Erickson. It is not, to my knowledge, historically accurate, but it sure is gorgeous.

Adielle's leaf-spring arming sword is an Oakeshotte Type XIV, probably French in design, based off an arming sword I handled once that was, literally, made through stock removal on a Cadillac leaf spring. (And yes, a piece of steel discovered rusting in a junkyard and finding new life as a weapon in the hands of royalty on another world is a reference to Jarrod's arc all the way back to the beginning of *Dragon's Trail,* you literary deconstructionist, you.) Adielle's sword is probably the most historically accurate of any of the swords in the series, although not representative of the swords in use in the world where the books take place.

The common sword in Gateskeep and Falconsrealm is an early-medieval sword with a shorter blade of about 26-30", a Viking-type pommel, and a spatulate tip.

The longswords of the Knights of the Falcon are based off of Angus Trim's Atrim 1509 design.

Jarrod's and Renaldo's greatswords brought from Earth are reflective of Michael "Tinker" Pearce's Great Sword of War, a massive, extremely fast weapon of alarming capability. If you hold one of these swords in your hand and feel the power inherent in it, you have no choice but to write heroic fantasy. Were I to travel to a medieval-era world and be allowed one weapon (at least, one that's not a cut-down Mossberg with a recoil-suppressing stock), it would be one of Tinker's greatswords. Jarrod's has what Tinker calls a "working finish."

Renaldo's is polished.

Carter Sorenson's two-hander, Celeste, is a custom configuration of a 15th-Century Irish two-handed sword, with a wider and longer blade, an egg pommel for balance, and a squared ricasso functionally similar to that of a Danish two-hander, the Oakeshotte Type XVIIIe. I know of no historical basis for Celeste, nor anyone making such a weapon currently. If you do get someone to make you a Celeste, please send pictures and let me know where you got it.

Jarrod's rapier is also a custom job, which I envision as a progenitor to the Schiavona with an overlong blade and a swept hilt of South German design circa 1570. A loose historical basis for such a weapon can be found in the sword used by the bodyguard of Christian I, Elector of Saxony, in the Late 16th Century. I needed to design a weapon for a relatively short *sabreur* with powerful hands, and this seemed to fit the bill. Since Jarrod's rapier is considerably longer than a typical Schiavona, I slimmed it down and added a few rings to the guard for balance.

Source validation is hazy on the quote attributed to Chief Aupumut in the closing chapter. It has been variously attributed to Tecumseh, Sitting Bull, and Crazy Horse.

While writing *The New Magic,* I stumbled across a genre of music, "gothic country," with which I was not previously familiar, and which contributed in no small part to the tone and feel. Blues Saraceno's "Dogs of War" and Robin Loxley's "Rain Down" run neck and neck for opening credits music when I imagine *The New Magic* as a movie. I'd also like to give a shout out to Lizzie No, whose song "Crying Wolf" was on endless repeat writing multiple scenes. The entire *Crying Wolf* album found its way into my writing playlist, with several tracks right up at the top.

I wrote Carter's denouement to Krista Detor's transcendent "Clock of the World."

I found the words *Sail On Gone* annotated in the margins of my notes for the ending scene, which led me to rediscover the song of the same name by Tom Catmull and the Clerics; I similarly looped the hell out of it for hours working to capture the vibe of the closing pages.

I don't formally endorse any companies, but I couldn't do my thing without Aeron chairs, Bulleit whiskey, and Brooks Brothers.

Thank you to Badger, Keeper of Stories.

Thanks to my writer friends, my horde of fans, and most of all, to you, my reader. You make it possible.

If you enjoyed *The New Magic,* please leave a review at your preferred retailer.

As a final word, I want to extend my sincere and heartfelt gratitude to the U.S. Army Human Resources Command and members of the 115th U.S. Congress. I finished the final draft of *The New Magic* during the January 2018 government shutdown, when HRC fucked up the orders of tens of thousands of mobilized Reservists and inadvertently recalled hundreds of teams from live missions, including mine. I was able to complete *The New Magic*—and start *Coin of the Realm*—while waiting for amended orders, and I was paid for all the time retroactively when HRC classified it as non-chargeable leave. Way to go, The Army. Keep being awesome.

– JM

Bonus Scene
featuring
Jerandra of the Wastes

AVAILABLE TO E-MAIL SUBSCRIBERS

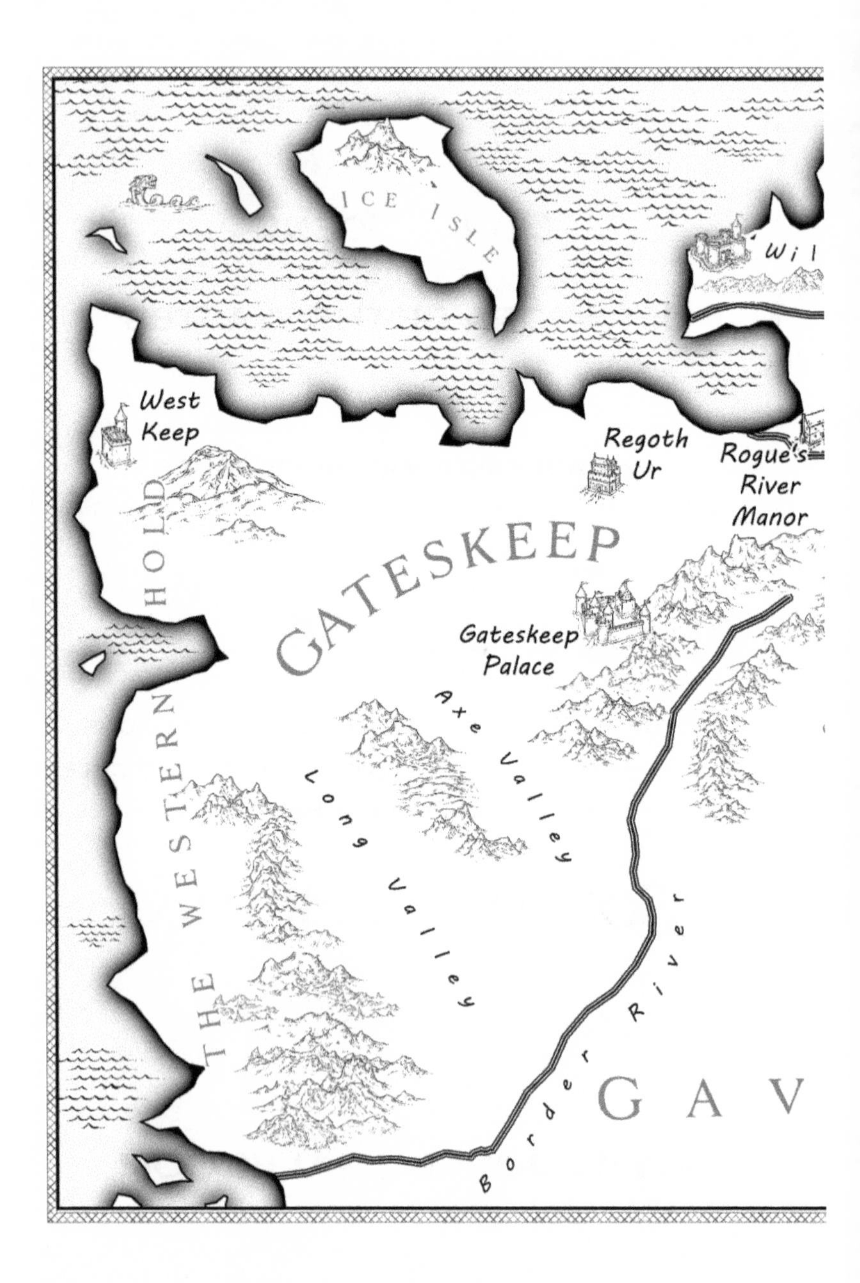
ICE ISLE
Wil
West Keep
Regoth Ur
Rogue's River Manor
GATESKEEP
THE WESTERN HOLD
Gateskeep Palace
Axe Valley
Long Valley
Border River
GAV

River Reach
The White Hills
Dragon's Trail
FAERIE STRONGHOLD
High River Keep
Sanctuary
High River
Horlech
FALCONSREALM
EASTERN FREEHOLD
THE SHIELDLANDS
The Teeth of the World
Silver Palace
ULORAK
Hold of Gavria
RIA

CPSIA information can be obtained
at www.ICGtesting.com
Printed in the USA
LVHW031047281018
595120LV00003B/442